Seer's Quest

BOOK ONE OF
THE DIVINE GAMBIT TRILOGY

CHAD CORRIE

AMI™

An Aspirations Media Publication

An Aspirations Media™ Publication
www.aspirationsmediainc.com

Copyright © 2004-2006 by Chad Corrie
Interior Illustrations Copyright © 2005 Ed Waysek
Map Illustrations Copyright © 2004 Jeremy Simmons
Cover Copyright © 2005 Carrie Hall
Layout Copyright © 2005 Nancy Kurzweg
Design: Nancy Kurzweg and Chad Corrie

LIBRARY OF CONGRESS CONTROL NUMBER: 2006920967

ISBN: 0-9776043-0-6

MANUFACTURED IN THE UNITED STATES

First Printing April 2006

Thanks to:

God, who has brought me this far.

*My family and friends for putting up with this
obsession of mine and supporting me in their own unique ways.*

Especially my father...this should be a fun run, dad.

Never confuse yourself by visions of an entire lifetime at once. That is, do not let your thoughts range over the whole multitude and variety of the misfortunes that may befall you, but rather, as you encounter one, ask yourself 'What is there so unendurable, so insupportable, in this?' You will find that you are ashamed to admit defeat. Again, remember that it is not the weight of the future or the past that is pressing upon you, but ever that of the present alone. Even this burden, too, can be lessened if you confine it strictly to its own limits, and are severe enough with your mind's inability to bear such a trifle.

Marcus Aurelius
"Meditations" Book 8 Paragraph 36

For now we are looking in a mirror that gives only a dim (blurred) reflection [of reality as in a riddle or enigma], but then [when perfection comes] we shall see in reality and face to face! Now I know in part (imperfectly), but then I shall know and understand fully and clearly, even in the same manner as I have been fully and clearly known and understood [by God].

1 Cor. 13:12 Amplified Bible

Prologue

Bloodied clouds clawed their way through the dark sky, shackled to the barren land below. Infernal gales slid through dead forests of mangled, black wood, grabbing the ash-covered ground to swirl it into noxious dust devils. The sulfuric wind traveled onward through the rotting, pervasive aroma of blood drenched fields until it came to a brimstone wall. The wall grew to be part of a dark tower rising from the ground like a skeletal finger. All around it, the land echoed with the tortured screams of hidden souls whose tormentor's visage alone would cause madness. Finding a crack in the worn wall, the sickly breeze poured itself into a room, more vile than the land surrounding it.

Crafted in the exact center of the tower; more square than round, the room was large and plain in decoration. Tapestries, long since turned over to moth colonies, rustled in the stagnant wind. Their ruined images lit solely by an eerie, blue incandescence from in front of them.

A stand in the center of the room stood before an archaic, stone throne made to appear as a monstrous obsidian hand grasping a time-worn skull. It was from the skull that the blue light issued into the room; it's bony surface possessing all manner of strange, red-glowing, etched runes.

The back of the skull faced a polished, red, stone throne. The front of the skull stared silently in the other direction, as if it tried to hide its empty eyes from the half-shadow swallowed figure who sat behind it.

The throne's occupant continued to patiently peer into the rune-etched skull as the last of the breeze tugged the hem of the seated figure's rotting robe.

The dying breeze scattered the decaying fabric about with small tufts of dust and debris fluttering from the garment; while expiring in its final effort. The occupant paid it little mind though; his attention was focused elsewhere, but not too far from the entity coalescing behind him.

Not even the incandescence glimmering from the horrid stand could illuminate this faintly humanoid form-floating just behind the great chair, ravenously devouring all the ghostly light of the room.

How much longer must I wait here? The image behind the throne asked without the use of natural words. His voice was a mental projection of his own thoughts into the mind of the throne's occupant.

"Do not anger me, Balon. My plans are reaching fruition, as I told you they would. Your presence here is unnecessary," spoke the throne's occupant, whose skeletal hand appeared on the armrest of the throne; bone fingers clenching themselves into a fist. Refocusing his thoughts, the occupant drew closer to the pedestal; its light penetrated his gloomy shroud revealing more of his decaying body.

A tattered hood, drawn over the figure's visage, concealed much of the fleshless skull in a dim shadow. The rest of him was illuminated by the cold, blue light glowing in the center of the room and from the small tongues of flame lapping out of his empty eye sockets.

Remember the agreement? We are both to leave. Do not forget that, wizard, or I shall be forced to render you limb from limb. Mage or not, you can't withstand my strength. With glowing, red eyes, the only source of color on it's dark, insubstantial form, Balon hovered in front of the throne and glared at its occupant.

He had no real solid form being little more than inky gossamer which gained a bit more solid seeming toward the center of his figure.

"Can't I? Need I remind you who built this tower and all that is housed in it, with the mere power of will? Your threats are more hollow than your frame," the seated figure snarled.

The swarthy, flimsy form of Balon, eyes flaring a fiercer red than before, arrogantly returned behind the polished stone throne. *Ah, but things change do they not? You've lost much of your bargaining power, and are not in the best of positions to make such threats.* The words, though internalized in the enthroned figure's mind, were still laced with enough caustic barbs to rouse his ire as if they had been spoken aloud.

"Be gone! I must have silence for my next spell to work."

Balon took a moment of delight from this anger he aroused. It told him his accusation was truer than he had guessed. With an animalistic scream of fury, the shadowy demon dissipated into the filthy air.

Stopping for a moment to scan the room with his vacant, flaming eyes the seated figure, who called himself The Master, returned to his spell. Once before the demon had made itself invisible rather than leave the Master's tower. It was a harsh lesson to learn as Balon was able to gain a greater understanding of The Master's plans, which put the wizard at a slight disadvantage and had contributed to the demon's recent arrogance when dealing with The Master.Because of this oversight he swore never to be as foolish again.

Though Balon could send his thoughts to The Master, he wasn't able to read the skeletal wizard's thoughts. No, that was the one area where The Master never let his guard down no matter what he was doing.

He couldn't afford it here- it was the main reason why he'd managed to exist as long as he had in the first place.

When he was finally content with his privacy, he began to trace strange, glowing runes and symbols on top of the previous ones lining the weathered skull's surface.

As The Master traced the runes, an aquamarine flame licked across the ancient bone. Starting with the eye sockets the fire flared across the top of the skull and up into the air. Speaking an archaic language, long since corrupted and almost forgotten by those of mortal years, The Master intensified the flame. As the fire grew, the skull's surface became more mirror-like, reflecting the fleshless face that had conjured it.

Speaking but one word, The Master lessened the reflective quality until the skull became clear. Pictures of another world played inside the transparent cranium, like reflections on a pool of water or mirage in a desert. Looking closely at the images, The Master watched a young man standing on a cold, weathered rampart, wearing a fur-trimmed cloak to fend off the chilled air. He appeared to be a Nordican, a human who populated the farthest northern lands of Tralodren, which had been the Master's former home.

"Yes!" The Master hissed. "Here is my champion; my key I shall mold. Yes boy. You'll have a special part to play soon enough. Soon I shall be free!"

The Master cackled insanely. The hollow sound reverberated off the walls and outside into the hot, putrid air. It joined the continuous screams and tormented howls of things and creatures best left to the shadows of reality to fathom.

"Free...." the voice echoed across the broken plains. "Free...."

Chapter 1

Soft whispers of late summer air licked the underbrush in which Dugan lay sleeping beneath a mid-afternoon sun. His dreams were awash with fire, blood and revenge. Years of slavery, abuse and combat reflected back at him as a prism, a kaleidoscope of death and carnage.

It was from these nightmares he sought escape, but instead they hounded him during the day, and hunted him in his slumber.

Dugan wasn't aware of the date. Time had been erased for him in terms of days and years-only moments mattered now. He devoured them as they came, like a ravenous dog with his fallen prey.

He was Telborian, a race of humans that dominated most of the central and eastern lands, called the Midlands, of Tralodren. They were a fair-skinned people, tall and robust; with light- to medium-shaded hair. To most other races, the Telborians represented the only form of human they would ever encounter, but they were only one of four forms of humans populating the wide, diverse planet.

The figure of Dugan was different than most of his kin. He was ripe with muscles and battle scars, stood slightly more than six feet in height, and looked to have been chiseled out of stone. Even as he slumbered, there was a certain sternness, a dispassionate grace about him. He was more animal than human; being trained to fight on command and for no other reason than sport. Compared to the normal Telborian, he was something of a savage.

The breeze rustled the leaves above his head, softly caressing his blond hair. The Telborian awoke with a jerk. His movements were sudden and swift as he scanned the surrounding forest. His eyes moved with his head and, at some intervals, it appeared as if he were sniffing the air.

He occasionally cocked his head, exposing an ear to the breeze, hoping to catch the smallest sound, perhaps a snapping twig or lone shout or cry of discovery. His training had served him well in the arena, where he slew beast and man at the end of a chain and whip. Now those same skills would be used against his former masters.

From his position he could see for a good twenty feet in each direction, his body somewhat camouflaged by the blooming undergrowth where he'd hidden. His muscles tensed, causing a myriad of scars to appear on his bare upper torso. Chief among them was a deep branding mark in the form of a stylized eagle, which was emblazoned on his flesh like a cattle iron to a cow. It was seared into his left shoulder to serve testimony to his service in the gladiatorial games of the Elven Republic of Colloni.

The Republic used slaves for all manner of services. Those who could work did so, while those who were suited for more sensual occupations became engrossed in those. So, some slaves found themselves as gladiators, fighting for the glory of the court and society.

A gladiator's only possessions were the scars they suffered in their bloody toil. The more marks a gladiator had, the more battles they could claim to have survived, increasing their popularity and thereby ensuring a longer life in the Republic. Those who couldn't claim battle scars found their lives ending in the grave. Gladiators who performed well were allowed to accumulate profit for their owners and in theory themselves. While their owners were free and gained great wealth from their suffering, they were allowed to remain slaves and gain fame to keep it as long as they could survive the rigors of their martial occupation.

Those who failed to meet expectations were either killed within the arena or spared the quick death by the Master of Ceremonies, so they could provide another form of entertainment; a slow and torturous public execution.

The Republic of Colloni was the homeland of elves, who called themselves Elyellium or Elyelmic. Once, they had the largest empire the world had ever seen. It dominated three-fourths of Tralodren-but countless wars, rebellions, and the loss of one great leader after another caused the nation to dwindle to its present size, which consisted of a more feudal status with satellite colonies in nearby islands and continents.

Remnants of a once mighty and powerful, echo of glory are all that remained. It held great influence within the Midlands of Tralodren and was often involved in various matters of trade with the Telborian kingdoms and cities to the south and west. However, none of these cities or kingdoms looked favorably on the gladiatorial games (at least in public). Such barbarous acts had evolved in Telborian lands to jousts and contests of honor; though many still relished such blood sport as the elven games.

A hawk screeched off in the distance. Dugan was well aware elven hunters often used hawks to aid them in tracking their prey. He also was aware he was their prey. Hunters seemed to have an affinity for the avians; some had even jokingly speculated they shared the same disposition.

Upon hearing the hawk cry, Dugan began running further into the forest, his massive legs pushing him onward. He'd been running from the hunters for five days now, and knew they would never give up on finding an escaped gladiator. As long as the gladiator was on the island of Colloni, he was fair game to hunt, and retrieve for a bounty.

The amount of the bounty was usually dependent on the fame of the escaped gladiator. In Dugan's case, he would fetch a fine sum. He was a deadly fighter, and drew in large crowds, much to his previous owner's delight. Dugan's escape meant he'd lost a great money-making opportunity.

To the Telborian, it meant he would have to get off the island or be killed. He was surprised more hunters weren't after him, but understood why as well. The manner of his escape, and the reputation he had earned in the arena would chill even the most avarice-inflamed heart.

Whenever a gladiator escaped from the coliseum he was treated as both stolen merchandise and a thief. His owners made money off him through crooked betting, and fixed games. They would often try to prevent his escape through harsh rules and penalties. By escaping, the gladiator had broken the rules of the Republic, and once recaptured, the former owners could still make money one final time as they charged admission to watch the offending slave get crucified in the coliseum.

The more popular the gladiator, the larger the crowd, and money purses gathered for the final event. Even in meting out justice, the Republic sought to turn a profit while it taught its bloody lessons.

Dugan knew he was nearing the end of the island from conversations he had heard in the coliseum. Another day or so of running westward would get him to his destination, along the coast. It had taken him longer than he had thought to cross Colloni Although it was the smaller of many continents that made its home in the Midlands, Dugan was finding it really was much larger than he had first thought. He knew if he kept heading west, he'd come to the coast as the city of Remolos, from which he fled, was in its center.

A carpet of new growth and decomposing matter were crushed beneath his booted feet as he ran. The Telborian was naked save for a lion hide loincloth adorning his waist, and a pair of well-worn leather boots. His titanic limbs continued to thrust him forward at a rapid pace, making pursuit difficult-but Dugan knew the hunters were out there. They were relentless in their pursuit of money, and a bit of their own fame for having caught him.

He didn't want to waste any more time than he had to. He wasn't even slightly skilled in the wood lore these hunters practiced from childhood, so he felt his greatest advantage was in speed, not stealth. He leapt over a fallen tree.

He thought he heard a hawk cry again. Not only was it hard to maneuver through the dense brush, but he left a trail so clear even a child could find it. He thought he had chosen the right path of escape. It was certainly the quickest route as far as leaving Remolos was concerned. The path had let him hide well, until he crossed the hills and into another deciduous forest some two nights ago.

He had no idea, until his escape that the whole Island of Colloni was spotted with large forests, but he could understand why. The Elyellium, in general, were a nature-loving race, and liked to be surrounded by it. Even their building style reflected this. They would build towering columns and huge, spacious buildings with openings in every wall so they could take in the beauty surrounding them. However, their love was for ordered nature. Gardens had replaced much of the natural flora of the land, and even the forests surrounding cities and towns had been hand-planted long ago and pruned to the whims of the elven emperors. Even leaf litter was cleared at regular intervals.

Dugan stopped suddenly in his tracks. His fiery green eyes squinted as he strained his ears. He thought he heard a barking dog in the distance. His face cringed for a moment as he saw movement in the underbrush behind him.

They were much closer than he'd thought!

Dugan ran for about thirty feet, and then jumped as high as he could up into a thick collection of oak. The colossal muscles in his legs gave him enough of a boost to reach the first branch of a tall tree. Using his great strength, he pulled himself up into the foliage, and further cover.

Within moments, two tracking dogs ran out of the underbrush. They stopped for a moment beneath the tree where Dugan was hiding, sniffed around the mossy base for what seemed like an eternity, then began to growl fiercely.

Their brown, sleek bodies clawed and pawed the tree as they spied the escaped slave from below.

Their jaws salivated with delight as they barked their find to their masters.

Dugan's heart began to beat like a war drum. His muscles tensed and his eyesight began to take on a reddish tint. To a gladiator, these were tell-tale signs the body was preparing for a fight to the death. Dugan had learned this soon enough in the coliseum, and had used them to test himself before each battle. Without these cues he wouldn't have survived as long as he had.

The first sign was reddened vision. Indeed, the whole world seemed to become awash in a spray of blood as the rage boiled from within. The second was the great bursts of energy surging though his veins and muscles like small explosions of lightning. The third was the feeling of eerie calm, though his body was a raging engine of war. Together, these skills of the arena, if understood correctly, would put victory into the hand of whoever heeded them. After feeling the signs wash over him, Dugan understood that the warlustwas with him, and he could now safely handle any threat.

The mighty Telborian closed his eyes and drowned the growling dogs from his mind, effectively dismissing their loud snarls so he could focus on his plan. It had to be timed just right or his life was forfeited. Straining his hearing beyond the frustrated hounds below, he sat as still as a jungle cat waiting for the arrival of the hunters.

Dugan easily caught sight of the first patch of movement amid the forest growth from his high vantage point. The patch was moving faster toward him with each passing moment. Soon he could hear excited voices and running feet approaching, plodding the ground with no apparent desire for stealth.

Though he spoke the Elyelmic language, known as Elonum, he didn't understand much of the conversation due to their rapid excitement. All he could glean from the yelling was something about rexiums (an elven form of currency), and enjoying his death. Drawing in a breath, he poised himself for the attack. There could be no second chances; no mistakes.

Elves were beings not far removed cosmetically from humans, though to Dugan they always seemed to look like children or weak feminine creatures. They were fair-skinned, but had a smoother, younger look about them, possessing straight medium to dark hair and thin eyebrows. Neither sex could grow body or facial hair (which Dugan found amusing and added to his thoughts of them being childlike) they all displayed pointed ears.

These points weren't that dominate, being little more than half an inch at best above the top of a traditional human ear, but easily noticed from some distance given the 'wolfish' or 'teardrop' shape to the formation of the rest of their ear. The two hunters also followed Elyelmic tradition by keeping their hair cropped short and combed forward into bangs resting slightly above their slender eyebrows.

As his final thoughts dwindled down to concentrate on the task at hand, Dugan saw the first figure move out of the forest's undergrowth. He was tall for an elf, about six and a half feet. He wore the leather armor common to all elves engaged in the hunt as it was called; the pursuit of escaped slaves. It was bleached slightly to a dull wheat-brown, instead of the common tree-bark color standard for all hunters Dugan had seen during his years in captivity. Observing this, he realized he was dealing with an experienced hunter, as the discoloration could only have been caused by constant sun exposure. Taking out a skilled hunter would be harder but he was confident he could do it.

A second figure then emerged from the undergrowth. He too wore the armor of a hunter but it looked newer, almost freshly-made. Though it is almost impossible for any human to guess the age of an elf, due to their long lifespan, Dugan surmised the first figure was the other's superior by the way the second carried himself around the first. So, with only one real threat presented to him, the golden-haired slave pre-pared himself for a fight.

The hunters' reached the tree within seconds. Their senses were heightened as each drew his gladii, a favored weapon of the Elyellium. This weapon was a hiltless blade a little more than two feet in length and half a hand's breath in width.

Both of the hunter's weapons appeared to have seen action in recent days, nicks and other subtle signs of conflicts shimmered from their steel surfaces. Dugan could spy such details even from his vantage point as such details had to be learned in the fights he'd seen– any advantage one could gain over their opponent was greedily hoarded. Dugan could also smell their aroma of sage, nutmeg, and pine sap as it mingled with their sweat and leather dress. Known as the hunter's scent, which was thought to aid them in blending in with their natural surroundings, and keep them from being sensed by animals. Dugan, however, had yet to prove the validity of those claims.

As they neared, Dugan watched closer, not even blinking, should he miss the split second which could serve him as his moment to act. The older elf proceeded to move forward with an even gait as the younger one stayed behind him, wary and observant of what was around him.

Seeing his opportunity, Dugan leapt from the tree. His mighty frame crashed down on the older elf like a lightning flash, knocking him unconscious. The older hunter's body was smashed to the ground, leaving Dugan standing on top of him. The older elf had been pushed face-first into the earth while the gladiator straddled him as if balancing on a log. Dugan's face then took on the scowling look of a wild animal that had found its prey. The younger hunter rambled off something in Elonum as he swung his sword at Dugan. Using his reflexes and years of fighting experience, Dugan dodged the blow easily.

Rushing to charge him head on, the hunter yelled an old elven chant of protection to Aerotription, god of the elven race. This did little good as Dugan grappled the young hunter's blade away from him by crushing the hunter's wrist with a crackle of tendon, bone and flesh. The gladius fell harmlessly at Dugan's feet.

The young hunter reeled away in pain and horror, grasping his wounded wrist with his opposite hand while rattling off a stream of Elyelmic curses.

It was at that moment the dogs bit into Dugan's tanned flesh. They were trained to take down their prey with the least amount of damage, for 'the better the prey, the better the pay', went the old hunter slogan. Most of the time this was achieved by attacking the legs, which caused their victim to fall. Unable to move, the prisoner could then be easily captured.

Looking down at the furry pests, Dugan picked both of the beasts up by the scruff of their neck. The vicious snarls and saliva splattering attempts at biting his hands and arms didn't even faze the Telborian. He had fought fiercer beasts in the arena and lived. This whole episode was nothing but a temporary distraction to him at best . . . and he had grown tired of it.

With a throw that could only be accomplished by the strongest of men, he hurled the protesting animals into the nearest tree. There was a thick thud, a shrieking bark followed by a small whimper, then silence. The only thing remaining was a smear of blood trailing down the thick, mossy trunk to the forest floor. At the base of the blood smear the two dogs lay still, their heads bent at awkward angles, their bodies already growing cold.

Dugan then turned his attention to the final threat. The young hunter looked in panic at Dugan's advancing massive frame, then at the older, unconscious hunter sprawled out beneath the Telborian. Panic washed anew over his pallid features.

Dugan paced forward, his face full of malice. The elf began to seriously doubt his survival. Everything seemed so surreal, so wrong. In desperation, the young elf charged headlong into Dugan, fists flying like bees on a rampage. It was the final effort of a man who knew he was doomed. The youth was met with trained blows striking his smooth skin.

The young hunter was unconscious in a few seconds.

With the setback overcome, the Telborian stopped a moment to catch his breath, release the warlust, and think... to listen. For a moment, he stood silent amid the fresh carnage, his eyes taking in the whole scene, all his senses in rapt attention. Confident he was once more alone in the wood, he bent down to snap the necks of his would-be captors. He cracked them as if they were simple twigs rather than sentient flesh. Better than they deserved, but the Telborian didn't have the luxury of time to do much else.

Following this, he quickly began to go through their belongings. Knowing the leather armor was too small for him, as it was often fitted only for its wearer, he picked up the two gladii. They seemed to be relatively new, despite their recent use, and in good condition. He spun them both in a clockwise motion, creating two circles of steel in front of him as he tested the blades. A grim smile crossed the Telborian's lips as he surmised they were workable.

Dugan preferred a longer, edged sword himself, but was familiar with all manner of weapons to a certain extent. He'd been introduced to different weapons to add variety to the games. At least now he was armed again, and could face whatever else came his way; since he'd lost the weapon he had used to escape, among other things. . .

Pawing further through the elves' belongings, he found rations that could easily last him a week. He was glad they were elven rations, as they were well-balanced between meat, grains, and sweets. The variety would help him remain healthy while also permitting him to make them last longer than normal rations he'd been accustomed to in the coliseum.

Hastily gathering up his findings, Dugan checked his surroundings once more, then was off again. Confident of his greater safety now, at least for a while, he settled into a comfortable jog. Looking around as he ran, he noticed he was getting very close to the ending of the forest by the thinning of the wood. It had begun to slowly recede, and had grown more delicate, as if one were walking out into a great garden. Thin plants, and bushes began to appear as the tall, massive pines, oaks, sycamores, and maples started to disappear.

The Telborian could only guess at what lay beyond here. It could be plains, or more forest, or it could actually be the long-awaited coast. As Dugan had been a gladiator for most of his life, he had never traveled anywhere beyond the coliseum, or his cell in its darkened bowels. To run through the unknown of the island nation where they called him slave was an adventure undreamt of by all his imagination... and frightening.

For years, Dugan had known only enclosed spaces as home, but as he was confronted with miles of open space and a real sense of unlimited freedom growing fast upon his soul and spirit, a strange sense of dizziness and weakness absorbed him. In his old home, he was the champion and master of his domain. Even if he had been a slave, in the places where he could rule and reign: his cell, the arena, he was lord and master. In the lands he now roamed, however, he felt small and insignificant, as a bird in flight is lost when compared to the sky it inhabits.

Dugan grew more cautious. If he was reaching the end of the forest, he would be that much easier to catch. In the open field or even hill country, hawks and other hunters would find him that much easier. Over the next few moments of his jog he drew closer to a green barrier which seemed to be comprised of vines naturally arranged to form a curtain of sorts before him.

From his past days of travel he had discovered this was a common occurrence with the vines along the edges of all the forests. It was the elven way of using nature to close off one section of terrain from another - a means of ensuring control, keeping order, even amid the randomness of nature.

Dugan knew beyond the vines lay greater freedom, but something held the Telborian back. It wasn't the fear of being in the open, and therefore easily detectable, nor was it the thought of dying as soon as he stepped through the stringy green curtain before him; skewered by elven blades and arrows.

What held him back was a sharp point in the upper right portion of his back. A point reminding him of an arrow tip. Dugan cursed himself for a fool, for not thoroughly watching his back as he had let his confidence get the better of his disciplined senses. He didn't hear him approach until it was too late. If it was another hunter, he knew he was a dead man.

"Turn around…slowly," a voice spoke Telborous, the language of the Telborians from behind him. It had a strange quality which Dugan couldn't place. It was a medium-ranged tone made to sound lower than what it might be, and had the ring of a strange accent with which the Telborian was unfamiliar with as well.

Chapter 2

Sunlight withdrew its slender arms across the growing broad night sky. The day was dying. Pinpricks of stars illuminated the frost-covered ground, creating an eerie alien feeling about the whole area. It was a strange calm, similar to the one before the storm - a stillness that wasn't about to release itself in shouts or screams from what it hid from view. That feeling carried over to the forested areas as well. Forests that kept a silent watch on a lonely keep near the coast.

The strange calm generated a feeling of horrors among the darkened areas of the wood. Horrors making short work of any creature foolish enough to venture into their murky depths. For here were the Northlands, and it could be a rather harsh place at times - harsher than the warmer climes of the lands to the south.

This keep though, belonging to the Knights of Valkoria, sworn servants of Panthor, goddess of humanity, was far removed from such fearful appearances. Crafted of fieldstone and rough, quarried rock, it rose some, two hundred feet from the frosted ground; the ramparts raising another five. It kept a sole vigil on the sandy coast where the forests melted away into plains, rocky hills and surf. This keep was also encircled with a fearsome wall built of solid granite and topped with cast iron spear points that had rusted some over the years.

The entire curtained barrier rose some twenty feet off the ground, and was interrupted only by a pair of old oak doors which were reinforced on both sides by sturdy iron. They closed over a dirt road which slithered away to be swallowed by the forests beyond, another branch turning toward the coast where a handful of weathered sailing vessels lay in port in a relatively calm sea.

A handful of squat buildings nestled around the keep, but still behind the wall, like rocks encircling a tree, or children seated at the feet of an elder. These lesser buildings housed the clergy, scribes, and other lay people who contributed to the continued success and existence of the Knighthood and keep itself. The rest of the buildings, tower included, housed the persons of greater importance and the place of worship in which all came to worship.

The Knights of Valkoria strove to better humanity, and give aid to other humans where they could. Living by a strict code of honor and discipline, they were often misunderstood by non-humans and even other humans. Their views of human superiority over all other races branded them bigots by some. However, this religious zealotry had helped to secure the knights a reputation of honor and wisdom among the Nordicans, where they had helped to meld the warring tribes of the Northlands into one loyal, loosely united nation, keeping them from falling into ruin and decay after many generations of schism and strife for years at a time.

The Valkorian Islands, also called the Northlands or Land of the Nordicans, were comprised of four land masses: Frigia, Baltan, Troll Island, and Valkoria. All were in the far northern waters of the Yoan Ocean, near what is called The Top of the World. Here, the light of day was almost non-existent during the cold months of winter; which was fierce and prolonged, lasting more than half the year, while summer and spring never reached above what would be considered autumn temperatures in more southern lands.

However, it was here, in the midst of snowy fields, sharp winds, and almost eternal night, the Nordican race flourished. Nordican men looked like any other human, except they were taller, paler, blond, or red haired, with blue or green eyes. Nordican males were also hairier, and stronger than most other races. Their women tended to be stronger and taller too than most other human females on Tralodren - the very environment formed them as such.

They were a sea-faring people, raiders and explorers who looked to the ocean and rivers as a great road taking them to riches and lands wondrous to behold. To travel on it meant hope, excitement, and life itself. They didn't venture too far south themselves - the Midlands, the homeland of the Telborians, being as far as they would travel in most cases. Arid Land, a nearby source of supplies and profit suited many travelers and traders well. Often isolated by weather, clans, and terrain, they had learned to endure and learned to prosper despite it.

It was because of this limited contact and harsh life, many saw them as barbarians. Few from other lands ventured into the Lands of the Ice Warriors, as the very word, Nordican, means in their language.

The moon had yet to rise, and the men keeping watch on the tower suffered for it. The cool night was a normal one for any citizen of the keep during this time of the year, cooler still at the higher altitude they now stood on the tower's roof open to all sorts of passing breezes. Rowan, a young, sandy-haired Nordican, looked out over the surf below, and drew his fur-lined cloak tighter around his body to shut out the frosted winds relentlessly battering his bones.

He stood at the far southern rampart overlooking the frothy ice-cold sea eating at the rocky cliffs.

The raging waves lofted their salty scent into his nostrils, a scent Rowan had grown up with for the past seven years. It comforted him during the bitter nights like a soothing blanket wrapped around a child by his mother. He had been born and bred to appreciate it like most Nordicans. And, like most initiates in the Knighthood, Rowan had been recruited from the inhabitants of the Northlands. He had come from the Panther Tribe, a people who often went on raids to other lands and tribes to insure ample food supplies, as food could rarely be harvested in the semi-arctic climate of where the tribe resided.

Both of Rowan's parents were highly respected within the tribe, and were often honored by the chieftain. Rowan's father had been one of the greatest warriors of his clan, standing a bit more than six and a half feet, and built like a bear. Even for the hearty Nordican race, he was an impressive being, and when it came to fighting, no one could best him. Due to his prowess, he was often the leader on many of the raids and trading expeditions his tribe made both toward Arid Land to the south and his other Nordic kin scattered about the Northlands.

Rowan's mother, a slender great cat of a woman, was also well known amongst their tribe. A hunter of great skill, she could track prey with the cunning of a wolf. Often she'd leave in the morning, and return home with enough food to feed half the tribe.

When Rowan was born to them, they loved him as they loved life itself. When he came into their lives he brought a sense of purpose greater than themselves, and greater than the tribe. Their existence expanded as it took on a great new meaning for them at that time, and had ever since as they watched their son grow into manhood.

As he grew, his father taught him to fight, his mother to hunt. Rowan took to these lessons instantly. He didn't have his father's large frame, standing almost a head shorter than his sire, but more than made up for the loss of brawn and height with cunning and intellect.

By the power of observation and strategy, Rowan had won many battles with relative ease, more so than physical confrontations ever could. Rowan also had a handsome face, which combined the soft, loving features of his mother with the sharp, chiseled visage of his father. He had the dark blue eyes, the same color of the sky which covered the land of his birth, and lightened up his reddish-brown hair and enriched his fair skin. He was the pride of his father, and the love of every young woman in the tribe.

Over the years, Rowan grew into a very fit and proud Nordican male whose life would change in his twelfth year. It was then, on a warm day in spring, while learning a new fighting move from his father, when he noticed a group of men enter their village...

They were dressed in ornate metal armor adorned with pictures and designs of panthers, very much like his tribal totem. Five in number, they were rugged men who seemed to be as hearty as any man who made up Rowan's tribe. Their plate armor might have been a strange sight, but they were Nordicans like all the rest who called Valkoria home. There was something else, though, about the men marking them as unique.

It was the way they looked around with eyes clear and focused from a dedication that the young Rowan hadn't known any of his fellow kinsmen to possess. They moved as one; an organized band of men rich in confidence.

This wasn't arrogance, but rather a humble security in who they were - what they were about. This is what drew the young Rowan's eye. Though they were all physically strong, each also possessed an inner strength seeming to radiate outward, absorbing Rowan's full attention so he was drawn to them more than his lesson. He was soon reminded of that lesson though when a heavy wooden pole swished by his head, followed by his father's cursing.

Unaffected by the outburst, Rowan watched as the armored men surveyed the clan's totem, a great panther statue resting in the center of the village. It was carved to represent a panther on its haunches, observing all that lay before its lifeless eyes. They appeared to be impressed with it as they spoke excitedly, looking around the village with feverish eyes.

One of the armored men's eyes rested on Rowan for a moment. He motioned the others to look at him also. Rowan smiled at this older knight. The knight himself only nodded with a satisfactory smile of his own as did the other four who had started to murmur around him. Rowan couldn't hear the words, but knew they were speaking about him. There was a strange energy about the air then as the young Rowan watched them with a fleeting eye. He tried his best to divide his vision between his father, who was instructing him for the next maneuver, and the strange armored men.

Finally, after a brief discussion among themselves, they marched toward the young Nordican.

"Young man, come with us. We will train you to be a brave and true warrior who will fight for the honor and health of all this land and the human race," the armored man spoke.

"Who do you think you are then, to be making such an offer to my son?" Rowan's father interjected. His massive arm entwined about a thick quarterstaff poised at his side. "I'm more than able to teach him the ways of the hunt and war." We are warriors who have chosen to follow a knighthood dedicated to the teachings and ways of Panthor, goddess of the human race." The lead knight's body grew taller with pride.

…Human race...human race…

The words trailed off into nothingness as Rowan was brought back from his daydreaming into the present. The wind tried another desperate grasp at his warm cloak, but his fists held it tight.

That had been only seven years ago, yet it felt like a different time, a different Rowan. He had been taken to the knight's keep. There, he was taught to read and write, to fight and honor the goddess Panthor. The Code of Panthor had been instilled into his mind and heart. He had been honed like a blade in the forge to prepare for the night he now faced. He was ready to be accepted into the Knighthood should he prove worthy enough - should the goddess grant him entrance into her order. It had certainly become a night of reflections both toward the past and toward the future...

"Come on Rowan. It's time to get ready for the ceremony," the husky voice of Holvar, Rowan's friend, came from a stairwell leading into the heart of the tower.

Looking back one last time over the ramparts, Rowan smiled. Holvar was more excited than he let on. He had been fussing with his ceremonial garments since he awoke that morning. He had arranged them and rearranged them on his bed, looking over them like a mother hen.

Rowan shared the same nervous excitement as all the new dedicates of the order. It was only natural. After seven years of training, they would be granted the highest honor a member of their order could receive: to serve their goddess.

Rowan had learned a lot since the knights had taken him in to be trained as one of them. They were his family while he was away from his own, and the lessons he had learned during his stay had given him a sense of self-betterment and purpose.

They had opened his eyes to the world around him, and had awakened the spring of destiny deep inside him. Wrapping his cloak tighter about himself, Rowan walked to the stair-well where music was flowing up from the main chamber below. His excitement followed him as the moon came into full view, and the sun was swallowed by the greenish-white waves on the horizon.

An hour later Rowan was standing in the altar room of the tower along with many other young men. The altar room was the largest room in the tower, and took up much of the first floor, and a hallway. There was also a doorway attaching itself to another building outside the tower where the priests and higher-ranking members of the Knighthood kept their residence. However, the altar room was open to all who should enter whether lowly dedicate, layman, priest and knight alike. Maintained by the clergy, it was a spectacle to behold.

The ceilings rose high above the occupants who had come from all over the Northlands to see their sons pass their final tests. Along with them were those knights who could get away from their duties to witness the dedication ceremony. There were no spots to sit in the whole chamber. Instead the place was open and ornate, dominated by a large altar on the far west wall, opposite the assembly.

Dangling from the two-story ceiling, hung a bronze cande-labra swaying in the meandering heat of the room; a forest of white candles affixed to each of the two light sources.

The altar itself wasn't very large, but the dais on which it stood was. It comprised of four large white quartz steps, a gray marble statue of an attentive panther at each of their ends, which rose to a rectangular block of granite upon which rested the dark mahogany altar.

Polished to a fine sheen, the rectangular altar was a simple affair, plain and unadorned save for obedient wooden panthers, which stood tall on each of the four corners. On top of the altar was a simple golden, round shield emblazoned with the silver symbol of the faith, also the symbol of the Knighthood: a profile of a panther's head in mid-roar.

Near the bottom of the altar stood small braziers lit with glowing embers and smoking with sacred incense to the goddess, giving the chambers a rich, earthly scent. Their aroma mixed with the imagery portrayed on the many banners and tapestries hanging from the ceiling, walls, and behind the altar itself.

This room was also windowless, and so only the candlelight illuminated the holy inscriptions and past deeds of the Knighthood - which decorated these cloth relics of the faith. Some were as old as the Knighthood itself, showing events of its founding. Others were more modern with recent decades being portrayed in needle-worked yarn. To the truly dedicated follower, however, the altar room was the most beautiful and humbling place in the whole land.

Rowan, like the other dedicates, was dressed in uncomfortable ceremonial vestments. He stood at the base of the altar; his back to the gathered audience. The Robes of Dedication were beige, stiff and coarse, tight, long-sleeved, garments with gray emblems of a pouncing panther stitched all over them. They also possessed a gripping waistband and even tighter pant legs under the robes allowing for only the most minimal movement.

As an initiate, Rowan was to wear the garments as a sign of his holy dedication of spirit, mind, and body to his goddess. He thought the real dedication was not giving into the compulsion of ripping them off his body as he had been feeling over the last hour. He began to also entertain thoughts he would drown in his own sweat before the ceremony even began. The heat in the room had become like an oven to him - all the pressing of bodies, candles, and his own nerves wringing sweat from almost every pore on his body.

Once a year, the dedication rite was performed for all the tribes to observe. It was the induction of new members into the ranks of the Knights of Valkoria when Panthor chose her next soldiers - a very holy and special event for all her faithful. Those found unworthy by their goddess were sent back to their tribes. A small number of those who were not chosen as warriors became scribes or local workers to help run the day-to-day operations of the Order itself, but they did not bear armor or arms for their goddess. That honor was for the knights.

Trying to find his parents in the crowd, Rowan was rebuffed by his tall, awkward collar which had to stand at least six inches above his shoulders. After trying several more times with no better results, he decided to just give up until after the ceremony. He hoped it was soon, because he didn't like the thought of sweating to death or the almost unbearable anxiousness swimming in his stomach.

As he roasted in anticipation, two ornately-carved doors to the far left of where he stood suddenly opened, which caused everyone present to jolt in surprise. Carved into each side of this solid pine portal was the profile of a sitting panther. These were the same doors connecting the tower to the lower-leveled keep of sorts beside it where the priests and higher-ranking knights dwelled.

Red silken banners with the symbol of the Knight-hood standing guard beside the doors flapped in the soft gale created by their opening. As they opened, Rowan breathed a bit of relief as he knew the ceremony had started.

A tall and broad figure stepped out of the carved doors. His heavily panther motif decorated splint mail clanging and jingling as he approached the altar. A billowing gray cape with an embroidered gold panther's head, done in profile, followed behind him. The man was well-groomed and carried a certain amount of dignity about him as he stepped down through a path of parting bodies. As he passed by the knights, they bowed with deep respect.

He was the highest-ranking knight in the order; The Grand Champion of Panthor, the head of the knights, second only to the High Father himself. Tradition dictated the Grand Champion proceed and announce the High Father along with an invocation. The Grand Champion neared the altar at a serene pace, bowed to it in homage, then turned to address the massive audience as sweat dripped from his clean-shaven face.

"I, Sir Draven Talec, Grand Champion of the Knights of Valkoria, ask you to pay homage to Panthor, great goddess of humanity, as we begin our service of dedication."

The room's atmosphere swiftly changed as a peaceful presence filled the altar room. It seemed to soar on the singing voices of all in the assembly. As they sang an old hymn of invitation to the presence of the goddess of humanity, the supernatural presence attached to it softly assured the congregation they were at peace, and safe from harm.

Even the heat seemed to lift as the comforting breeze of the holy presence moved softly about the room. Rowan and his fellow believers knew enough from their instruction to understand the goddess herself was now present. Her spiritual being was near them, and she was ready to bless and commission the dedicates on their new path toward knighthood.

Throughout the hymn, which was sung with voices alone, all eyes focused upon the altar. The dedicates took a final moment to focus their thoughts. Each prepared for a powerful introspection and spiritual encounter they had been told would leave them changed for life.

Rowan felt his heart increase in rhythm as he focused on such thoughts. As the song drew to an end, a soft rustle of robes drew all eyes present to the new figure that emerged from the pine doorway.

This figure's beige robe was tied at his middle with a red belt, accentuating his thin waistline. Long white hair hung in tresses from the brilliant gold headband that encircled his wrinkled brow. His flesh was wrinkled and deeply tanned like the bark of some ancient tree. Though he looked old, his bright blue eyes spoke of the great vitality and spirit still driving the man onward.

The knights bowed as he passed with the deepest of respect. The others present immediately went to their knees. Though he was just above five and a half feet, he possessed a presence that made him seem colossal.

This was the High Father.

Deemed the highest-ranking priest of Panthor, and the spiritual center of the Knighthood itself, the High Father was said to be the most holy Nordican alive. As leader of the Knighthood and head instructor of the one true faith of Panthor, he was seen as a god-like being himself. This image was always discouraged by the High Father whenever he got wind of it, but it was still murmured amongst believers, as it had with his predecessors and theirs before them.

As he approached, the thumping of the High Father's old, worn, cedar staff fell in rhythm with the beating of Rowan's heart. He'd heard stories about the High Father, but had never seen him in person. Not even in the long seven years he had resided with the Knighthood had he laid eyes upon the holiest man of the Northlands.

The High Father spent his days sequestered in meetings with the lesser priests of the faith, worshiping in solitude, interpreting the will of the goddess, or running the affairs of the Knighthood. Rowan found himself more than amazed by the sight of the elder priest. The young Nordican thought he'd die from the sheer excitement of it all as the old, bent figure shuffled toward the altar. With a massive flourish of his staff, more for dramatic style than practical means, he bid the people to rise.

"We are here to bear witness," the High Father began in a strong, raspy voice, "to these young men who have chosen to follow a higher path, serving Panthor as her men of arms. They were called from their old lives to be taught how to help humanity on a larger scale. Their training complete, now they stand before the goddess' altar, ready to dedicate themselves fully to her cause, for the rest of their lives. Each of them deserves our deepest respect. For who among us could ever take on such tasks as The Queen of Valkoria will ask these young men?"

Sir Draven raised himself to the altar to stand one step below the High Father and addressed the crowd. Even when compared to the aged High Father, the strong warrior seemed the weaker of the two. The holy eminence of the high priest overshadowed the martial and physical prowess of the mature knight.

"These young men have been tempered and shaped like the swords in our smithy. Each one of them has been instilled with what Panthor and the Knighthood expect of them, and it is now a great pleasure to begin their dedication and induction into our ranks. Every one of them is more than worthy in our eyes," Sir Draven began his speech in high Nordic spirits.

The room suddenly exploded with jubilation and excited responses as parents supported the Grand Master's interpretation of their child. After a few moments, the High Father then raised his arms in the air, and the room fell silent once more.

"Panthor rejoices with you, young dedicates, as you are brought closer to her presence than any other warrior. Step forward so you may receive the blessing of Panthor and enter this sacred trust of service for the greater good of humanity."

The Grand Champion silently gestured the young men to step up toward the altar.

The young men, solemn faces hiding excited but uncertain grins, slowly walked toward the altar platform. They formed rows to allow everyone a place on the altar steps. None would be left on the floor when the dedication began.

Rowan swallowed hard as he stood as still as he could. He had found room for himself on the third altar step, just a breath away from the Grand Champion himself, and within sword strike of the High Father. He hoped neither could see his legs shake, or hear his racing heart and erratic breathing.

Though he had dreamt of this moment often, he always had pictured himself more calm and noble-looking, not so scared and excited. He wanted to be a knight - more than anything in his whole life - but he was fearful of what the dedication process would reveal.

Rowan knew the beginning of the ceremony was simply a show for those gathered. The last stages really tried a man.

Here there were three tests the goddess demanded of her dedicates during the asking of blessing. These three tests were the means by which the true merit of a knight was proven Should he pass all three tests, he would then be granted acceptance into the order.

These tests were divided into the three aspects of a man. One was for the body, one for the mind, and one for the spirit. Each was different for the individual dedicate. Though

Rowan had prayed and studied as best he could, and had practiced as hard as his body would allow, he was uncertain how he would fare when it came to the testing of his spirit.

He had searched himself as deeply as he could, but still was uncertain of what would befall him, and what he would be forced to discover about his deepest self. The time had finally come though. There was no turning back.

"Goddess of all that is right with humanity, hear us today," the High Father began in a somber tone. "Fill these young men with the holy tests of your devising so each may merit his own worth and come to you in understanding of himself, and of your favor or displeasure in their attempt to join our holy order."

As the High Father finished his prayer, a great wind overwhelmed the altar room. Slowly at first, it licked the candles and caressed the High Father's thin hair, then rushed itself into a lofty gust flying upon the faces of the dedicates.

Rowan gasped as he realized the tests had begun.

He prayed he would be worthy.

Then the altar room disappeared and the whole world - as Rowan knew it - vanished.

Huge birds, the likes of which Rowan had never seen, swooped down upon him; brushing his dark brown hair with their multicolored tails. He looked around and discovered he was in the midst of a strange jungle. A fat sun hung low above him adding to the already oppressive heat and dingy, greasy hue of daylight.

Tall, thick trees and vein-like roots clustered before him with wide-bodied vines tying it all together. Flying insects buzzed around his head and dipped their appendages into his sweaty flesh. He took off his ceremonial gown and vestments; stripping down to his thin undergarments: a pair of breeches and shirt, and began to look for a way out of the strange terrain.

He didn't know if what he was experiencing was real or not, as the tests of his goddess were often in the mind of the dedicate, though some dedication visions had taken on physical manifestations in previous ceremonies. He would just have to be observant, and do his best at proving himself.

As he began to move through the jungle, a faint whisper floated toward him. It sounded like the brushing of leaves on a tree when touched by a gentle wind. At first it was weak, and he dismissed it as a figment of his mind; but then it grew in volume.

come......come......Come this way.

The voice seemed to emanate from the jungle's interior, but Rowan heard it clearest in his head.

The noise, heat and activity drained his mind for a moment. He had to realign his thinking to concentrate, to make sure he understood what was going on, and if he had indeed heard a voice. What was his goddess trying to tell him? Assuming it was his goddess speaking to him...

Though he didn't want to go deeper into the jungle, Rowan found himself being drawn to it, as if a strange force had taken over his body, moving it like a puppet into the mysterious, humid, vegetation. As he was drawn on he noticed all the birds that had previously been present when he had first arrived had now suddenly vanished. The sun too, which had beaten down on him constantly since his arrival, had lessened to a soft warmth, and the very air itself was charged with a pulsating energy.

It felt to Rowan as if he was entering the mouth of a hungry beast. A beast ready to devour him body, soul, and spirit.

Come....come… The voice called on.

Chapter 3

Dugan slowly obeyed the command he had been given. He wouldn't be taken easily, and readied his gladii for a fight. If he was going to die anyway, at least die outside the arena - on his own terms. He could also get the pleasure of taking his would-be captors with him.

"Don't even think of using those swords." The strangely accented voiced ordered.

"Drop them." The words were a strong, low growl. "I said drop them - and I mean it. You'll be dead in an instant at this range."

Dugan knew in the heat of the moment accuracy could be lost entirely. He also knew at this range, it was impossible to miss with any weapon.

The Telborian reluctantly complied.

The weapons fell to the forest floor below with a muffled rustle.

He then silently turned to face his captor. As his eyes met his assailant's, Dugan was shocked to find his foe was not a man - as he had assumed - but a woman. An elven woman had captured him where two male hunters had failed. But this was not just any elven woman. She was like no other elf he'd ever seen.

She had long, shimmering silver hair whose brilliance was enhanced by her radiating sapphire eyes. The deep pits of color seemed to draw Dugan into them like magical gems, taking hold of his mind - forcing him further and further inside their recesses. Lithe, tall, and graceful, her light frame seemed to float when she moved. However, Dugan also saw and understood that she knew her the short bow she held before him; arrow tip centered on his person.

Her skin was of an alabaster hue with a soft gray tint adding warmth to her pallid complexion. Her pointed ears were also more angular than the elves the Telborian had known, and she had an even more refined and fragile look to her.

Who was she? A hunter? If so then she didn't have the hunter's scent, and she wasn't dressed like them either. Why hadn't he seen the likes of her among the elves he had known before? He wasn't even sure if she was a being of flesh at all. more a spirit that took on flesh. The Telborian kept a steady eye leveled against her as she stood defiantly facing the mighty gladiator. Her short bow, which was carved to look like it was a twisting set of horns from some type of strange animal that Dugan didn't recognize, at the ready.

"So I suppose you're going to take me back to Remolos then? What's your take on the money you're claiming after my crucifixion?" Dugan did his best to hide his amazement upon learning of his captor's identity.

"Shut up! I'm here to save you," she spat out. Again the accented Telborous seemed strange to the escaped gladiator.

Dressed in a dark brown hooded cloak, the hood of which was now down, she didn't grant the Telborian any further information to discern her nature. Only in a few instances of movement could he catch a glint of a sword strapped to her waist, and flashes of some type of leather armor not common to the hunters - or even Elyellium, for that matter.

Was she an elf from outside the city? Perhaps she was a country bounty hunter looking for fast coin to advance her station in life. But why hadn't he heard of other elves in the land then?

"Look," Dugan started, "I don't want to kill you, so just get out of my way. I'm not going to be worth the trouble I'm going to cause you... so just leave me be."

"Would you listen to me?" The elven woman's words were rushed and frustrated. "I'm not a hunter! I'm not here to collect your bounty. I'm your only way off this island."

The arrow point remained fixed on the Telborian, just above his heart.

"Do you think I'm dumb enough to believe you?" Dugan snorted. . "Listen, I don't know who or what you are, because the elves I know sure don't look as strange as you, but I have to get out of here. I've lost enough time with you already."

Dugan turned to pick up his weapons and began to leave through the vine curtain behind him, Suddenly he was pulled back by the impressively strong grip of the elven maiden; her fingers digging into his left shoulder.

His strong chin clenched tight with anger as his eyes smoldered into slits of burning cinders. The Telborian turned once more to face the bothersome woman. He pierced her with his gaze, causing her muscles to twitch tighter in anticipation. Her grip still remained. The arrow, though, relaxed from its former aggressive position. He could strike now... should he wish. He didn't need a blade to kill, and his hands could make short work of that frail swan-like neck of the elf before him...

Dugan kept himself ready.

"You don't understand. I've got a boat nearby with people willing to help get you out of here. I'm with a group of people who want to free you. We can get you out of here, if you will just stop being so pig headed!" This time there was a petition in her eyes - a frustrated pleading for the Telborian to hear her out and believe her words.

"I don't need your help!" Dugan returned. He tore himself from the elf's grip, and took a few steps away from her. "I got this far on my own and I don't need anybody's help to see me through the rest of the way! I'll be damned if I would ever accept the help of your kind for anything."

Dugan growled, turned to leave again but was halted by a sudden noise. The woods were abruptly filled with the shouts of other elven hunters calling out their location. Dugan's eyes grew wide. The elven woman's violet eyes glimmered with urgency, but her bow remained relaxed and lowered from the Telborian.

"I knew I should have just killed you," Dugan hissed to the woman, as he turned to pick up his weapons, and resume his run out of the forest. Before he had fully arisen from bending down to pick up his discarded weapons, he heard the release of a bowstring, and then felt a sudden pain in his back, which quickly flowed into numbness.

Dugan turned to face the elven woman but didn't make it all the way around to face her before he began to get lightheaded, and then was enveloped in darkness as the world was lost to him.

The Telborian fell to the ground with a thud.

"Why do you males have to be so stubborn?" The elf maiden's voice echoed in his head as everything faded into nothingness.

Darkness had fallen on the Republic of Colloni. A soft breeze and warm temperatures made for a blissful night. It seemed the early autumn winds were banished for a while, and the breath of summer still held on for a spell.

Dugan appeared to be asleep. His tanned body was sprawled out like fresh kill in a small clearing of hilly grassland outside the woods through which the Telborian had just been recently running. Though his face could be seen by the cold glow of the stars above him, it was hidden mostly by the thick blond tangles around its strong contours, allowing him to peer out of his half-closed eyes undetected.

The ravishing elven woman sat a little ways off from him, polishing and tightening her bow. She was everything an elven and human male desired in a female. Be she god, demon, or another mortal, her blood could not be pure elven - she was too different. Dugan was sure of it.

Her cloak had been discarded, allowing his vision to roam over her toned, leather-clad frame. Her dress was definitely foreign. The stitching of her leather pants, armor, and boots all seemed to be backward, and more interlaced than the elven garb he had become accustomed with seeing. Even her sword, which now lay close by her side, and near a simple traveler's backpack, seemed exotic. It curved slightly at the end of its medium-range progression to end in a fat dollop of steel. Added to her short bow's unfamiliar design, she seemed out of place for this land altogether.

As Dugan watched her, she looked up from her work at him. The only sounds were of his breathing, and of crickets in the blackness beyond the starlight. They were alone on the open plains between the forest, and the ocean no more than two miles to the west. They didn't have a fire as to remain as hidden as possible, and it wouldn't get as cold for them to really be worried about its absence anyway. She was just happy she'd been able to hide them so well both in avoiding the hunters in the forest, and now here amid the grassy hills.

It wasn't easy to move the Telborian to his current place, as he had to weigh as much as an ox. Furthermore, she had to grunt and groan through the terrain with the excess baggage, covering her trail as best she could as she went. She had been assured by the same person who had told her where to find Dugan if she made it this far, she'd be safe for the night. So far her allies' information and insight had not been found wanting.

She glanced around the area for a moment, making sure their location was secure, then turned back to her work. When she did, she saw the gleam of moonlight on one of Dugan's two swords laying beside her. She'd taken them off the brute when he was knocked unconscious by one of her magical sleep arrows. The arrow had just enough strength to knock out a large animal; allowing her to put Dugan to sleep and carry him without a struggle. Lacking access to his weapons, she hoped he wouldn't be much of a threat to her. She also hoped it'd make him more cooperative; and willing to listen to what she proposed.

Looking closer at the blades a second time, she was suddenly filled with alarm. She'd set both blades down beside herself, out of Dugan's cold reach, yet there was only one now. She began to frantically search the area for the missing blade, but it was nowhere to be seen. Then it found her as it pressed up against the front of her neck; the hand wielding it reaching out from behind her.

"You have some explaining to do, elf," Dugan whispered in her ear, his hot breath stripping any courage from her being.

"I find it a little hard to talk with a sword against my neck" she feigned what bravery she could.

"I'm sure you'll find a way; you're the resourceful type," Dugan growled.

The woman swallowed hard then relaxed.

"For starters who are you? You aren't like any elf I've seen. What type of hunter are you?" With each question Dugan tightened his grip on the sword just a little more.

"I'm Clara Airdes, and you probably haven't heard of my people. I'm from another branch of the elven race called Patrious who live far to the west. We have little love for the Elyellium, let me assure you.

"I was sent by my people to find you, and take you off Colloni. I'm in need of your strength and training to assist me in a task I have been given." She tried to get a bit more room to breathe, but Dugan's other hand gripped her left shoulder and withered the effort before it could begin.

"Elves sent you to retrieve me from other elves?" Dugan wasn't believing any of this.

"Yes, from the Republic of Rexatious- my home-land." Clara did her best to measure her words- to keep the gladiator calm. She wouldn't be able to reason with a man given over to strong emotions.

"Never heard of it." Dugan drew the blade a bit tighter above Clara's neck, this time drawing a thin trickle of blood. "How did you know where to find me, or when even?"

"I wasn't quite sure... only had a vague location for where you might be. I had to track you for a few days before I found you." Clara grimaced under the pressure.

"I see. And what if I don't accept this 'call for aid' from this Rexatious? What if I simply go my own way? Surely then you'd have no objections," Dugan mocked.

"No, I would have no objections," Clara swallowed hard.

"Where would you go, though?" she asked. "Or better yet, how? You think you can just walk into a city and pick up some kind of transport off Colloni with that wonderful scar on your shoulder, and hunters on your back? If it wasn't for me, you would be back in Remolos right now, getting ready for your final performance in the morning."

Her forehead had started to bead up with sweat. She was running out of options.

Clara cringed as Dugan turned her head to the side, forcing her to look into his cold and mirthless eyes. She felt the small trickle of blood grow a bit larger; like a claret stream now running down her throat. She had been foolish in underestimating the skill and speed of the golden-haired human. It seemed now it could cost her very life. She needed to keep to the plan, and get back control, or she'd never get out of the situation alive. She needed Dugan.

She just prayed he would be as worthy a final piece as she'd been told he was. She didn't want to have gone through all this suffering for nothing.

"What if I told you I would help you off Colloni first, before you had to decide," Clara's visage was calm and businesslike. Even her eyes were still ponds, though under them a current of chaos seethed. "It would be a good-will gesture of my intentions."

Dugan pondered Clara's words deeply. He knew she was right. He hadn't given much thought to fleeing Colloni once he reached the coast. Instead, he'd just assumed a situation would present itself allowing him to leave without detection. His impulse-driven escape didn't allow him the luxury of much of a plan besides getting out of the arena. Perhaps this strange elf was of some merit after all. Even if he did get free of Colloni with her help, he was under no obligation to join her 'cause', though he doubted such a thing really did exist. It seemed like a fair offer unfortunately, though it came from an elf.

Dugan hesitated.

What did she really want?

"So you're not a hunter?" He repeated.

"No." Clara flatly answered.

"You want me to join you on some mission you're on as decreed by your homeland?" Dugan studied her face.

"Yes." Again the words were flat.

"You're willing to offer me freedom without any strings attached," Dugan intensified his steely gaze.

"Yes. It is up to your honor and conscience to decide where your obligation lies after that." Clara's eyes again had begun to plead with the Telborian to take up her offer.

Dugan smirked. "You assume much about my conscience and honor then."

"Maybe, but it is a risk I'm prepared to take." This time her words were bold as well as true - and Dugan believed what she said.

"So then, why did you attack me back there instead of telling me all this?" He asked.

"I believe I tried to," Clara did the best she could at hiding her frustration, "but someone was too bull-headed and bent on running to listen. Besides, we didn't have time to stand around and talk - the hunters were right on your trail. You left a swath of tracks even an elven babe could have followed. I drugged you with my arrow and carried you out of the forest to here."

"You drugged me? It must have been some drug," Dugan chuckled to himself.

"Not really," Clara's matter-of-fact tone broke the Telborian's levity.

"Well, I don't think you could have dragged me this far all by yourself without snapping in two," Dugan darted a quick look about him to see nothing more than the hills. "Where are the others who helped you? "

"You'll find out I am full of surprises. We'll be safe here until morning. Right now, we both need some rest." Clara's eye's darted down toward the gladius at her jugular.

"Assuming I agree to follow you tomorrow, where are we going?" Dugan didn't move.

"If you decide to come with me, I have a boat waiting for us in Ino. It's a small port city on the coast, about two miles west of here," Clara tried to swallow. " We'll be safely out to sea before any hunter can come close to us."

The gladius then relaxed a bit across Clara's neck. She hoped it meant Dugan was beginning to trust her, and possibly even agree to come with her.

At the very least, a return to reason was a blessing.

It was this return to logic that emboldened Clara to push again for her own safety.

"I'm risking my life for your safety and freedom, at least put down the gladius."

Surprising, the weapon came away from her neck. Dugan remained behind her, though - ready to strike should anything not sit right with him.

"Thank you." Clara carefully wiped the blood from her neck with her hand. "You can leave anytime you want, but it would be foolish to try. There's nowhere on Colloni you'd be safe. As long as you're on elven soil, you'll be tracked down like a dog. The best chance you have is my proposal, even if you don't fully trust me or believe my offer, and you know it."

Dugan swallowed hard, and then locked his jaw firmly in place. He may have been a gladiator, but he wasn't stupid, especially where matters of self-preservation were concerned. What option did he have? The elf was right. He simply detested the fact of having his salvation handed to him by the same race which had once enslaved him. After much thought, he had failed to see any worse-case scenario for himself by going along with Clara's offer, and so reluc- tantly accepted.

"All right," Dugan wiped the flecks of Clara's blood off his gladius on his loincloth as he rose and stood before her. "I'll go as far as the boat ride, but then I can choose where to go after that. I'll be no one's slave anymore."

"That is the deal," Clara's sapphire eyes looked up and into the Telborian's hard green orbs. "If anything, I'll have earned some blessings from the shade of Cleseth for my service to a human slave. I think you'll consider joining though, once you understand the nature of the situation."

"What is this task you are undertaking then, if you think it will convince me to stay? And how did you know my name?" He watched the elf pull a corner of her cloak to her neck to clean up the rest of the blood that had still managed to run down her throat, and would for a little while longer from the small cuts.

"I'd rather not say out here, it would be best if left alone until all those concerned meet together." Satisfied that the worst of the bleeding had stopped, Clara returned the cloak to its resting place beside her.

"Why? What are you hiding?" Dugan questioned her as she began to unroll a simple brown cloth sheet on the ground, unpacking it from her nearby backpack as the Telborian stood over her; watching her all the while.

"You'd better get some sleep, Dugan, you'll need it," Clara remarked, ignoring Dugan's inquisitive stares. She lay down on her blanket, covering up with her cloak, and prepared for sleep. Her bow and sword lay ready at her side, but she didn't make any move toward them nor even search them out with her eyes. She was confident all was well for the time being, and would put her faith in that.

Dugan walked a few feet from the elf. Obviously he wasn't going to get anything out of Clara tonight. He would keep himself armed though just the same. He could play her game. As long as it guaranteed him his freedom, and his life in the end. He stepped off a few paces more and made his bed with dirt and grasses, taking his rest opposite the elf, facing her; blade near his reach.

He didn't sleep though. His eyes stayed open, staring at Clara. As he watched, he felt for the wound the arrow had caused in his back. After several minutes of searching he discovered, much to his amazement, there was no wound.

"If you're looking for a hole in your back Dugan, you won't find it," Clara spoke as she lay still on her blanket, eyes closed tight. "That arrow I hit you with was enchanted to cause sleep, not to harm a person. You're perfectly all right."

"Elven magic," Dugan cursed through a hoarse whisper.

On the outskirts of the makeshift camp, Clara smiled.

Chapter 4

"Are you sure this is the safest route?" Dugan whispered to Clara in the morning breeze. The pair found themselves overlooking the wonder of the landscape of Ino. They had traveled during the early light of dawn to the outskirts of the city. There they stood a short distance away from the hustle and bustle of the port's brick walls which rose more than twenty feet from the plains surrounding it.

Ino was a small city used mainly as a harbor for importing goods to the Republic. It exported little, save Elyelmic ideas, ideals and a few soldiers to refresh the forts dotting the nearby Telborian lands to the west. It was also a place where danger lurked, waiting to erupt.

Hunters often patrolled the cobblestone streets in search of prey by pirates of human and elven descent, looking to make a coin or two off the suffering of others. It wasn't unheard of for people to be kidnapped and sold off as slaves to the Republic or used for other forms of entertainment in varying localities across the Midlands.

While some imperial presence was made known with guards and soldiers patrolling a few streets, the reality was many, if not all of them were on the take of someone who paid them for blind eyes and deaf ears when the need arose. It was common knowledge that even governing elves of the city were bribed; serving the wishes of whoever gave them some decent piles of rexiums as if they were the wishes of the emperor himself. Of course, should the 'good graces' of the

Republic be tramped too hard and some 'reform measures' needed to be implemented to please the higher powers that be, then these corrupted forces would put on a good show of reform … for a little while … before reverting to old habits. In short, Ino wasn't a place you'd want to call home if you were a rather decent person, and could afford to live elsewhere.

"Yes I'm sure. My boat is here, and waiting at the docks. All we need to do is stay hidden until we get there." Clara dug in her backpack, and pulled out a common-looking brown cloak.

"Take this," she shoved the cloak to Dugan, "It will keep you hidden as long as you don't speak. Slump to break up your frame and keep your face in the hood."

Dugan looked at the garment with a scowl. "It reeks of the hunter's scent."

"I know, I got it off a hunter while I was tracking you. The scent should add to your disguise. You should have had enough experience with them to be able to pretend to be one." Clara cautiously looked around their location. They were still some distance from the walls of the city; perhaps a quarter mile.

Not many, if anyone was about this time of day. They had chosen a little area secluded by a clump of waist-high bristling bushes to make the final preparations before they entered Ino. If anyone was out, they were on the main road leading into the open gates of Ino, which was a good many yards from them still. Those that were out, though, would care nothing for the two strangers, had they seen them - but none did.

"Great," Dugan groaned beneath his breath. "That's all I need."

"Just stop worrying," Clara's tone seemed maternal, "You're completely safe with me.

48

With us being cloaked and smelling like hunters, we are less likely to be hassled by anyone. Are you ready?"

"So you killed an elf?" Dugan took in her angelic face. "No hunter would part with his cloak unless he were dead."

Her face had grown solemn at the Telborian's comment. "I had to at the time. There was no other way."

"Why are you cloaked, though?" Dugan raised an eyebrow.

"I'm a Patrious elf. The Elyellium don't favor my race too highly. For the safety of us both, it's better if I assume the role of a hunter as well."

"So then, I'm not completely safe with you, then am I?" Dugan stared into her eyes with his own stern orbs.

"As long as you stay with me you're safer than if you were left to your own devices." Clara was short.

"Why do they dislike your race so much?" Dugan eyed her slender body like a jungle cat.

Clara was silent. She pulled up her hood, and started to walk toward the front main road that made its way into the gate nestled between the dark gray walls of Ino. "You'll find out soon enough."

The gladiator simply looked toward the distant city in silence as the wind blew at his golden strands like wheat stalks in a field. With the wind came some doubt about what he had gotten himself into. He felt he could go on, and had enough faith in Clara to at least trust her not to turn him in or harm him, but he was beginning to wonder how long this journey might last. If she was indeed as welcomed in Colloni as an escaped slave... well, perhaps it wasn't a good omen for any favorable end.

"We haven't much time! Come on!" Clara called back to him.

Dugan shook his head to clear it of his thoughts, and then followed. If this mission she kept referring to was real, as were the other things she was telling him, then Dugan found himself wondering anew at why she was doing this, and going to all this trouble to help an elven slave escape. Something didn't make sense here, and before things went too far he was going to get his answers... one way or the other.

He checked the gladii which he'd holstered in the belt of his loincloth, and then broke into a jog to catch up to Clara.

Beyond the thick, iron-shod, wooden gates of Ino, a whole land appeared. Swallowed behind the maw of the dark, weather-worn wall, shops and commerce bled about the stern stone edifices, columns and walls.

A foul odor also wafted up from the cobblestone streets of Ino. To the resident, used to living many years with the noxious scent, the only distinguishing smells were those of fresh-baked bread, mixed with exotic spices from the far-flung islands of the south, and the salty sea breeze from the port.

That wasn't what the traveler experienced though, especially if they were unaccustomed to city life. Putrid aromas of decaying food, dung, and ill-washed people assaulted Dugan's nose.

Though Ino had wide streets open to the air, building placement, and the outer walls made it difficult for the wind to travel through, and remove the smell of unwashed feet and feces, it far outlasted any other pleasant fragrance. The Telborian was barely able to stifle a retching cough as he followed Clara through the streets, both of them cloaked in their stolen disguises. He now tried to use them as a means to filter out the stench.

"How much further? This city is making me sick," Dugan rasped from out of his hood.

"I thought the odor would be similar to the dungeons of the coliseum," Clara's nose wrinkled as she darted small looks here and there as they walked through the thinly-populated streets, careful to take notice of anything or anyone who might hint at causing them some difficulty or harm.

"No, the Elyellium aren't stupid. They kept the animals on the lower levels. They wanted to keep the gladiators healthy to fight, so we were on the upper levels. And let us bathe often and kept our cells clean too," Dugan's voice was a low growl. "How can elves live here with such a stench?"

"This is a smaller urban area." Clara whispered as she continued to survey the area with a studious gaze. "They have different rules here than most Elyelmic cities. Ports are hard to keep clean. They have too much activity and too many visitors to keep up with. The walls don't help either. They're here to stop raids from marauding pirates, and other rogues."

"Fine. Just get me out of here. If this is civilized freedom, I don't have much to look forward to," Dugan coughed into the cloak.

"We're near the docks, "Clara informed the Telborian. "I can smell the water. About another two streets, and we should be there."

As they walked, Dugan studied his surroundings as best he could, while remaining hidden from passersby. He noted many taverns and inns around the streets, which were bursting at the seams with rowdy human, and elven sailors. The number seemed too great to be gathered in such a small section of town, even by his outsider perspective.

Peddlers and beggars laid claim to the various inter-sections the duo passed, and he could also make out structures lined with priests. He assumed them to be temples.

A few of the temples had symbols he recognized. One was the symbol for Perlosa, goddess of the waves and moon; her symbol had been on a warrior he killed recently. Her sign was of a full moon overlaid with a crescent moon. Often the full moon was made of silver, the crescent moon black, though they had been known to be reversed in places.

He also noticed the symbol for Aerotription, who many said was the god of the elves. Dugan had seen this symbol more than a thousand times draped from the walls and entrances of the coliseum. It filled his heart with the blackest of rage to see it again here; so far from Remolos. But this was still Colloni and the land of the Elyellium, and their god.

The symbol was slightly complicated: a four-pointed white star, over a purple background, crossed by two silver-tipped, purple-fletched arrows. Dugan's rage was stoked further when he witnessed the smiling faces of the clergy ushered in and out of the temple, as though it was a place of peace, not a symbol of a god hungering for the blood of slaughter. Had he a death wish, Dugan would have charged into the temple and slaughtered all of the elves he could find inside; slaying those smiling priests until he himself was slain. For now he simply walked past while his rage seethed in his gut.

As Clara walked through the throng of people inhab-iting the city, she paid close attention to the crowd's reactions to them, especially to Dugan. Much of the population were elves, but about one fifth were Telborian sailors and mer-chants who sold their cargo in the markets.

She studied their faces as they passed, and found none of them were curious - or even concerned - about their presence in the city. Apparently their disguises were convincing. Clara was pleased, and hoped it would last until they got on the boat, and were safely away from the Island's grasp. She spied the entrance to the harbor a little ways ahead of them, and started to look for signs of concentrated hunter activity. She feared they'd be stalking the docks in search of fresh prey, as this was one of the few ways off of the island. She didn't see any, and took it as a good omen.

"Aghh!" Dugan spat out.

Clara quickly turned her attention to the cloaked Dugan, who had stopped, and was looking at his boot.

"What is it? Are you hurt?" She spoke while looking around herself nervously.

"No," Dugan muttered in a hoarse whisper. "I stepped in a pile of-"

"May I be of some assistance brother?" A voice speaking Elonum quickly drew both of the duo's eyes to a lean figure of an elf wearing the outfit of a hunter. He appeared middle aged, and of average appearance for an Elyellium. His manner, though, spoke of some training and experience that came only from the more aged of hunters.

Clara cursed under her breath as she managed a smile. They were so close.

"Are you hurt, sir?" The elf spoke to Dugan, who was still deeply-cloaked in the dark hood.

The air seemed to draw itself closely around the pair as the elf continued to stare at Dugan's cloaked form. Clara sweated profusely as she tried to think up ideas to get them out of the hunter's grasp without arousing too much unwanted attention.

The seconds seemed to drag on in agony as her mind raced for solutions. They never came. She was running out of options, time and space as the hunter drew in closer to Dugan to offer his assistance at what he believed to be another hunter.

It would seem odd to refuse the aid of a fellow hunter. At the very least, they had to be civil to each other.

As Clara continued to rack her brain for an idea, Dugan saved them.

"That's all right my friend," an old Elonum speaking voice came out from Dugan's hood. "I am quite well. I just stepped on a bad spot of road, that's all. Thank you for the offer."

Clara couldn't believe what she had heard.

"Very well, take care- and you too sister." The hunter's expression then took on a bit more concern. "You appear very pale and tired, perhaps from a long trip? At any rate, I must be off."

"Good hunting," the congenial words were more unnerving than his presence.

"G-good hunting," Clara stammered in disbelief.

As the hunter walked off toward the harbor, Clara stared at Dugan in astonishment. The color slowly returned to her gray-tinted flesh, but her eyes still remained as big as cartwheels.

"How did you do that, Dugan?" Clara whispered her amazement.

"When you've been a gladiator as long as I have, you tend to pick up the native language...and a few tricks and minor theatrics." Scraping the sole of his soiled boot on a nearby wall, he looked up into Clara's frightened expression. "Now let's get to this boat of yours."

"Are you sure you won't join? That's just the kind of thinking we need," Clara looked over at him with a hopeful grin.

"The boat," Dugan's stoic face peered at the Patrious elf.

"It's up ahead in the harbor, another five hundred feet or so," her manner became business-like again.

"Good. I'd like to be out of here by nightfall" the gladiator made his way forward.

"Fine," Clara pulled into the lead. It was obvious he would have to be convinced of the importance of her cause after they had left the city. For now though, she just had to concentrate on leaving the city.

Silently the two started toward the harbor, trying to keep to the shadows. Neither wanted any more attention like the kind they had just received. Clinging tightly to their cloaks, they neared the docking area.

The salty smell of the sea overcame the pungent aroma of the city as fresh air rolled in with the waves. The harbor was just starting to come awake with the rising sun, fishermen and traders were beginning to set up their shops and wares for trade. As the day grew older, the harbors would become packed with people looking to get the catch of the day or the latest bolt of cloth, spices or gems. If they could keep themselves hidden, they'd be able to get to the boat, and off Colloni without any more complications.

The harbor was a simple collection of docks constructed from wood and stone. Many ships of varying size, from small fishing boats to massive trading vessels, were tied up indiscriminately at every pier. Men, like rodents, scurried up and down the gangplanks with crates and barrels filled with a multitude of goods. Others hauled thick nets fat with fish and other delicacies of the waves. It was all carried out in a self-contained little world; a whole clockwork motion of people and things set to its own rhythm.

Clara unconsciously breathed a heavy sigh of relief. It appeared as if they were going to make it to the boat without further incident. Now all she had to do was get on her boat and flee this corrupt city. Looking back, she noticed Dugan wasn't behind her. Frantic, she rapidly scanned the area until she caught sight of him walking back into the city.

"Dugan! What are you doing?" she hissed out in Elonum as she chased after the bulky man as inconspicuously as she could.

He didn't respond, just continued to walk back toward the city, reaching out his hand into empty air. Then suddenly he stopped, and drew his gladii as if facing a fellow combatant. Clara stood in shocked horror as she watched Dugan begin to swing wildly into the air, the motions of his thrashing causing his hood to fall back.

The gladiator's further erratic behavior attracted the attention of the human merchants and sailors milling about the harbor, as well as the eyes of an elf entering the docks, who upon seeing Dugan, ran off into the city shouting excitedly.

"What did I get myself into?" Clara wondered aloud as she ran for Dugan.

Dugan was caught up in a fight. He'd been following behind Clara when he'd heard a whisper. It was seductive, and although he didn't know exactly what it said to him, he was compelled to follow it. All other things paled in comparison to the soft voice and the coercive power it held over him. He found himself following it back to the city, his feet obeying the whisper instead of his own commands.

As he realized what was occurring, Dugan began to fight for control of his body, and was met by an apparition shimmering with an azure light. The image was of a decayed humanoid figure, robed in what once could have been a white gown and hooded cloak.

Dugan discovered it was more skeletal than flesh when it held out a bony hand toward him. The form then hissed out a strange and archaic jumble of words causing Dugan's eyes to ignite with a stabbing pain. For a moment he saw a land of swirling, blood red clouds, and dark shapes.

The vision revolted Dugan. In disgust and pain birthed rage, he unsheathed his swords and prepared himself for an attack... but the attack never came. Instead the burning in his eyes ceased, and he found himself looking once again at the decomposing image. It laughed at him with bone-chilling malice, and then - to his horror - spoke. "Soon... soon I shall be free," it hissed in an icy breath. The decomposing image then made an attempt to claw the tanned warrior in the chest. Dugan dodged the attack, and returned one of his own, but it passed through the image as if it were nothing more than smoke.

He thrust and slashed again but to no avail. He grew angrier with each failed stroke of his swords as the apparition laughed at his pathetic attacker. Suddenly it enveloped itself into nothingness, freeing the Telborian's senses from its grasp.

Dugan shook his head, trying to free his mind from the muffled buzz and disorientation the experience had left him with. When he opened his eyes again, he found himself facing an outpouring of hunters coming right at him.

Shaking his head once more, he cursed under his breath as he realized the hunters were real. With no understanding of what had just happened and the reality of things as they were coming back under his mental control, Dugan could do little but curse his situation, and prepare for the worst.

"Are you mad, Telborian?" he heard Clara shout in Telborous to him as he felt her arm on his back. But there was no time for explanations as the hunters, and a few human pirates, closed in on Clara and Dugan like sharks smelling blood in the sea.

"The slave in the cloak is mine!" an Elyelmic male with a husky voice spoke up to the gathering group of ruffians as they neared Dugan and Clara. He had a crooked nose and twisted smile.

Dugan looked at Clara with a squinting gaze. His first thought was to wonder if she had led him there to betray him to the hunters now encircling them, but his many years of studying body language in the arena told him this was not the case. She was just as prepared to fight for her life as he was.

They were both in deadly peril, and Dugan dealt with the danger the only way he knew how: He called upon the warlust and ran to meet the first of the assailants. He began to feel the warlust growing in his veins as a small gathering of humans on the docks, who had stopped from their labors to sit on some crates and containers to begin cheering on the approaching fight.

"Run while you still have a chance!" Dugan shouted to Clara as his sword clanged heavily against the first hunter's blade.

Swinging his second sword, Dugan pushed violently against the hunter as he managed to use his large muscles to gain access to the middle of a circle of hunters quickly overtaking him. He estimated their numbers at half a dozen. He had faced worse odds before.

Clara watched as Dugan was suddenly lost in a flowing ring of steel and brown cloaks. Some of the elves continued to move forward, advancing on Clara but their threatening posture faded as they realized she was an elf.

Her hood was still drawn, hiding much of her distinguishing features, but she kept her own unique sword drawnand readied for any attack leveled against her.

The hunters were hesitant.

"We mean you no harm. Please lower your weapon, and we will take you to safety, away from this human slave," a thin elf spoke to Clara in Elonum, lips curled in revulsion, obviously thinking Dugan held her captive. "You will be compensated for his capture when we all collect the payment. We hunters have honor."

"I'm afraid I can't. You see, I'm helping the human - and if you are going to get in my way, then may Aerotription have mercy on your souls." Clara threw back her hood.

"A Patrious in Colloni?" The thin elf gasped as the other four around Clara stared at her in shock, their eyes widening to the size of rexiums.

"She's a spy!" said another.

"Her kind want nothing but our death; we must kill her for the protection of the Republic!" Still another of the number, this one a haggard, scratchty-voiced thug, moved forward with his cutlass firmly in hand.

"No," the thin elf spoke up again. "We'll take her to the emperor so he may deal with the situation as he sees fit. He may even reward us. Take her alive."

So they wanted her captured? Clara had been warned about this. She had hoped the element of surprise would work to her advantage when she had revealed herself, but it was too late to worry about it now. She had to concern herself with their escape from the docks, as she had no intentions of being taken captive, or losing Dugan to the hunters. If they wanted a fight, she was prepared to give them one. She still had a few surprises she could use.

"Don't come any closer," Clara's stance grew rigid and treelike; feet being planted into the ground while she held her sword level before her. "or you'll be dead. Stand down and I'll be on my way; none of you will be hurt."

Dugan had been surrounded by a motley collection of fellows. Each one held his ruin in their well-oiled swords. Human pirate joined elven hunter as they encircled their prey, hoping he would be an easy take. They swung wide for their first attack, giving Dugan the time he needed to ready his stance, and begin a great volley of deadly blows. He unleashed two deep thrusts from his gladii, sending two hunters to their graves. As the two elves fell, the rest of the hunters attacked with a vengeful fury birthed by the slaughter of their fellow hunters.

With blades enhanced by rage, they cut deep into the Telborians' war scarred flesh. Experience and the warlust had taught Dugan how to ignore pain during a fight; to give into it made the enemy much stronger. Instead of crying out in pain, or becoming distracted by it, the gladiator grit his teeth in a determined grimace. Stronger than ever before, the warlust guided Dugan's actions with the fury of sheer will. Four Telborian pirates had also joined the fight. Of the four, two were hopelessly drunk, and missed Dugan so much they nearly managed to cut off their own heads. Another one jabbed into the fray, making it through an attempted block Dugan tried to establish.

The attack pierced Dugan's side. At the same time a blow from behind lodged itself in his back. Dugan felt the blood begin to flow from his wounds like water, and he knew he wouldn't last much longer at this rate.

The hunters drew closer, and laughed as they celebrated the gladiator's upcoming downfall.

Dugan's mind rebelled at the hunters' impending victory, he wouldn't give them such satisfaction. A new surge of war-lust filled him, which flooded his muscles with white-hot retribution. Shouting a deep-throated roar, he swung his blade wildly, cutting down the last of the elves who tried to take him.

His swords laid waste to much of their flesh, cleaving to the bone in one blow. He yanked out the weapons in seconds, and turned to face his new challengers who stared at him with open mouths.

Seeing the carnage Dugan was capable of, the pirates decided any money they might gain from his capture or death wasn't as important as their lives - and so they ran off into the city streets, to merge with the shadows that had spawned them.

Watching the fleeing thugs, Dugan grinned wickedly, then spun himself around to see where Clara had gone. He saw some other hunters had surrounded her. She was holding her own, though, for the moment - but appeared to be in danger of losing at advantage rather quickly.

With fierce determination, he leapt toward the circle of brown-cloaked elves. This wasn't for any love of the woman, for indeed he had no such sentiment, but for the love of slaying some more elves while he had the chance.

The fact Clara still might be able to get him off the island - should she survive - was well in his mind but the matter of slaying those who had once called him their property was his driving compulsion at the moment.

Kill me and you'll be sure to join your fellow slave in the arena!" a hunter shouted at Clara, "Get her!"

The hunters began to encircle Clara in a tighter grip. She prepared to plunge her sword into the heart of the lead Hunter.

The four surrounded her with their blades readied for anticipated resistance. They were cautious, and strategic in their moves, more so than what Clara thought they were capable of, but she dismissed the thought as she took a lunge
forward.

The hunters didn't move. Instead she felt the unmistakable pinch of a dagger point at her kidney. A rough arm then suddenly encircled her neck in a choking grasp and hot, foul breath slapped her ear.

"Not so tough now are you?" a voice sneered. "Nothing says we can't have a little fun with you before we turn you over to the emperor. I can think of one way to entertain" He was cut short by a sword strike cleaving right through his neck, then parting bone from flesh. His severed head fell beside Clara's feet with a hollow echo as blood spurted all over the elven maiden and the three other hunters who rapidly backed away from the sudden attack.

The beheaded hunter lost his grip around Clara's neck, then slumped to the ground to join his head in a growing pool of crimson.

Dugan ran out from behind the shocked and blood-splattered Clara toward the other hunters. He raised his bloodstained weapons in his gore-covered hands. Behind him lay the bodies of the others who had tried to impede his progress, but all had fallen to meet the gates of Mortis, the realm of the dead.

He swung his two swords in a great arc, and sliced through all three of the hesitant elves.

Their insides were sprayed out onto the docks.

As soon as the final hunter fell, Dugan's warlust began to fade. With it ebbed some of the gladiator's strength and focus.

He turned his attention to Clara.

"Where to now?" He coughed in a brief spasm, then spat out some blood.

She raised her dazed eyes at him, her face and attire painted with claret ichors. The ferocity of his attack, and the gore around her feet had left her near the point of collapse. She was certainly not ready for the violence she had gotten herself into, and had a new respect - and fear - for the man who had dealt it. Taking in a deep, shaking breath, she knew she had to concentrate. They still needed to get off the island.

"You don't look so well. I -" Clara began to move to help the gladiator with this injuries.

"Boat," Dugan snarled through his bloody mouth.

"There," Clara pointed in a non-directional manner to a general clumping of boats, docked for the day.

The dock had become deserted during their fight, only a few brave souls watched the final result hidden away in shadowy corners, and from behind crates and barrels they so recently had sat on and cheered. The pungent stench of death and fear was too thick in the area to do little else.

"Where?" Dugan spoke as he squinted in hopes of finding the boat in question.

"That small one over there," Clara motioned as she spied her vessel. It was a sloop, a tiny vessel, perfect for short trips and small enough to sneak in and out of docks unnoticed. It had one mast and two sets of oars with red sails rolled up tight, and tied to the riggings. The boat couldn't have been more than a glorified rowboat, but was a boat nonetheless…and a way off Colloni.

"Come on," Clara sharply snapped at Dugan as she ran off toward the boat. Seeing it would do little good for them gaping and gawking about this opportunity they had been given, she knew it would be a only a matter of time until the city guards were called and set against them. Best to be about the things needed to get out of this city while they could. There would be time for interrogation and introspection later.

Dugan followed closely at her heels, his hand gripping at his side, which was bleeding grievously. He had begun to feel weak too as his life continued to filter out of him. His only goal was to make it to the boat. That, and nothing more. Should he die after that, at least he would die at sea, and off the land where he had been enslaved for so long.

The boat and nothing else.

Chapter 5

Rowan had been wandering in the jungle for what seemed like days. The unrelenting voice continued to usher him forward as the humid air sucked the strength from his body, just like the mosquitoes constantly draining his body of blood. Swatting at another swarm of the pests, he thought he heard something up ahead.

Several times before he'd tried to pull himself away from the jungle, but was unable to shake the controlling force pulling him closer to an unknown destination. Tensing with anxiety for what could lie ahead, he prepared himself for the worst. His feet no longer acted of his accord.

During his compulsive venture into the jungle, he'd heard very little noise, save the voice calling him onward - not even the wind seemed to be present. He thought it strange how no animal could be heard - not even a lone bird or similar denizen of the terrain. It sent an odd feeling of apprehension down his spine. That, coupled with the inability to regain control over his body, filled him with the greatest sense of uncertainty he had yet known.

As he moved into a small clearing amid the leaning giant trees, he saw what appeared to be a large stone formation. It shone through the dense, green growth like jagged bones amid a dirt heap of an unearthed grave. Roughly half the size of the tower from which he had so recently been, it was made of white marble and carved with a collection of strange symbols and designs which Rowan couldn't quite place.

It spoke of an older age, something before the creation of mortal man. How Rowan knew this, he wasn't sure, but the feeling was strong. The knowledge simply seemed to fill his brain and spirit like the breathing in of air.

As he walked closer, he heard another sound. This one emanated out of the marble building itself. It was a bestial growl, and yet it also sounded like a warrior's scream. Rowan's apprehension suddenly grew as he felt his blood grow cold. The little light filtering through the canopy of surrounding trees suddenly dimmed into darkness, and the stars began to appear.

A cool breeze whisked by him, sending him into shivers as it chilled his sweat. Still his feet walked on, taking him to the mysterious building.

Stairs stretched up from the green carpet of jungle growth before him, which led him up to an empty shell of a doorway, long since fallen to ruin and decay, void of any proper door.

The door frame was made of two huge logs, looking more like two stunted trees which had naturally grown together in an arch rather than forced into shape by human hands. The organic feel of the doorway was oddly familiar and comforting, yet somewhat haunting, as if he had walked underneath the arch many times before.

Again, he couldn't place the reason why he felt the way he did.

Rowan mouthed a quick prayer to Panthor, asking for strength and courage as his body continued to move forward against its will. If this was a test, he most certainly wanted to be found worthy.

The growling sound grew stronger as Rowan crossed the threshold. The faint smell of musk reaching his nose marked the entrance as an opening to some type of animal lair.

Forced inside this den of sorts, Rowan tried his best to control his stealth, limiting the noise of his entrance. Nevertheless, a force stronger than a hurricane spun wind, blowing him back onto the stairs, causing flashes of pain to flare across his chest. Rowan was too shocked to move as he found himself staring into the fierce, black eyes of a giant gray panther. Its height at the shoulders was at least six feet, its width seemed twice that. Its muzzle was pulled back into a drooling snarl of malice, and its claws were dug firmly into his flesh.

The weight of the creature was immense, like a huge boulder pressing on top his chest. The youth could do little more than struggle for breath as he lay under the subduing pressure.

It was the most impressive animal Rowan had ever seen. He found it more than a coincidence he was struggling with his own totem and symbol of the Knighthood! Was this part of the test? And if so, how should he pass it? What did it mean?

The searing pain of another claw attack on his chest brought Rowan out of his contemplation. The great cat was incredibly strong. He had to think of a way to get it off him before he was mauled to death. He couldn't move because the cat had him pinned down on both his arms and legs. His strength was no match for the great beast so brute force was out of the question.

The only thing left was cunning and wit; areas in which Rowan was well practiced. As he began to think of solutions to his current situation, the panther's drooling jaws snapped at his head, narrowly missing his face as he turned it just in time to avoid the crushing vise. He had to think fast.

Desperately, Rowan searched the ground for anything he might use to free himself from the colossal beast. As his hands were the only parts he could move, he had to settle for anything near them. Fishing around the hard surface of the marble slab where he was pinned.

After some frantic moments of searching of this surface, Rowan discovered a loosened corner in one of its sides. It wasn't much of a weapon, but he had nothing else to use. He was without sword or fist. The pointed rock would have to serve him well enough.

Turning the marble in his hand so the sharp tip faced upwards he focused all his energy into what could possibly be his last action. Using his wrist as the sole source of power Rowan thrust the jagged rock at the massive underbelly of the panther.

The sharp point bit into the soft stomach of the great cat, and dug deep into its flesh. The panther reared up in shock, howling in pain and anger. It snarled at him one last time before it slowly turned into a gray vapor that trailed off into the air, and then nothingness.

The young Nordican stared in amazement at the vanishing trail of mist. The animal had felt so real. His shredded chest was proof of its existence. Unfortunately, Rowan wasn't granted the time to reflect on the validity of the panther, or its meaning. He was raised to his feet once more by the unseen force that had brought him here, being compelled to continue his trek inside the ruin.

As he was forced deeper into the building, the animal scent grew fainter, and the hint of steel began to fill the air. It smelled as though he was now entering an armory, though the scent was also mixed with the musk of dust and mold.

Deeper inside the ruin, Rowan found himself in a room which had lain empty for some time. Dust covered the marble floor in a thin blanket, undisturbed, even by small rodents as cracked walls struggled against decay to hold the ceiling and floor apart. Nothing living had touched the room for what could have been millennia, and darkness had swallowed most of it long ago.

"Welcome fool, to your death," A voice echoed out of the dimly-lit room.

Looking around for the source of the disembodied voice, Rowan could find nothing.

"Choose your weapon," the voice spoke again.

With those words a grouping of weapons appeared on the far wall, emerging from the shadows opposite him. Rowan approached them, again under the compulsive influence, studying them. A broadsword, dagger, mace, and pike were laid out on the wall like a merchants wares on display, each in pristine condition.

He looked closely at them all, weighing the strengths and weaknesses of each weapon. He had a feeling, a very strong conviction, he would need one for his protection. If the recent encounter with the panther hadn't shown him then his concern over this current situation did so. He wanted to choose a weapon he had some experience with, but the choices offered were slim. The only weapon he had ever come close to being good at was the broad sword. As he reached for the blade, he heard the clank of a metal-soled boot upon a hard surface, and spun around to find an armored man charging toward him.

The man was tall, and covered with plate armor made of shining silver. It caught the low light in the room, transforming it into a shimmering aura around him. Like the ruin, he too looked as if he belonged in a past era. His armor was ancient, made in a style of metal working no longer in use by Nordic smiths. He wore a helmet hiding his face, and carried a great two-handed long sword.

The strange attacker ran toward Rowan with his great sword raised. Rowan was barely able to throw up the sword he had chosen to deflect the blow.

Instantly, he was sent flying back into the wall behind him, knocking over the collection of weapons, which scattered about the floor with no more noise than if they were made of silk. The heavy blow against his sword had caused it to slice into Rowan's arms, creating a deep wound cutting into several layers of muscle.

The youth lay senseless on the floor in shock before he heard the grating of armor, his attacker raising his weapon again.

Frantically, Rowan struggled with the sword he had dropped to the floor, slick with his own blood. By sheer force of will, he managed to raise the sword again before the second blow struck.

Sword clashed with sword as sparks of incandescent green light flew off the blades - dancing briefly on the floor before fading away. The armored man was strong. Each blow he delivered severely weakened Rowan, as if each strike were absorbing a little bit of his strength and will, regardless if he hit Rowan's flesh or blade. He knew he couldn't last for much longer as each blow brought him closer to defeat. The youth took a deep breath and closed his eyes in a silent prayer to his goddess he would be found worthy to receive her aid to win out over his foe.

The armored attacker was well versed in the art of warfare. He knew how to read every movement Rowan made, and Rowan felt the shame of not being his equal, regardless of the lessons the knights had burned into his mind. He also felt foolish for not being properly armored; even the clothes he had removed at the beginning of his journey would have helped to provide some protection. The flimsy undergarments he now wore were useless against the strike of a sword. One good strike, and his life was forfeit.

The armored man continued to attack Rowan with vicious swings Rowan barely managed to parry. Each strike propelled him back a step or two, and took more of his strength. The young Nordican was almost out of space as he was pushed closer to the wall behind him. A cool draught of water assaulted his back, seeping in from an unseen crack in the wall, like the hand of death caressing his skin.

"I shall enjoy hanging your head up as a trophy," the armored man's voice echoed from his helmet. "You've made a useful training exercise.

Another heavy swing sent Rowan to the floor. He had grown weak in the brief battle with the armored man, and his wounds were making the situation worse. He had begun to feel light-headed from the loss of blood and darkness had started to over take his peripheral vision. He knew he had to keep his mind active and alert in order to take advantage of any opening his attacker might give him, no matter how small. He had to win this battle to pass this test.

As the armored figure lifted his sword up high for the final blow Rowan realized his chance had come. His foe had miscalculated Rowan's determination, and had left himself wide open for attack. Rowan struck just as the opposing sword swung down in a final arc, and slid his blade with a quick thrust, into the unprotected midriff of his assailant. It went through the body as if it were air, coming out of the other side without any blood or sign of injury. Rowan drew in a shocked breath as the armored man laughed.

"Hah! A valiant effort but now you are mine! Prepare to meet your god."

Rowan jerked his muscles in an effort to pull his weapon from the man but found he had no strength left.

As darkness filled his vision, he caught the glimpse of steel flashing in his eyes, and then heard an echoing crunch.

All was then silent blackness.

The familiar smells and sounds of the altar room suddenly returned as Rowan's vision began to clear. He found himself once again standing on the altar steps before the High Father and the Grand Champion.

It was as if he had awakened from a dream like trance to discover he'd been given the three tests of Panthor. He prayed he had passed them. However, when he thought back to his ordeal, he thought it strange he was not able to count three tests. The panther and the armored man added up to two encounters. Where was the third? Had there been another test of which he was unaware?

Tomas, a young man who was ahead of Rowan on the altar steps, ascended the stairs to the top of the dais. The High Father greeted him with a smile, and a sign of blessing. It was then Rowan realized he had been found worthy, otherwise he wouldn't have been on the altar steps preparing to be welcomed into the fold of knights.

He would have fallen to the base of the stairs to lay prostrate before the altar like a few of the others he witnessed slumped at the bottom of the steps, sobbing at the rejection of their goddess, and their impending ejection from the Knighthood. He thanked his goddess for her mysterious ways of choosing, even if he didn't understand it.

The blessing ritual was brief. The initiate approached the altar to be blessed by the High Father and to be knighted by the Grand Champion. It was at that time the parents of the newly-confirmed knight announced themselves, symbolizing the pride they had for their son.

Seer's Quest

After the knighting, the new representative of Panthor was made to wait in a closed-off hallway, away from the altar room. This was done after he'd been allowed to meet with family and friends and allow the new knight time to reflect into what he had entered.

Approach, Rowan Cortak." The High Father's voice drew Rowan back from his fog-enshrouded mind. He heard his parents' acknowledgment of him, and wished he could have turned around to see their faces. Protocol forbade such an action; his attention was to be focused solely on the altar.

He looked up at the High Father and Grand Champion standing before him, both peering down at the youth with solemn faces. He took the first step up and sensed the presence of Panthor flowing from the altar and into his being. He felt as though he was being brushed with soft grasses and feathers. The sensation birthed a great joy deep inside his spirit.

Looking up again, Rowan found himself in front of the High Father, whose hands were outstretched in a welcoming gesture. He approached the space allotted for him to stand before the old priest, the air around the High Father thick with reverence.

The High Father then began to chant in a strange language unknown to all but the priests of the order. The motions of blessings were placed upon the future knight as well as prayers of protection for his long years of service ahead.

Rowan was then led to where the other new knights stood, facing the gathered audience and the Grand Champion. One by one each of the new knights were touched on the shoulders with the Grand Champion's blade as they were dubbed Knights of Valkoria by the grace of the goddess of humanity.

A shrill, piercing note of a trumpet then rang through the room prompting the knights to face the altar to pay their respects, and to declare homage and dedication to their goddess. At the end of the ceremony, speaking a few final words of benediction, the High Father raised his arms in a sign of triumph and turned to the crowd.

"Behold!" he told them, "Before you stand, men who are no longer warriors of simple faith, but Knights of Valkoria; proud men of piety and welcomed additions to our brotherhood. Panthor be praised!"

"Panthor be praised!" The echo of the altar room reverberated in Rowan's head with the responses of those present.

Rowan felt as if he were dreaming. Never in his life did he ever think he would attain knighthood! The thrill of the ceremony filled him with unbridled energy and excitement; excitement he needed to share with his family.

Shortly afterward, Rowan was allowed to step down from the altar with the other new knights to accept congratulations from the crowd. Desperately, he squeezed through the people, hoping to catch a glimpse of some familiar clothing, or hear a loving voice that he would recognize. Then a flash of a brown cloak caught his eye. Rowan smiled.

"Mother! Father!" Rowan ran through the wall of bodies to the brown-cloaked figure of a middle-aged woman. She wore goose feathers in her amber hair along with a set of colorful glass beads around her neck.

Her clothing was made from animal hides and homespun fabrics of bright colors. Behind her stood a massive man who was taller and more muscled than most other Nordicans in attendance. He had a red face, burned from the icy winds, and long brown braids trailing down his back. He wore tanned leather breeches and a pair of well-worn boots. His chest was covered with a simple vest of bearskin.

Both figures smiled as Rowan approached, and hugged him; almost smothering him with their deep affection. It felt good to be with them again. In some ways it even surpassed his joy at being accepted into the Knighthood.

"Son, I'm very proud of you. You do your mother and me honor by joining the Knighthood," Rowan's father beamed.

"I've missed you so much, Rowan," his mother said, as she kissed his cheek. His own tears were a mixture of joy and relief. "I thought we would never get to see you again. We thought you were locked up in this walled community for good!"

Rowan laughed as tears formed in the corners of his eyes.

"I've missed you too. As soon as I can, I'm going to take some time off from my studies, and come stay with you so we can be together for a little while. Come with me, I'll take you to my quarters where we can talk in cooler and quieter comfort."

"...and then I took the beast by its tail and spun it around in the air until it howled like a fiend, then threw it into the lake. Best fight I've had all year, I tell ya!" Rowan's father spoke with a sparkle in his eye.

"And your father thinks he's losing some of his strength as he ages. Can you believe it Rowan?" His mother asked with a laugh making Rowan's smile deepen.

"Well, it was only a cub. I couldn't have done it to a full grown beast cat, not even when I was in my prime." Rowan's father puffed out his chest.

"Father, any man who can do that to a raging beast cat, no matter his age, is as tough as the mountains. You'll be the strongest elder in our tribe's history if you keep this up." Rowan gave his father a hearty slap on the back.

The three of them laughed as they watched a fire burn in the small hearth of Rowan's room. Rowan, as did all the other dedicates of the Order, made their residence on the upper levels of the tower, above the altar room below. The living quarters where Rowan resided were sparse but cooler, and he had made them his own with some mementos from home, brought with him when he entered the Knighthood.

Dedicates weren't allowed outside the keep walls during their training, except once a year, when they were allotted a family visit. Even then, it was a brief sojourn, lasting for only a week. Discipline was of the utmost importance to the knights. Constant vigilance to training and adherence to the Code of Panthor were to be the only pursuits, but short family visits were permitted to make sure they never lost complete touch with the people they were to protect.

Rowan and his family had suffered through this and survived, but it was taxing on both of them, Rowan especially those early years as he had never felt so alone and forced to grow up so fast under such conditions. The brief visits home allowed him to catch up with tribal issues, and generally stay informed on anything else of importance. He was also able to watch the passing years touch his parents with gray.

Rowan looked again into the loving eyes of his parents where the sparkle and joy of youth was still apparent. It had seemed like a short time had passed during his stay with the knights, but when he was with his parents, he realized time was running faster than what he had first thought.

Rowan assured himself things would change now that he was a Knight of Valkoria. He'd be able to travel the lands, and perhaps go where he wished. It was just a matter of time.

During the last two years of his training he began to realize he missed his tribe and family to such an extent he was half tempted to leave the Knighthood for good. Now he was free to do so, and much relieved because of it.

"So when do you want to leave for the village?" Rowan asked his parents.

"Are you sure you can leave, son?" His father's brow was wrinkled. "You're now a Knight of Valkoria. You have battles to fight, and causes to champion for the might of Panthor. I doubt we'll see you for some time. Your actions now have greater responsibility than they once did."

"What are you saying? Do you mean Rowan will never return to the village with us? You mean we'll never see him again?" His mother looked toward Rowan's father as he finished speaking. Her eyes were wet and quivering.

"No, my dear," Rowan's father shook his head softly, taking in his wife's tear streaming cheeks with his own stoic face. "I mean Rowan probably has tasks to perform before he can even think of taking leave from the Knighthood." The knight's father laid hands on his wife's shoulder.

"No father." Rowan drew both his parent's gaze to him. " I can get a brief rest before I start my rounds for the Knighthood. I'm sure of it. Who would order a mission so soon for a new member of the Order - and on the very day of their admission ceremony at that?"

Rowan's father looked into Rowan's eyes as his boy finished speaking, then drew a solemn and quieted breath.

"Son, I fear you do not understand the duties you have undertaken. Your commanding officer will probably have a mission for you already. We know you want to come back with us, but you must understand, as I do." His arm encircled Rowan's mother as she hugged her husband tight.

You have a service to perform. A service is not only indebted to man but to your goddess as well."

"Surely the Knighthood lets a knight choose when he wishes to start?" Rowan half-whispered, but it was a fleeting hope; his faith in his previous plan of a brief respite had been dealt a strong blow by his father's hand.

"Maybe for a higher-ranking knight, but not to a dedicate like yourself. You have to go to where and when you're told to go, Rowan. Right now you have very little say."

The youth walked closer to his mother, and laid a hand on her arm. She turned to look at her son with a tear-soaked face.

"Don't worry," Rowan comforted his mother. "I'm sure I'll be able to stay at the village for a while, or at the very least be posted close to it." He didn't really believe himself though, but hoped against hope anyway his words would become reality soon enough.

Rowan's father shook his head as his wife tightened her grip around his massive waist.

"What?" Rowan asked in shocked disbelief.

"You are to leave Valkoria at once, Sir Cortak." The hulking form of a Journey Knight named Fronel spoke to Rowan from behind a large pine desk carved to look as if four panthers bore the weight of the thick table above them.

To his right stood a tall shelf lined with books and scrolls - records which had been kept from all the knights and their quests over the years, of which Fronel was one of the chief chroniclers.

Behind the Journey Knight, next to a narrow, clear glass window, was a small bronze shield emblazoned with the Knighthood's crest.

"It is vital you leave on time to fulfill your mission. Speed is of the essence," Fronel addressed the young knight with the dry formula that hierarchy often instilled in ranked officers of any institution.

Journey Knights were the mid-range administrators of the Knighthood. Lesser knights, like Rowan, were under them, and taking on tasks they dealt out as the orders of the higher knights above the Journey Knights. These higher-ranked knights were called Champions and numbered a smaller percentage of the overall Knighthood. The Champions served as a sort of council and advisory group to the Grand Champion, whom they were all under, and acted in harmony with the priests of Panthor.

Rowan had been summoned to the Journey Knight's room a few hours after he had spoken with his parents. He thought the Fronel would offer his congratulations. He never expected to be ordered on a mission, to an area of the world not of his choosing...especially so soon.

He began to realize how naive he had been, and what kind of a pact he had made with these men and his goddess. He'd sacrificed a large piece of his own personal freedom, and time spent from his village and family to be the servant to a larger and more demanding cause. This was something he hadn't envisioned.

Any facade of a hopeful outcome more to his liking had begun to topple away before his very eyes. Somewhere amid the excitement of being in the knighthood itself - being immersed in the training, he had lost sight of this truth, this responsibility.

"Journey Knight Fronel, I think there's been some type of misunderstanding. I was under the impression I could have some brief time to enjoy my new admission to the Knighthood with my family." Rowan stood confused and doing his best to hide the crushing defeat he felt had been dealt to his previous joy.

Fronel looked gruffly at the young man.

"Then you were misinformed, Sir Cortak. Only the tenured and higher-ranking knights choose their placement, and when they go under most normal situations. It is the newly-ordained who are made to follow the path the goddess chooses for them. In time, by the will of the goddess, you may rise in rank and gain the ability to make your own missions - at your own time."

"I see." Rowan did his best to swallow his disappointment. "Will this mission take long?"

"That is a question only you can answer. It all depends on your abilities as a Knight of Valkoria. If you're strong, and run into few distractions, it should not take you long. However, if you are sidetracked and prove weaker than you think, it may take some considerable effort." Fronel's encouragement was lack luster at best.

"May I ask where I am going then, sir?" Rowan did his best to swallow the massive lump of disappointment in his throat. Maybe this wasn't so bad as it sounded. Maybe it was some easy task that wouldn't hinder him too long from seeing his family. After all, didn't Fronel say he would be able to make the task easier and faster if he wished to?

"You have been chosen to go to Takta Lu Lama," replied the Journey Knight.

"Where is that?" Rowan asked with an emotionless face, though his heart was bleeding inside. It wasn't near anywhere he'd ever heard of before.

"It's a wild region of terrain jungle and swampland in far western Talatheal. Reports have reached the knights saying there may be elven imperial movement in the area."

Fronel had come flat in tone, like a sage reciting figures and dates to a pupil, as the Fronel rustled through some parchment on his desk.

"Rumors gathered by some agents we support there have spoken of an ancient ruined city, probably elven by the sounds of it, holding information to rebuild an empire, or start a new one.

"You are to travel to Talatheal and find out if what they say is true, to act upon that information, then report back to us. A rather simple task, but one of great importance." He had stopped his scavenging of parchment to look up at Rowan.

"Why me sir?" Rowan dared. "Surely there were others who could have done this mission in my place, other knights more worthy perhaps." Rowan hoped that this might be true. Talatheal was a great ways away from the Northlands. The travel alone would take some considerable time. Maybe if someone else was worthy, he'd be given some lesser assignment maybe…

"You should be honored, Sir Cortak. Few newly-appointed knights are rewarded with a task so soon after their dedication. Have you forgotten the way to excel in the Knighthood is through service to her Celestial Highness?"

"No, I haven't forgotten, Journey Knight Fronel. Forgive my outburst." Rowan looked down at his feet for a moment, trying to get his warring emotions under control.

"You are forgiven, Sir Cortak. Your boat leaves within the hour. Pack what you can and get to the docks. May Panthor bless you."

Rowan bowed to the higher-ranking knight, then turned on his heel and abruptly left the room. He told himself on the way to his room if this was how life in the Knighthood was going to be; being moved to and fro at the whim of some bureaucratic ideology, then he was beginning to want no part of it.

Unfortunately, he had to comply with the order, or face severe punishment. The longer his eyes were opened to the truth around him, the less he liked the world he thought he knew. He slowly walked to his chambers with a heavy burden resting on his shoulders and sadness in his heart. He wondered to himself, as he entered his room, if this was what being a man was all about.

However, he also knew he was whining about not getting his way, and that wasn't right either.

He wasn't totally blind to what he was getting into when he joined the Knighthood, even at the young age of twelve. He knew then this was the life for him, and it would take much sacrifice to live it too. This had been instilled in him by the seven years of training he had received up until now. It was now finally time to live out that reality - to put to proof what he believed, and become a fully functioning member of this body of which he was called to be part.

This was the struggle, and Rowan knew it. He had to come to terms with the fact he wasn't really living for himself anymore, for he had been dedicated to his goddess; made a possession for her to own. He didn't hold claim to his life anymore; it was Panthor's and it was to her that he now had to spend the rest of his days in service. It was an honor and privilege to do this, but to Rowan at this moment, it was a time of great struggle and conflict.

His mind warred with his heart and the wish to return to the way things had been, even if he knew that wasn't what he really wanted, and it couldn't happen anyway. Still, these things danced about his mind like shadows on a cave wall. Despite this struggle, though, he was still leaving, and had to pack.

Chapter 6

In the gloom of an underground room, Kylor moved
in silence, his flickering torch haunting the walls with
dancing shadows. He was a Telborian of average height,
about six feet, with long, brown hair falling to the middle of
his back.

He was thin and pale for his race whose body had
long ago reacted to the strains he put it through in his search
for hidden secrets. The long nights and years for his pursuit of power had left him hidden from civilized folk and a
stranger to the sun or proper health. His bone-thin fingers
glided over the smooth surface of a cylindrical object resting
in the center of the room.

This column stood fifty feet tall, and was as wide as
Kylor was tall. It was crafted of blue marble, the veins of
which looked like the arteries of a decaying arm: thin and
web-like; all of it encased in an old steel cage stretching
toward the ceiling.

Etched into its smooth surface were runes and symbols of archaic magic, a language only mages could decipher
and use in their understanding of the cosmos.

These runes glowed a soft red and were the source of
light in the subterranean room, save the torch the mage carried with him for extra illumination in reading his tomes and
scrolls.

Outside the cage rested a podium stacked high with
large books and scrolls. It was here the wizard worked to

uncover the mysteries of the blue column. So far he had met with little success, but he was far from surrendering his pursuit just yet. This column was an artifact of ancient power, and he was determined to unravel its mysteries at any cost. Kylor's carefully-measured stride carried him over to a desk in the far corner of the room. This desk was carved out of ancient granite, and made to look as if petrified vines and thorns had intertwined to form it and the detached seat resting beside it.

Kylor wore robes of bright silver, reflecting the poor light of the room. With every movement, the material would send flashes of light cascading about, slicing through the gloom like falling stars in a sea of night. It seemed he alone was the only sense of life in the room; the rest being left to die centuries ago.

The room was was quite large, with books and scrolls in musty shelves lining the walls. Some of the literature had been here when Kylor moved in, and some he'd brought with him. The dark mage was confident with such a collection at his disposal his lack of progress would change quite rapidly... it had to. He couldn't bear going on in his quest for discovering the secrets of the column much longer without going mad.

Picking up a quill resting on the stone desk with some other scattered parchment papers, scrolls and time worn tomes, he wrote some notes in a large book which lay open in front of him, then inclined his head...someone was coming.

Footfalls echoed from the stone steps snaking up the far wall, into an antechamber above this chamber. The antechamber was guarded by two hobgoblins; preventing any entrance through the secret passage leading to the lower level where Kylor was now working and living.

"What is it?" he spoke with a dry tone of authority.
"My apologies, but I bear news," a shadowy form in the darkness responded. It was rough Telborous with a strong accent, but Kylor was still able to understand it. He had forced himself to patiently teach the rudimentary parts of the Telborian language to this creature and its kin.

"Out with it, Relforaz," Kylor barked. "I have no time for your games today. I'm in deep study."

The figure bowed again. As it did so, tiny streaks of light stroked his head and protruding horns.

"We have not been able to capture the escaped elf." Relforaz's low growl was hot with digusted rage. He continues to elude my troops, and uses the jungle to his advantage."

Kylor looked up from his desk, and into the shadows, outside the strongest of the red glimmer of the column, where Relforaz pretended to cower.
"You had better find him, Relforaz, or I'll be forced to use the powers of the column on you and your tribe again." The dark mage's deep green eyes blazed a powerful hatred.

The figure of Relforaz bowed once more before vanishing back up the stairs. Kylor returned to his book, resuming his scribbling. Once he had completed his task, he proceeded to the massive column in the center of the room. For moments, the mage stood in silence before the structure. It filled his mind with thoughts of promised power and divine rule.

For three years he had been occupying the column room, studying its potential. Twenty years before his discovery of the pillar he had searched for power and wealth by traveling the world, looking for rare magic tomes and training for his own advancement. He had seen and done much, but had never really gotten close to his true idea of success. His body told him the winter of his life was coming;

he had needed something more tangible than mere spells and trinkets of enchantment. His magic had slowed the effects of his fifty-five years, so he appeared to be a man of thirty-five. However, he wanted more than the mere slowing of his age. He wanted all the column promised.

"I will discover your secrets yet. Soon, I shall be granted your greatest gift!" He whispered to the column as he began to stroke the marble again, muttering words of magic beneath his breath.

Relforaz ascended the twisted stairs to the upper levels, beyond Kylor's domain; his body hidden in the darkness of the stairwell. Two other forms were also hidden in the shadows, waiting for their chieftain to appear at the top of the stairs. The shadowy duo began to speak in whispered tones of Goblin, their native tongue, when they caught sight of Relforaz.

Hobgoblins, a larger version of their smaller goblin kin, populated the forgotten, wild, or forsaken lands of Tralodren. They tended to form tribes, which are ruled by the most powerful figure around, and looked to get what they wanted by showing how tough and resilient they were by dominating others.

They have minds predisposed to warfare and conquest, and little else. This was reflected in how they built their homes, like small forts with thick walls and protecting doors. Further, no member of their race ever traveled without a weapon of some kind. They will often improve upon great forts and structures they come to inhabit, from their experienced mindsets and strong military training.

Some bands of hobgoblins roamed the world in wild hoards like heavily-armed locusts. A very deadly wave of disaster and fear, few of these bands were left in the world but they did rise up to cause trouble every odd generation or so. Because of the hated of their evil nature and tendencies of war and destruction, they were hunted and killed on sight by their non-goblin neighbors. Many tribes had taken to finding permanent dwelling places to inhabit. Some were rumored to be on the verge of forming nation-states in some lands if tales could be believed.

Possessing pointed elven-like ears and sprouting yellowed canine fangs from roughened lips, hobgoblins appeared more feral and bestial than intelligent and cunning. Where goblins had a lime green complexion, a hobgoblin's skin was more of a yellow hue similar to a ripe pear. They were also known for their great strength and sturdy body, resembling a human's frame standing around six feet, with long, thin, dirty black hair often adorned with beads, strips of leather, or the fragmented bones of their victims.

Adding to the unsettling nature of the species were eyes with yellow irises and red pupils and thick, talon-like claws that could slice into the flesh of a lesser creature in a single swipe, or wield an axe with similarly deadly accuracy.

"What did he say?" One asked in his guttural tongue.

"He wants him found, and brought back here. Otherwise, we're to be used as experiments again," Relforaz responded in the same language.

"I'm sorry my lord," Drogg, the other hobgoblin spoke from the gloom. "I have dishonored you. It was my fault the elf escaped. Let me take a small force with me so we may track him down, and bring him back. Please allow me to restore my honor, and yours."

Drogg was an average-looking, war-scarred warrior within the tribe, and for many moons had also served as sub-chieftain, a position held by only four mighty warriors at one time.

It had been Drogg's duty to keep watch over important captives and when the elven prisoner had escaped, Drogg had to take responsibility for the loss. His punishment was the demotion from the position of sub-chieftain. Since his loss of power two days prior, Drogg had been trying to find the means by which to reclaim his place in the tribal order.

Relforaz thought for a moment in silence. Though it wasn't light enough to see his face, distant wall-mounted torches traced out fine white lines of horns as he turned his head toward the stairs. The horns had been a gift from Kylor after having offered himself as sacrifice in order to save as many of his people from the fate of the blue column as possible. The effects from the ordeal had mutated him into a different creature.

Though Relforaz still looked like a hobgoblin in many respects, his skin had taken on a reddish color; his hair had become a light grayish-white and two white horns jutted from his forehead in a curved arc. He had suffered much, but he had lived.

Those of his tribe who had been forcibly subjected to Kylor's demented experiments had fared far worse than minor mutations or even death. The boldness in of the dark mage in taking these past actions was a constant sore spot with the hobgoblin chieftain and not a day went by when he didn't try to figure out a way to be done with the mage, and liberate his people from his mad lusts and whims.

However, he knew to anger a wizard was to tempt certain death. Legends and stories had been told amongst his tribe for centuries illustrating the folly of such actions. For now he would have to keep buying time and pray to Khuthon the fool mage might blast himself into oblivion.

For now Relforaz had been unable to do much of anything to slow Kylor's machinations over his tribe. The elven prisoners they had taken captive recently had helped, but now the stark reality of the situation had once again become dark, and dominate in his foresight. This only rose Relforaz's already high level of vexation higher still.

"The sooner Kylor gets himself out of here the better. Go, take a small band of troops, and return with the elf," Relforaz answered Drogg dismissively.

"Yes, lord," Drogg bowed.

Malice burned in his ruby-tinted eyes as Relforaz closed the door to the lower room behind him. The echo of its closing traveled down the twisting spiral of darkness to the object of his hatred below. He wished he could close that door forever, sealing it with brick and mortar.

Relforaz walked out of the hallway and bumped into a small mass. It jingled and yelped as he hit it with his booted foot. The hobgoblin looked down at the quivering shape of Hoodwink, his goblin jester, a shorter race developed from the same primordial line, the hobgoblins thought of the race as inferior to them.

Hoodwink was decked out in a wild display of orange leggings, purple tunic, and a multi-pointed hat of green, which dangled silver bells from each bent tip. His dark, green complexion added to this putrid, visual sensation, as did his yellow cast eyes looking up at Relforaz; his tarnished teeth showing, as he began to widen his mouth into a smile or sorts.

"Is there trouble, my lord?" His spit-covered smile gleamed in the darkness of the room.

The chieftain snarled his reply. "The elf we were holding prisoner has escaped.
If we don't find him soon, Kylor will begin his tests on us again."

"No need for panic, my lord. Perhaps a story is all that is needed to sooth-" Hoodwink was cut short by Relforaz's boot. It embedded itself deep into his cheek. The blow sent the small figure flying into an adjacent wall, blood pouring over his lips.

"Save your stories, Hoodwink. You'll be the first to be tested upon if Drogg should fail. You'll have no excuses left then when it is time for you to face the blue column once again, will you jester?" Relforaz stormed out of the darkness which clung about the entrance to the secret passageway to the stairs into Kylor's chamber, and up into the more adequately-lit areas of the hobgoblins' lair.

Hoodwink gave a huff through his damaged teeth. A fine bloody mist flew out of his mouth, covering his clothes in a red dew. He got up from his slumped position, and managed to walk to a door at the other end of the hall. It was old and worn, one of the few that had not been replaced over the years.

"No tricks left, jester?" Hoodwink mocked in a perfect imitation of Relforaz.

Slamming the door shut Hoodwink continued to walk down a long and dark corridor. The bells on his hat jingled as he proceeded through the dim walkway until he reached another door with light issuing from a thin crack beneath. He flung it wide to let daylight stream into the dirty hallway, shielding his squinting eyes.

"I'll show him." Hoodwink huffed. "I know more about this place than any hobgoblin. I'm the smartest goblin here."

Hoodwink walked into an open area which had once been a beautiful courtyard before the hobgoblins took it over, along with the rest of the ruins they now made their lair. Prior to their habitation it had been left abandoned to the mercy of the jungle surrounding it. Now that it had been reinhabited, it had been cleaned up of much of the old debris and choking growth of the jungle around it to bring back a faint shadow of its former glory...

Hoodwink sulked around a collection of tall, faceless statues, something he did practically every day, spitting more blood on the ground as he did so. He could still feel his jaw throbbing, and knew it would begin to swell soon enough. All for the joy of keeping his life...what a great blessing. At least he still had his forehead, and not those horns Relforaz possessed.

"One day the laughter will stop. One day I'll be free from this place, and command my own fate," the goblin mused aloud. "Then things will be really different."

Each day was often spent in the same manner; Hoodwink being mistreated by those around him, causing him to retreat to this quiet place where he was left alone to sulk in silence until he regained his composure and was able to rejoin the hobgoblins.

He felt at peace in this place, which he called a garden - though it didn't have anything of a garden in, or about it. It did have a great many statues, though - timeless figures that didn't judge or mock him.

He was fairly certain none of the tribe cared about his secret place. Hobgoblins were not known for their love of nature or the arts. The garden had become the goblin's own imaginary court, where he wielded absolute power and could daydream about the day he would get back against all those who had tormented him, his so called betters. Of course this was just fantasy, and Hoodwink knew it. He didn't dare do too much, or press for better treatment too hard, or else he might find himself in worse situations than he did now. No, he could bear what he could for now, but should Kylor raise that spectre of more experiments, Relforaz had sworn Hoodwink would be first in line...

He turned his attention to the statues around him to clear his mind of such troublesome thoughts, though he knew he'd have to deal with them much sooner than later. Hoodwink would often look up into the faceless statues, and wonder who had carved them.

Certainly it was not goblinkind. The statues looked like no other race Hoodwink had even seen. They were strongly built, crafted from hard stone and depicted bodies well-muscled, yet slender in form, coupled with solid stances. This all made them seem more mythical than real representations, he thought.

None of them had any heads though. Both men and women statues were decapitated by what appeared to be swordstrikes if the goblin had to hazard a guess. Just who had done this, and why, Hoodwink didn't know. He had searched for the heads out of curiousity to see just what they might have looked like, but found nothing anywhere in the area.

Goblins, and hobgoblins for that matter, had never been very interested in the tales of the ancient past, or how they related to them in the present. Only tales measured in generations were the stock and trade of the firelight tales-things noble and true to goblinkind about goblinkind. Hoodwink was the exception to the overall goblin race. It was through his experiences with the hobgoblins he'd come to know of a higher culture, and the importance of history as a tool for understanding the world around him.

He had heard tales of the Great Ones, who were also called The Ancients or Dranors, which was usually a collective term covering all the ancient ancestors of the present day. However, it also was a term to describe a race who had founded vast territories and empires, making a great name for themselves before they vanished long ago.

The small goblin looked up at the statues, and wondered if these were the Great Ones who were often spoken of in conversations among some of the hobgoblin priests. Often the jester would look at the headless statues and envision his own head resting on their mighty shoulders, a body full of strength and power commanding authority, not the boot heel of his hobgoblin masters. Ah, but this was fantasy again it did little to sooth his fearful ponderings today for they were very dark indeed, should things progress as they were set to be played out currently. If the elf wasn't captured, he would be the first to be handed over to Kylor to experiment on as he pleased. The thought filled him with dread as he began to think of the pain and disfigurement. Death would be a blessing compared to what awaited him.

He had talked his way out of the initial rounds of testing, when Kylor had first appeared to the tribe, telling them they were to become his subjects or die. Relforaz boldly sacrificed his body for his clan, as any chieftain would do, but Hoodwink found it a vain and useless gesture to perform for a tribe that had mistreated him. So he'd avoided the same fate by declaring his position as chief chronicler of the tribes history, should they survive their subjection to the ancient device, was important enough to keep him from such a fate. It had bought him enough time to hide and think for a while. He didn't fully resurface from the shadows until the elves started to arrive in large groups some two months previous. They had been a godsend. They had come looking for power and glory, believing the hidden ruins were a lost shrine of their empire, or so one of them had told Hoodwink before he died in one of Kylor's experiments. They had been more than sixty strong. Now they were gone.

Soon the experiments would be started anew upon goblinoid flesh and that chilled Hoodwink to the bone. No, something had to be done and done soon, or he might very well be looking into the crazed face of that dark mage Kylor as the last thing his eyes would ever see...

Yornicus, last survivor of an elven exploring force, ran without thinking. The sun had set low in the sky with a bloody oozing, and seeped into the horizon.

The elf's legs felt like jelly, his lungs burned in agony, yet he continued to slaughter his body with continual effort. He had to force himself onward. There were no other options left to him. To stop fleeing meant certain death and he knew he'd suffer greater pain meeting his demise. He would rather die fighting for his life, fleeing from the ruins within the accursed tropical jungle of Takta Lu Lama.

The dense undergrowth did much to hinder his movement. Roots tangled his feet, sending him sprawling to the muddy ground. Many times he had to counterbalance himself by placing his hands on nearby tree trunks that were slick with precipitation. The air was thick with humidity, and he had to practically swim through it in order to continue moving. At every step, he was plagued with phantom footfalls of pursuing hobgoblins.

Yornicus was strong. He hailed from the Elyelmic lands of Colloni, and was regarded as one of the finest of his race. He had been trained within the ranks of the army of Colloni, and was more fit than his pursuers - or would have been - if he had eaten within the past week. Having not been beaten on several occasions by his hobgoblin captors would have helped out as well.

Yornicus had been sent to the ruins with a large exploration team to search out any ancient knowledge that might lie entombed inside. The priests of Aerotription had won the ear of the emperor with talk of great riches, and hidden truths of absolute power. Naturally, the emperor had sent out his best men to search for the ruin, and recent tales had placed it in the jungle of Takta Lu Lama.

The dark mage was something of a surprise to the experienced force, which had only been expecting to recapture an ancient ruin from a tribe of hobgoblins who had recently inhabited it. Death had never been wished by so many before they had met Kylor.

By using his powerful magic, the wizard was able to subdue the whole unit, and imprison them while he performed a number of macabre experiments on each captive. Yornicus was the last one of his unit to be used as a guinea pig, and knew his fate had been fast approaching as, one by one, each of his comrades had perished in front of his eyes. He had chosen, in that moment of desperation, to die in a flight for freedom rather than during an unknown length of incarceration and torture. He had escaped into the woods soon after.

It wasn't easy, but with a patient eye and traditional Elyelmic discipline, he found his way from his cell ,and out of the ruins to the jungle. He knew his captors would be close behind, however, and so kept up his running for as long as he could. To stop would bring about his death.

Yornicus' ears throbbed with pain from the intense pounding of his heart. His head screamed hysterically with an inner voice, driving him on, even though his body was almost spent.

He had to get word back to his commanding officer. Time was fleeting. If the mage was to work his dark magic again, he would almost certainly be unstoppable, especially, when he found what he was looking for. While lost in thought, the elf was grabbed around his ankle by a thick tree root, pulling him to the green ground below. For a moment the throbbing in his ear stopped, and in a brief space of time, he knew quiet blackness. It called him to rest in its peaceful embrace, and the elf was tempted to do just that.

Then the noises came.

The elf rose from the ground with a start. He heard the thrashing movements in the forest behind him, indicating the hobgoblins were closer than he realized. He began to panic, but caught himself before he took off in any direction, and truly lost himself in terror. Steadying his weakened frame, he took a deep breath, got his bearings, and then continued his frantic run through the dense jungle once more.

Farther back, the hobgoblin company, headed by the scarred and massive Drogg, heard the fall of the desperate Yornicus. The troop leader motioned the seven others with him to advance, as he readied a jagged collection of rust-colored steel beside him. Past victims' blood and teeth were still on the blade, having never been cleaned off. He would enjoy slicing into the elf with its putrid edges. He knew just where to cut so as to not kill the elf, thereby saving him for Kylor, but still allowing for his fun as well.

The troops quietly closed in on the spot where they thought the noise had come from. Their reddish eyes were lit with gleeful anticipation at the retrieval of the prisoner. As they neared the location though, they discovered it to be empty except for an impression in the tangled underbrush allowing them to see just where Yornicus had fallen. Drogg cursed by Khuthon, the god of warfare and strength, under his breath.

Yornicus ran on and on, his feet losing all feeling, his legs powered by a heart which may burst in the next beat. Sweat filled his eyes so only visions of light and shadows could be distinguished.

It didn't matter.

He had no choice.

He had to escape.

He could no longer recall what the trees looked like or if he was in a jungle anymore. All he knew was he must get a warning to a commanding officer. Though his will wasstrong, his body was unable to keep up the pace he had set. His beaten frame fell once more and his mind tumbled into the great expanse of silence. This time he welcomed its embrace.

Drogg poked the lifeless form on the jungle floor with his deadly blade. He had been doing this for the past few minutes, and had finally come to the conclusion the elf was thoroughly unconscious. Motioning to the other hobgoblins, the grinning Drogg sheathed his sword. They circled the fallen warrior like vultures.

"This one is a pathetic excuse for a warrior. If he was a true warrior, he would have faced us in combat. Truly, he was nothing of an elf; not even a man," Drogg snarled.

The others laughed as they tied his feet and arms with crudely-fashioned rope. They slung him over their shoulders like a sack of grain, and began to carry him back to the ruins. With their prize in hand, they had been infused with a new spirit of levity.

"You're right Drogg," one of the shorter hobgoblins remarked. "This elf was truly not even worth the effort to catch. We should have left him alone and spent our time figuring out how to get rid of that blasted wizard."

Drogg snarled at his subordinate.

"Relforaz knows what is right for the tribe, and I don't question his orders. I let the scrawny elf escape, and now I have recaptured him. My honor will be restored once Relforaz sees my valor."

"Drogg, honor isn't something to throw away, as money to a tart, like Balen did last night," another hobgoblin spoke up.

The group chortled amongst themselves.

"Shut up, Sen, or I'll tell the others what you do to those sheep behind the walls at night." Balen lunged an accusing finger into the other's face.

The other hobgoblins bellowed in laughter at the retort.

"Silence!," Drogg bellowed. "Have you forgotten what we are doing? Where we are? The longer we are away from the city, the better the chances are the bastard mage will take another of our kin to be tortured in that damned artifact of his.

"We will march back to the city in silence, or by Khuthon's helm, I'll have your sorry hides turned over to that mage instead of this elf.

"Now move!"

The small band of hobgoblins immediately got into line, fearing for their own safety. They trudged on through the dense undergrowth and moist air until they reached the rebuilt stone gate of the ancient city, which their tribe had come to inhabit. Carrying Yornicus past the restored walls, Drogg and his crew proceed to a massive building deep within their new home. This impressive structure was referred to by the tribe of hobgoblins as the King's Tower.

The city had once been home to the Ancients, or so their priests told them before Kylor killed them. When the hobgoblins found it more than four years ago, the city had been overgrown with mosses and plants, forgotten for centuries, and unused for millennia. With help from their priests, and sweat from their brows, they had reconstructed most of the ruins back into a secured dwelling. They used it more like an encampment than city, but it still served their needs. In the past four years, it had become almost rebuilt into its once great luster. Only a few holes survived here and there in the walls and floors. It would serve to protect them more and more as they grew more hostile toward the dark-skinned humans dwelling in the forests. Once the elves ran out, they would have to go and get these humans opposing him until they could find a way to attack the wizard haunting and hindering their lives.

At least that had been the plan Relforaz was working with at the time.

The King's Tower stood about fifty feet high, and appeared as if it had been the bastion of defense in the once mighty city. The hobgoblins, always militant in mind, had realized the potential of the tower, and had turned it into their command center from where Relforaz could give orders with relative security.

Most of the tower seemed to have been well repaired, except for a crumbled section of masonry on the southwest corner, which hung open like a festering wound. It would not remain open for long, though, as plans were underway for the tribe to finish up the last repairs quickly, to secure the entire building.

Two double stone doors, carved in worn and defaced friezes guarded the entrance to the tower. Their beauty was forever lost to the observer. Sadly, much of the ruins had eroded into faded memories neither the hobgoblins nor the few goblins in their service cared to study. The massive ten-foot tall doors were pushed aside and two hobgoblins, dressed in chain mail, ushered Drogg's band inside the tower.

They entered a small antechamber with two strange statues standing at attention on each side. The statues were devoid of any detail save for their legs; their heads missing and much of their upper bodies marred. Drogg and his men strode by the statues, and went straight for the stairs at the end of the room leading to Relforaz's throne room.

He and his group climbed upward through small, roving bands of guards and their vicious, sadistic dogs dressed in spiked leather armor. The dogs had been bred from wild wolves, providing a more volatile and tougher breed of guard dog than the standard domestic stock that might be found in the nations of mortalkind.

Drogg and his band stopped their ascent before another set of stone doors. Unlike the previous stone doors, these still held their carvings. On the left door was a gleaming spear, suspended in mid-air. On the right was the image of a large, grinning skull.

Both illustrations were intertwined with vines and small people who were scattered around the images. They appeared to be a combination of all the peoples of Tralodren, running around, performing various tasks. Not one hobgoblin could decipher the meaning behind the carvings, but many liked the chaos depicted within them, including Relforaz, as he felt it was a favorable omen of some sort.

Drogg stood defiantly before the door as another two hobgoblins on sentry duty in the musky, humid enviroment demanded to know his purpose and the legitimacy of the tribal status he claimed. A brief discussion followed in the goblin language. When both were confirmed to their satisfaction, they opened the heavy stone doors, letting candlelight from the chamber spill out before them.

Drogg strode in with his small band close behind him. They wanted to share in the glory Drogg would receive from recapturing the prisoner. Being seen with him would also increase their rank in the tribe. It was only natural.Drogg would allow it; for he too knew how the inner workings of politics were in his tribe, and it was wise to have all the allies one could.

When Drogg arrived near the foot of the throne dais, four other hobgoblins, all elders of the tribe, turned away from the throne, and parted to either side so as not to obstruct the chieftain's view. There, atop a throne of deeply-etched gold, the horned visage of Relforaz loomed. He looked down at Drogg and his band, and took careful note of the cargo they carried.

Beside his right boot was the terribly-dressed Hoodwink, his lip had swollen to double its normal size, but the goblin didn't seem to mind much. He had more of an interest in the events playing out before him.

"You've done well, Drogg." Relforaz's admiration was genuine- almost fatherly in its approval. "This pathetic excuse for a warrior has just saved our tribe from further torture. I am pleased to restore to you the honor you lost when this elven worm fled. Hold your head high today Drogg, for you are once again one of my advisors." Relforaz's voice made sure that all the others gathered in the room took notice of the redeemed hobgoblin.

Drogg smiled triumphantly. He approached the throne surrounded by the gathered elders.

A small nod by Relforaz toward the others who had accompanied Drogg told them their faces had been remembered. They would also be honored by their assistance with the recapturing of the elf.

"Leave us, and take the elf to Kylor so he can do what he wants to him," Relforaz snorted as the circle of elders formed again around the throne.

"Yes, my chieftain," the other hobgoblins saluted, and then left the room with Yornicus over their shoulders.

Amid the semi-rebuilt ruins of the ancient city, one structure still retained its original luster from when it had first been built. Carved from white granite, this building was covered in friezes of defaced men and women of heroic stature who wielded great weapons against villains and monsters that were only best described in myth.

Twenty feet tall and seventy-five feet wide on its longest side, the time encapsulated building was supported by sweeping arches and fanciful stonework. Light and airy, the stone - though old - was still fresh and clean as if newly-carved the day before.

Natural images of vines and roses, birds and serpents all lived amid its pillars and walls. Daily events of faceless forms petitioned giant figures as if they were great divinities. The whole building was a holy, living relic at times that seemed to breathe with the morning light and fall into slumber at the beginning of night. It stood not far from the King's Tower. It had become Kylor's dwelling place, the dark mage slaying the priests of the tribe to claim it as his own when he had first arrived.

The small party of hobgoblins treaded up to the golden doors sealing the white structure from the world. The three passed a small protectorate of four guards who were dressed in chain mail and carried sharp spears at the ready. They were posted there to keep an eye on Kylor for the tribe, as much as protecting him from intruders.

Within the building itself, statues of powerfully-muscled humanoids, devoid of heads, lined a forty-foot section of wall. Each statue wore unique Armor, and depicted a different type of military stance. The hobgoblins traveled along the far wall of the temple, opposite the statues.

As they moved deeper into the structure, they passed collections of radiant, multicolored glass windows, most of which had been shattered by forces of nature or the hands of an unknown vandal, for the hobgoblin priests wouldn't dare strike out against such a place. Indeed, many held it to be a scared spot even before they dedicated it to the worship of Khuthon.

Some small scraps of glass still clung tenaciously to the lead lining of the windows, like wounded flesh on bone. In some windows, clusters of color had been preserved, forming vivid pictures of glorious deeds and heroic battles but once again, all humanoid figures were devoid of heads or faces. One partially-complete picture formed a vague image of a horrific beast slaying a giant-sized Telborian male by rending the victim limb by limb.

After a brief walk, the party halted by a granite statue. It stood at the far end of the temple, and had been carved to represent a Telborian male of fair features. Unlike all the other artwork within the city, the male figure's head and face were unmarred. He had short hair, was of medium build, and was dressed in a long, flowing gown.

"Push it open," the hobgoblin carrying Yornicus said to the other as he motioned to the statue with his chin. The other approached the carved image, and pushed it to the left with heavy grunts, uncovering the dark opening of a doorway some seven feet tall.

Strange odors limped out of the opening; strongest amongst them was the charnel stench of death. Another hobgoblin took a torch from the wall, and proceeded down a flight of stairs illuminated by the flickering light. The remaining hobgoblin stayed behind to act as a guard while his comrade, carrying Yornicus, followed the torchbearer into the maw of the stairwell.

Halfway into their descent, the stairs became illuminated by soft, warm, red light. It pulsed from the stone steps like a heartbeat. The light intensified slightly as the duo approached Kylor's chambers. Reaching the bottom step, the hobgoblins found they didn't need the torch anymore as the red light from the glowing column blanketed everything in its crimson glimmer.

They stopped when they neared a metal cage erected around the pillar, whose runes had taken on a powerful red incandescence. In front of the bars, Kylor, in his silver robes, was bent over a tome atop a stone pedestal, also carved with runes of a long forgotten language. When they saw how near the wizard was, they drew silent.

Just as fear had taken their tongues, it also caused them to wait.

"What is it?" Kylor said, his face still implanted in his book.

"Brought you the runaway slave," the hobgoblin spat out in rough Telborous.

"Put him inside the cage," without even looking up from his studies, the mage caused the cage door to open of its own accord.

Not wishing to test the mage's wrath, the hobgoblins hurriedly walked inside and threw Yornicus to the floor in front of the red glowing blue column. Kylor withdrew from his book, and looked at Yornicus then at the two hobgoblins.

"He better not be dead or damaged too badly." The dark mage's eyes narrowed into slits, chilling the blood of the hobgoblins. "I have need of strong specimens."

"No, he is not. He is ginshsaw," one of the hobgoblins sheepishly responded.

It took a moment for the mage to understand the term. He had been around the hobgoblins long enough to pick up key phrases and words, but he refused to take precious time away from his studies to learn their tongue.

"Unconscious?" Kylor translated.

"Yes," the other nodded.

"Then wake him up dolt!" Kylor venomously spat out, causing both hobgoblins to jolt a bit as if a serpent had just bitten their heel.

The hobgoblins proceeded to slap the elf's face until he groaned awake.

"Good. Now place him in the column." Kylor motioned to the blue cylinder.

Yornicus screamed bloody curses at his assailants, who lifted him up in the air and carried him - kicking and screaming, over to the column where they threw him into a rectangular opening in the artifact's base.

Landing on his back, Yornicus quickly righted himself and attempted to maneuver out of the cylinder, as best as his bound limbs would allow, but the exit was blocked.

Though he didn't see a door, he felt a barrier of some kind press against his face and shoulder as he struggled for release.

"Don't waste your strength trying to escape," Kylor cackled as he held up his hands. "It's quite secure, I assure you."

The wizard then stepped back from the podium where he'd been standing. The hobgoblins, now familiar with the mechanics of magic, realized Kylor was about to work his dark powers, and cowered back behind the bars, outside the cage itself, which eerily closed of it's own accord instantly following their fearful departure.

Kylor's raised hands began to gyrate at strange and untimely intervals as if moving to some weird rhythm. As he moved, he spoke the ancient language of magic from what he had read from the ancient tome before him.

"Thoth ron heen ackhleen lore uylchyre uylchyre...."

The mage's voice was drowned out by a rising hum coming from within the artifact. Yornicus struggled to thrust his shoulders up to his ears at an attempt to block them from the agonizing noise, but was hindered by his bonds.

As he sat in the column, the small room he was in began to glow bright red. He knew his life was forfeit in mere moments and so decided he would die as best he could, with as much dignity he could muster. It was his only weapon - the only way he could fight back.

The erratic movements of the mage continued.

The runes on the cylinder flared into life. Blazing hot light singed the walls of the chamber. The humming grew louder, as did the light, until the room was completely swallowed in red murk, blocking anyone from looking inside the artifact.

The dark mage escalated his chant, taking it up to the next pinnacle of energy. Then suddenly, his chanting halted.

Small rivers of sweat poured down his face onto his silvery robes.

The hobgoblins twitched with fright, but they couldn't avert their eyes from the compelling scene. They watched in immovable horror as the opening in the artifact stopped glowing. The runes on the tall cylinder of rock ceased to flare, and the hum stilled to a minuscule noise, then silence.

Kylor took a deep breath and rushed to the artifact. The mystically-sealed doorway had cleared, allowing him to look inside and see the results of his work.

"No! By all the dark gods!" Kylor rushed to his tome. He tore through it wildly, and muttered to himself. "So close, so very close. How could this happen?"

After a few more frantic page turnings, Kylor fell silent, and looked at the hobgoblins who continued to stare stupidly at the column.

"Clean up that mess," he said, motioning to the cylinder's interior. I want it ready for another test when I return!"

Timidly, the hobgoblins neared the cylinder; iron gate opening again of it's own accord as they neared. Kylor ascended the dark stairs behind them. As they entered into the cage the hair on the nape of their necks stood up, and their heart rate quickened. Something told them not to go on, but they knew the alternative was worse.

They treaded closer.

A smell filled their nostrils, reminding them of roasted rabbit. Curious to see what the source of the aroma was, the hobgoblins peered inside the opening in the column where they had thrown in the elf.

The smooth, curved interior walls of the cylinder were splattered with blood and innards. Small chunks of anatomy hung on the walls in sticky globs. A great pile of ruined mess congealed in the center. The molten mound of flesh lay like a pile of butcher's garbage. Sinew and bone crossed over each other like a macabre sculpture. Both barely managed to suppress the instinct to run.

What held them captive was the sight of a skull in the pile of flesh. Though it was noticeably a skull, there was something very awkward about its appearance, as though it were looking inside itself.

Pondering it a bit further, they finally came to the hideous conclusion the skull, and the rest of Yornicus, had been turned inside out.

Chapter 7

The cold, salty air slapped at Rowan's cheeks as he looked out over the frigid waves highlighted by the setting sun. He had already endured three weeks of what would be a two-and-half month-long journey to Talatheal quite well. Though it was already getting colder in the Northlands, he would experience milder temperatures, as the Midlands would be just entering into fall when he'd arrive. Something to look forward to, he supposed.

Rowan's mind reflected the turmoil of the rough waters passing before him. He'd managed to pack up his things in the time allowed, and had taken the next boat heading south to Talatheal. He hated the fact he had to part with his family so soon after their reunion, but knew his oath was greater in importance than family ties. He belonged to Panthor now, and it was his responsibility to fulfill her missions until he was no longer able to do so.

Rowan prayed for a swift completion to his task. He already missed the shores of his homeland. Such was the way of the Knighthood though, to all who had sworn their allegiance to the Queen of Valkoria. He prayed he would find peace in his heart before he returned home, but that blessing was proving elusive to him...

As the cold waves of the Yoan Ocean lapped at the sides of the sailing vessel, he began to also doubt his worthiness toperform the task ahead. After all, what did he know? He was a young, beardless warrior from the Valkorian Islands.

His life before was the hunt, tribal shamans, and the harsh realities of bitter weather. What business did he have being a knight in the first place?

But he had been knighted, hadn't he?

And Panthor had accepted him, hadn't she?

Rowan continued to wrestle with these things in his mind as the boat moved further south, and he came closer and closer to what one could call, their destiny...

The Frost Giant was an older carvel with two masts flying deep blue sails, striped vertically in a shade of brownish-red resembling dried blood. Knowing the temperament and superstitious nature of his people, Rowan had no doubt it probably was dried blood. More than one victim had run afoul of the Nordicans over the years - and even past months - he supposed.

It was a rather simple vessel, with three decks. The one below was for cargo, and had a space where some of the men could sleep, as well as places to prepare and protect the food and gear. Another deck lay above; the main deck allowing the ship to function - where many of the sailors slept during the nights.

Above this second deck, connected by some narrow stairs, was the captain's deck, housing the captain's personal quarters, as well as navigational and rare, expensive goods. This smaller deck, comprising not more than a quarter of the ship, also held a guest quarters, where Rowan was allowed to stay for his journey.

The Frost Giant's crew of forty strong Nordicans busied themselves around the seasoned deck and rigging as the rolling waves of chilled salt water carried them and their cargo along their trek south. The crew was rugged and tempered from many years of exposure to wind and waves, and the men had grown dense beards to protect their faces from the ravages of the salt and wind.

Ragged hides and simple, yet thick garments of waterproof cloth covered their leathery skin. Each also carried a sharp knife at his side, and a few even wore a charm of protection from Perlosa about their necks. Indeed many a sailor held that the goddess of the sea would protect them if they possessed the amulet - a faint superstition still held strong among the two battling goddess' who warred over control of the heart of the Northlands.

Rowan sighed in his thoughts as he watched the captain appear on the main deck. The plump Nordican sailor was top-heavy and looked as if he could only walk upright for very short periods of time. He swaggered over to the troubled youth, his pungent aroma carried through the brisk air, unmasked by the cold, salty wave's own fragrance.

The captain was an older sailor, a merchant who had met with good fortune for many years. His wealth had allowed him to grow lazy. It had given him time to think. So much time, he had begun to fashion himself an epicurean philosopher of sorts.

"Don't worry lad, the trip won't take much longer. You'll go ashore, do what you must, and be back to Valkoria before the beginning of summer. It will be like you never got the kiss of Perlosa." The rotund man slapped the back of the youth. The rousing words of the aromatic captain did little to comfort Rowan, who looked intently out to the churning waters, still deep in thought.

"You're right," Rowan half muttered, "it won't be long at all." The knight feigned a smile to get the captain to leave him alone with his thoughts.

"That's the spirit lad! There be Nordic blood in ye yet, I reckon." The captain raised himself from his seat, after giving Rowan a final pat, and slowly waddled back to his cabin, stopping every now and again to look over a few crewmen and some of the ship's rigging.

Rowan continued to look out to the sea, lost in the memories of a faded coastline.

"Not too long at all..." the words echoed in Rowan's mind.

The day had been a long one. Rowan, who was a little older than twelve, was hunting bear with his mother. The winter months were fast approaching, so the beasts would be slowing down for hibernation, making them an easy kill. The meat, hide, and bones would be very helpful for the tribe as the months began to turn colder when food and clothing became valuable.

Rowan's mother turned to him. The beads in her hair and on her buckskin made no noise with her movements.

"Time to be quiet," she whispered to the overzealous youth. "There's a bear still in the cave. I'm going in to flush him out; you lead him to our trap."

"Yes, mother," Rowan chirped. His legs were like water pumps; bopping up and down as the body they supported waited impatiently.

Rowan had watched in childish awe when his mother moved into the cave without making a sound. He had tried to strain his eyes in hopes of finding her form moving about the dark maw of the rocky opening, but she had vanished like a specter into the night. Time passed in slow, excruciating silence.

Rowan began to imagine himself leaping into the gloomy opening in hopes of saving his mother from some horrific disaster, when he heard the deep roar of the massive beast. The bellowing grew louder until a black furry shapecharged out of the cave's mouth.

Rowan was new to hunting; his mother having taught him the skill for only a few weeks. She had wanted to train him in the ways of the hunt in order to get him used to the warrior life he was destined to pursue. The warrior was a time-honored and worthy pursuit for any male of the tribe, and as a mother, she had wanted to give her son the best training possible.

For two weeks, they had tracked and captured smaller, more docile animals to teach Rowan how to move silently and to out-think an opponent. Bears were the next level in his education. Now, with one charging toward him, he was paralyzed with fright.

"Get ready, Rowan," his mother's voice echoed from the cave."Lead him to the trap."

Though he had been immobilized moments before, his mother's voice snapped him out of his paralysis, and Rowan jumped into action as the bear charged at him. The huge black bear easily dwarfed the twelve year old, but it was up to Rowan to lead the bear to the trap he and his mother had made out of a pit they had dug in the forest floor.

The youth was quick to take flight with his well-developing legs, goading the bear on by shouting and throwing rocks at it. His mother had told him if the bear got severely enraged, the creature would not pay much heed to its surroundings and, as such, be easier to trap.

Even though Rowan was a fast runner, the enraged bear was more determined, and quickly gained on the boy. The trap had been set on the opposite side of the trees lining the rocky boundaries of the cave. Rowan knew he had to reach it soon, or be mauled by his enraged pursuer. As he neared the pit, Rowan began to daydream of the hero's welcome his tribe would give him over his first kill. Though his mother had helped, he could still claim some ownership in the task.

The pride swelled in him.

The massive beast gained more distance. As it did so, Rowan faltered and fell. He hadn't paid close enough attention to his footing while he was daydreaming, and had tripped on a root at the lip of the trap. He toppled beside the opening, fear rising anew.

The bear raised to full height, readying itself for an attack on the youth.

Within moments, arrows filled the air, embedding themselves into the the animal. The bear howled in anger as he turned around to face its new assailant. Another shaft flew through the air, into one of the bear's eyes - embedding itself in the beast's brain. Blood flowed like water, and for a moment, the bear gave out a slight whimper of protest, then convulsed into a heap beside the prostrate boy.

Rowan looked from the dead bear to the source of the arrows. His eyes opened wide at the sight. On a small, raised, area were footsteps at the pit's end, and there stood Rowan's mother. Her hair blew softly in the breeze as she lowered her bow.

"Are you all right, son?" Though taut with the recent energy of the encounter, her maternal concern still showed through.

"Yes," Rowan answered in a daze as the whole event began to sink in.

"Good. Thank the spirits you weren't wounded." She lent a hand to her son.

Rowan got up and looked at the dead bear, and a sense of sickness washed over him.

His mother noticed, as all mothers notice such subtle things in their childern.

"Ah, you taste fear, Rowan. Don't savor the flavor; it's far too bitter to nourish anything. Once you have mastered fear, and only then, you will be on the road to becoming a good warrior and hunter for the tribe." She peered down at her son with a loving eye.

"When will that be, mother?" He returned the gaze.

"If you're truly dedicated, not long at all son, not long at all." Rowan's mother stepped around the pit to comfort her son.

....long at all....long at all.

Rowan returned from his daydream to look out over the sea. Ever since he had gone through the knighthood's training, he'd felt slightly different, than what he had felt like growing up- even in that daydream he just had. He couldn't figure out where this thought was coming from - or what was different. He just knew something had changed.

You're a man now, Rowan. That's why you feel different. His father's voice echoed in his mind.

It wasn't that - or was it? He'd grown up over the last seven years in the knights' care. He came to them a boy, and now was leaving on a mission for them as a man. He didn't feel that different from the youth who had started out on the knight's path on other levels, though, which made this uneasy concern more confusing.

Back then, he thought becoming a man through the glorious ascension to knighthood would be something wonderful and mystical in itself. He didn't feel that now, nor did he feel any wiser or more intelligent as he thought he would when he became a man. All he had was fear, constant worry, and regret at not having become more than what he'd thought he should have been in his previous visions of his future self. Somehow he thought when he'd reached this time in his life he'd be a little greater than he knew himself to currently be.

Rowan had been taught what was right and wrong by his parents, and he was quite convinced of its truth. Enforced by his tribe, it served him well in his development and functioning in the lands held by his tribe. To him, it was the total truth of the world around him; it made absolute sense. Then he was taken to the Knighthood, where he was taught a new definition of right and wrong: a divine definition. This definition added some new insights to his old concepts but also reinforced what his parents had already taught him.

But there was still that nagging, deep-seated doubt...

Rowan walked back to his cabin to escape the frigid mist. He pondered his doubt in silence, as he was taught to do by the order. It was through self-examination a knight came to know himself and, in so doing, be better at fulfilling his task for his goddess. The youth plunged deeper into his subconscious as he entered his compartment. It was a simple room, with a single porthole window and hammock, and a heavy wooden chest beneath it. He took some furs from out of the chest, and began to wrap himself in them. As he did this, he chanted a prayer to Panthor, in his native tongue.

He knelt beside his hammock, and proceeded to pray to the divine force he had dedicated his life to, hoping for some guidance. In the old ways of his people, Rowan bowed his head, resting his forehead on his bent knee, as if swearing allegiance. His psalms of reverence spoke of pride and strength, two traits the Knighthood advocated above all else, and pleaded for direction and protection,

The praying continued until Rowan finished with the customary removal of the furs before he got up. When he had done so, he let them lie as they fell off of him. After this, he removed his clothing down to a thin, light gray, cotton undershirt and pants. Though it was cold outside, it was warmer inside the cabin, and under the furs of the hammock he often got too hot to rest.

His pale, lean form stood out from the dimly-illuminated interior of the ship's cabin as he slipped into the hammock. Rowan took one final look at the garments he had taken off. In the morning, he would look at them to try and devise a method of insight left by Panthor for him to discover. Such were the superstitious ways of his people they found their way into everyday usage as well as religious customs of even the Knighthood. From the fate he read in his garments, he would interrupt them to fit into his day.

Sliding beneath the furs covering the hammock's surfaces, Rowan closed his eyes tightly, and listened to the shudder and creaking of the ship. It was a gentle rhythm, like the beating of a maternal heart.

It lured him into a peaceful slumber where his troubled soul could be at rest. He hoped Panthor would speak to him as he dreamed, providing him with a vision that might lead him on the right path, or at least rid him of his doubts. As sleep won over the last bit of consciousness, Rowan felt a foreign, even hostile, presence in the cabin with him - but the alarming thought quickly fled as sleep gained control. In moments, he had left the waking world.

When Rowan passed out into unconsciousness, an opaque form shimmered into being. At first it was incorporeal, flickering in and out of sight. Within moments, though, it began to solidify; its smoky shape coalescing into a tall figure, clothed in torn robes of soiled white. A moth-eaten hood camouflaged his ruined face in its shadows. Only two small points of bluish light crept from the dark cover illuminating traces of white bone.

The Master's skeletal frame drifted silently toward Rowan to inspect his slumbering form.

The young Nordican was fast asleep.

"Dream now, young knight, while I attend to your belongings," the lich cackled softly.

As silent as the night, the Master moved the chest out from under Rowan's hammock, spoke a few words of an incantation and the chest opened of its own accord. It began to spit its contents into the air, where they floated before the robed figure's outstretched, skeletal hand.

With strange motions, the Master swirled the contents around in the air. Tunics and boots flew by, followed by capes and rations, and then all but a few articles fell to the floor with a soft thud.

"Here we are," The Master leered at Rowan's armor and weapon as they drifted before his glowing eyes. He laid his hands flat against each item and allowed the flow of mystical energy to pass through his arms, and into the sword and armor. They began to glow an angry red as this power coursed through them, growing hot like freshly-forged metal. Then, a sudden flash erupted from them, bathing the room in a white light before both armor and sword grew as cold and gray as the weather outside.

The Master muttered to himself again, and pointed to the collection of clothing he had let fall to the floor. One by one, tunics, boots, and the newly-altered armor danced through the air to rest once more within the confines of the chest, in the exact order they were in previously.

"All is ready, my young knight. You shall not fail in your task, not now. I have given you the key to my freedom." The Master's bony face twinged in what could have been a smile when he spied Rowan's garments laid out for divination. The lich took his staff and twirled the garments around, laughing as he did so.

When he was satisfied, he muttered more words of ancient lore beneath his breath, and then his rotten form disappeared into a vortex of azure light.

In the morning, Rowan awoke to a musky odor of the cabin. Swinging himself out of the hammock, he wiped the sleep from his eyes, and stumbled over to a small bucket containing cold rainwater, hoping to splash his body back into awareness, gazing down at the bundles of clothing he had left the night before. The curiosity of the custom's outcome outweighed his doubts on the matter of its validity.

The youth peered at the simple hodgepodge of clothing, and his eyes widened at what he saw. Though he was new to the learned custom of divination from such objects, he had mastered some small insight into the method of interpreting the results he found before him.

They looked quite favorably toward him. Most times they did, in fact in almost every outcome he had looked into through this ritual, and by talking with others who still practiced this custom, there never seemed to be a day outright set against a person.

He looked further into the folds and fabric. The young Nordican could sense, something today, or very soon, was going to bring him great advancement and enjoyment in life. Quite a common and easy to spout off answer, he thought.

Scoffing at the result, once he found he could stand relatively straight without dizziness, Rowan opened his chest to select a new outfit for the day. Rummaging through his belongings, he stopped to examine his armor and sword. For some reason, he thought the weapon had gleamed for a moment - a flash of luminous azure. Holding it up to the meager light filtering in from the filthy porthole, he discovered nothing out of the ordinary, and decided it must have just been a trick played on him by his still-awakening mind. Repacking the sword back in the trunk, donning the garb he had shed last night, he strode out of his cabin into the cool air of the deck.

The morning sun was clear and bright, free from having to battle against any trespassing cloud. The ocean was calm; the larger waves being produced by the bow of the ship. All around the boat, sailors sat and joked with their mates as they devoured their meager breakfast rations of salted fish and dried bread, washing it down with flagons of slightly sour wine. The poor meal would be their rations for the entire day unless they caught more fish in their nets.

The past two days had turned up nothing of value, which was odd as they were in the waters near the outskirts of Arid Land, where the sea began to teem with life. They would probably make sight of the pine-bedecked continent some time later that week if the winds held, and the sea was kind.

Rowan strode to the port side of the vessel, and looked over the railing into the slowly-passing waters below. He noticed the color of the sea had changed from the frosty blue-green of his homeland to a deep, murky green of the warmer climates.

He was delighted, for the temperature change meant he was halfway to his destination. The Yoan Ocean, which covered much of Tralodren, bridged the gap between the Valkorian Islands and Talatheal.

The youth was starting to get agitated, being cooped up on a ship with very little space to move. The agitation had lessened over time after he had settled into a pattern to help focus and balance his mind and hours. Each day seemed to be a little better than the last. He was sure with a few more days he would come to see a peace descend upon him as he accepted his situation through a regulated pattern of events. His troubling thoughts had faded from the previous night, but were still with him, lurking in the shifting shadows of his mind. For now, he tried to focus his mind on the peaceful waves beneath him.

Suddenly, he noticed something beneath the waves. It was large and dark; a black stain swimming amid the tranquil emerald waters. Rowan knew dolphins and whales frequented the area, but the shape of the shadow was unfamiliar to him. Curious to know what it might be, he called to a sailor who was coiling rope nearby.

"What's that down there?" Rowan asked.

The middle-aged sailor finished his task before making his way to Rowan's side. Thinking it would just be an ignorant landlubber fascination with barnacles on the hull, or some other such nonsense, the sailor took his time approaching the young knight. The less time he spent talking to this new salt about barnacles, the more he had for his duties and his wine.

"What is it lad?" The sailor bent over the railing, and peered into the water. For a moment, he saw nothing. Then, his trained eye spotted the dark blotch moving alongside the ship. It seemed to swim as fast, if not a little faster than the ship itself.

The sailor paled as the shadow began to surface, and grow in size. Looking deeper into the water, with eyes trained by years of sea travel, he turned white. The beast was the largest thing he could have ever imagined. It ran further beneath the waves still, and seemed to be a mass larger than a whale. As the sailor continued to look, he saw two red glowing eyes return his gaze.

Fear gripped his heart.

"All hands on deck, linnorm off the port bow!" The sailor screamed. "All hands-"

He never finished his sentence. A massive force struck the port side of the ship, and sent all on deck to their knees; Rowan fell onto his back. A deep roar erupted from the starboard side, followed by a hissing sound. Then a large cloud of boiling mist engulfed all those on the port side of the boat.

Rowan stared transfixed as screams of sailors and the sound of sizzling meat could be heard from within the cloud. Men began to run out of the mist, covering their tortured eyes with hands of boiling flesh. Their clothing and weapons had melted away in some parts, leaving behind smoking, dripping remnants.

Before Rowan could think further, the captain appeared behind him and grasped him by the shoulders, his chest heaved like a mad bellows.

"What are you doing standing about on the deck, lad? To arms! We need all the help we can get, and there is none better than a trained Knight of Valkoria is their now? Now off with ya. Get your weapons and get back!" He pushed the youth, almost throwing him, to his cabin before running to starboard to shout orders.

"To arms! To arms! We have a linnorm against us!" The captain kept shouting as he wobbled onto the starboard deck, which was now pitted and worn as a stone after a fierce sandstorm. He raised his own broadsword in challenge, and peered over the partially-eaten away railing.

Looking below, he almost lost his legging and fell headlong into the sea. It was good he didn't, for he would have fallen head-long into the gaping jaws of the reptilian beast whose eyes were dripping with malice.

The linnorm's maw was huge and reptilian, much like a crocodile's with thick, deadly teeth poking out of scaly lips, like jagged reefs. It had the long neck, and sleek body like some great eel or serpent, with grayish-green scales, highlighted with a soft blue. The eyes were wide, slightly elongated, and glowed an intense sea green.

Rowan had heard stories about dreaded beasts, but he never thought he'd see the day where he would be staring into the eyes of a linnorm itself. They were said to be the first dragons created by the gods - beings of raw power aligned to one of the elements of Tralodren. For years, nobody had seen the creatures. Bards had even begun to tell tales of the race's extinction.

The skalds of Valkoria, however, still sang ballads of deadly encounters with the Midgard - the linnorms of the sea, prowling the Nordic waterways. If any linnorms still lived, then they were in the sea, and who knew how deep the great waters really were?

Rowan and the ship's crew could now attest the linnorm's existence. Even as they managed to flee the attack, many of the crew quickly jumped back from the eroded railing before an enormous webbed front claw knocked them overboard.

"Change our heading toward the east, lads!" The captain bellowed. "Then w-."

Another blow struck the side of the ship sending water, crashing up and over the vessel. The force of the tidal wave knocked the crewmen about, but many of them managed to grab onto rigging or railings to prevent themselves from being washed overboard. When the sailors regained their footing, and attempted to lay in the new course, the Midgard slithered up out of the salty depths to loom above the deck.

All on board scattered like mice before a cat.

"Where's that boy knight?" The rotund captain shouted above the linnorm's bellow. "We could use his sword arm right about now!" Fear clenched at his heart like an icy hand of stone.

"I'm here!" Rowan shouted over the clamor of the crew. He had quickly dressed himself in his leather armor, and was equipped with his long sword.

"To work, boy, you have a beast to help us slay!" The captain shouted.

Rowan looked at the huge monster towering at least twelve feet above the railing of the ship. He watched as a sailor at the bow of the boat took a sword swipe at the serpentine body of the beast, cutting deeply into flesh.

A thin river of deep blue blood ran down from the cut.

The other men began to rejoice at their comrade's well-placed stroke, taking courage in his victory, until a shower of crimson burst across the deck.

So quick was the occurrence many turned their heads to and fro in confusion, then up, as their minds finally came to realize the Midgard had struck. The only proof, there indeed had been a crewman at all who once challenged the linnorm, lingered from the beast's teeth as a set of helpless feet.

They dangled much too loosely from between the Midgard's toothy maw to rekindle any ray of hope. Then, in a swift backwards motion of the neck, the monster flipped his victim down his throat to disappear behind scaly lips.

The crew grew ashen and still.

"What can I do against such a beast?" Rowan shouted at the round captain.

"You're a knight aren't you? Use your powers," the captain responded.

Rowan didn't want to explain to him what the captain really wanted was a mythical hero, not a recruit freshly out of the Knighthood. Yet the youth knew he had to represent his Knighthood to the best of his ability; he was considered an ambassador for the Order and all of his actions reflected back on them.

He had sworn an oath to uphold the Code of Panthor, and therefore the Knighthood's image, and now he felt its burden on his back. After all, these people were humans. He had avowed to protect and aid all humans as best he could. Furthermore, they were kinsmen - brothers of the North-lands. He owed it to them to fight alongside them.

Another hiss cracked through the air.

More screams arose from the men as they fought off another attack from the Midgard's acidic breath as it claimed more lives. Rowan could smell the burning fumes, and feel traces of it eat at his face and hands, stinging his eyes, as the sea breeze carried it to him.

He had to do something.

The young knight raised his sword high into the air, screaming a war cry at the top of his lungs, he charged the massive creature. The Midgard lunged forward at the new threat, and attempted to swallow the young knight whole as he had done to his previous attacker. Rowan saw the serrated jaws rush for him, and anticipated the strike.

He somersaulted low, and to the right, as the mouth snapped with an echoing clap inches away from his side. At the same moment, he stood up quickly, and swung his blade. It seemed to be lighter and better balanced than he last remembered. He brought it down behind the beast's head, severing a vein, and causing a spout of blood as cold and blue as the sea to erupt from the wound. The cheers of his fellow Nordicans increased his nerve - allowing him to delve into reserves of courage he never knew he had.

The linnorm howled in pain. It reared its head just as Rowan attempted a second blow. It landed short, for the beast had raised his head out of range. Rowan could no longer reach the monster, but the other crew members who were hanging from the rigging were within striking distance, and attempted to hack away, with very limited success, at what the young knight supposed to be the Midgard's neck as though it were a tree trunk.

Rowan shouted in fury against the wounded monster; a part of him excited by the success of his fellow Nordicans.

Blood flowed freely now from the Midgard's neck and head. The combined efforts of crew and knight severely weakened the creature. It was time for one more strong strike to make the victory decisive.

Rowan swung in a wild, slashing arc which unbalanced him enough to cause the knight to lose his footing. In spite of attempting to right himself with a mad dance, Rowan fell to the blood-coated deck with a wet thud.

The final blow Rowan meant to deliver never came.

Despite this, the linnorm suddenly sank down into the water with a cascading splash of foam and bloody water flooding the deck, rocking the vessel, and the crew.

For a long moment nobody moved. No sound was made. All braced for the beast's return.

When they were convinced the menace had finally gone, the men all rose and gave a shout of victory. Rowan bent his knee in prayer to his goddess. Others began to clean up the mess the battle had left.

After his prayers, Rowan looked around the vessel and tried to survey the damage. Scattered about the thirty-foot deck were the wounded, lying on their backs like freshly-caught fish. They stared blindly into the sky as their flesh bubbled like a rigorously-boiling stew. He tended to the wounded, and helped where he could, but there was little aid he could give, except for slight comfort to the dying.

The captain hollered orders over his swollen tongue. His sword was clean and his gelatinous flesh unmarred. Sailors moved like ants to try to salvage the ship, and keep it seaworthy. Rigging was replaced and pieces of wood from below deck were brought up and nailed into the gaps. Others set to the gruesome task of swabbing the now-purplish-blue blood and still smoldering acid, which had collected into a few smatterings of small puddles, from the deck.

Rowan was distracted from this seeming frenetic action by the moaning of a wounded crewman near his foot. His eyes and nose had melted like lard in a fire, leaving behind a very foreign visage. The crewman's hand clenched at the air as if grasping for the remains of his life. Rowan could make out glimpses of bone and muscle beneath the ruined flesh; tangled cobwebs of veins fell and raised themselves over the wounded flesh.

The fallen sailor grabbed onto Rowan's foot.

"Kill me," the crewman spat out from bloody lips.

Rowan looked at the wreck of the man, his mind torn between respect for life, as the Knighthood taught, and the honor of a mercy killing the Nordic people embraced in dire situations.But what was his duty?Where was his alligence? He wasn't ready for this. He wasn't sure what to do, and not being ready was what scared him most of all. He just wasn't ready.

Yet something in him, a small spark of light touched his mind. It told him he was ready, and this was as ready as he'd ever be. Rowan couldn't accept or rather, he didn't know if he should. He took to his feet quickly, and walked to his cabin briskly. He needed to be away from the moans of the dying, and the stench of acidic blood.

Let another do what was needed for the dying man- the dying human. Rowan had too much to wade through in his heart and mind. He needed to think.

Chapter 8

Dugan felt the sharp sting of the elf's spiked leather glove on his left eye. Warm blood trickled down his face, burning it with a river of crimson continuing to fall onto his lip and mouth. He felt the pulsating heat around the eye itself, and knew it was red and swollen.

The elf dragged the jagged-edged glove across his face once more. The sharp metal fastenings gouged into Dugan's youthful cheek, where it made a myriad of red canyons.

It was fourteen years since Dugan had first been captured by the Elyellium. All that time he'd served in the work yard of a minor noble, dying wool at one of his factories. His parents had been murdered, and his town had been razed to the ground by Elyelmic forces when he was nine. A few weeks after that, he had found his way to the factory.

Why the elves had attacked his town, he never knew. Dugan had lived in a very secluded fishing community on the coast of Colloni. Still predominately Elyelmic, it had a good mix of Telborians calling it home as well. Because of this racial mix, Dugan had long put away thoughts of his parents' slayers doing this all just to rid Colloni of human blood. He had also given up long ago trying to figure out what motivated them as well. There was little benefit to him as he toiled away to care why they had come in the first place.

They simply appeared one day and laid waste to all he held dear. In their final efforts, the elves had taken his freedom and future by making him a slave. Dugan had been one of a handful of other humans, and Elyellium who had been spared death. Where those others were now Dugan could care less. Probably dead, they wouldn't help him out either in keeping himself alive.

When the minor noble was murdered by some rival political faction, the factory was reorganized. A few prominent slaves noted Dugan's strength and size, for he had grown into a very strong man over the ten years he had been sentenced there.

It didn't take those interested in him long to acquire him like so much property. His new owners were rather well-to-do nobles who were very involved in the arena, and its spectacles. And it was to his current owner he had to be reckoned with deep below the coliseum.

"You will learn respect, human," the elf spoke in accented Telborous.

The remark was followed by another wounding blow.

This blow was the last Dugan could take. He was barely held by the manacles biting into his feet and hands, anchoring him to the wall behind him. Though the Telborian was chained by both hands and feet,the links allowed him some slack. This distance was made much shorter by two stalwart elven men who held him at each wrist. They were the guards assigned to keep order, protect and maintain the coliseum.

Even in his heightened rage, however, they wouldn't do much to prevent him from tearing into the Captain of the Games like a lion going for a kill.

Since his arrival, the Telborian had been beaten to teach him his place. His face was a massive patchwork of bruised and broken flesh. His body was splattered with blood and more bruises. Though his frame had been nearly broken, and his hair was matted with gore and sweat, his eyes still held a defiant glare.

"Now you will learn what it means to serve as a slave. You're nothing but property; a trinket. Your new owners can buy and sell you like herds in the market," the captain continued with a cruel eye and sour tongue.

The last comment of the captain earned him a round of laughter from the guards holding the massive man. Dugan had begun to notice the smell of searing metal through his blood-caked nose. It seemed to grow more intense as the captain stepped away from Dugan, and was replaced by a bent, smiling elf, with a toothless maw. He had the look of one who lived his life close to a forge; for he was covered in a light dusting of soot; his wrinkles transformed into black lines as they held the grime in their fleshly folds.

Moments later, Dugan felt the searing pain of another blow. Little did he know then this one would wound him deeper than any other strike dealt to him in his life. The sound of searing flesh, as well as the oily aroma of burning skin, filled the room.

The elderly elf smiled another empty grin toward the broken youth as the throbbing agony of the searing rod clawed its way into Dugan's skin, then burned deep into muscle.

Dugan cried out in fury, and though he was nearly successful in his pain wracked struggles at freeing himself from his holders, in the end he was subdued by a fist from the captain. The blow ended in a crunching sound as it connected with the Telborian's face, but it didn't usher from Dugan.

"Tripton's bow!" The captain shouted as he tried to open his broken hand as it leaked blood onto the rocky floor.

"Oh, you shall pay human! I shall see to it that you are treated worse than the hounds! By Aerotription, Ganatar, and Rheminas, I swear you will suffer!."

The captain left the small chambers with the slamming of a door; a trail of blood following his rapid departure. Dugan was left to ponder the new pain he had acquired, the first of many. The bent old elf turned slowly, inspected the still glowing rod, then he also proceeded out the door. This left Dugan alone with two coliseum guards, who still held him fast at the wrists.

They let go at the same time, both making a mad rush for the sturdy oak cell door. Dugan let out a howl of anger and pain as they slammed the thick, wooden barrier to be locked into place, then barred it with a heavy iron latch. The iron fetters and chains barely managed to restrain Dugan as they groaned against his strength. Laughing, the two guards looked in again at the 'helpless animal' in his cage; so easy to control, so easy to maintain... from behind closed doors.

Dugan cringed in pain as he delicately touched the burn on his skin with his right hand. The burn was made on his upper left shoulder, as all slaves of his rank in the gladiatorial games were marked. As he gingerly touched it, the wound seeped brownish drops of searing sorrow. He drew back his fingers and witnessed they were coated with the same sticky brown liquid.

He drew in a deep breath, but quickly bent over in pain and spasms, and began to cough. His fit lasted a long time. When it had subsided, he noticed a small puddle of blood had chilled between his feet on the cobblestone floor.

With the danger passing his adrenalin was wearing off, and the full gravity of the beating he had received was revealed to him with each passing moment.

The Telborian grit his teeth together and made a solemn vow to himself he'd get revenge on his captors for doing what they had done to him - what they had stolen from him. He was a proud Telborian from a now-destroyed village, and would be damned by the gods if he was going to bend to his captor's will when he had witnessed the end of his family by elven swords. He had been here for four years so far, and had a new owner who treated him even worse than all the others. This beating was just the first of many, and Dugan knew it. He had to do something soon, or he wasn't so certain he would be able to hold out for another four years.

Licking his broken, blood stained lips, Dugan whispered.

"Rheminas, god of revenge, hear me. I ask you to grant me one final request before I die in this god-awful pit. I ask for revenge on my captors and the slayers of my kin and family. Grant this to me, oh great Lord of Flame, and I will be content to live with whatever cost you wish to place upon such a gift."

To add strength to his resolved commitment, he hit himself hard on his burned shoulder. The pain was like lighting, coursing through his being.

He screamed, and closed his eyes as blackness overtook his senses.

Clara started at the sudden jerk from the nearly comatose Dugan. She hadn't been expecting movement from the injured man for quite some time...if at all. The Telborian's wounds had been bound with light cloth torn from her blanket. The simple bindings were stained a deep rusty red, and were leaking in some places.

"Sit back. You'll break the bandages I managed to put on you," Clara spoke with a shaky voice. "I thought you'd be out for days from your bleeding."

She had managed to clean herself off from the bloody splatterings in Ino, even changing her cloak as such a gore-stained garment would attract too much unwanted attention where they were going. She had seen to Dugan's cleaning as well, as best she could as she had tended his wound.

Dugan looked up at the elf with a groggy expression. He felt light-headed and was having trouble focusing on images clearly, but still managed to force out a question.

"Where are we?" He asked hoarsely.

"On the boat," her own voice was measured.

Dugan fell back onto the hard, wooden deck with a thud and groan.

"Ngh! How long have I been asleep?"

She looked out over the waves before them. "We've been at sea for at least half a day already. I'd wager we'll be able to dock on Altorbia by nightfall, and stay there until I can get the others. Then we'll be off to our final destination."

"Which is?" Dugan half-whispered as he closed his eyes tightly and reconfigured himself slightly on the wooden deck.

"Talatheal." Colloni wants to increase its hold on the land through peaceful agreements with the local Telborian kings. What they really seek is an empire once more; though now through a mercantile nature. However, a slave is still a slave." Clara's sapphire eyes flared with rage for a moment, and then returned to normal.

"You should be safe there," she looked back toward the wounded Telborian.

Dugan's eyelids fluttered as he tried to keep a grasp on consciousness. He was still leery about what he had gotten himself into. He felt even more apprehensive now that he was weakened, and in a boat in the middle of nowhere.

Still, it could be worse; he could be back at the coliseum. He told himself with a grim sense of optimism that the choice he had made was the only solution. However, he was puzzled at how weak his wounds had left him. He had sustained worse in the arena, and still managed to walk off the bloody sand.

Something wasn't right.

"The hunters sometimes use a rare drug on their swords to keep the wounds bleeding, and make their victims dizzy," Clara said to Dugan, seemingly anticipating his question, as she attended to his drenched bandages. "The drug will run its course, but only if you remain still and asleep.

"Rest and you'll feel better when we reach our destination. Of course, we wouldn't be in such a mess if you hadn't been as stupid as you were back on the docks."

"What do you mean?" Dugan cracked one eye partially open. He could make out shapes better now, but they were still blurry around the edges.

"You know full well what I mean, Dugan. Why, in the name of the Abyss, did you start attacking the air? You gave away our cover," her demeanor took on more an authoritative air.

"I saw a man. He started to attack me. You mean you didn't see him?" Dugan sighed.

"No," Clara studied the Telborian carefully.

"Then what did I see? Hunter Magic?" Dugan shuddered in pain, and tried to hold back a muffled groan through clenched teeth.

"Rest now, "Clara's words had taken on a soothing quality. "We'll find out later. All that matters is that we got out of that encounter alive."

"You...never told me...how you knew my name," Dugan grunted through a stiff jaw.

"Later. Just rest," she hurried the conversation to an end.

And though Dugan fought it as best he could, slumber came over him once more and left Clara alone with her thoughts.

The sun lingered in the center of the horizon before it plunged into the land of night, fighting as it fell, bringing up great rust-colored clouds in it's wake. Clara sat in the keel of the little boat, watching a bird which had been circling the boat since it first arrived a little more than an hour ago.

She thought of the tales of Endarien, god of the sky, who was known to use birds to act as his servants and his eyes and ears. She wondered what the old god was thinking, should he be watching, at the sight of her and Dugan and smiled at the silent answer. Birds also meant that land was close at hand. She figured they were close to the island of Altorbia, and so began to start to think of what she needed to do next.

The boat continued to float onwards.

Soon, Clara began to see a faint haze outlined on the multi-colored horizon. It was small and fleeting at first, as the waves would block it from view with their crests, then release it to sight once more.

She speculated they would reach the island close to the tenth hour, well under the cover of darkness.

The darkness would be her ally, as she would need time to get herself off the small boat and into the company of her other recruits without being seen.

Although Altorbia was somewhat diverse in terms of its racial makeup, it was still considered part of the Republic, and hunters frequently passed through there. Elves populated more than half of the tiny isle, with the rest of the inhabitants made up of Telborian merchants, getting fat off the rich commerce passing through the island's ports each day.

Clara knew Dugan still ran the risk of capture on Altorbia, but the risk was greatly reduced by the fact information on his escape had yet to reach this far. It would be a few more days still until news would reach over the waves. Hunters didn't like to give up any possibility of capture on their home territory before they were totally certain their prey had escaped them.

She also knew she had to act fast and get off the island by daybreak as the harbors and docks were watched very closely. If she were going to run into any trouble, that is where it would happen. And given the recent set of events with Dugan, she didn't want - or need - any more trouble.

The boat silently coasted on, aided by Endarien's breath, into the sleepy western harbor of the island. The cobblestone wharfs were dimly washed in an orange glow flowing from lamp posts lining the docks.

These lamp posts were a unique feature of the island as they had thick, square bases jutting out about five feet from the ground, and were covered in fat glass domes overlaid with metal netting. Their wicks went all the way down the interior of the posts, into the bases, where the oil was stored. The lamps had been crafted so they wouldn't be knocked down in a heavy wind, storm or turbulent waves. Their tiny fires emitted just enough light as to outline the docks, preventing ships from ramming into the wharfs and keeping guards from losing their footing in the darkness of night.

Clara tried to quietly maneuver the boat to a dark, secluded section of dock about fifty feet from the island's end. She had made prearrangements for the dock to be empty, and ready for her arrival. She didn't want anybody to witness her entrance or exit from the port. The Patrician maiden moored the boat to a slab of granite jutteing out of the platform, and prepared to head into the city center.

Farther out to sea, a soft air ushered forth, which traveled through a sandy beach stretching for some twenty feet before turning to rocky ground, then went inland. The dark trees of the coast, a short distance from the rocky ground, swayed in the starit wind, and softly carried the off key notes and swanky banter of sailors spending their evening in the taverns further inland. Apart from the drunken sailors, all was silent. Not a guard was in sight.

Clara remained cautious, however. She had quickly learned that things could go wrong in a split second. She looked down at Dugan once more. The Telborian was trouble waiting to happen, and because he was wounded, she didn't know what to do with him.

Dugan had slumbered through the entire voyage. Periodically, she had checked his wounds, and found the poison had run its course as his bleeding had slowed, then finally stopped and replaced any bandage saturated with blood.

She worried he would be too weak from the blood loss to move from the boat. The elf wanted to be sure, though. The last thing she wanted now was to have gone to all the trouble of getting the Telborian to have him die before they even started their journey.

She slapped his cheek softly.

At first he didn't stir. She began to panic until she saw the tanned chest raise in a mighty motion. It was followed by another, then his eyes slowly opened. Even with these positive signs, it took a few more good hits before the gladiator wakened.

"Wh…," he tried to speak through a hoarse voice.

"Shhh," she whispered. "Be still. The poison has gone, but you're still weak. We made it to the island, but I don't want us to be discovered. How are you feeling?"

Dugan struggled to sit up, and felt the world swim in his head. "I'm fine. Just tell me where we're going."He grit his teeth to fight down the nausea.

Clara quickly glanced around the docks before speaking.

"I'm going to a tavern called the Musky Otter to get the others, then…."

"We're going," Dugan finished with a snort, as he clutched his bandaged side. "I won't stay here."

"Dugan, you're in no condition to come with me. You need rest and food. I'll bring you back some meat from the tavern when I return with the others," she argued.

"You're half right. I need the food, but I've had enough sleep. If I slept any more, I'd be dead." His eyes were gaining an inner flame of strength. He also found his vision was back to normal too.

"You almost were, so don't go risking your life trying to check up on my integrity," Clara looked back toward the harbor to make sure it was still empty. "Gilban was right about you; you are stubborn beyond all reasoning! Just stay here, and I'll bring back some food for you."

"Gilban? Who's he?" Dugan's sense had fully returned.

"Gilban is the one who told me where I would be able to find you. He's a priest of Saredhel, the goddess of prophecy." The elf's gaze returned to Dugan.

"Another elf then."Dugan's eyes focused more on Clara.

"Yes. He's Patrious like me," her reply was curt.

"How did he find me then, and what does he want from me?" Dugan struggled to sit up with a groan.

"Dugan, we're wasting time here. Gilban can tell you himself once I return with him, and the others. Now, I have to go, please understand. You've nothing to fear."

Clara moved toward the stony dock, but fell short as she was held back by Dugan's grip around her ankle.

"Let go you big ox! We've wasted too much time already," Clara whispered back as she shook her leg.

"We both go, or neither of us," Dugan grunted from a seated position where he held her fast.

"Let go, or you'll ruin my timing!" Clara's shaking increased.

Dugan let go of her ankle and raised himself to his full height. Clara turned to rebuke the thoughtless gladiator, but he stood defiantly in front of her, eyes blazing fiercely in the dim lamplight. She also noticed he'd miraculously managed to gain access to both of his swords again, which he held in each hand in tight clenched fists.

"Fine." Clara reached down onto the deck beside her bow and quiver (she won't be needing them on shore) and threw Dugan a hunter's cloak. "Come on then. But if you fall over from your wounds, I'm not stopping to pick you up!"

"Two then, eh?" Dugan donned the cloak, and noticed it was newer than the one he had last worn.

"What?" Clara let out a frustrated whisper.

Dugan shoved the gladii into the belt of his loincloth as he stepped off the boat with a weak grin.

"This cloak is newer than the last one you gave me to wear. You must have killed more than one hunter then - another to get a new cloak for yourself , unless you laundered it on the way."

Clara was silent as Dugan crossed over to the docks, and followed Clara through the shadows onto the sandy streets. . This silence lasted until Clara cocked her head to one side and whispered back at him.

"What have I got to do to prove to you you're safe?"

"I'll answer when you show me this Gilban, and finally tell me what is going on," Dugan drew his stolen cloak over his head, and wrapped the scented cloth tightly around his body.

Clara turned back to the dark path shaking her head.

The two of them reached the Musky Otter without incident. Clara had joined Dugan in drawing her hood up around her silver locks, masking her appearance. From the noise emanating out of the tavern, it seemed as if the island's entire population had migrated to the ale house.

"Are you sure you want to go through with this? There's still time to go back to the boat," Clara whispered as Dugan drew up behind her.

"Don't press me." Dugan clenched his jaw beneath the hood

For a moment, his eyes closed in silence but when he next spoke, his voice was a hoarse whisper. "Are your friends supposed to be inside there?"

"Yes. I told them we would meet here, after I found you," she returned.

"Then let's get inside, I need some mutton and ale." Dugan's face was unreadable to the elf.

"Remember, don't talk if you don't have to, and if you do, speak in Elonum. We can't afford another fight if anyone notices us here."

"I don't plan to do any talking. Let's go, woman! My stomach may be sliced but I'm still hungry," he began to make his way toward the tavern door.

Clara glanced hesitantly about them before advancing farther into the light leaking from the tavern like sour milk onto the sand littered cobblestone street.

As they entered the rundown building, they had to walk through a curtain of smoke and grease before bursting through into the main room. Drunken sailors filled the tables, laughing at bawdy jokes, or trying to grab the serving women who flitted in and around benches and chairs with the ease of dancers. A few patrons glanced at the newcomers, but all they saw were two hunters and since their like was common enough, the few curious sailors simply continued on with their business.

Soon, obnoxious singing began to grow louder again from distant corners of the room. In time, even more vocal drunks swung their ale-filled mugs in an offkey salute to maritime ballads, spilling their ale as they did so around them in amber cascades.

Clara scanned the interior. It was a good-sized tavern, holding many patrons around large barrel tables, and shabbily-constructed stools. At her rough guess, she thought it was about forty feet wide, and about ninety feet deep. It was also the ideal setting for those wishing to stay hidden from prying eyes, and so would suit their needs quite nicely.

Both she and Dugan walked over to the bar to order food, and get a better view of both the entrance, and a set of stairs leading to the guest rooms above.

A tall and well muscled man, of Telborian descent, appeared behind the mahogany countertop of the bar. He had the rugged looks of a local tough, but these were softened by his aging face, gray hair, and laugh lines.

"What be your poison, strangers?" The barkeep greeted his patrons.

"Ale and mutton," Dugan replied in perfect Elonum.

He turned to Clara, "How about you?"

"Wine," she replied coolly.

The barkeep left the duo, and went into the kitchen where the sounds of flaming grease and the odor of foul milk lofted out into the dining area.

No one had decided to take a seat near them. To most, the hunter was not always a welcomed dining companion. Due to the nature of how they secured their wealth, namely by the exploitation of others, they tended to keep an aura of unpleasantness about them at all times. This obviously worked well for the duo, and their current needs.

As soon as the barkeep left, Clara turned to Dugan.

"I don't see anyone yet, but I think we're a bit early." She kept her voice low as she spoke in Telborous.

"Who are we supposed to be looking for?" Dugan whispered.

"You'll know him when you see him, actually," her eye caught the movement of a familiar shape, "There he is now."

An elf, dressed in coarse brown robes tied with a simple hemp rope, was making his way slowly down the stairs. On his feet, he wore high-necked sandals of black leather. He carried an oak staff in his left hand, which thumped in succession from stair to stair as the elf made his descent. His eyes were white, devoid of sight, and there was a look of calm wisdom to his features.

Like Clara, he was a Patrious elf, although signs of aging had changed the shape of his face. His hair was as white as his eyes, and the top of his head had been shaved bald. Dugan could also make out a silver necklace of ornate design hanging around the elf's neck as he drew closer, but failed to see any finer details about it from his location.

"Gods! You didn't tell me this group of yours was made up of invalids and half-wits! What kind of mission are you going to accomplish with that sort?" Dugan nodded in the direction of the robed elf.

"Hold your tongue Dugan! That's Gilban. He's the one who started me on this quest," Clara's eyes flung a dart into the Telborian.

"You mean he's your leader? That blind old elf?" The Telborian half laughed.

Clara glared at the Telborian through her hood, like a cobra ready to strike. "That blind old elf told me where to find you, your name - not to mention how to find the others at the right location, and right time."

"So he's a wizard then." Dugan's eyes studied the strange figure more closely. "I've seen their kind before. They're devious and shifty, they don't fight like true men; you can't trust them."

"He's a priest of Saredhel - and we can trust him." Clara retorted. "She is a goddess who enlightens chosen servants with visions and other prophetic gifts. Gilban was one who received such a vision - but I'll let him tell you of it, when he reaches us."

"If he reaches us. I doubt he'll manage to get himself safely through this drunken rabble without being lifted of coin, personal items, and balance."

"Then you don't know the power of Saredhel, Dugan," a rather low and aged voice, possessing the same strange accent as Clara's, whispered in Dugan's ear. The

Telborian jumped in surprise, spinning around to face the wizened elf, nearly knocking his hood off in the process.

"How did you get here so quickly?" He whispered to the blind elf, forgetting to use Elonum, reverting to his human tongue instead.

"Such is the power of Saredhel, a perception can be peeled away to see the truth." He turned to Clara with a blind stare. "He is wounded, is he not?"

"Yes. It happened before we reached the boat," she answered.

"How did you know that? You haven't even touched me," Dugan looked wide-eyed into Gilban's sightless face.

The elf simply smiled again in response as he accepted a stool beside Clara offered by the elven warrioress. Gilban prodded the floor with his staff, which hit onto the legs of a stool. After a few moments of adjusting the stool, one he had laid his hands on, he sat down. He then placed his staff at his side so it rested against the counter before turning toward Clara.

"Why aren't you cloaked like she is?" Dugan motioned to Clara. This time, he remembered to use Elonum, but thought only after making the gesture how the blind priest wouldn't be able to see it in the first place.

"Altorbia has no care about my presence. If I was a buxom young maiden rather than a wrinkled blind priest, things might be different. I pose no danger, and most would just as soon ignore me than notice me. It is therefore unnecessary for me to be cloaked. I have to hide from nothing," Gilban answered.

Dugan was silent.

"I trust you found him as I instructed," the old priest turned to Clara.

"Yes, he was where you said he would be," Clara smiled gently at the priest.

"Good. Where are the others?" The pure white eyes seemed to almost look right into Clara's own sapphire orbs.

Clara looked around the tavern once more. "I have yet to see them. They may have encountered some trouble."

Gilban closed his eyes a moment. "No, they are fine, though the dwarf seems to be moving more sluggishly than usual."

The two elves talked further, stopping only when the barkeep brought Clara and Dugan their orders. As Dugan ate, he studied the strange elf Clara called Gilban.

There was something odd about him. He matched the general traits of the elves, at least as he assumed them to be for Clara's race. This one was different, though. He was older and looked to be about a human male of sixty, maybe seventy - though Dugan knew it wasn't the case. He was probably far older than what most humans could live to - even in their ripe old age. Dugan had never seen an old elf before, and so had nothing with which to draw a comparison. The priest could be the oldest elf in the world for all the Telborian knew.

He was also taken by Gilban because of some strange pull hovering over and working through him. Another worldly sort of essence made him seem very wise and observant of all around him, though he wasn't graced with normal sight.

Additionally, the Telborian found himself drawn to the priest's necklace. It was unlike any other he had seen before. Crafted of silver, it was inlaid with a clear crystal resting at its center, reflecting the dim light falling upon it. The crystal was surrounded by a coronet of mother of pearl, from which radiated a multitude of gold lines. The center of the crystal seemed to swim in a sea of milk and gold. The longer Dugan stared at the pendant, the more he was convinced it looked like an eye. The crystal was the pupil, the mother of pearl the whites, and the gold lines the iris. Truly, it was a wondrous symbol.

The Telborian's mind then returned to his food. Uncertain of everything around him, he drank down the ale. At least he'd be as confused on a full stomach. He continued to eat as he slowly scanned the tavern instinctively looking for signs of trouble... especially hunter trouble. He had never known of such a lifestyle like had been portrayed around him. All he could see was decadence and debauchery. He had seen these traits in his captors, but with them they seemed much higher and removed from the common approach of men. Here, they were so close, grounded to the touch of everyone who should reach out and grab them. Such frivolities of life he had yet to experience.

As a slave, Dugan was taught life was a stone cell where he was chained to the wall, his bed cold dirt, and straw-covered stone. Food had been nourishing gruel-served luke-warm. Now he was in a new world, and he determined to make the best of it as long as he could. Should he find his way off this island, he'd delve into more of what the world had to offer a free man.

His meat was devoured quickly, and it began to make him sick by its richness, yet he continued on with the gorging. He took much pleasure from it. His greasy hands grabbled onto the common goblet, and drained what was left of its contents into his stuffed stomach. The ale was of a Telborian brew, hearty, but mild compared to most.

To Dugan, it was the richest drink he knew. He'd never known the feeling called satisfaction before until he awoke from his trance-like gluttony to see his plate empty and goblet bone dry. He had to admit, it was an addicting and pleasant sensation. He would have to give it more practice with freedom. All the eating had stretched his muscles a bit, which caused him to whine once in a while as a jab of pain shot out from his wounded torso.

"Is he ready yet?" Gilban asked Clara with slight impatience in his voice.

Clara turned to the Telborian. What she saw shocked her. The Telborian was licking his greasy fingers, trying to get all the flavor he could off of them. His fork and knife lay beside his plate, ungreased and unused.

"What are you doing?" Clara asked.

"Eating. This is the best food I've ever had," his slightly shadowed grin mimicked that of a great cat after a successful hunt as it gorged itself on it's kill.

"It could be your last. Did you ever think to use the fork or knife?" Clara sounded like a mother chiding her child.

Dugan stopped for a moment, then looked to his plate. "No."

"Well," Clara looked around, filled with worry, "elves and other civilized folk use them, so you better hope nobody saw you eating, or we'll be in trouble soon enough."

Trouble came before the trio was ready.

The tavern grew quiet for a moment as another cloaked form fluttered through the open door. He was of a taller, thinner build than most of the sailors in the establishment, and at first glance it was hard for the trio to tell if the new arrival was friend or foe until the smell of pine sap, nutmeg, sage, and leather reached them.

"Who is that?" Gilban asked.

The smell hit Dugan's nose instinctively when he turned toward them.

"Hunter," he whispered in Telborous.

"We have to get out of here before we are seen, hurry!" Gilban spoke up.

"Too late!" Clara whispered. "He's already seen us. Dugan, try not to talk. Let us handle this."

The gladiator wiped his hands on the cloak, and sat motionless by the bar, resisting the instinct to attack the advancing threat.

"Hello, friend!" The hunter addressed Dugan, as he approached the counter.

"Might I join you for a bit?" He spoke in Elonum.

Dugan nodded quietly.

"It's nice to have somebody to talk to who enjoys the same profession, is it not?" The hunter took a seat and then turned to Dugan for conversation.

Dugan nodded again, this time pretending to look for something inside his cloak. In reality, he had turned to Clara, motioning frantically at her with his eyes to warn her of the growing danger of the situation. Clara signaled with her own eyes to be calm. Looking beyond her, Dugan noticed Gilban had vanished, and gave Clara a questioning look.

She shook her head slightly, warning him to concentrate solely on the hunter, not to worry about others around him.

Dugan returned to his hunter friend.

He wondered what the crafty devil, Gilban, was up to. He never did like priests much, nor the gods, nor what they served. They were never fair fighters, and unable to be properly gauged; for they always had the power of their faith. Dugan learned to both hate and mistrust them in the coliseum and elsewhere when his wounds would be treated by them at various times throughout his career.

He just hoped he could last with the hunter long enough until he could think of a way to escape.

"Yeah, I haven't caught one bounty this year," The hooded newcomer continued. "The way I figure it, one has to cross my path soon enough, and when it does, I'll be living well for the rest of the year. How about you friend, found anybody yet?"

"No," Dugan said in a rough voice, hidden by the Elyelmic tongue.

"That's just the way things go, I guess. The gods just hand out blessings differently to different people. You'll get your fair share eventually, I'm sure. You're certainly large enough to take down just about any foe I should think." The hunter's eyes narrowed as they searched his body loosely, then relented.

From the opposite side of Dugan, Clara cringed.

The Telborian slowly prepared to react. He was ready for anything, and was looking forward to pummeling the hunter.

"Aero's eternal crown! What's your secret to getting so large? I have never known, or seen, an elf as large as you before. Surely if I was as sturdy as you, no slave would stand a chance! The hunter reached over and grabbed Dugan's upper arm. The Telborian wasn't able to move his arm fast enough and the hunter's hands quickly encircled it.

"Gods! It's like iron!" The hunter exclaimed as he squeezed Dugan's bicep.

Unfortunately, when the hunter grabbed Dugan, the front of his cloak shifted, exposing part of his bare chest. Dugan's jaw locked in anticipation.

The warlust rose within him.

Clara had managed to get herself off the stool, and was heading for the door. She would give Dugan as much cover as she could, but didn't want to put herself in harm's way by standing behind the gladiator. She trusted Gilban was safe, and had gone to protect the others from harm...or so she hoped. Otherwise, it was going to be a very short mission indeed.

At first, the hunter didn't notice the gape in Dugan's cloak, and continued to admire the gladiator's strength. Then, after a few seconds, his trained eyes found the exposed skin of the Telborian, and the branding mark that seemed to shine like a beacon under the cloak.

A smile traced its way around the hunter's lips. "You're mine–slave–"

The hunter didn't finish his sentence. Dugan's fist rammed straight into his mouth. The quickly-dealt blow shattered the elf's teeth, and sent a shower of misty blood into the air. The hunter desperately struggled to hold onto Dugan's arm as he tried to draw his sword.

Then Clara struck.

She jabbed a dagger into the back of the hunter's neck. An eruption of spasms and crimson spurts followed with lightning speed. The hunter struggled for a final moment. He tried frantically to remove the deadly weapon from his jugular, but to no avail. Eventually he slumped to the floor; his life leaking out with each spasm.

"Come on!" Clara shouted to Dugan over the growing commotion in the tavern.

The Telborian didn't linger. He took one big stride and ran from the inn like a hunted beast, Clara at his heels. Cries of outrage and disorder erupted from the door as they burst out onto the street. Filtered throughout the chaos were cries for the guards.

Once again, Clara's dealings with the gladiator had ended in violence. She didn't like the unhealthly pattern she was beginning to see developing. All they could do now was run wildly into the night. They would have to find a place to hide until she could figure out another way to regroup with Gilban and the others. Without them, they'd be unable to complete their mission.

Dark streets flew by as they ran. Clara tagged closely behind Dugan, frequently looking behind them for signs of pursuit.

"Go to the right, Dugan!" She ordered.

He obeyed without any hesitation, even though the strenuous action of running had caused his wound to leak and burn. He could feel tiny streams of warm liquid trickle down his waist, but he ignored the blood loss, continuing to run with all his might.

The moon was the only source of light in the alleyways, barely illuminating the path ahead. Nevertheless, Dugan was able to spot movement off in the gloom of a nearby alley.

Dugan stopped suddenly.

Clara was so close she was unable to stop herself in time, and ran straight into him.

With lightning-fast reflexes, Dugan drew his swords.

"What are you doing Dugan?" Clara panicked.

"There's someone in that alley." Dugan shook his head to clear his blurring vision.

"Are you sure?" Clara's breathing was shallow, ever part of her body and mind ready to leap into action at any moment. "We don't have time for you to start fighting air again. I can't see anything!"

"Someone is there. I'm sure of it," the Telborian's eyes narrowed, continuing to fight off the fuzziness of his peripheral vision.

"So? Let's get out of here. The guards will be upon us soon if we wait any longer."

Dugan remained motionless. His face contorted into a visage of anger and warlust.

"Who goes there?" Dugan shouted in Telborous.

Nothing stirred. The only sound was the footfalls of the advancing guard.

"Come on you dumb ox!" Clara cursed. "The guards are almost on top of us!"

Just as she was about to push Dugan on, the figure moved out into the moonlight. The lean form leaned on a staff it held in it's left hand and wore a brown robe, tied with a hemp rope belt.

"It's Gilban!" Dugan hissed. "I told you he wasn't to be trusted! He set us up to be captured by that hunter! Now he wants to finish the job!"

"That's nonsense, Dugan. I already told you Gilban is our ally in all this - are you feeling all right? You look pale," her panic deepened.

"Believe what you will. I-" Dugan staggered for a moment.

He felt his mind go black and his legs become numb.

"Gods above, you're bleeding to death!" Clara rushed to try and prop up his muscular frame.

"It's nothing," Dugan didn't need to look down at his wound to know it glistened in the starlight.

"Hurry! Gilban can help you, but we have to get off the street," she moved to Dugan's side to try and help him get to the priest.

"I....won't trust....that devil," Dugan struggled to speak through his dimming mind.

"Don't be stupid! Clara persisted and helped him struggle to Gilban's alleyway. Behind her she heard the boots of the local guard coming nearer.

"I need...no...help...I'm fine," the Telborian collapsed with a thud.

"Bring him Clara, and hurry! There isn't much time," Gilban spoke from the darkness.

Desperately she struggled with the dead weight of the fallen Telborian, managing to only move him a foot before she stopped to catch her breath. If Gilban thought this task easy, then he was gravely mistaken. She was still sore from moving him the other night on Colloni. Pulling him across the dirty street was no different than trying to get a stubborn mule back to his pen.

Driven by desperation brought on by the approaching illumination of torches coming up the street, however, she lugged the Telborian into the alleyway with the last of her energy.

Gilban's empty stare fell upon Dugan's chest. His wound had grown deeper with the deadly run from the tavern, and continued to bleed profusely.

Clara squatted down beside Dugan as a group of torch-carrying elves, bearing the sign of imperial guardsmen, ran past the alleyway.

"Remove the ruined bandage, Clara," Gilban spoke after they had passed.

Without question, she unwrapped the wet dressings and exposed the hideous gash drooling out its murky contents.

"Place my hands on the center of the wound, then step back," the older elf said.

Gingerly she gripped the elder elve's hands, helped him get down to a kneeling position, then slowly placed them on top of the red mess. Then, obeying the priests command, she stepped back.

Speaking a few mutterings into the air, he caressed the wound.

Dugan grunted beneath him.

Then, the miracle began.

Gilban placed one hand on his amulet, the other he left on the wound. He began to speak in Pacoloes, tongue of the Patrious, a goddess few knew.

"Saredhel, Mother of Prophets, Seer of All, I ask from you a favor.

"I ask that you wrestle the life of this man from the gates of Mortis, the realm of the dead. You can see the end of all things, and know the things this man is fated to perform.

"Heal this man's wounds, and make him whole - so by this action he will be further able to serve the cause he was called to do. You alone know his fate and how he shall tie his life in with those who have been called for this holy task. Please, Spawn of Dreams hear me and grant my request."

The priest's hand began to glow slightly, and the wound beneath it slowly closed. It folded together like wax, melting back into healthy flesh until it was completely knitted together.

Not even a scar or blemish remained.

Dugan's eyes fluttered, then opened to find Clara and the old priest peering over him. Clara was shocked, she'd never witnessed such a feat of faith. Given that Saredhel wasn't known to be a healing goddess, this new, wondrous thing shocked her further. She began to wonder what else Gilban was capable of, having experienced only a fraction of his interactions with his goddess thus far.

"Thank you goddess," the old elf smiled calmly. "You have kept him alive to serve his fate, I ask you will keep him safe to see it come to pass."

Dugan stared up at Clara, speechless.

Chapter 9

The Frost Giant rolled gently in the warm waves of the Yoan Ocean. It had been three weeks since the encounter with the Midgard, but nobody had forgotten the horror it had wrought upon the ship. Every so often, Rowan would notice a sailor looking nervously at the water surrounding the boat, eyes wide with anxiety. Tentative men also walked around the ruined wood of the deck making the sign of Perlosa's protection from a watery death. It would be a long while – if ever - before the attack stopped haunting them.

Few repairs had been made to the ruined deck and rigging. As the ship was a merchant vessel, it tended to carry more goods for trading than materials for repair. This was due to poor foresight on the part of the captain. The crew had managed to salvage enough resources from packaging crates to patch up the most ruined areas, making them some-what seaworthy, but there were still weaknesses in the pitted wood. The sailors had to be careful where they stepped, or they might find themselves in the cargo hold with half the deck on top of them.

The dead had been dumped into the sea during a quick funeral where the captain and crew sang a hymn to Perlosa and Asorlok, the god of death and the afterlife, to take care of the departed souls and guide them to their eternal reward. They further pleaded with Perlosa to secure the journey ahead of them, keeping it free from any further entanglements. No sailor worth his salt would dare try to chance a crossing by sea without beseeching the goddess.

Her realm was vast and mysterious. Those who dared cross it without her approval risked grave danger. The crew had offered up the sacrifice of a precious ring and necklace before they left port, committing it to the waves, as a sign of their payment for safe passage in honor of Mistress of the Waves. In the funeral rites, they had added a silver bracelet to further stay in the goddess' favor. It had been a dangerous journey so far, and none wanted to have it get any worse.

Rowan though took no part in these rituals. His goddess was Panthor, not Perlosa or Asorlok (though all faiths gave at least some minor thought to the god who was said to usher you into your final afterlife) and he was called to worship her alone. He wouldn't hinder the ceremony of the sailors to their god, but won't take part in it either. The others seemed to respect his stance on the matter for none spoke either one way or the other about it all.

Rowan had finished his prayers for the morning, and was eating a stale biscuit as he studied the sunrise on the distant horizon. Within a few more weeks he'd be in port, and free to stretch his legs on the land known as The Island of the Masses. He had heard all manner of races lived there, selling their wares and practicing their culture and religion in a rather large social mixing pot of sorts.

Growing up, he had heard stories about the inhabitants of the southern lands. Along with the other children of the tribe. He would gather around the feet of an old adventurer and raider named Tricky Dick. The old man would tell tales of how he had acquired so many of his injuries through chance encounters with islanders from the south.

Most of the old man's encounters involved those of elves.

Tricky was a testament to the sturdiness of the Nordic race. Either that, or he was damn lucky to be alive, if you could believe the pedigree of his wounds. When he grew older, Rowan dismissed many of the tales as yarns made up from the old man's over consumption of warm wine rather than from reality. Now he was about to find out if Tricky Dick was right on his other accounts, and Rowan was nervous for the answer.

He'd never left his homeland in all his life. While before this would have given him a burden of worry and concern, a new joy had began to fill him up instead. The burden he'd been feeling since leaving his home had lifted, and he now looked forward to meeting humans who looked and acted differently than those in the Northlands. While Talatheal could never replace his homeland, a sense of pragmatic optimism helped convince him over the last few weeks to make the best of the situation he'd been given. And so he did, and had.

The climate continued to change as the vessel sailed farther south. Warm breezes replaced the cutting wind. Rowan was so enthralled by the temperature change upon their first arrival he spent all his time on deck. He wanted to be near the wind and surf, to experience everything different from the new environment. It proved to be a learning experience.

The youth rubbed his neck in painful memory. His fair skin had never been exposed to intense sunlight, and he received a severe sunburn for his over indulgence.

Already Rowan's mind prowled the waves for the first faint glimpses of Talatheal. In about a month, Rowan would be free of the boat, and then the real challenge would begin. It seemed longer than what it would actually be, he knew, as almost all journeys seemed to those who were taking them - though they always seemed shorter returning home than traveling from it. The past six weeks had proven to him the benefit of having a routine to make the day seem to go by faster. It also made for some predictable days, though.

Rowan went to his room and looked over his equipment once again with excited eyes and nervous hands. As his arrival drew near, he began to check over his equipment almost hourly. The habitual cleaning of his belongings made him feel better and more in control of his fate than simply sitting by and waiting for everything to fall into place by itself.

His sword had been oiled and polished so many times it gleamed with a luster putting gold to shame. His armor too had been well polished. He was ready to face any challenge arising during his journey. Content, he put them back in the chest, and went to walk the deck once more.

After another month at sea, the Frost Giant finally managed to maneuver itself into the Talathealin port without falling apart. The vessel of wounded wood quietly limped into the busy port of Elandor and pulled up to the docks on calm waves. The boat would be making repairs, and then wintering for the next three months in Elandor. Rowan figured his trip to Takta Lu Lama should take him about the same amount of time, if not less. He planned to be back to the repaired vessel then and back to Valkoria with little trouble at all.

The crew of The Frost Giant weighed anchor, and prepared for unloading as Rowan paced about the deck where the gang plank rested to be lowered to the dock once the ship had been properly secured. Almost upon the gang plank's descent, Rowan leapt off the boat, and onto the docks of Elandor. Coveting to be able to move about on land again from his long confinement at sea, the knight almost took to running about the place just to gain some greater distance than what he had been able to experience until recently. His eager legs took him from the stale odors of the ship to the spiced winds of the cities and towns of Talatheal.

Rowan had managed to stuff most of his belongings in a pack he'd swung over his back. He was officially dressed in his armor with his sword strapped to his side. As soon as his feet touched the wooden planks of the dock, he moved off toward Elandor's interior at a slow trot and watched the activity around him.

Fishermen cleaned and gutted their catches on the docks, dumping the waste in the water below them as a motley collection happened by them. Men, women rich, and poor, all made their way through the narrow paths toward the inner gates of the city.

All manner of races appeared there as well. Elves and dwarves scattered, with a few halflings making their appearance amid the collage of flesh and fabric. Spices and perfumes were being unloaded from far-off Belda-thal and elsewhere. And always, there were weapons, cooking utensils, bolts of fabrics and buckets of fresh produce, all making their way to the central square for trade and purchase.

Elandor was the capital city of a powerful Telborian kingdom sharing the same name. It wrestled in shared existence with its sister kingdom, Romain, to the south. Both claimed they were the direct descendants of the Telborian race which had long been thought to have come from the ancient city of Gondad, which lay in ruins many miles to their west.

For centuries each had disputed the claim and set up their own doctrine as to why they were right, which led to a few wars and minor skirmishes. But for many generations since, not many have challenged the notion so harshly.

Nevertheless, it was a sore spot between the two kingdoms.

Rowan knew of this legend for he had been taught all humanity came from Panthor long ago. All humanity was descended from the ancient city's inhabitants. The city itself had become ruined and lost. Not even the odd expeditions the Knighthood had sent in the past could find it. Since then it had become more of a symbol than a tangible artifact of humanity's past.

Elandor was a spacious port city dealing mostly in trade and ship building. It was a highly multicultural island where elf, dwarf, humans, and handfuls of other races commingled peacefully. The success of the city showed in its opulent scenery.

Sculpture, fountains and wonderful works of architectural delight sprung up and over the city like ivy. It was as if each street were the pathway into a royal palace. They were lined with modified braziers affixed to walls of buildings surrounding the streets, allowing a glimmering tongue of flame to dance on its surface. At each intersection, there was a tall oil lantern converted to serve as a streetlight to passing traffic in dark surroundings. It was typical of many Telborian cities of the land, but to the young Nordican it was amazing.

When he neared the city gate, he slowed to a walk as the wheel-rutted road became congested with merchant traffic, as people were held up at the gates while guards checked for official documents, illegal merchandise, and many other matters. Rowan had to stand in the line for what seemed like an eternity, while exotic smells of sweet perfume and tangy spices enticed his nose.

Once he was looked over and deemed permissible, Rowan was allowed through the gate into the city beyond. The young knight was assailed by so many sights and sounds he was left dizzy from the assault.

The streets were mazes of shops and stalls. Vegetables, meats, brilliantly-colored cloth, weapons and furniture crowded tables and windows. Everywhere he saw people, scurrying like a plague of rats, hurried about with their purchases, their arms overflowing with produce.

Commerce, the life-blood of a city and indeed a nation, surrounded the youth. He knew about the city life of the southern lands from his texts and teachings in the Knighthood, but to gain it first-hand through experience was a different matter entirely.

As the young Nordican wandered the streets, his wide eyes took in all the strange merchants selling their wares. One in particular was tall and slightly gaunt; with a slender, frail look about him. It wasn't until the merchant threw back his head in laughter that Rowan discovered he was an elf. The pointed ears, previously hidden by straight brown hair, protruded from his dark tresses as he laughed.

Rowan had never seen an elf before, and found himself drawn to the merchant. Tricky's stories had depicted the elves as cold and vindictive; a gaggle of weak-armed sissies who threw a good punch when you weren't looking. Yet Rowan couldn't help but feel slightly entranced by the figure. Truly they were a beautiful people. The Nordican found himself making the merchant into a living statue, so seemingly majestic was his form.

Stranger too was how the elf seemed ageless, almost eternal or immortal in his being. That was a trait Rowan had never known in his very human realm of Valkoria. Just as soon as Rowan began to praise the elven merchant, however, another voice spoke up inside him. It began to show him they were weaker and lesser skilled in weapons than he was, how the merchant probably was a cheat in his dealings with others, and he wanted nothing more than to raid the world and make Rowan his slave. The words were heavy, hard, and scraped his heart and mind like a mighty plow shear.

Rowan had no idea where these feelings and ideas came from. From someplace deep down, they bubbled forth. He soon found himself not even thinking of the elf as a thing of beauty, but as a flawed gem needing to be recut. As he stared at the elf, he felt a nudge on his leg.

The knight looked down to see a dirty Telborian child dressed in rags, her hand around his coin purse. She looked no more than ten winters old, but the rough life she must have lived had aged her prematurely. Her eyes were ringed with thick black and purple circles, her skin sallow from malnutrition and exposure to the outdoor elements.

"And what do you think you're doing?" Rowan asked the young girl in her native tongue. His training had included the comprehension of all human dialects, both past and present.

Without speaking, the tiny child bolted off into a dark alley. Rowan shook his head in sorrow as he watched the little girl go. He wished he had time to help all the poor humans in Elandor, but knew it would only detract from his mission. Learning from the experience, Rowan reached for his coin purse to shift it to a safer location, away from prying fingers, should any thief come his way, and was surprised to find there was nothing to move.

The girl had managed to take it from him.

"Hey!" he exclaimed as he broke into a run. "Come back here!"

The girl, whether she heard him or not, continued to run through the maze of alleyways and tight streets, managing to avoid the grasping arms of the pursuing knight. The money was important to Rowan's mission, without it he would have no way to secure the tools and aid he'd need on his journey- and he needed desperately to get it back, even if it meant chasing the girl to the end of the country and beyond.

They ran onward, deeper into the city, the conditions of the buildings growing steadily worse, until the housing was nothing more than tree limbs held together by crude nails and baked mud. Dead animals, and nearly dead people huddled in the corners and other areas where their pathetic and soiled frames wasted away through despair, hunger, and poverty. These corners and realities had been hidden well off the main beaten path of the roads and major commuting routes of the city. It was the same effect as pushing dirt under a rug. Everybody knew it was there, but they didn't have to look at it with unshaded eyes.

The girl finally stopped when she ran into a dead end. Rowan caught up with her, and wrapped an arm around her shoulder.

He turned her to face him, and looked into her eyes, which were tearing up in fear.

"I just needed the money to eat," she sobbed. "Why can't you just leave me alone? I'm sure you have plenty more where this came from."

Rowan was moved by the sorrow in the little girl's voice. He stooped to his knee to wipe the tears away from her soiled face, and managed to smear some of the grime away, leaving behind smooth, tan skin.

"I mean you no harm," Rowan spoke gently. "But that's all the money I have. It's not even mine; it belongs to my Order. I'm on an assignment for them, and I need it to complete my duties.

"If you return it to me, I'll be very grateful and give you what I can."

The girl glanced at up at Rowan as he spoke for a moment. He felt like he was being looked through, though. Suspicion took him further as her eyes darted over his left shoulder - high left. Acting on instinct, he spun around with his blade in hand, prepared to defend against an attack. The block managed to stop the descending club of a heavily-muscled Telborian thug.

"Good work, Sally. Go run off to the meeting spot while I take care of this idiot." The girl ran off as Rowan raised himself to face the cutthroat.

He was a large man, fully a head taller than Rowan and covered in a layer of street grime. His beard and long hair were both unkempt and greasy from lack of washing; housing particles of his last meal even in their bristly briar.

He grinned at Rowan, revealing a number of missing teeth.

"You're going to be a tough one, eh? Well, I like to have fun once in a while." The cutthroat swung again with the heavy club.

Rowan blocked the cumbersome swing easily and sidestepped to the left of the miscreant. With every down-swing, the thief exposed his left side, a weakness Rowan was more than happy to take advantage.

With a quick thrust, his sword slid into the cutthroat's chest and skewered his heart on the Nordic steel.

The man's piggish face went placid and wide-eyed in amazement and disbelief. Like a broken child's toy, he tried to raise his club in a final defiant swing, but the heavy oaken log fell out of his lifeless fingers to the ground beside him. Rowan jerked his sword free, and the dead man fell to the muck-covered street with the rest of the garbage.

Rowan was amazed by his keen reflexes. It seemed his training had taken him to a new level - he could fight without even thinking about anything else.

Wiping his blade clean, he began to look for a way out. He didn't want to be around when the dead bandit's friends came looking for him - and his sort, like wolves -

always traveled in packs. He had no idea where the child had gone, or even how to get back his money should he know how to find the meeting place the brigard had spoken of before his death.

This wasn't good. Not good at all.

He had read great fortune in his garments just the morning and now this...

Rowan decided he'd have to be content with his own means to get him through the mission now. He had a small pouch of personal monies just for very minor purchases, or in emergencies, but he would have to make it work somehow in place of the coin entrusted to him by the Knighthood for his mission. At that thought, a thick wave of depression fell upon him.

This was going to be harder than he had first thought.

"May Panthor guide your steps," Rowan blessed the corpse before turning back down the alleyway.

As he wandered the twisted back ways of the shantytown, Rowan assessed his situation. His shoulders sagged with the weight he placed upon them. He'd failed the Knighthood; he hadn't even managed to be in Talatheal for one day, not even for one hour, before he failed in his mission. Without supplies and a guide, not to mention mounts, he would never find Takta Lu Lama in the time allowed, unless he had a miracle from his goddess.

He wandered down the twisted back ways of the city and beseeched Panthor for forgiveness, in his failing. By the time he had reached the area where he was first lifted of his money pouch, he was so laden with sorrow and deep regret he scarcely noticed an old, worn sign swung over the doorway of an even older building.

Rowan's attention was drawn to it when a drunken old sailor staggered out of a tavern into the sunlight, shielding his eyes from the burning light. The sailor almost collapsed into Rowan as the knight hustled through the street, but with a stumble to one side and a small spin on one leg, the inebriated man staggered out of the way before falling face first into the muck. Had the youth been in higher spirits, he might had laughed.

The drunken intermission brought the youth to the door of the Broken Oar. The sign was painted in Telborous, and under it Elonum script. The picture on the sign was plain enough: a simple bed with a broken oar above it. Since he had nowhere else to go for the rest of the day, and the ship would not be ready to sail again for weeks, he decided to use his meager personal funds to get a place to stay for the night while he decided on a plan of action, unless he wanted his armor and sword stolen too. He might as well turn some good fortune from the bad he'd just been dealt.

Rowan's arrival into the hazy room of the Broken Oar was acknowledged by a few wandering eyes of elves and a number of other races unknown to him. It was hard to say who was the more shocked, the patrons of the Inn, or Rowan himself. Not many Nordicans made it down as far south as Talatheal, and even fewer of the races chose to venture up to the 'frozen wastes' of the Northlands. The tavern wasn't much different from those of his homeland. Simple wooden chairs circled reinforced tables and tall stools surrounded the bar. Most of the chairs exhibited battle scars from many drunken brawls. The common room itself was a little more ample than most taverns and had a staircase leading up to the rooms the tavern rented.

Rowan walked up to the bar. The heavy aroma of strong perfume descended around him, strangling his throat and making his eyes water. He barely managed to suppress a gag as he motioned for the scruffy Innkeeper.

"I need a room." The youth greeted the innkeeper kindly.

"Two gold pieces for one week," the Innkeeper grumbled as he eyed the Nordican youth with mistrust. He'd heard tales of the fierce raiders from the north, and was far from trusting when it came to their kind. Still their money was the same color as the rest, but he wanted to keep his inn safe from the random riffraff as much as possible.

Rowan dug into his pack, and pulled out the required amount.

"You can have the room at the top of the stairs," the Innkeeper dismissively motioned to the general location of the stairs once he had pocketed the money. "You'll have it for one week at the most, if you ain't get any money after that or cause me any trouble then yer out on yer ear."

Rowan was taken aback by the Innkeeper's uncouth manner. Back home, a tribesman was welcomed as family in another tribesman's house. The rude and uncaring ways of southern civilizations left him quite perplexed. Shaking his head in bewilderment, Rowan turned toward the stairs. He wanted to stow his equipment before getting a meal.

As he turned from the bar, the curtain of perfume grew heavier and a feminine arm encircled his waist and drew him against slender hips. The youth looked down into the green eyes of a heavily made-up woman. Her raven hair was braided with beads, and her body was barely covered in clothing. A skirt of gauzy material dangled to her knees and was slit up the sides to her waist, exposing her entire right leg. She also wore a strange brassiere made of bronze, holding her overflowing chest, and a silken scarf of purple was tossed across her bare shoulders.

Her green eyes were penetrating, but clouded to some degree. Her intentions, however, were instantly apparent to the youth.

"Those rooms can get very cold at night. Perhaps you need someone to help warm your bed?" The woman teased as she twined a strand of her hair around a finger and licked her red-stained lips.

Rowan was shocked at the brazenness of the woman, and yet her offer did make his stomach twinge with anticipated excitement of what she might have in store for the night....No. He caught himself before his thoughts led him down a road that would sully his morals or vows. He also didn't have the time or money to waste on meaningless pleasures. He struggled from the woman's grasp, and lunged from her toward fresher air.

"No thank you, I prefer the cold," Rowan struggled to breathe.

The woman shook her hips at the Nordican youth. "You don't know what you'll be missing, boy."

"I'll survive," Rowan made his way toward the stairs at the far end of the Inn.

The Innkeeper laughed as the woman sat down on a stool beside the counter.

"You'll be back," she shouted over the din of the room.

"Looks like your losing your charms, Vilisha," the Innkeeper smirked as the sultry woman eyed him like a panther about to strike.

"He'll be back, Grobo. They always come back to Vilisha sooner or later. He's a young one, too. Just the kind I like; they're so full of energy." A feline smile crossed her lips as she watched the youth disappear into the hallway upstairs.

Rowan found his room with ease, but struggled with the lock in his haste to be away from Vilisha. Once the door was open, he dashed inside and slammed it shut, leaning against it in relief. He stood against the door for a few minutes before looking around the room.

Given the size of the cabin he had stayed in on the Frost Giant, the tavern's accommodations were spacious. It had all the bare necessities: a bed, a chest with a lock and key for valuables, and a set of drawers for his clothing. There was also a small window, but it was nailed shut, perhaps to prevent non-paying customers from escaping.

Rowan spent some time putting his meager belongings away. This done, he opened his purse up on the bed, and fingered through the coins, counting thirteen pieces of gold and ten pieces of silver. Hardly enough to buy supplies and hire a guide, but it was all he had. The youth sat in deep thought for hours. He didn't want to return to the Knighthood a failure on his first mission just because he was lifted of the funds the Knighthood had given him to get him started. He would be here all through the wintering of the Frost Giant too so he might as well make use of that time for some positive use.

He needed to find another way, and find it soon. He sat for a few hours, as day turned to dusk, thinking of ways out of his situation before he was drawn from his thoughts by a knock on his door. Rowan cracked it open, expecting to find the heavily perfumed Vilisha. He was surprised to find himself instead looking at empty air.

Nothing was there.

He poked his head out and checked the hallways, looking in both directions, shook his head in confusion, then turned back to his room.

He almost shouted with fright when he found his bed occupied by a massive gray panther, similar to the one in his vision during his initiation. The muscular beast fixed its intense gaze on Rowan's face, locking eyes with the young knight. The great cat purred as it coiled slowly down from the bed and snaked its way over to Rowan.

As the beast drew closer, it began to growl sharply. With each step toward Rowan, the menacing rumble increased in volume. Rowan stood as motionless as he could. He didn't want to be attacked by the beast as he was unarmed and unarmored. The youth prayed to Panthor for protection just as the great cat leapt at him.

The beast tackled him with a leap that was as quick and powerful as lightning, throwing the knight into the floor. Pain erupted through his skull, pounding like a festival drum.

Then darkness overtook him.

When he awoke, the panther was gone, and moonlight was filtering in through the murky window. He lay on the floor, head resting against the hard surface. He instantly found himself wondering if the panther had been real or if he was going crazy. He could hear the patrons in the common room below shouting and singing as if nothing had happened. He was sure if a huge gray cat had walked through the inn, people would have been screaming in panic.

The youth rolled up off the floor, rubbing the back of his head. He didn't know exactly how long he had been unconscious, but he estimated it had been at least two or three hours, time he needed to make up for.

Grabbing some of his coin, and locking up the rest, he followed some sort of Nordic logic, and descended to the lower level of the Inn where he thought he might possibly find some good leads on finding a cheap guide, or failing that, a map to his destination.

He had little experience doing such a task, but wanted to give it his best. After all, how could he get better without trying? He was becoming convinced the panther had been an omen. Whether it was for his own good or to serve as a warning, he didn't know for sure, but he knew he would find out in time...hopefully the best. He wouldn't fail the Knighthood, and some thought echoed in his mindscape: I will not fail humanity.

Rowan went back down to the common room to get something to eat as he thought what to do next. He had managed to purchase a flagon of ale and a meat pie and to get a solitary seat in a quieter section of the room when a familiar strangling perfume clawed the back of his throat.

Panthor's claws!

The woman didn't know when to stop!

He turned to face the tavern wench with a clenched jaw.

"Now that you've had time to see how cold the rooms can get, you've come to see me, huh?" Vilisha smiled coyly.

"Look- I told you once I was not interested in any of your services. I have no time right now to argue with a bed wench- especially one who lacks the ability to understand when her advances aren't welcome." Rowan spat.

He realized too late his Nordic blood was pulsing through him with the speed of a raging stag. The same blood that screamed for open, bloody conflict and was in direct opposition to what the Knighthood had taught him about resolving conflicts.

"Fine!" Vilisha half-shouted in defiance. "I just thought I would give you a second chance. I thought you might be too timid to approach me yourself, thinking I'd laugh at you because of your fear to spend some quality time with a real woman. I thought I'd be kind and save you the humiliation by asking you."

"The only one humiliated around here is you," Rowan blurted out, though his mind tried to withhold the remark, his fierce Nordic blood was winning the battle of control.

Vilisha's cheeks exploded in red, and her forehead creased.

"Do you think you're some kind of hero, or seasoned warrior, or something? I've been bedded by noble men who had more bearing and probably a purer bloodline than you'll ever have." Vilisha stormed away from the youth in a flurry of silk and exposed skin.

Though his blood boiled, and told him to go after her and teach her respect for a man of the north, his training told his rage-quivering limbs to calm, and his racing heart to slow. He wasn't about to be the slave of his emotions as his other kin were. He had the Knighthood to represent.

He sighed deeply, and thanked Panthor for the resolve of his nerves.

Nordic instinct told him the best deals were made in taverns and inns, and so this was where Rowan scoured for answers and/or aid on his quest. He started in the Broken Oar, and then moved from tavern to tavern, hopping from inn to inn. He spent the better part of the evening turning up nothing.

He could only return to his room to sleep, gaining enough energy to start fresh in the morning. There he removed his garment to be divined in the morning, fell into his bed, and said his evening prayers with a tired mind and heavy heart.

Sleep overtook him as soon as he closed his eyes.

The next day found the young Nordican hard at work looking for a guide. He had spent a good portion of the morning searching and, so far, Rowan hadn't come across anyone he felt he could completely trust. He was now convinced he was on a fruitless trek - most of the people in the area were only operating out of greed, with little care for what happened to the rest of their kind.

His feet had grown tired, so he sought out a bench to rest on. From there he looked around the town square he had wandered into, observing the strange races coming and going. Slender elves and short, stocky dwarves were of particular interest to him.

He was somewhat familiar with dwarves, as he and his tribe had seen them from time to time in the mountains near his tribe's holdings. It was the elves who were the true enigma to him.

Rowan's eyes trailed to an older dwarf who was leaning up against a nearby wall, smoking a pipe. His white, chest-long beard was braided into four coils and his almost-black eyes scanned the crowds passing by. The normal charcoal-gray skin of his race was a darker, deeper shade than most of his kin from his constant sun exposure. His dark eyes and light beard made him look very skilled and knowledgeable.

The dwarf had a simple enough face, marking him as a guide. He had a seasoned look about him. The youth guessed the dwarf had to be middle aged, though the youth wasn't very skilled in telling the ages of other races. Rowan knew when the elderly dwarf turned his head in swift sweeping motions, the old dwarf was a guide, or at the very least could work as one. It was simple Nordic logic when one came down to it.

At least it was for Rowan.

It suddenly dawned on Rowan though he had been searching diligently for a guide throughout most of the city, he'd been looking for a human guide. He hadn't even thought of asking for aid from one of the other races. He found it odd he had not even allowed him to consider hiring a nonhuman for a moment, but the thought soon presented itself.

Just by looking at the dwarf, he could tell he was twice as experienced as some of the other guides he had spoken to. Why hadn't he asked him? It was the second time he found himself questioning the worth of another race.

Why? He couldn't find the answer. He had never had the same outlook before, yet he'd never been surrounded by the different types of races in such abundance before either. As he got up to approach the dwarf, his mind began to turn him from the idea. Something tried to persuade him to leave the dwarf alone and look for a trustworthy human. The dwarf would probably betray him, the little voice insisted. Rowan caught himself again before his mind wandered into dangerous waters.

The dwarf wasn't his enemy. He hadn't acted against Rowan in any way. What was going on? Why were his feelings turning him against dwarves? He knew from his training and upbringing he should never be judgmental of someone he had no knowledge of personally, and yet his mind seemed to be pitting him against nonhumans with a will of its own.

Rowan was pulled from his thoughts by a ruckus erupting in the square. Another dwarf, two elves, and two humans were being attacked by a large band of brigands.

The ruffians circled their prey with cutlasses drawn, ready to slice into their victims. As Rowan watched, a fire took hold of his brain. He saw humans who needed saving. All else was forgotten as his body flared into action.

The taller, more muscular human was obviously a warrior, for he kept the rest of his party behind him as he faced his enemies. The female appeared frail, and therefore unable to defend herself effectively. And though Rowan knew mere moments ago that he'd seen others with the two humans for some reason they had vanished from his sight. All he saw now were the two humans surrounded by the brigands.

All else was forgotten.

With this in mind, Rowan raised his sword high in the air, and charged the gathering with a war cry on his lips. At least he would be able to do something worthwhile on this trip and help out some fellow humans for the glory of Panthor.

Chapter 10

Clara looked down at the healed Telborian and smiled slightly.

"By the Lord of Light! I feel like a new man!" Dugan coughed as he looked up at the aging elf.

"It seems your destiny is yet to be fulfilled; it was stronger than the pull of Mortis and so Saredhel was able to barter with Asora for your spirit," the elder elf replied.

Dugan sat up from the cold ground and rubbed at the side where his wound had recently been.

"My destiny, huh?" Dugan stared at the clean and undamaged flesh as his hand passed over it. A quick check at the wound he had on his back revealed the same thing. The Telborian now held Gilban in an even more intensive stare of examination.

"There are higher levels of existence than just this material life and higher matters of importance than just going about the daily routines in it," Gilban commented.

"I had no idea that other priests could heal besides Asora," Dugan ignored the old elf's comment as religious esoterica. He was curious as to how the priest had done what he had done. No priest, besides those of Asora, as far as he knew, had the power to heal.

What sort of goddess did Gilban really worship? Truly she was more powerful than his own demon, maybe even strong enough to...Dugan stopped himself from completing the thought. The memories burned him like the hottest flame.

"Not all of the gods heal - or care too," Gilban nodded slightly, "but sometimes persuasion can be had, and Saredhel is well received and respected by the Pantheon."

"It's nothing short of miraculous!" Clara exclaimed!

"So where are we to go now?" Dugan asked Clara.

"You've decided to come with us then?" Clara smirked.

"It seems I've been convinced to stay." A rough grin peeked out of the Telborian's lips.

"Then as soon as you're ready, we'll find the others, and get off this island," Clara said.

"And when we do get off the island, what then? What is this mission you're on?"

Clara took a hard stare into the Telborian's eyes, then gave him answer.

"You are to aid Gilban and I on a matter of dire importance to the Republic of Rexatious. You already know Gilban and I are Patrious elves, and are unlike the Elyellium with whom you are acquainted. It is the Elyellium who have sought to build a vast empire over the past ages, and it is the Elyellium who took you as a slave. We Patrious departed from their fold thousands of years ago, which, even to an elf, is long ago.

"Recently, Gilban received a vision from Saredhel of the Elyellium calling for the rebuilding their empire through the discovery of some ancient ruins in the forests of Takta Lu Lama, on Talatheal. If they get their hands on these secrets, they can use them to expand their empire and the Elven Republic of Colloni will become the Elven Empire once more. We must make sure the Elyellium don't get a hold of those secrets."

"What powerful secrets lie in these ruins? What arethese ruins? More importantly, what will you do with this knowledge?" Dugan broke Clara's stare to peer at Gilban.

"We Patrious have long known that before mortalkind first emerged, there was one single race from which they all came," said the elder elf. . "They were called the Ancients or Dranor, in our tongue. They were powerful beings blessed by the gods, able to do things we mortals can only dream of, but they fell into disgrace.

"They became self righteous, and self worshiping - and in their arrogance, attempted to control the world - which they did for countless centuries. Some even claimed themselves to be gods, until the true gods punished them for their sins and sent them to their deaths. However, before eradicating the Dranor, the gods used their blood to create the new races of Tralodren. That is the true history of the world very few know, save the Patrious.

"The ruins hidden away inside Takta Lu Lama contain information on how to build and maintain a strong empire for countless millennia, if not an eternity. They are the remaining skeletons and ghosts of a once-powerful Dranor stronghold.

"We need to stop this information from passing into the hands of the Elyellium, for it was fragments of this information which enabled them to establish their empire in the first place and what caused us to split from one another. To gain greater insight into such information would be to assure them the new empire they'd build would be mightier than the current races have ever seen," Gilban sighed and shook his head.

"I've foreseen the time when all I have told you will come to pass, and it is fast approaching."

"You believe him about this vision then?" Dugan returned to Clara.

"The Priests of Saredhel don't lie, and Gilban is one of the strongest in the faith. I trust him with my life, as do those who sent us - who chose him as their representative on this mission."

"But what will happen to the information once you get it? What are you going to do with it?" Dugan kept an eye toward Clara as he stood to his full height.

"The Patrious have always been lovers of knowledge and history." Clara replied with some small degree of pride. Since the days of Cleseth, our nation's founder, we have sought to record what has transpired in the world, both mystical and mundane. Through our efforts, we have managed to help restore the lost insight from ages past after the various dark ages which have covered the world. We also look to keep potentially harmful knowledge or information which could be abused, and used for a great evil, hidden from those unworthy of such insights.

"We respect peace, and don't want to see another war for domination of Tralodren. We love this world and hate to see it destroyed by foolishness."

"That's true lad," a gruff voice spoke from the darkness in Telborous, "at least as far as I've come to understand it."

Dugan instinctively spun around to meet what he thought could be a new assailant, but all he found was shadows.

"Who's there?" He brought up his swords, and planted his feet firmly in the ground. "Show yourself."

A small figure slowly materialized out of the darkness. Dugan was amazed to see a dwarf coming toward him. Dwarves didn't normally frequent the coliseums, so he had only learned about them through exaggerated tales from other gladiators. They had tended to give them mythical qualities this dwarf apparently didn't possess, such as fiery eyes and a frosty breath capable of freezing a man solid.

The stocky man stood four and a half feet tall. He was stout and strong, with thick muscles bulging from his arms and legs. His skin was tough, leathery, and tinted a charcoal gray, darker than the Patrious light gray tone. His stern mouth was enshrined in a salt-and-pepper beard braided in three distinct strands with the tips of each braid dyed a deep crimson.

He carried a large axe whose keen edge reflected the moonlight. The double-headed blade was decorated with stoic, lonely runes, carved deep into the metal surface. The runes intertwined down the handle of the deadly weapon, which stretched down to the dwarf's ankle. He walked toward Dugan with a shortened gait and slight limp, which Dugan suspected was the result of the dwarf trying to counterbalance the weight of the axe.

It wasn't until Dugan looked straight into the dwarf's eyes when he noticed the small figure only had one steel gray orb on the right side of his face. The other eye should have been on his left was covered in a black leather patch decorated with golden runes, similar to those on the axe.

"Dugan," Clara gestured to the new arrival, "this is Vinder, one of the others we've gathered for this mission."

"Well, what have we here?" The dwarf tugged at his braids, which cascaded over his copper-studded leather armor. "This wouldn't be the fella who has raised all the ruckus with the guards I saw a few blocks back now would it?"

"I'm Dugan," the Telborian studied the dwarf, but made no motion to lower his weapons or relax his stance... not just yet at any rate.

Vinder squinted his eye as he observed something about the Telborian then huffed out his displeasure at his discovery.

"Don't tell me I have to work with an escaped slave!" The dwarf motioned to the mark on Dugan's shoulder. "I won't join this mission if he's along."

Clara studied the short figure, then looked at Gilban. The blind elf stared blankly into space; a thin smile piercing his lips.

"Why Vinder?" Clara moved out of the alley more to get a better view of the short warrior. "I told you I was getting another sword arm; you knew he was coming. So why back out now?"

Vinder stepped back from the towering Telborian. "We have enough to worry about without having to keep watch for bounty hunters. Trouble follows this one... I know his type. We don't need trouble. I don't need trouble."

"But he's a good fighter," Clara rebutted.

"I'm sure he is; most gladiators are. I just don't want to be watching my back more than I have to with bounty hunters following our trail. I have enough to worry about," the dwarf crossed his arms. "You've seen what happened with the guards here. I'm not looking forward of a repeat of that wherever we go."

Dugan said nothing, he just simply studied the dwarf with a stoic glare.

"Once we get out of the Elyelmic lands, we'll be less likely to run into any bounty hunters at all," Clara tried to assure the dwarf. "We'll be safer once we get off this island, and to the mainland, trust me."

Vinder lowered his head for a moment, closed his eye, then looked up again at the elf with a contemplative expression. "You haven't dealt falsely with me yet. I suppose I can afford you a little trust then...at least to the mainland.

If we start getting more than our fair share of unwelcome guests, then I might have to reconsider some things."

"Your trust isn't misplaced Vinder," Clara's faint smile helped ease over any further unease which might be present.

"I wouldn't worry about it too much," Gilban added. "You, as well as Dugan, are all intertwined in this thread of fate, and we all are part of the goddess' plan."

"He has those flowery speeches a lot," Vinder nodded to the blind priest as he addressed Dugan.

"I noticed," Dugan was curt.

"Yeah, I suppose you want the armor now too, huh?" Vinder huffed as he disappeared into the shadows. "Probably need it sooner than..."

"Armor?" the Telborian questioned.

"You need to be properly outfitted if you're to be put to an effective use," said Gilban. "I sent Vinder to go and fetch some for you, along with a few other supplies."

"We already spoke about this, Gilban." Clara's face echoed the slight frustration in her voice. "I thought once we reached Talatheal, we would be outfitting him with armor there."

"I have foreseen…."

"You told me confrontation could be avoided if we moved in haste," Clara interrupted the priest.

"The future is always in motion, Clara - you should know that. When I told you of possible conflicts, they could have been avoided, but the future is always changing its course. He needs to be outfitted for further travel. That is why I sent Vinder out to retrieve some suitable armor." Gilban glanced down at the short warrior.

Dugan raised an eyebrow when the dwarf emerged from the shadows once more toting a large sack he dragged across the cobblestone street to the mouth of the alley.

"Took me awhile, but I found it, and got it here too, just where you said to take it," the dwarf huffed.

"Good. I trust the funds where enough, then?" Gilban asked.

"To the last copper piece." Vinder nodded. "I'm just surprised they had such a suit for sale."

The dwarf opened the sack after he had tugged it a good degree what light there was in the alley. "I just hope it fits."

Dugan watched Vinder pull the armor out of the sack.

"Your armor, Dugan," Gilban invited Dugan's gaze toward the suit. "Go ahead and try it on. You'll need it in the time to come."

Dugan tentatively, rested his swords at his feet, picked up the armor and held the metal shirt up against his body. The armor was chiefly a scale mail shirt appearing to be fresh from the forge, and shimmered in a rainbow incandescence in the moonlight. It also appeared to match his frame perfectly. The spiked and studded leather sleeves reached his wrists and the body completely covered his torso. The weight of the armor was deceptive, however, looking lighter than it really was. Accustomed to donning all forms of armor rapidly, Dugan flung on the armor as easily as common garb.

Cotton and leather undergarments slid over his well-muscled flesh to protect it from the chaffing metal. Next came the metal suit, which slid over his form with ease. His loin cloth hung out just a bit from under the long coat, which stopped just at his mid-thigh. It was nearly a perfect fit.

Clara helped to adjust the leather straps at his sides as the final adjustments were made, but it did seem a fine fit for him.

Once donned, the gladiator flexed his muscles to test the give in the armor. In the moonlight, the armor shimmered with a silver aura. The shoulders and back were tight, but still allowed him some flexibility.

"Khuthon's Axe!" Dugan swore in delight. "It fits like a second skin, but I'll need a pair of pants to keep me from standing out too much,"

"Gilban thought as much," the dwarf rummaged through the sack. "Here, take these." Vinder thrust a wide leather belt and a pair of trousers into Dugan's grasp.

Dugan laughed. "So Gilban sent you shopping for me, huh?"

"Just be thankful I did it," Vinder growled. "If you had the mage shopping for you, she'd never get here in time. That girl keeps her head in the clouds."

"Mage?" the Telborian questioned as he slid on the pants and belted them to his midriff. They, like the shirt of armor, almost fit him like a second skin as well. He had become very impressed with Gilban. To have gotten all the people together they now had and to have secured clothes for him...it was quite a feat. And of course his recent healing.. He must serve a very powerful goddess indeed.

When he had finished dressing, he felt ready to battle with anything standing in his way. He belted on his gladii, then turned toward Clara.

"Yes, we needed two strong sword arms, and an extra hand in the matters of magic as we have reason to believe the knowledge we seek might be protected by magical forces of some kind as well," Clara addressed Dugan's question.

"Speaking of her, have you heard anything about Cadrissa?" She asked Vinder.

"I'm here," a voice, soft as rain, spoke from the dark.

A woman of Telborian descendent entered the dark alley. Her hair was cascading pitch with a blue sheen, and she was dressed in gold-colored robes which flowed gracefully around her slender body. As she neared, Dugan also noticed her robe was embroidered with strange silver symbols and runes.

Her manner was womanly, but her face and soft green eyes spoke of youth, and a naive nature amid a mystical aura and insight which she also seemed to radiate from her pores.

Dugan guessed she was something of a young woman, probably fresh into the bloom of womanhood by no more than a few years. Her smooth, pale skin, and soft, delicate hands at her slim waist attested to as much. Still though she was something of a rare beauty...Though he wasn't so compelled to act upon such urges - especially given her youth, and their current situation - he did enjoy what he saw nonetheless. Indeed, it had been a long while since he'd seen a lovely Telborian woman.

"So this is the mighty warrior you went through all that trouble to get?" Cadrissa eyed the armored Dugan as if she was sizing up a prize bull; a slight turn at the corner of her lips.

"Cadrissa, this is Dugan," Clara introduced the young mage.

"I'm impressed," her voice was calm and measured, as if she restrained herself from some emotion or saying that lingered close to the surface.

"You seem a bit young to be a mercenary," Dugan spoke to Cadrissa.

"Mercenary?" She was taken aback a bit by Dugan's appraisal.

"I prefer to think of myself as an explorer - an adventurer. You can only get so much knowledge from books. The rest you have to glean from the world around you."

"Great," Dugan moaned, "another philosopher."

Vinder chuckled beneath his breath. "She does well, Dugan. If you can get her head out of the heavens more than an hour, she actually is somewhat able-bodied too."

"Just because I don't rush headlong into every situation brandishing an axe doesn't mean I'm useless," Cadrissa retorted.

"Nobody said you were," Clara came to stand between Cadrissa and Vinder, easing any tension that might have been brewing with her presence. "Each of you is vital to the success of this mission," the elf continued. "You all have your own special place in this group - a place ordained by fate, and your own unique skills."

"Indeed," Gilban added. "Now, we haven't much time, so listen to me carefully," Gilban motioned everyone to approach him. "You have all been told about the reason for your selection regarding this journey. You've been promised certain rewards, but only upon completion of this mission. Failure is not a destination we wish to visit, so it is vital that you listen to the following plans.

"We are to leave this island tonight on the same boat that brought Clara and Dugan here. We head to Elandor, the port kingdom of Talatheal. There, we shall use our money to purchase supplies and proper provisions for the trek before setting out into the jungles of Takta Lu Lama. Once we have retrieved the information from the ruins, we will go back to the Republic of Rexatious, and you three will be free to go, with a monetary increase."

"So we will truly be free?" Dugan took a hard look into the blind elf's milky eyes.

"The Patrious are masters of no man or woman, as we have told you before," Clara reassured him. "Once your task is completed, you can go anywhere you like, do anything you like."

At this, Dugan nodded.

The conversation continued but Vinder was lost to it now. He stroked his graying beard, deep in thought. This was the final mission he would have to undertake in order to gain his dearest wish, and it was so close to completion. He could also almost taste it - to the point it almost flowed out of him like a broken dam.

Vinder rubbed his moist eye and shook his head as he watched the others silently walk into the shadows, away from him.

He suddenly realized he had been daydreaming and had missed the others' departure.

He took a deep breath, then ran to catch up to them, his moist eye left to dry in the wind.

Chapter 11

Sunrise broke over the horizon as Dugan shook himself awake from a night of uneven sleep. He looked around the boat and noticed the others were just as exhausted, save for Clara, who tended the rudder. She greeted him with a brief smile. Even though she didn't seem the least bit exhausted, her smile betrayed her some by showing some degree of strain.

Dugan stood and stretched. He was shirtless, wearing only his leather pants since he took his armor off the night before to rest. The Telborian rubbed his face, and tried to adjust to the growing light, as he strolled to the bough of the vessel, where he stood and looked out over the wobbling waves of green. The strong wind blew his long tresses out in wild bunches, mimicking flame.

Clara watched Dugan rise, and studied him as she continued to steer the boat, as she had done for the past six hours; since Vinder had given up the position to get some sleep.

Dugan was the strongest human she'd ever encountered. His back pulsed with muscles, each one hard as iron, and many scarred with deep lacerations from whip markings which had healed to cruel scars. Sword strikes, claw marks and other injuries made Dugan's back a map of puckered trails. A momentary twinge of sadness overtook her upon seeing this. The Telborian had suffered much by elven hands.

Though it wasn't her kin who had done it, she felt slightly responsible nonetheless.

So, that is what a few thousand years of imperial power did to a culture. Clara shuddered inwardly at the bestial nature of her closest elven relations. The Patrious had separated from their brethren at the formation of the Elyelmic Empire. They knew nothing good could come out of it, so they left to form the Republic of Rexatious.

The split had been long in coming. Sparked mainly by two brothers, then princes of the unified elven nation, it had led to brutal war, and distrust between both nations ever since.

At first, the Republic of Rexatious mimicked the Elven Empire with a semi-imperial ruler, but it quickly changed over to a more representative form of government with many commoners running the affairs of the Patrician state. Within time, however, this ideal started to decline. Harsher climates of warfare and struggles began so an autocratic ruler was imposed, though the various ranks of representation still held. These representatives didn't have much governing power, but the name Republic still remained.

Despite this change, never had the Republic stooped to such cruelty as the devious rulers of the Elyelmic Empire. This was one proud star of many the Patrious held up over the Elyellium in present day arguments. To many others, it served to show yet one more rift failing to keep them from reuniting.

Clara wasn't exceptionally tired, but knew she had to rest if she wanted to be effective in meeting any future challenges. The previous evening had been a nightmare.

Things had started out as they had planned: gliding silently through the city like prowling wolves to the docks where the boat was anchored.

That was the easy part.

The waterfront was quiet as the group approached the boat. The only sound was the slapping water against the hulls of the moored vessels and the occasional drunken sailor staggering back to his ship.

Then the night erupted in a flurry of activity.

In spite of Gilban's prediction of the attack, Clara was still taken by surprise. Somehow a small band of hunters had been waiting by the docks. They must have been tipped off by recent sightings of an escaped slave in the city. Dugan certainly was a memorable character. The killing of the hunter in the Musky Otter didn't help the situation either. Clara knew how quickly word spread in cities. The hunters must have figured the docks were the last place left for Dugan to escape to, and had set up their ambush accordingly.

Dugan had been the first to notice the attackers overflowing out of the darkness. His keen senses amazed Clara. Vinder was the second person to notice the danger, and within seconds his axe was drawn, and stained red with the first casualty, cursing all the while that Dugan was nothing but a flame to these moths who were attacking them. Though they refused to admit it, Dugan and Vinder worked well together. It was a good sign.

The hunters had numbered twenty, if Clara recalled correctly. Two of them moved into Dugan's path, but with two swift swings, his blades cut through them like sheaves of wheat. The others attempted to surround them.

Five hunters faced off with Vinder, two immediately cried out in pain and slumped to the ground, clutching bloody stumps where their legs had been. It was then Clara lost sight of Dugan and Vinder. Three of the crafty elves surrounded her, forcing her to defend herself. She swung her falchion at the first assailant, but it swung wide, and her intended victim easily avoided the first blow. However, the second strike hit, digging into the hunter's head with a wet, crunching sound. He was dead before he hit the ground.

Three other hunters laughed as they circled Gilban.

"This one won't be much of a challenge," growled one.

"It might give us a good warm up, though," replied another.

They drew closer to the blind prophet, snickering, as Gilban caressed his medallion and mumbled to himself. The hunters stopped their mocking when the old elf was suddenly outlined in a glowing white aura, and began to shimmer and fade. Gilban became less and less corporal, until he vanished completely.

Stunned, the hunters ran to the spot where he had last been and poked at it with their swords.

"He's a wizard!" one exclaimed.

"Or a servant of some dark god," another voiced.

"It doesn't matter, he's gone now and there are others to subdue," the group's leader said as they quickly ran off to join their comrades.

Cadrissa found herself in a similar circumstance as Gilban. Three hunters surrounded her too, taunting her with lewd remarks.

"I think I'll knock her out," one of the attackers luridly winked at the mage. "No need of harming her if we don't have to, eh, men?" Laughter then erupted as they closed in around her. Cadrissa merely raised her hands in surrender.

None seemed to notice the snide smirk on her face. The hunters immediately rushed to collect their prize. They knew such a beauty could be worth more than an escaped slave, as Elyellium and even some noble Telborians were known to keep hidden harems in their private residences. As they groped for her, Cadrissa violently threw out her hands, causing an eruption of searing bolds of lighting to fly toward her attackers.

All three hunters flew backwards through the air, landing fifty feet from the wizardress, their bodies twitching and smoking. Charred holes were burrowed into their chest where their hearts once were. This done, Cadrissa gathered up her robes and ran to the aid of the others.

The small group continued to fend off their attackers. Dugan blocked a sword strike and in response, he stuck his blade into the hunter, digging deep into his chest.

The elf cried out in pain, then fell into death. Grinning evilly, he turned to face another challenger. As he did so, Dugan noticed, out of the corner of his eye, Vinder gloating over a small pile of mangled bodies lying in a pool of blood at his feet.

The electrical charge in the air grew heavier as Clara slid a body off her sword. The hairs on the back of her neck began to stand on end as a light touch of static breezed over them. Turning to look behind her, she caught a glimpse of something shimmering in the darkness of the night not more than a handful of paces from her.

Gilban then materialized out of the air.

He smirked in self-amusement, his milky eyes looking off into the distance. Clara took in a ragged breath at the priest's sudden entrance.

"I trust all goes well?" Gilban asked the startled Clara.

"We've nearly defeated them," she replied before chastising him for the sudden appearance. "Where did you disappear to?"

"Had I really left I would not have chosen to come back. Rather fate would see to my preservation to guide and protect us onward. Such is the way of Saredhel." The priest answered.

Before she could say anymore, Clara heard the fleeing feet of heir elven attackers; her eyes searching them out as they fled into the swimming shadows of the night.

"The cowards are running away!" Vinder shouted.

"And the battle was just starting to get good!" Dugan exclaimed.

Cadrissa remained silent, watching the cloaked elves flee into the darkness of the night, leaving their fallen comrades and any plans they held of gold and glory behind. She seemed to be focusing her attention on something else at the moment, but Clara was uncertain just what that was - perhaps a spell...

It had been a vicious battle, and one which could have been very deadly for the small group - had things taken a different turn. However, some good came from it, as the fight for their life had begun to form a bond among them, and they now knew they could trust each other.

A faint coughing brought Clara out of her reverie.

Vinder was stirring. He had leaned against the mast the night prior, after resigning the rudder to Clara. He stretched and rubbed at his eye, but weariness still showed in the lines of his face. The journey had been quite taxing, and now everyone was tired.

They'd quickly boarded the small boat, while Dugan and Vinder took up the oars, their muscles bulging as they worked double-time to get out of the harbor, and onto the open ocean. Once the sails were unfurled, Cadrissa conjured up a strong wind, sending their vessel speeding off into the anonymity of the night, vanishing before any pursuit could be organized.

As the lights of the island disappeared, exhaustion quickly overtook them. The waves lapped at the hull of the boat and lulled most of them into sleep.

Clara only remembered waking up when Vinder tapped her on the shoulder, ending his shift at the rudder.

Out of all of them, Gilban was the most haggard looking. From the very first moment he had received his visions, he worked tirelessly to rally supporters to his side, trying to convey the seriousness of the situation to a mostly skeptical audience. After constantly disputing with Elucidator Diolices, the ruler of Rexatious, he had finally won the elven ruler over by stating if the Elyellium began their campaign to glory again, it would be Patrician blood spilled in ready supply, as they would surely come after their distant kin for past grievances. Diolices had then quickly given Gilban the supplies he needed.

Gilban then, knowing he didn't have the strength or the blessings of a whole, youthful body to complete the mission himself, also requested an assistant. Many capable and experienced elves were introduced to him, but he turned them all down.

Until one night, he was visited by his goddess, and given a vision of a fair-skinned, silver-haired Patrician woman of budding militant skill. The image of a wilderness or farm accompanied the visions. This information was passed on to the leadership the next day, and parties of scouts were sent out to look for this mysterious person, bringing back many candidates who fit Gilban's description. One by one they were brought before the old seer, until Clara appeared before him.

Clara was the daughter of an elderly artisan and farmer who had married late in life. She had two brothers, Isciles and Percula, both of whom trained to become soldiers. Clara, on the other hand, was deemed suitable for household work, and tending to the animals. When her two brothers left home to fight in the army, she remained to help her mother with the farm, while her father worked from inside his studio, carving away at his pieces of wood and rock.

When her brothers spent time in the yard training, Clara would watch them while she tended the goats and sheep. Then, when she was alone, she would mimic their movements, learning how to fight on her own. As the years passed, she grew competent enough to engage in real combat. Though she never told her parents, many nights she would leave their home to seek out thieves on the roads, or in the woods surrounding the village, using them for battle practice.

Because of her clandestine adventures, she also became adept at treating and binding wounds, so that her parents would never see the damages inflicted on her by her nightly attackers. By the time she was called to answer Gilban's summons, she could easily hold her own against a trained warrior or soldier of the army, much to her family's surprise.

Since joining with the blind seer, Clara had grown up quickly. The outer lands of Tralodren held no special love for elves. It was a rapidly changing world, ruled by races who lived and died so quickly three or more of their generations would pass before one elven life was lost.

In those first few months of travel, Clara had learned that not everything was solved with a sword swing, and with Gilban's aid, had become as skilled with words and diplomacy as she was with her weapon.

She and Gilban had been through a lot together since then.

Clara looked over at the priest and watched his eyes rapidly twitch back and forth under their closed lids. His wizened face was scrunched up in a deep furrow of concentration. She had seen those mannerisms before, enough to know the priest was having another vision. She wondered what it would be this time. Clara took a deep breath and stared back at Dugan, who was walking toward her.

Gray mists danced and twirled before the priest's sightless eyes, and yet he managed to see as any normal person. Shapes and colors joined to make complex images until the vision took form. Before he entered Saredhel's service, Gilban had been a strapping youth, full of ignorance and foolishness, as well as keen sight.

It wasn't until he was middle-aged he found the priesthood of Saredhel. When he had entered the priesthood, he was promised access to its ancient knowledge, to gain insight into the workings of destiny and the future. However, he was told to receive such a gift, he would have to give up one of his other senses in sacrifice.

The petitioners never got to choose which sense they would give up. Destiny took a hand in the matter, and one was weakened as the sixth sense, the sense of supernatural insight, was strengthened. For Gilban, it was his sight that was weakened to blindness.

Since the day, he had experienced each of his visions in a similar manner. They would come to him in a moment like a flash of light which often aided the seer in finding lost items, recalling spoken phases, or having insight into the inner workings of a person.

The other means was a longer version - which at times could take hours or days as Gilban watched the movements around him as though they were a play. For his journey thus far,and what led him to the understanding of his mission to stop the Elyellium from getting the information, he had received many longer versions of the visions. This vision he was having was proving to be no less difficult.

In the vision, it was night. The stars and the moon could be clearly seen from his vantage point, which was unknown to him. There was a cool breeze, and the sound of frivolous laughter, as one would hear at a brothel, or lower-class tavern. Then Gilban saw a massive panther bound into his sight. It was gray, and larger than any cat he had seen or heard about. It had to be as wide as a man was tall, and twice that in length.

It approached the priest at a slow lope before suddenly springing at him. Taken back, Gilban started in his sleep as the great cat lept at his face, only to fade into a cloud of vapor.

The old elf's heart raced and his breathing came in shortened rasps. Then the smoky mists cleared again, and out strode a young human male. He was quite young, of Nordic decent, and dressed in ceremonial clothing making Gilban think he was some type of knight or priest.

The young man raised his sword, and a ghastly new form arose beside him. It was dressed in decaying flesh and tattered rags, and hung about the youth as a ghostly, pestilent cloud. Wherever the young Nordican swung his blade, the decomposing form traveled with it, to strike out of its own accord with withered, taloned claws; a dark soul living within the steel.

The vision distressed Gilban deeply, but as he tried to study the strange spectacle playing out before him, he felt the warm and soothing tendrils of the waking world drag at him. As he was pulled from the dream, the young Nordican spoke out with deep pride:

"Through me is the door to destiny."

Gilban, shuddered awake, a name teetered on his lips as the salty morning air, tried to tear it from him. "Rowan..."

He felt the warm sun on his checks and the briny air stroke his silver-gray hair as he closed his eyes once more to study the vision he had just received. If the vision had been correct, then it would seem another would cross their path. Be he friend or foe, Gilban didn't know. If he were friend, the vision could indicate Rowan would aid them in their mission. If he were foe, then there was something vile trying to influence the outcome of things and would cross their path in the future.

Gilban pondered the matter deeply. He knew enough not to jump to unfounded conclusions. He'd seen so many other amateur diviners of fate fall into that trap. Once someone over reads or worse, under-reads a vision, then it is destined to become false, or unfulfilled. The matter required more time to ponder.

Time was the great bestower of wisdom and insight.

As he dwelled upon the meaning of his vision, Dugan's shadow crossed his path. The blind prophet heard his heavy steps across the wooden deck, Gilban smiled to himself, and proceeded to get up.

"I'm finally a free man," Dugan addressed Clara as he came to halt before her.

Clara looked at him with a cheerful smile. "And that's the way it should be, with all people."

"Some are destined to be slaves. Their very actions and spirits declare it," Gilban said as he felt his way into the conversation, his vision forgotten for a moment. His words were not welcomed by the Telborian, who lost his whimsical smile.

"It's not in my destiny, let me assure you," Dugan turned toward Gilban.

"You may be right, Dugan. Destiny is never certain for those who have the strength to shape its path. Very few are those with this ability, and fewer still that choose to use it... and know how to," Gilban spoke as he felt his way over to Clara who rose to help him should he trip.

"You should be sleeping still, Gilban." Clara's tone became minorly maternal. "I noticed you were having another vision. Surely you must be tired."

"No, Clara, I must be awake. My mind needs to think on things." He came to stand beside the elven maid.

"You had a vision?" Dugan interest in the blind elf was piqued. "What was it about?"

Gilban laughed a dry laugh. "We priests of Saredhel swear a sacred oath to keep secret the things our goddess shows us. To the untrained mind, the images we would relate would cause confusion and misinterpretation. Only when the timing is right do we reveal what we have learned."

"That may be a good rule, Gilban, but what if the vision pertained to a person who would need its message in order to make a decision wisely? Wouldn't it be better to tell the person about this vision then?" said Dugan. "For the sooner warned a person is, the better he can prepare."

"And if the vision is catastrophic to that person? Let us say, his death. What if I, or one of my brothers or sisters, told someone of their approaching death - how and when it would occur. How could that person prepare to face it?" Gilban replied.

Dugan was speechless as he struggled for a thought.

"Throughout my time of service as a preist of Saredhel, nearly everyone I have come into contact with has

199

asked the same question of me at sometime or another. This is why I laughed. I find it amazing so many wish to leap into things which are not ready for them yet.

"Would you plant a field without first plowing it?" The priest had taken on more of a scholarly tone now - like an instructor in some academy.

"No. I guess not," Dugan lowered his eyes to the deck trying to understand the old priest's parables, and get the conversation back under his control somehow.

"Exactly," Gilban nodded. "You wouldn't get a crop. Instead, you have to let life make ready the field by plowing it with experience. Then the vision can be planted, the word shared and allowed to grow through time and understanding. If you didn't follow this method, you would do more harm to both the seed and the soil than produce a bounty of richness for life.

"However, you must learn what to plant in a field - what will grow. One could not escape death, if he was destined to die, as all things are. Some as blackened cinders." The priest's pure white eyes fixed upon the Telborian's face before closing upon the utterance of his last spoken sentence.

Dugan raised an eyebrow. He didn't know what the priest was saying, or what he could be implying. It was fruitless to continue the discussion, as Gilban wasn't going to answer what he wanted to know anyway.

"I see. Maybe we can talk later, then," Dugan's words were brief.

"The answers will still be the same," Gilban bowed his head.

Dugan sulked off to the bow of the boat again. Clara turned to Gilban, who silently stared in Dugan's previous position.

"What was that all about?" asked Clara.

"There are great wars being fought inside him. Battles which would put the Imperial Wars to shame," he confided.

"Will he be okay?" Clara took another worried look toward the retreating gladiator.

"It is difficult to say. A brick wall falls with time to the ravages of outside forces" his eyes followed the gladiator with the eerie echo of natural vision.

"Don't you ever get tired of speaking in metaphors?" Clara returned her gaze toward the priest, who she noticed had moved to take a seat near the rudder.

"Not when they answer so potently," he smiled.

The boat needed to be hurried if they were to get to their destination in time. That would mean Dugan and Vinder would have to row, and Cadrissa would have to mind the rudder while she slept.

Chapter 12

Cadrissa's golden robes shone brilliantly in the sunlight, washing across the morning sky. Scattered in a neat semi-circle all around her were scrolls and tomes of all sizes. The young mage always craved knowledge, and read heavily whenever she got the chance.

Cadrissa was about fifteen when she discovered she possessed the potential for magic. Unlike stage magic, which anyone could perform if they practiced hard enough, true magic was something one was born with an affinity to wield. Not all who were born with this affinity, however, were able to wield it effectively. That was where the need for training came into the picture.

Cadrissa's parents had saved up what little money they had to send her to a school of the arcane arts, where she absorbed all her lessons like a sponge. The more she learned, the more she advanced, so it was no small wonder the money sent to her by her family over the next five years after her enrolling was used to buy herself more tomes and scrolls on an array of subjects. These would further her mystyical abilities and general knowledge about the world around her. They would also contribute to her growing habit - rather her addiction, to possessing as much knowledge as she could.

When Clara told the mage to take the rudder, she gladly obliged by casting a spell on the rudder to steer the ship, so as not to interrupt her studies. At least between then and their landing in Elandor she'd be able to get in a few more pages. After that it would be much harder to take to her texts, and she would be limited in what knowledge she could gain from them. So for now, she read.

She took a bite of her dry biscuit, and looked up at the muscled Telborian who manned the oars. His sweat-soaked body glowed as a freshly-bronze cast statute. Cadrissa pushed a windblown lock of her dark hair out of her face. In all her texts and studies, she had never come across a man like Dugan. He seemed to possess an inner fire fueling him onward in ways that other men she had encountered so far seemed to lack.

All she'd been surrounded with for the past five years were frail men, with as much strength as a dead mouse, but Dugan was another story. She finished her biscuit, then returned to her texts, a strange giddiness in her lips and stomach.

She'd read texts on love from the tomes of Causilla. The goddess of love and her priests had much to say on the subject. She was confident this was what she was feeling, as well for the Telborian. But to what degree? Was it lust, or something more? It mattered little, though. Dugan would be gone soon after this mission was completed anyway, and he seemed to not be that interested in her at all. He had his own life, and seemed to live in his own world. Besides, she had her books and knowledge to keep and help her develop into an even greater understanding of her natural talents. Still though, it would be fun to dream a bit more about the potential of possible mutual interest during the rest of the mission...

She sighed to herself, and returned to an old tome about the land of Talatheal. Cadrissa wanted to be well-informed about the environment she would be visiting. The book was slightly cracked along the binding, but the vellum pages themselves showed no evidence of damage. It was a

copy of a gnomish book on travel, trade, and political institutions of interest in the lands far to the east of their own
nations.

The gnomes were famous for their robust economic
state, trade, and scholarly insights. Perhaps most famed
was their development of a new type of government called
democracy and the development of a free enterprise system
of trade. The writer of Cadrissa's text had included various
insights into the climate, flora, and fauna of the continent.
She read:

*...Talatheal is by far one of the most wonderful lands
in all of Tralodren. A warm, temperate climate dominates
the varied terrain, giving the inhabitants and visitor a most
blessed stay. It is one of the few lands boasting of racial
diversity without bitterness and hardship. All manner of
races can be found living together scattered about the land,
which some have nicknamed 'The Island of the Masses'.
Never before has this old man seen so many different people
and races forming a tight group of culture completely its
own. I am quite impressed with the whole result...*

Cadrissa scanned further down the text and stopped
when she caught another phrase piquing her interest.

*...Takta Lu Lama is a rare tropical forest situated
on Talatheal. Though the land itself is temperate, for some
reason, this jungle exists. Some sages claim it to be magical
in nature, others point to lava underground, or some other
natural answer for this unnatural occurrence....*

*...Those few who have returned from the jungle tell
of dark skinned humans, called Celetors. These savage men
and women pierce their body with bones and rare metals
as decoration. They are scantly clad in hide loincloth or*

other simple attire, and rely on simple tools and weapons of
bone, wood, or stone to seek out a living in the thick forests.
Tales also abound about expeditions failing due to attacks
by rather large and ferocious lizards. It is said these lizards
stand on their hind legs and rip men apart with their vicious
claws and deadly teeth....

Cadrissa closed the book and drifted into thought.
She looked up once more at the brilliant sun and drank some
fresh water resting beside her in a tin cup.

As she drank, her excitement grew.

She, as well as the others in the party, had also come
along on the journey to work on a personal goal of her own.
Her's was to find evidence, and even touch artifacts of the
Dranors. She had become consumed with the quest in the
latter days of her schooling when she first discovered the
whereabouts of the ancient race. She wanted to touch and
experience this unrecorded time in history - and learn from
its hidden secrets.

If she was right, then a great deal of insight was
going to be revealed about a very powerful race of beings.
A race said to have had the understanding and power of will
to shape the very elements to their whims, and they were
going to walk right into their city to take away the knowledge they had once possessed. How could she turn down
such an opportunity?

Cadrissa had come to learn the Dranors were very
close to being gods themselves. In fact, it seemed there was
almost nothing they couldn't do. Indeed, many theories had
even put forth that the only reason some people had the ability
to wield magic in the first place was because they were in
some way connected to the Dranors, either by descendency
or some other means. The thought then of traveling through

the ruins of such a majestic race, to learn their secrets was a dream come true, and brought a smile to her lips.

"What are you so happy about?" Vinder trotted up beside her.

"What..,?" Cadrissa awoke from her trance-like state to find the shirtless dwarf peering into her face. He too was a mound of muscle and scars - like Dugan in miniature only a charcoal gray in hue and a coat of thick graying black hair on his chest.

"Have you found something in your book then? I saw the way your face lit up when you read it just now. What did it say?" The shorter warrior drew closer still to the wizard-ress.

"Shouldn't you be minding the oars?" She grumbled irritably at the interruption.

"I'm taking a break for a moment." Vinder's voice, like his face, was emotionless.

She didn't know what to make of the dwarf yet.

Cadrissa had met up with the stout warrior in Altorbia, after being recruited in Haven near the school of arcane arts where she had recently studied and hoped to return to again once this excursion had run its course. Neither talked to each other much, tending to keep to their own interests, and selves most of the time. So Vinder's sudden interest with her, let alone her studies was quite out of character for the dwarf.

"Would it concern you if I didn't want to tell you?" She tried to be congenial as she could. Interpersonal interaction wasn't her strong suit.

"Yes," Vinder grunted as he sat beside her, amid her collection of books. "Especially if it affects me, and my safety,

"I trust you're boning up on where we're going. I can read other languages you know; I saw the title: Localities of Tralodren.

"I think anything you read about that subject would pertain to me, as I live on the same world," the dwarf huffed.

"Very well." Cadrissa let out a small sigh of defeat upon the dwarf's seating. He didn't appear to be leaving anytime soon, so she decided she might as well humor him, and be done with it then. "It seems Talatheal is a very interesting, and almost certainly dangerous land. It would appear we have our work cutout for us."

"How so?" Vinder searched the mage's face with his eye.

"Well, the land we wish to travel to, Takta Lu Lama, is a vast jungle of incredible size and density. It's also full of dangerous lizards the size of dragons hunting in the green lands who like to tear everything they meet to shreds. We should be on our guard."

"Good advice at any time. Think Clara and Gilban already know about this?" The old dwarf rubbed his bearded chin, and turned his head over his shoulder to spy on the two elves who sat toward the back of the boat.

"They must," Cadrissa nodded, "I think they've probably kept quiet about it to insure our aid. Very few people would follow them into such a dangerous place."

"Either that or they know how to combat the lizards and other challenges we might come across in our travels," Vinder touched a book at his side.

"So you're scared then?" The dwarf asked as he picked the book up.

"No, not really," Cadrissa tried to grab the book away from Vinder, but he held his grip. "What are you doing?"

"Reading, lass. It will be a long voyage, and I thought I would take a look at what you have here." His lone eye caught her two orbs with a sheen that revealed his hard center as both clung tight to the book; wrestling over it for a moment more before Vinder tugged out of Cadrissa's struggling grasp.

"Be careful!" She cautioned as it the book were a newborn. "These books are rare treasures. I got many of them from my schooling. I even had to copy some myself because of their age."

Vinder ignored her pleas, opened the book to a marked page, and started to read aloud:

"...and so it was that in the Third Age of the Wizard Kings, there arose the two paths to higher arcane pursuits: The Path of Knowledge, and the Path of Power. It was from these paths that new evils and greater goodness erupted in a celebrated dispersal of mystical delight..."

Vinder closed the book and handed it back to the distraught Cadrissa. She clasped it tightly to her chest; happy to have her child back in her arms.

"So that is what history was like for your people, dry and simple; nothing like our ballads." Vinder was stoic.

"Why did you have the page marked, I wonder though?" The dwarf's lone eye dug deep into Cadrissa's own green pools with a hard, penetrating stare. "Could it be you secretly long to be something you shouldn't be?"

"I don't understand." Cadrissa hurriedly gathered up her precious tomes and scrolls and began to place them in a wooden chest sitting at her feet. "What do you mean? I'm just reading up on the past."

"You and I both know, lass, it's been forbidden to unleash the power of the Wizard Kings upon Tralodren once more. Their age is finished, and they are to be remembered only in written history, not the present. Even the dwarven histories have said it was decreed by the gods themselves."

"You're wrong," she weakly rebutted.

"I thought so," the dwarf flashed a sideways grin at the mage.

"Why else would a mage as young as you come along on this journey then unless they were foolish or ambitious?"

"I don't understand," Cadrissa had become confused by the conversation.

"I was uncertain at first to which of the two you might be, but now I see you're foolishly ambitious." Vinder grimly nodded. "What better place to go than to the heart of a ruin said to hold ancient knowledge? Knowledge which just might aid you into the path of the very people you have been reading up on: The Wizard Kings. The gods have forbidden what you seek.

"It was a divine decree. The stories of my clan, and of the sages, all speak of the terrible anger the gods directed toward the Wizard Kings and their followers. It was so important a matter to the Pantheon they decimated the ability of mortals to even use magic, until this recent age.

"You must have read about it in your books. If you seek their goals - which I now believe you do - then you are doomed to failure, and probably damned by the gods as well." He ended his sentence with a strong nod to back up his claims.

"I don't think you know me very well at all," Cadrissa became flustered by Vinder's accusations and innuendoes. "What I seek is not what you said it is. Besides, you speak of the days before the very dawn of the new era, when fear and misunderstanding of the arcane arts filled people's hearts and minds with dread. I just want a chance to be enlightened. I want to be able to help make the world better than what it is now. I want the lost knowledge of the Ancients to benefit all."

"Bah!" Vinder scoffed. "Curse yourself then, lass, but don't let anyone you care for, or myself, be anywhere close by when you become 'enlightened.' Just be a help to this mission, and you'll get rid of some of my fears. After that, do what you want to."

"Don't worry," Cadrissa snarled to the retreating dwarf as he arose to move to the farthest end of the boat, "You won't be anywhere nearby, I promise."

"See to it," the dwarf's answer floated back to her.

The mage was so upset she didn't even notice Dugan leave his seat, and come toward her. Nor did she notice him as he stooped beside her as she continued to feverishly pack away her books.

"Excuse me, Cadrissa, but may I ask you a question?" Dugan's voice interrupted the mage's thoughts.

Cadrissa started. "What...? Oh. Come to lecture me too, have you?" She stared up into the Telborian's eyes, and felt her heart flutter and pulse like it had never done before. Her sight locked upon the Telborian, and she smiled - though she had no intention of doing so. It was if her body was acting on some impulse other than her own.

"If I've caught you at a bad moment, I can come back later," Dugan turned to move away.

"No-no. I have some time. I have all the time in the world." Cadrissa sputtered. Get control of yourself, Cadrissa., she thought.

"What would you have me answer?" She managed to secure herself once more though her emotions and body still warred against the effort.

"I have a question regarding the gods," Dugan knelt before her with an emotionless face.

"I didn't take you for a scholar, Dugan," her grin remained.

"I'm not, except when it comes to things I have an interest in," he replied dryly. "I simply need some insight. You appear to be one of the more learned of this group, and you don't speak in strange riddles," his face was calm and peaceful now as he looked into Cadrissa's own green wells. She could feel herself drowning in his gaze...

"I understand," the mage's smile deepened. "What's your question?"

"You've heard of Rheminas, I'm sure," said the Telborian.

"Yes. Some call him the Mover of the Sun," answered the mage.

"Others call him the Vengeful One," Dugan stated flatly.

"Yes," Cadrissa was still locked into his deep green eyes. Nothing else was really important but them...

"How much power does he hold in this world? Years as an elven slave have kept me from knowing my human heritage and customs as much as I should. I just want to know all there is about him."

Cadrissa took a deep breath and pondered. Her love of sharing knowledge was almost as great as acquiring it. This love was even greater in strength within Dugan's gaze... Within a heartbeat, however, Cadrissa's mental clarity had been regained.

Dugan looked around to see if any others saw him at the moment. Relieved they did not, he returned to Cadrissa's admiring eyes as she spoke.

"There are gods more powerful than Rheminas, and there are many who oppose his will and actions. Just who you believe on the topic is up for debate - as all priests will tell you their god is the strongest.

"However, even gods of lesser power don't hold him in the highest of favor. Drued, Aerotription, and Panthor all hate him - but are weaker than him. Ganatar, Asora, Dradin, Olthon, Causilla, and Perlosa care little for him, also. He is mainly worshipped by more distant persons who hold him up for his more peaceful boons. It's only the few select individuals who worship him for his darker, destructive aspects - and his gift of revenge."

"Does that help?" Cadrissa looked up into Dugan's eyes again but felt her heart stop for a moment at the dark images, and thoughts she saw brewing behind them. They frightened her as much they as called to her in some unsettling way she didn't quite understand.

"It'll do for now. Seems I've got a lot of planning to do."

"Are you looking for a new faith to follow, Dugan?" Cadrissa couldn't help but blurt out. Her curious nature had to be fed.

"Something like that," the gladiator then left the company of the wizardress, and went to overlook the water once more, deep in thought. Cadrissa had given him much to contemplate.

"If you need anything else, I'm more than willing to help," she assured him.

"Thanks," he looked back to smile at the mage. "I'll remember that."

She held herself rigid until she was sure Dugan wasn't going to return. With this assurance, Cadrissa then shook her head for how foolishly she had acted, and how stupid what she had just said sounded.

Chapter 13

The Master paced the tormented silence of his dark keep. His rotting robes made light trails in the dust-covered floor, which met in a circle around the pedestal holding his scrying skull.

It was there the concentrated thoughts of the ancient mage were focused. He could barely hold in the excitement welled up in his bones. His plans, after centuries of toil, were coming to fruition and, with them, his rise to glory and power. True power, the thought filled him with a violent seether of energy he felt would shatter his skeletal frame if not released.

It was nearly his!

It was almost as if he was alive again; as if he felt the sensations of breath or touch again. Nothing could come undone or go awry in his moment of approaching victory. No one could destroy his triumph now, except Balon. Balon was just the tool which could stop him. The Master saw the rising confidence in the demon's ability to best the lich - and so he knew that the fool had now almost outlived his usefulness.

The demon had worked well for The Master, keeping the various factions of abysmal denizens always plotting against each other, busy with inconsequential subplots and counterplots. They had been so preoccupied with their own little petty bickering they had failed to pay the old lich much thought, if any. Since the dawn of time, when the demons had been imprisoned in the plane for their crimes against the gods, they'd never united or worked together, only squabbled and warred among themselves to fruitless ends.

That gave The Master a great break in the rigors of his exile to work his plans to their full potential. Now that he was close to leaving, it was time to tie up loose ends and he was happy for it.

He picked up his weathered bone staff beside his throne.

"Come," he commanded.

The eye sockets of an infant's skull, which sat on top of the time-worn staff, suddenly glowed with a murky green light. At the same time, a dark green billowing vapor appeared before the lich. Then, from within the misty-green cloud, a form began to appear.

The collection of putrid smoke dissipated quickly as this form grew more solid, leaving behind an impressive figure. It's skin was a deep cobalt blue and it's eyes burned a hot white, like iron in the forge. It's muscled, humanoid body had the head of a jackal (also blue), purple bat-like wings covered in a horrid display of hundreds of ever-searching eyes of various shapes and sizes, and a set of deadly claws - both on it's feet and hands. Only a red silken loincloth added any more color to it's frame.

The figure, who was an Enveal, a form of creature many uneducated would incorrectly call a lesser demon. The Enveal was smaller than Balon, and just a little taller than The Master in height. Among the lowest of ranked demons in the fiendish hierarchy, he wasn't noticed that often among the more prominent demons, which is very unfortunate for them, since his eye-covered wings saw all.

This, of course, worked to The Master's benefit, who used this lesser demon very effectively to his own means. He needed someone to keep track of what Balon was doing.

Moreso, he needed to keep informed of how the winds of power were blowing in the Abyss. Should they turn to his disfavor, he would have to act quickly. He also used the Enveal to feed misinformation, when the Enveal was able, to Balon to keep him off chasing rumors. This left the lich alone to work his own ends. He smiled to himself when the creature appeared. He'd now be able to tie up two loose ends at once.

"Why have you summoned me?" The demon's voice growled and it's countless eyes, nestled in the flesh of it's sapphire wings, scanned all before them in a scene that would have driven other mortal men to madness, but did little to unnerve the mage - who stood before it.

"Tell me of the progress occurring, Covis," the lich addressed the demon.

"Balon doesn't suspect a thing," said Covis in wicked delight. His voice sounded like the whisper of serpents. "His time is spent planning - conquests of the other realm. He creates battle plans, rallies his troops, and is already deciding how he will bring about his empire to Tralodren."

"The gullible fool!" The mage's teeth came together. If he had any flesh left, a grimacing smile would have been on his lips. "Have you planted all my false reports with him?"

"Yes," the jackal's head smiled its own unsettling brand of abysmal mirth which only added to the unnatural nature of the animal visage. "Each day I deliver more intelligence information to him, and he absorbs it as truth. He believes the whole world to be awaiting for his arrival, like some dark god. Your trickery has paid off. For a mortal, you are almost as fiendish as we are. Truly, you belong here with us." Covis stretched his eye-covered wings; fluffing them up before folding them behind himself to rest.

The Master was silent.

His jaw clenched with irritation and the blue light in his sockets intensified to a near blinding brilliance.

"Don't you ever suggest I will be here forever!" The Master screamed in rage. "I'll turn your blue hide into searing ooze, and watch your spirit slowly die if you ever speak to me of this prison again!

"I, who have fought and won battles with wizards whose powers rivaled gods in strength - I, who have watched worlds die and new empires reborn - will never be held in such a place as this. You'll remember this the next time you address me, or learn true obedience to my will." The ancient mage spewed out his anger.

All of Covis' eyes enlarged, his cold, feral grin replaced by a wondering, fright stained sobriety. The abysmal incarnate had taken his fair share of tirades in the past dealings with The Master, but none had rivaled the one he had just completed, and he new it was about time to be done with this rotting mortal. The lich seemed to be getting more unstable the closer he came to completing his plans. It was then that the Enveal knew for certain he had to get out of the magical servitude by which he had been forced to serve this wizard before it was too late.

"Very well," Covis' two white eyes narrowed to slits as his muzzle wrinkled just a hair. "But I shall have your word once you leave, I shall be free of this forced servitude you've bound me to since your arrival."

"I will give you your freedom readily," The Master waved such concerns away with a bony hand.

"Never to be called upon again?" The Enveal maintained it's stare.

"Are you implying, Covis, I will not honor my word, and keep my spell of servitude on you even after I have left this place?" The flames in the Master's sockets grew white hot.

"You haven't for Balon. Why should you for me?" Covis' growled.

"I'm a practical man, and I keep my word, as I see fit, to those who have served me well. You will have your release from the spell with my absence." The Master would be done of this pointless posturing, and pressed to get his answers from the Enveal.

"I have done all you have asked now let me return to my own abode," the Enveal's white eyes grew cruel with it's snarl.

"Good," with another wave of his hand, The Master dismissed the multi-eyed, repugnant creature. "Go back to doing whatever your kind does best. I care not what you do, just so long as it doesn't affect me. Be gone!"

With a screaming sound resembling the pathetic cries of a howling jackal, green smoke erupted from cracks in the floor and out of the air around the Enveal, enveloping him in an opaque haze. Then he vanished into the cloud, leaving nothing behind but a wispy trail of mist.

The Master moved to the pedestal, which contained his scrying skull. When he thought it safe from those many prying eyes and any others who might be about, he waved his hand over the skull. He then took a deep look into its smoky outer covering peering into a collection of swirling colors and sounds.

Slowly, the twirling vortex sucked The Master's mind deep within itself, and an image of Rowan began to appear. He was battling with some cutthroats, and The Master was pleased to see the youth was using the sword and armor he had enchanted earlier. Then, to his amazement and rage, he noticed the youth was fighting alongside others who were of various races.

The Master even thought he saw a priest of Saredhel beside him.

Why he had never seen it before, he couldn't fathom, but there was some greater part of
destiny being played out in the lives of those who fought within the vision. Something seemed slightly off kilter, as if another shadow lurked in the background with the lich. Balon? No, he wasn't smart enough, and no other fiend would dare intrude upon The Master's actions.

The gods perhaps then? It was possible...but it didn't feel like something they might do. It was too subtle, almost like it didn't want to be noticed or intrude upon the lich's actions; almost like it didn't want to hinder the lich in anyway, just observe.

Odd.

The gods, though, would try to do anything to stop him from meeting his final goals once The Master started getting closer to Tralodren - and he knew it. He would deal with them when the time was right, though...

As the mercenaries battled on, a glimmer of gold swam across the scrying skull.

"It cannot be!" The Master shouted. "After all this time! To have the pieces to my plan within my grasp - and now this!"

A young woman appeared in the golden light, a wizardress of seemingly great skill... potential which he could mold to his own needs even more so than that boy knight. The Master grew excited. He would use her as well to bring himself to his one great goal. He had plans to search out for such a person once freed, but with the onset of this wizardress, though, things became much easier.

Again, it seemed a bit too easy, a bit too fortuitous, all this fell into line - but no matter. He'd soon accomplish his plans. Surely destiny was on his side, or at the very least traveling the same road he was treading. He had to make sure Rowan continued to do so, though. If anything should happen the intricate spindles of his dark plotting would unravel and the millennia spent working on his escape would be for nothing. Then he truly would be stuck in his prison - a powerless undead for all eternity.

Intent on the outcome of the battle, The Master took a seat on his throne, and stared transfixed at the skull.

"I shall mold you too, my golden-robed mage," he said. "I have great plans for the two of us, my dear. With your skill, I shall complete my final ambition, and be free to take my revenge!"

The Master cackled with his hollow and frightful laughter as the image in the skull became more intense. As he did so, he felt another force at work in the scrying skull. While there was still one he couldn't place that just wanted to observe there was another now, a new force, that wanted to seemingly hinder his efforts, even block his scrying attempts.

"Is that you Endarien?" The glowing within the skull continued to intensify. "Or Ganatar perhaps, or even Dradin... or is it all of you? Is the entire Tralodroen Pantheon now so terrified of my return that you all have taken to stand against me?"

The Master would have to stop his scrying, or the skull would be destroyed from the sheer energy exerted upon it by this new opposing force.

"I'll come in and lay waste to your temples and eradicate all your followers!" The Master shouted. "From their ashes, my followers shall erect new temples to my glory. I shall reign over you forever! I shall reign supreme and reign alone!" He hit the pedestal with his bony arm, causing the scrying skull to topple to the floor.

Its brilliance dulled, and then fluttered out in a thick, oily smoke. Time had grown shorter, and now things were progressing too quickly for them to stop. He had to prepare.

Even with this opposing force, whatever or whoever it may be, he would succeed. The Master left his throne room for the darker recesses of his tower. He had to be ready for when the events he had set in motion fell into place. There was much to ponder, much to plan, and not a great deal of time to do it in.

Chapter 14

The rag tag company slowly began to pack up their belongings as they glided into port. Daylight was half spent when the group managed to go ashore. The boat ride had been mercifully peaceful, with calm seas and strong winds providing a safe and speedy passage to Talatheal. Clara silently thanked Perlosa, for her generous spirit on their passage as was the custom of sea travelers - even for those who didn't call the goddess their own. The journey had taken a week to complete, but it would have been longer had the weather turned against them.

As the group strode through the streets, the smells and sounds of the lively city filled them with excitement. Rich, salty aromas of the sea, mixed with freshly-cooked meats and spices from the far south mingled with soft music, and the chorus of voices around the docks themselves. It was a collection of many a varied race that met their eye. Telborian mixed with Elyellium, a few outlandishly-dressed halflings milled about the pools of people, and even a handful of dwarves made their appearance amid the bright colored sails and screeching gulls.

The port city of Elandor had stood for countless generations, growing richer each year off the elven and spice trade, as well as the abundance of fish found in the surrounding ocean. Elandor was also the capital of a Telborian kingdom of the same name covering a good portion of the upper continent of Talatheal until it ran into Romain, the kingdom to its south, and the Marshes of Gondad to its west.

The city itself was wonderful. Where elves had placed a standard of design and blending with all the elements of nature, Telborians had been content with pure function and practicality. There were no overly-decorated buildings following the same code of style and look, rather each one was unique and special, a gem in its own right. Through the chaotic setup of Elandor, a systematic form of beauty and wonder all its own was formed, and Dugan loved every inch of it.

The Telborian smiled softly to himself. In this city, in this country, he was free. No more elven slave masters, no more of the tortures and killings he found himself reluctantly accepting over the years, and no more worrying about bleeding his life away on the sandy floor of a coliseum. He laughed inside at the thought of this freedom.

An elf saving, an elven slave. The thought was amusing. Once he had completed Clara's task, he could live in any Telborian land in the world as a free member of society. He could reclaim his life, and make a new one for himself. He hadn't experienced life in a human city before, not since his capture and enslavement, and was eager to explore it as well as seek out a few places of particular interest while he could.

"You can all rest and look around before we meet up again," Clara addressed the others.

"When and where do we meet again?" Dugan asked as they walked down the wide and crowded streets of the market district, just east of the docks.

"We've made reservations at the Sea Otter this evening. It's off to the north of the docks, just past the temple of Ganatar, and before the granary." Clara helped Gilban along the crowded and uneven flagstone pavement. "Feel free to explore the city - and keep an ear open for any rumors regarding the ancient cities or recent elven activity in the area. We'll meet back at the Sea Otter before dusk."

As the group dispersed, Dugan approached Gilban, who freed himself from the thick crowds by moving into a large plaza where he'd seated himself on a delicately-crafted fountain of blue quartz. Clara left the old priest for a moment to briefly look over some wares at a local shop while Gilban rested. The fountain had been sculpted to resemble a dolphin carrying a small male Telborian child on it's back. His hands were thrown up in the air with excitement, and water spouted out of his mouth, as well as that of the dolphin's.

"Yes, Dugan?" Before Dugan reached more than seven feet from Gilban, the old elf turned his head in his direction. "I wondered how long you could hold out from your troubles. You have done well so far, a mark of true inner strength and dedication."

"What do you mean?" Dugan asked with an air of hesitation.

"Don't be so ill at ease," Gilban motioned the Telborian toward him with an open palm. "Come sit beside me, and we will talk. Yes, you can sit closer; I'm not a leper; I cannot harm you."

When Dugan had taken his seat Gilban continued. "I understand the feelings you are experiencing, and can tell you there is only one remedy for them."

"You understand my feelings?" Dugan's face soured slightly at these words. "How can you when you don't even know me?"

"Oh, but I do. As well as the fiery serpent dwelling within you," Gilban's eyes narrowed slightly when he took in the full figure of the man beside him as if he had natural sight once more.

"How do you know about that?" Dugan's face lost all shade of color at the seer's words. Indeed, the abilities of the priest were staggering.

"My goddess has entrusted me with the knowledge. Just as she has allowed me to tell you of a possible remedy to your dark fears." There was no judgement in the priest's words just a calm timbre relaying the facts of Dugan's life.

"A remedy? What is it?" Dugan nearly leapt up at the old elf's words; almost grabbing his robes with both hands to demand an answer.

"In this city there is a temple dedicated to the god you serve," Gilban gave answer. "Hidden away in the shell of a forest, east of the city, a few people chose to worship the dark deity you have chosen in the same manner you do. Like you, they find out the price of their worship."

Gilban made a motion with his hand to rise, which Dugan found himself doing by reflex.

"Go there. Confront the god's voice through his servants, and face his will. It is a sorrowful thing to witness a man destroy himself by the searing flames of revenge," Gilban motioned Dugan away as he heard Clara approach. "Go quickly, for I fear there will be much to answer for - and the time you are allotted is limited."

Dugan didn't know what to say, or how to feel - and so he silently left the fountain and traveled eastward at a quickened pace.

"Is everything okay?" Clara asked as she sat next to the priest.

"Yes. Why do you ask?" He turned with a smile.

"I just noticed you with Dugan. Is there anything I should know about here? He wasn't causing you trouble was he?" Clara looked back at the tall warrior quickly making his way down a street which lead out of the plaza.

"Have no fears. Even now he has gone to clear his mind, and finally deal with the troubles burdening him. For now, let's travel to the inn. I have to quench my thirst, and I think something will soon unfold there very favorable to our cause… " Gilban began to rise.

"What now?" Clara groaned as she helped the sage up from his seat. "Hopefully a little less violent surprise than what we've been getting of late."

"Events are yet to be unfurled,." the old priest looked blindly before him as he steadied himself with his staff. This done he then made a quick glance over to Clara as they made their way to the inn. "Listen to your heart, but don't be ruled by it when the crucial moment comes - else you might miss your way, and cause to stumble another whom you mentor."

"More riddles?" Clara sighed. "Come on, Gilban, the inn isn't too far from here."

"No riddles," Gilban spoke to himself. "Only blindness to the truth awaiting you to discover it."

Cadrissa walked the swarming streets of Elandor at a rushed pace, as if being followed by an unknown pursuer. At every corner, she'd look behind herself, as if she felt a cold glance upon her, then tense up in fear - and quickly look away. She cursed herself for acting like a fool, behaving in such a manner, but she felt as if something was very close to her, and was trying to catch her in its cold, insubstantial hands. The thought made her shiver to the bone.

Her garb was certainly different too than what most others wore around her, and they glanced at her, adding to her growing sense of unease, but she was still safe. There weren't any cold, clammy hands racing out to lay hold of her as far as she could see, and Elandor was far from the sort of place were young women had to fear for their safety…at least she didn't think that was the case.

Nevertheless, she had tasks to attend to, and worrying about an unseen or seen assailant was only going to slow her down. She had read up on Elandor,and there were a few things she had wanted to see while she was able. One of them was a shop of mystic wares in the older part of the city. Few knew of it, and even fewer frequented it.. As with many things with the modern-day structure of mages, and their various academies, there was a network of information and persons and places - such as this shop - that were hidden away from the common eye.

Had not Cadrissa been allowed access to the shop's location, she might not have even known that such a place existed. It was the way of the newly-reformed Tarsu. They were an archaic order of mages who stretched back to the Shadow Years, and only in the last two centuries had reestablish themselves, chiefly with the handful of academies scattered over Tralodren. Cadrissa wanted to put this knowledge to her advantage. .

Turning another corner, Cadrissa suddenly stopped. She had entered a run-down part of city, and the population had dwindled from a swarming mass to sparse smatterings of vagrants and lower-class citizens…just the sort of place tha criminals liked to inhabit.

Just keep going, Cadrissa, you're almost there, she told herself.

The paved streets had given way to a rancid, rust-colored, soupy soil Cadrissa's booted feet sank deeply into with a hollow, sucking sound. The sensation of a foul pen for livestock suddenly flooded her mind. In many cases, the inner city of Elandor was similar to such an analogy. All the lowest beings of the city, those unable to afford a station, were herded into the fallen streets and facades to wander aimlessly in their pen.They kept mindful not to stray too far, and risk the change of having their keepers come back and put them in their place, should they get any bright ideas about leaving the hovels they called home. Such was the way of many Telborian cities.

Cadrissa brushed her long, black hair back with her hand. She scanned the area, knowing her golden robe would probably attract even more unwanted attention here. To remedy this she began working a spell in her mind.

Bending down, with one eye on the lookout for trouble, she gathered some filthy earth from her feet, and holding it high above herself, she began to chant.

"Analor khasem ytren ytren obdol."

As she chanted, she sprinkled the earth over her head. As it fell, it burst into colorful sparks of light reflecting outwards in ray-like mirror shards. Once she had emptied the contents of her hand over her head, a soft glow began to outline her body. Slowly, Cadrissa's frame started to warp and bend, while her clothes dulled and tore.

Within seconds, a wizened old hag, dressed in faded rags for clothes, had replaced the vibrant young woman. In her hand, she held a cane of worn and shoddy workmanship completing her disguise. Looking around for any trouble, or witnesses to her changing, she found none. She proceeded to walk through the quiet ghetto into one foul alley after another, the cold presence still haunting her all the while.

It seemed to intensify after she worked her magic, and now caused the cold to be marrow-cracking. Shivering to stay warm, the wizardress hoped she would reach her destination soon, or she felt she'd freeze solid.

As she moved deeper into the older part of town, a stale and pungent aroma rose steadily to linger in every nook and street. Just as she was ready to gag from the stench of refuse and feces, a sign caught her eye. Hanging askew over a seemingly poorly-kept establishment, was a sign written not in words, but in arcane symbols so only a worker of magic could understand it, declaring the building to be a shop of mystical wares.

Cadrissa stepped inside.

Immediately there was a noticeable change of atmosphere. The smell of decay and urine was gone, replaced with the sweet and soothing aromas of balms, flowers, spices, and rare plants. There were no windows in the shop, yet the interior of the shop was as bright as day. Light radiated from a globe in the center of the establishment, which rested on top of a bronze holder sculpted to look like two large hands holding a miniature sun aloft.

When she entered the shop, however, the intense cold became almost unbearable.

"May I help you?" A young, male voice asked from behind a wooden counter off to the side of the room. He was dressed in a long, flowing, gray cloak hiding most of his features beneath a large hood.

"Yes, you can," Cadrissa said as she released her spell, and returned to her natural form. The man behind the counter was not impressed; he simply continued to stare out of his hooded robe.

"What are you in want of, fellow sister?" His voice was even-toned and calm.

"I have need of some rare powders and a...a....Spellbook," the last word was in a voice not her own. As Cadrissa stood, trying to figure out what had just occurred, the coldness that had hounded her aggressively overcame her; so all she knew was excruciating pain.

Cadrissa convulsed with the frightful acknowledgement she was no longer in command of her body, and struggled to regain control. The cold enveloped her completely.

Suddenly she heard countless numbers of screaming people searing her mind as they withered in torment. She then saw a vision flash into her mind of these same people's painful existence in a red-tinted land. Even as she saw all of the vision, the voices grew louder and louder, and Cadrissa lost hold of her body and mind altogether.

"What spellbook are you looking for?" The cloaked man still held his composure.

"I have come for a dark brown book, sealed with the mark of Kurahi the Dark. Bring it to me," Cadrissa spoke, but the words were dry and cold, filled with an evil malice reflected in her now-shimmering, azure eyes.

"Who is looking for this book? Who are you, spirit haunting this woman's form?" The cloaked form moved slowly from behind the counter.

"You dare question me? Do as I command and fetch me the tome, or you shall see how painful death can be," Cadrissa's body spoke as her eyes began to burn red hot, like a poker in a fire, and glared at the man with intense rage.

"Do you know what's in the tome?" The other countered. "I have been honored to guard it from those who are unworthy to lay claim to it, save its rightful owner. It has been in my family's keeping for generations."

"Do not test me further, boy! The book. Fetch me the book!" The hollow tones of the possessed Cadrissa turned even more rancorous. Small flecks of white foam curdled on the corners of her mouth as the dominance of her body continued.

Ignoring the irate attitude of the possessed Cadrissa, the man went through a secret door behind the counter. He lingered inside for a few moments, and as the moments went on, the possessive spirit grew even more intense in it's anger.

"Don't try to switch the books or work any other-tricks to deter me! Even in this weak vessel my sight can distinguish the true book from any forgery. Hurry and bring me it!" Cadrissa's unnatural voice commanded.

"I have been charged with its protection by the ancient scrolls of the Tarsu, as has every member of my family to keep the book safe. As I said, it awaits for its past owner. If I am to give you this book, which I and my forefathers have safeguarded, I must know if you are the one to whom the book belongs," The young wizard spoke as he came out the dark portal with a large deep brown book clenched to his chest.

The book was as long as a dagger, half as wide as tall, and three fingers in thickness. Its cover was made of deeply-tanned leather, and though it looked aged, it held no cracks or flaws in its design. It was closed fast by a golden clasp bearing a rune inscribed, silver medallion lock on the cover.

"Closer! Bring it closer. I must inspect the design. Ah, yes! This is the book. I am the one whom the scrolls' speak, rest assured of that. It was I who signed the scroll assuring its safekeeping. Hand it to this girl's body, and give her your collection of rare powders as well." The unnatural voice grated against the gray robed mage's flesh.

The gray robed mage shook his hooded head. "I must know the secret phrase inscribed upon the scroll by which the true owner would prove his identity,"

"Very well. The phrase was: 'Power and glory are bound unto me,'" the cold voice ushered out of Cadrissa's lips.

"Then you are he. You are...." the young wizard stood in amazement.

"The book," the voice commanded.

The gray robed mage complied, handing over the large tome. When Cadrissa's hands touched the tome it began to grow smaller until it was no larger than her hand. She mechanically placed it in one of the many hidden pockets in her robes, and smiled an empty grin as a collection of rare powders was brought to her.

"Here are the powders you requested," the gray robed man humbly brought the items forward.

"Good. Place them in a sack, and hand them to her, then let her leave without incident. You have done well, and your life shall be spared," the spirit possessing Cadrissa said.

"Yes, Great Lord," the gray robed mage bowed his head. "I am honored to be in your presence, and to be able to help you achieve your goal." The young wizard prostrated himself before Cadrissa. "Remember me when you come into your rightful power, as the scrolls said you were destined to do."

"I shall," the possessed Cadrissa then turned around without another word, and walked out of the shop like a child's toy caught up in strings. Her gaze was distant and glazed, as she sloshed through the muck of the streets like a drunk. Her path was uneventful as each step brought her a clearer head. As she walked, the possessive spirit whispered to the mentally distant Cadrissa.

"You will remember the book in time, child. Every time you look in the sack, you will not see it. It will be as if the book does not exist, but when the time is right, you shall hand it over to me. Do you understand?" The voice spoke to the submissive wizardress.

"Yes," Cadrissa replied hypnotically.

"Good. Now forget about the book. Mention it to no other. If asked what occurred, you simply tell them you went to buy some powders for your spells for you'll have need of them in the ruins. That is all. Do you understand?"

Cadrissa nodded sleepily, closed her eyes for a heart-beat then opened them again revealing her natural green eyes once more.

A gentle wind birthed of magic transported her frame far from the location she had been, to the other end of town in a matter of moments. The same wind which had carried her off also removed the chilling presence of the dark spirit who had possessed her, allowing her to regain her body.

At this Cadrissa shook her head and stared at her surroundings. How had she gotten to the other end of town so soon? What had she purchased in the sack she held? She looked through the sack, and found the rare powders she went to buy because she knew they would come in handy when they get to the ruins.

Strange though, she couldn't recall actually buying the powders. All she could recall was stepping into the shop, and asking for some powders. Perhaps it was an effect of a spell placed upon the shop. Maybe a customer's mind was wiped as they left the shop to keep its location secret. She had never read or heard of other shops doing this, but there was always a rogue shop or two dealing with a certain type of clientele, and therefore preferred to remain anonymous if possible.

Whatever the reason, Cadrissa had her powders and with dusk approaching fast, she had more pressing issues than trying to figure out what had happened to her, namely rejoining the others. She did notice one thing as she traveled through the busy main streets of Elandor: the bone-numbing cold was gone. Dismissing the absence of the cold that had once so worried her before with a shrug, she made her way to the Sea Otter Inn. Things seemed to have a new perspective. In all honesty, she really couldn't focus her mind long enough to even contemplate the last past few moments of her life. There were other things a bit more important to think about, she discovered.

Vinder trotted down an alley in a more dismal part of Elandor than where he had come ashore. He'd wanted to be alone with his thoughts, and in his distracted musings, the dwarf had managed to walk into an older part of the city. He trailed behind a lose fold of men, women and children, all dressed in tattered rags and hunched over in hunger and desperation. They all did well to stay clear of the one-eyed dwarf though, even if Vinder made no effort on his part to steer clear of them.

The buildings around him were of stone, chiseled many years before Vinder's great, great, grandfather had been born. They had begun to crumble from misuse, neglect and centuries of abusive weather. This area seemed faintly familiar to the dwarf ,for Clara and Gilban had found him in an alleyway similar to the one in which he was walking before he had agreed to the mission at hand. That had been in a village on Altorbia.

He had ended up there after his last job. A political family in the area wanted some hired help to wage a private little war with a local, rival family that had been growing in power. The pay was good, and Vinder didn't know or care about the elven families involved, and so he took the task.

The battle was short and deadly.

The rival house was all but decimated, and their climb to power was halted in its tracks. Vinder had just about healed up from his slight wounds, and was growing restless, when Clara and Gilban appeared. With the amount he stood to make off of this mission, he would finally be able to return to his homeland and retire from the cutthroat life he led.

As he thought back on his past, the old dwarf was drawn deeper into the architecture and ran his hands along the walls of the buildings, feeling the history of their stone. Even though they were falling away, Vinder noticed the mark of the dwarves who had laid chisel to rock so long ago. He looked past the facade of decay to what once had been smooth, clean sheets of rock covered in friezes and sculpture of forgotten times...perhaps happier times.

He walked closer to a partially-preserved wall that had caught his attention. Stepping over a puddle of murky rainwater, he discovered a stout statue of a small form. Unmistakably dwarven, though it had been ravaged by vandals and time, it had fallen from a higher balcony above long ago. Vinder looked into its cold, empty eyes and suddenly saw a face he had nearly forgotten.

"By the gods!" Vinder whispered in reverence, and knelt before the figure.

Vinder's heart started to race in his chest.

It was an omen for sure.

It had to be.

Carved out of granite, it was made to look like a strong dwarf dressed in ornamental armor with a mighty axe hanging at his side. The edges of the statue were chipped and marred, but the main visage and powerful image it conveyed spoke volumes to those who knew how to read the stone.

The eleven braids of the statue's beard were all chipped at varying intervals, but his eyes still held true and stern appraisal falling upon all who walked by the carved figure. It'd been so long since Vinder had been with his own kind, he'd almost forgotten what the image of his god looked like.

Drued was the god of the dwarves and protector of the twelve dwarven clans. Vinder had been so long from his home, he had lapsed in his reverence to his deity of his youth. It shamed him deeply, as many other things of his life now shamed him.

As the dwarf knelt down in front of the figure and hugged the statue's legs, a tear formed in his eye. This had to be an omen he was close to the reconciliation and forgiveness he sought. There still was hope in his desire to be reconciled to his clan.

"Forgive me, Drued," Vinder prayed. "I've learned from my mistakes and past sins. I beseech you to forgive me and lead me back to Clan Diamant. I have gathered a tribute worthy enough to honor those whom I have offended. Please bless me on my journey so that I meet up with favor."

Soft, whimsical chuckling filtered through the air as Vinder pleaded with the statue of his god. The old dwarf turned around to find the source of the sound and saw a stocky dwarf, dressed plainly in clothing of muted browns and grays, and older in age than himself, with almost solid gray in his hair and beard.

Vinder rose from his kneeling as the figure approached. The other's laughter at his prayers was causing some ire in the lone-eyed warrior. The closer the strange dwarf got, however, the better Vinder's recollection became.

"Heinrick?" Instantly the ire left Vinder. "What are you doing here? I thought the clan disliked venturing outside its home? Then again, you never were totally devout to the clan's outlook on outsiders." Vinder was astonished to see his old friend.

"Been away so long you forgot already, eh?" Heinrick smirk. "I'm picking up the few supplies we've run low on before winter sets in. Mostly cloth, and a few other trivial items that only come in through the sea trade, but as you know Vinder, Diamants strive for self-sufficiency - and in time we will meet that goal. For now though, I'm here to help supplement our needs. You also knew I am, and always will be, a true supporter of the clan.

"However," Heinrick made his way to stand beside the Vinder, "it is good to see you again, Vinder. It's been a long time.

"Too long." Vinder solemnly mused.

"It sounds though as if you've finally come to your senses, if what I've just seen is any indication."

Heinrick had been a good friend of Vinder's when he had still made his home in Clan Diamant. Heinrick was fifty years Vinder's senior, but still looked as young as a strapping youth of 120, apart from the graying hair he kept in a pony-tail that trailed down to the upper portions of his shoulder blades. It was the color of limestone dust and matched his grizzled beard, which was frayed and striped with flashes of silver and white over the gray limestone hue amid five braided strands of dark-blue dyed hair. His flesh was a darker gray than Vinder's, and his eyes were a brilliant, fiery blue.

Vinder always remembered his friend's blue eyes, and the way his crooked teeth showed when he smiled- a hint of mischief about an ever-studious face. Those days were in a time when life was seemingly easier and held deep joy for him. He still recalled how Heinrick had warned him not to leave the clan, but had respected his decision nonetheless.

Vinder never really knew exactly how much he had missed him until this chance meeting. Perhaps this was yet another favorable omen for the dwarf. He could only pray to Drued it was and be encouraged by it.

"What news of the clan?" Vinder asked his friend.

"The same as always," Heinrick bore his crooked teeth.

"Oh. I was afraid of that. But I'm willing to come back, if they would have me," Vinder held out his tough, worn hand to Heinrick - who looked at it hesitantly. "Come, forgive me. I must have at least some hope I can return. I have been collecting a tribute to offer Konig Stephen and the elders on my return."

Heinrick cautiously raised his hand, as if he were about to grasp a deadly serpent, then clasped the worn leather skin of Vinder in a sturdy grip.

"I've heard from your own lips which I needed to hear. You have learned the lesson you needed to learn. While I can forgive you old friend, it will be another matter all together to see if the Konig and the Elders be so merciful.

Heinrick spoke by means of strong dwarven tradition calling the two of them to make, and accept the formal apology, if it was so warranted.

"However, I'm starting my journey back to the mountains tonight. Will you join me?"

Vinder's face grew sad.

He longed to travel back home with his friend, but he was sworn to another task, and even with the coin it would bring in, he might not be allowed back into the clan. His personal pride and honor would not let him forsake that oath. Dwarves were known for keeping their promises. Their word was their bond. Vinder was no exception. As much as his heart moved him to give up the quest and go to his homeland with Heinrick, honor prevailed.

"No," Vinder gently shook his head. "There is one last thing I have to do first. I've given my oath. Once it's done, I'll take the tribute, and go join you and the clan."

A slight peace settled upon Vinder's features. "Seeing you again has been just one of many favorable omens. I have new faith now for the fate of the future. For if you have forgiven me after all this time, then surely my family and the Konig can too."

Heinrick looked at the one-eyed dwarf in a sullen expression.

"One can only hope so. Should you not meet with Stephen's good graces though you might be walking into a death sentence."

"That's a chance I'm willing to take," Vinder nodded soberly in understanding. He knew the stakes as well as Heinrick. He also knew the stakes of remaining outside his ancestral homeland as well, and had made his choice.

"I've never had the chance to thank you, Heinrick, for standing by my side all those years ago even to the last moment before I was banished. You are a true friend indeed.

"When I return, we'll feast like we have never done before. The very mountain itself will reverberate with our merriment! I've been away from my roots for too long. I realize now the clan was right, and Drued's always is in charge of our destinies.

"His ways and laws as true and right even when we think them chains about us."

"Sounds like a celebration I'd love to attend. When that happens I'd love to hear your stories. Namely the one on what happened to your eye." Heinrick pointed out Vinder's patch.

Vinder lowered his head. "That one is a long and sobering tale."

"No doubt. Still it couldn't hurt to pray some more to Drued for protection and guidance. After all, he is the father of our traditions. But don't offend the Lord of the Twelve Clans by using that - that statue as an inspiration for prayer," Heinrick pointed to where Vinder had been kneeling before he arrived.

"Why?" Vinder followed his friend's finger.

"You've been away so long you've forgotten the face of the treacherous Drexel?" The other dwarf's voice grew a bit concerned. "Drued always has twelve braids, never eleven or seven – the numbers of Drexel."

"Drexel?" Vinder's face was suddenly overrun by suprise. Drexel had lived on in dwarven legend for generations as the infamous leader who broke the once-united dwarven nation into what would later become twelve clans. Because of this, he was seen as a pox upon their race; the ultimate traitor to all dwarves.

"I had no idea. Father Drued forgive me! Thank you once more my friend. I've come so far, the last challenge I need now is a divine one. I don't need his wrath or the spirit of the foul Drexel upon me. Seeing you again has given me so much hope when I thought it was lost, and has led me down a brighter path."

"Here. You'll probably need a little more illumination before this matter is resolved," Heinrick took off a necklace he wore around his neck, and tossed the religious icon toward Vinder. ."This will help give you more guidance and protection in your journeys."

The one-eyed dwarf caught and then clenched it fast in his hand. Vinder looked down at the necklace in his open palm and noticed it was of excellent workmanship; a carved figure of crystal on a gold loop which dangled from a leather strand. He took in the figure closer, and noticed the form was of Drued, the real Drued with all twelve braids detailed into the opaque stone.

Twelve braids, the number of unity; wholeness over Drexel's fractious eleven or seven as he was also sometimes portrayed as having.

"Thank you," Vinder said with tears forming at his eye.

"I look forward to seeing you soon, Vinder. Fare thee well."

"Farewell," Vinder's face had taken on a bit more shadow as the weight of his current situation took hold once more; the emotions welling up inside and churning about upon this recent encounter.

Heinrick walked off into another alleyway. His footsteps echoed in the soupy pools of the dirt-packed streets for a few more moments, then faded into silence. Vinder held the crystal up to the sun. The figure shimmered brilliantly, reflecting the light into a thousand shards of pure white beams.

Tears flowed down the dwarf's cheeks as he made a silent prayer to the god he had forgotten for fifty years because of the arrogant pride which had brought him nothing but ruin and heartache.

In that moment, he felt a burden lifted from his heart, as if a great stone block had been flung off his back, restoring inner peace to his soul.

In that moment, he had felt and latched onto hope.

"Drued be praised," the old dwarf whispered.

Chapter 15

The sun was kissing the horizon when Dugan made his way to the edge of the ailing pocket of woodlands east of Elandor. The sickly saplings, scraggy bushes, and green shoots erupting through the ash-covered ground were all that remained of what looked to have once been a small section of wildland set about for a park of some kind. All around him were blackened stumps and the charred remnants of hapless creatures which had been unable to escape the destruction of their homes.

All around the area was silent and empty.

Whenever Dugan's feet shuffled over the burnt earth, they kicked up plumes of dust smelling of ash and smoke. What remained unscathed was a lone temple in the heart of the charred territory - a temple dedicated to the force which had devoured the terrain around it.

Dugan traveled out of the city with a growing weight upon his chest. Each road leading further toward his destination caused his heart to groan, and his breathing grew weary as the pressure of his task started to overwhelm him once more.

He'd felt this way before. No battle glory or past memory of victories over other challenges could ever drive the pressure from his heart. It flung heavy chains upon his neck and back, weighing him down even further. Why had he been so foolish?

The Telborian stopped to admire the craftsmanship of the temple. Standing fifty feet high, it was constructed of volcanic rock, and painted in shades of red and yellow. Four pillars supported each of the corners of the square building, and every one of those columns was inlaid with amber and rubies, so when the sun reflected off of them, it seemed as if they were engulfed in tongues of flame.

The crowning achievement of the whole temple was a bronze dome, which was carved in such a way as to appear as it too was on fire - stretching its searing tendrils up to the sky, and glowing a brilliant orange when it caught the light of the falling sun.

The sight of the temple conjured up memories for the battle-worn warrior. Already at his distance of one hundred and fifty paces, he could smell brimstone, the by-product of the Flame Lord's passing - so stories said. Dugan stood silently and kept his distance as he made up his mind.

Silently, his thoughts journeyed back to darker days.

Dugan's broken form was shackled once more to the wall by short, biting, iron chains keeping his feet and arms trapped against the cold stone - a trophy over which the elves could gloat. He'd just defeated a Celtoric warrior, and his injuries were left to be repaired with very little care. The dismal cell where Dugan was chained reeked of old blood, rust and sweat. Dim light, provided by a small torch on the opposite wall, near the door, barely gave enough illumination to make out vague shapes fluttering silently around the cell.

He was convinced this was the lowest he'd been in his whole life - the true depth even beneath the pit he'd been in before.

The Telborian silently cursed his predicament, as he'd done for countless years. The branding he'd received, like a common beast, when he was first brought to the coliseum some ten-odd years before, had healed into a pink, puckered marking of disgrace.

Though his body hung in silence, each passing moment found his mind dwelling on the possibility of freeing himself, with the added pleasure of killing his overseer and owner, a cruel and pale elf named Gilthinius.

Through his harsh years of confinement and forced slaughter, Dugan had prayed to the gods for help, but he had never received a reply from them. The Telborian truly felt as if the gods had forsaken him. Surely he was damned, his life slowly being leeched out of him. He knew he was nothing more than a dead man, a corpse doomed to walk these catacombs for eternity; rising to an occasional sun to slaughter again before being banished to the gloom once more.

Something had to change very soon or he might never get free of his despair, and wind up finding solace in the embrace of his own blade when next his captors gave him one. He'd been able to hold the blackest of this depression at bay with thoughts of escape, and by feeding his fantasies of revenge but that would only help him through a bit longer - and he knew it…

Dugan was haunted by his dark thoughts every night in his dank cell, and every night he would dream of escape, formulating a new plan each time, almost believing it was possible. While he was chained, Dugan studied each stone and hinge of his prison. His dedication to his desire allowed him to become observant to the routines and regular duties of the guards, arena managers, and overseers.

He could almost navigate his escape route from his cell with his eyes closed, while at the same time factoring in the exact times and places the guards would appear during their rounds. He had to evade capture at all costs. It was his last hope of freeing himself from his bonds to a life shackling his pride, and debased his value to animal stock.

Then, his mind would turn on him, finding fault with every one of his ideas. This is how then slowly, Dugan's craving for revenge began to replace his desire to escape. Little as he liked being labeled an animal, it was what Dugan was becoming, and he knew it. It was another turn on of the key in the lock on the chains of depression which were ever coiling about his person - ready to take him whole one day soon.

Until then, he wanted to see his tormentors, chief among them his owner, suffer as much as he had throughout the years of his enslavement. At certain times, his hatred grew so overpowering it transformed each victim he fought in the arena into Gilthinius. He didn't care about the person behind the projected image of his most hated foe. His zealous emotions led him to crave the carnage more and more, like a sick addiction of twisted pleasure. A pleasure that was his only comfort in this depleting life.

The Telborian stared at the flickering torchlight on the wall. The anemic flames flickered and danced, always changing their form; all consuming in their makeup. Dugan found the similarity between the fire and his rage ironic, and as he pondered the orange glow, a voice filled his head.

Dugan.

He looked around in bewilderment to find no one in his cell. He shook his head and returned his attention to the torch.

Dugan. This time the voice was louder, but still soft and seductive.

"Who's there?" Dugan shouted as he strained his sore muscles against his chains.

Peace, proud warrior. I mean you no harm. The voice seemed clearer in his mind now.

"Where are you?" The gladiator scanned the empty room. "Show yourself!"

Very well, look into the flame.

The torch flared into life with a crimson burst to the ceiling, another three feet above the stationed torch. Thick curls of black, serpentine smoke rolled off the stone, as the towering flame stroked the cool rock above it.

I am here Dugan. I have heard your prayer, and have decided to aid you...personally. The last word of the sentence slithered around the Telborian's thoughts.

"Who are you?" Dugan stared at the red flame.

I am Rheminas, Lord of Flame. The words burned into Dugan's skull. The flame lowered itself slightly and turned a brilliant yellow, illuminating the entire room in glowing daylight.

"Is it really you? I've prayed for so long…" A faint ray of hope burst up into the warrior's heart to weaken the bindings of despair.

Yes, ten long years of suffering and hardship. Never knowing how much longer you could hold out against the biting of swords and lashings of the whip. I felt your pain, but there is something stronger in you that I have felt: your hatred. You crave revenge don't you?

"Yes," the Telborian clenched his jaw in a tight sneer.

Impressive. I haven't felt such rage since Aerotription himself. Truly it was wise for me to come to you in person. There was a jovial quality about the internal voice.

Dugan looked around the room again in frustration. "What do you want of me? Why help me now? I've prayed for aid for ten years, even swore an oath by you - and now you find the time to aid me?"

Do not question me! It is not often the god of flame transcends to the mortal realm. You should count yourself blessed. A fierce band of pain seared across the Telborian's head.

"You can talk all you want about your power, I couldn't care less. I'm not in the mood to hear another being rave about his authority over me, even if that being is a god. Now, either tell me what you want, or be gone," Dugan spat out amid the pain.

Choose your words more carefully mortal, or you shall find there are fates worse than the one you are now suffering. The pain subsided.

Suddenly, the torch's flame leapt from its roost and landed on the ground. Like a serpent, it wound itself up Dugan's shackles and around his leg. It twirled up the muscular appendage with a fiery vengeance. To Dugan's surprise, the fire wasn't hot. There wasn't even the sensation of a touch or a whisper across his skin as the flame continued it's climb. The bound warrior looked at the being now twisting itself around his arm, near the very mark that had been branded into his flesh, with awe.

I will give you the revenge you seek. You have a fire deep within you, and it has been stoked long enough. You shall conquer this elven owner of yours, along with anyone else who should cross your path, and win your freedom as you desire. All I need is for you to repay me for this gift I grant. The fiery serpent looked straight into Dugan's face, but the tempting offer was still made by the voice in his head. The Telborian was amazed at the detail the firey serpentine form- it was lifelike down to the smallest of scales and red glowing eyes.

"What's your fee for such a favor?" Dugan stared back unflinching.

Your soul.

"What will happen to me, then, once I'm dead then?" Dugan didn't show the emotional blow the answer had dealt him.

You shall pass into my realm where you shall spend the rest of eternity. replied the voice.

"Isn't your father Khuthon?" Dugan's forehead began to break out in a sweat. The flame was beginning to heat up rapidly. "Could it be possible I could have your blessing to turn to his realm, but you could still hold my soul?"

The Telborian had little knowledge of the structure of the afterlife and how it was ran, apart from a few smatterings of myths and tales he'd heard over his years in slavery to the elves. He'd heard the legends Khuthon, Father of Giants, was the patron of the mightiest warriors, those who had fallen in battle. These chosen warriors were taken to his realm. Rheminas, on the other hand, lived in a kingdom were eternal fires blossomed like weeds, scorching all who passed their way or so the tales he'd heard had said.

More so, Dugan had been told stories claiming Rheminas to be petty and cruel to those who worship him - and to those who didn't just the same. Though he wanted revenge more than anything in the world, Dugan knew he wanted a better afterlife, too. He wasn't a priest or sage though; his understanding of the realm beyond death was fragmented sparks in a great darkness at best. He would learn the truth later, after his freedom was granted.

Dugan you insult me. The tone was wounded now but still serpentine in nature. *Wasn't your vow to allow me to attach any cost to the answered prayer? Have you no love for this gift I give you of my own goodness, and personal sacrifice?*

The Telborian was silent; he merely stared back into the glowing red eyes of the serpent coiled about his left arm.

Your fears are in vain, Dugan. You will have an after-life befitting any brave warrior, I assure you. What is your decision? You must make it quickly, for I grow tired of this conversation. Will you accept this gift I am so generously offering, or will you deny it, and live out the rest of your days caged...as an animal...in suffering...forever?

Dugan closed his eyes, and felt the blaze slither from his shoulder to his massive chest. The flame was smooth as velvet, and as warm as a beam of sunlight upon his skin. He knew he needed to think very carefully about his decision. He had wanted freedom for a very long time. However, was he willing to pay Rheminas' price?

He didn't want to trade one form of servitude for another, but the chance to finally have his revenge upon Gilthinius was a powerful temptation. And to be free from this place as well...

Blood began to rage through his head as he imagined the vengeance he would exact upon Gilthinius. He knew he had always wanted to run the elf through very slowly and very painfully; looking into his eyes as he did so to take in the full effect of his actions. The Telborian licked his fevered lips in anticipation of the sweet flavor of retribution, and smiled with devilish glee. His need for revenge had overcome his concerns.

Well? The voice was growing impatient.

"I'll do it."

Excellent. You won't be disappointed. Now, open your mouth.

"What?" Dugan's eyes suddenly focused from their daze.

I won't harm you. I must fill you with my blessing in order to fulfill our bargain.

Dugan hesitantly did as he was told, and slowly opened his mouth. The burning serpent, who had coiled around his neck, twisted over his tongue and down his throat. Dugan suppressed the gagging sensation which overcame him as Rheminas went deeper into his chest, all the while intensifying in heat.

Revenge. Revenge. Revenge. Dugan thought in rhythm with his heart.

Suddenly, he felt a small part of his heart go numb, then screamed out in pain as his chest was engulfed in flames. Smoke poured out of his mouth, nose, and ears, and his vision became blurry and tainted red. Dugan fell to his knees to cough up spatters of blood, along with his new master, who hit the floor in a shower of sparks, coiling and twisting into a towering seven-foot-tall red inferno.

I have given you the power and strength to meet your goal. Now embrace your hatred and rage! Break your bindings! The voice in his head commanded.

Dugan, though his chest throbbed with pain, strained against his shackles. The chains, crafted of iron, looked as if they were centuries old, and yet, though he tugged with all his strength, he was met with resistance.

Release my gift to you. Use the warlust. The voice continued.

Dugan grunted as veins pulsed from his head and neck. The gladiator fought for the warlust he had used so many times in the arena, but when it came, there was something different about it. It was more intense, all-consuming, and uncontrollable.

His chest and mind were alight, with a fire fueling his blood with incredible power. It was the power to take back control of his life, the strength to rule over his oppressors, and the means by which he could extract his revenge from those who so dearly deserved this retribution. With a bestial roar, Dugan shattered the chains binding him hand and foot

to the wall. The ancient iron links exploded into shards of useless metal.

Good!. You have taken the first step - now take the last. Approach me. Deep satisfaction richly-covered the words from the column of fire.

Dugan paused, recalling the pain he had just been dealt by the god of revenge.

"How? I'll burn myself if I touch you."

You have already been burnt, Dugan. You cannot be wounded any more than you are now.

"What are you talking about?" Dugan's face and heart grew troubled.

Approach me! I thought you wanted revenge, Dugan. Isn't that what you sought after all these years? The longer you remain indecisive, the more time your captors have to react to the noise those chains made. You best be ready for them.

Dugan's eyes glazed as Rheminas' hypnotic voice entered his mind, like soothing music calming all his fears leaving him without any doubts.

"Yes...revenge," Dugan chanted as he stepped closer to the towering flame, illuminating it all in a blood-red light as warm as the sun.

Take this weapon and use it to get your vengeance, Dugan. Once it tastes blood, I shall owe you nothing, and my debt to you, and your hopes for yourself shall be done.

The flame shrunk to about two and a half feet in length, then began to glow bright white, like metal in a forge. The heat in the room intensified, making the cell feel like a blast furnace. Sulfur permeated the air, as did the acrid perfume of burning metals.

The heavy smoke clogged Dugan's sore lungs, and caused him to cough up even more blood still. The smoke also obscured his vision, causing his eyes to water, and lose sight of Rheminas.

Take the weapon, Dugan, and claim your revenge. The voice cheered him on.

As soon as Rheminas' words had faded in Dugan's mind, the smoke cleared to reveal a sword standing where the flame had been. It was crafted from a strange black metal. He grasped the hilt and found it to be a perfect match for his hand. He swung the blade, and noticed it was also well-balanced; as though it was an extension of his arm. Even more peculiar was its ability to increase the burning sensation inside the warrior. The longer he held it, the more enraged he became, and the more he wanted to slaughter Gilthinius.

Take the weapon. Extract your revenge. The thought whispered to him, as if from some distant land.

Dugan snapped out of his stupor when he heard voices coming from the outer hallway. The guards had been alerted to the noise from his cell. The Telborian smiled as he heard their approaching footsteps and raised his sword in anticipation. He looked forward to demonstrating just how much of a killing machine they had made him.

The lust for retribution pumped through his heart, and veins like a tidal wave. He channeled it into a great bellowing charge, and brought the black blade down upon the sturdy wooden door of his cell. It split in two before bursting into flames, toppling to the floor like pieces of kindling. The echo of the massive blow traveled throughout the hallways.

"What was that?" one of the approaching elves shouted as he neared the fallen door, another elf right on his heels.

"I don't know, but it came from Dugan's cell!" the other responded.

They neared the gaping hole leading to Dugan's cell with caution. Years of training had taught them to respect the gladiators. Even when they were wounded from a battle, they were deadly. They had learned to keep the slaves in line, and show them who was their master, but never went so far as to risk the fatalistic ire some gladiators would release if driven to the breaking point with beatings, verbal abuse and worse. In Dugan's case, many guards had made this mistake and never knew it. The Telborian had stored it up deep inside himself behind a great dam that was now ready to burst.

"Die!" Dugan yelled as he ran out of the cell, blade arcing down with the accuracy honed by countless kills. His first series of blows sliced into the nearest elf's stomach, spilling his intestines out onto the floor in fiery pools lit by the touch of thefirey sword.

The second guard was slashed deeply across his upper torso. He fell to his knees, gripping his wound in horror, blood pouring out of the flaming gash, he fell face down onto the dirt floor as a scream ripped from his lips. His hands clenched at the wound in a pathetic attempt to keep his heart from exploding out of his chest.

Gloating over his first victims, the seething gladiator stopped long enough to ensure they were dead before running off to find Gilthinius. His feet were swift, and his mind was keen in its calculations. It was just as he had practiced so many nights in his cell.

Everything seemed so surreal.

He ran down another hallway and climbed up some stairs to the upper level of the coliseum, following the smell of spiced meat and sweet breads; the food of the privileged. It came from the upper levels, where the gladiator owners and lesser nobles kept personal suites to host parties and private fights, should they so wish.

As Dugan drew closer, he began to hear music, and even the night calling of birds. Once he cleared the top of the stairs, the Telborian ducked into some nearby shadows as a patrol of guards crossed his path. Silently he watched them, but refrained from killing them. He knew if he did, he'd alert Gilthinius and the elf could very well find time to escape, distancing himself from Dugan's wrath quite probably forever.

Gilthinius had the most opulent quarters in all the coliseum, and as Dugan stood still in the shadows of the hallway, he listened to the well-fed elf sing as he moved about the room. Gilthinius fancied himself a bard many said, and quite the illustrious one at that. He was the son of a renowned general, whose family had taken over the coliseum from its previous owner years ago. Rumors at the time said it was lost in a game of dice, but the old owner could have also just as easily been murdered. Such things were not uncommon even for the nobility. For indeed, if they watched, and even promoted such violence it was no small wonder some would take the next step and do it themselves.

Dugan hated them all. His pain was their reward, and he vowed to put an end to it that very night. The rage and hate flared throughout his body.

"Oh, the rose is a beautiful flower, but on them many a thorn does roam." The musical voice of his enemy drew out further ire.

The song went on as the guard passed, and Dugan ran farther up the hallway.

"That is the way my darling, I feel when you're not at home." Dugan moved closer to the door, preparing himself to break it in as he gave himself enough distance between himself and the guard who had just passed.

"Glades and meadows are charming, but not as charming as you. Like the shiny fairy I love you…"

The gladiator raised his sword, and brought it down - shattering the wood into flaming splinters with one mighty sweep of his arm.

254

"GILTHINIUS!" Dugan shouted with such hatred and bloodlust the company inside the room; musicians, half-naked dancing girls, and other overseers of a lesser rank, turned white and sought the nearest refuge to crawl into. Many tripped over each other in their haste to get away from the madman descending on them, screaming in hysteria and panic.

Dugan had become berserk. The warlust overshadowed all reasonable thought. He ran through the scattering crowd, cutting down those who got in between him and his target like rotten fruit. The Telborian wouldn't be denied his justice. He took countless lives of those who happened to cross his path by some ill wind of fate before he even found his victim, cowering behind a thick, purple settee.

"Don't hurt me," Gilthinius whimpered, his face covered with inky rivers of mascara. His soft cheeks were smeared with thick, pink blush, and his lips were painted a gaudy red. He was dressed in a loose-flowing white cotton shirt, open to reveal his pale flesh, a tight pair of black leather pants, and tall black leather boots. Each finger sported a jeweled ring and mounds of gold chains were draped from his neck to fall on his hollow chest.

"You pathetic dog!" Dugan screamed. "I'm going to enjoy running you through very slowly."

"No! Have mercy. For the sake of Aerotription, spare me," the motley-faced elf begged.

"Elves and their weak gods no longer have hold over me," Dugan plunged the tip of his blade into Gilthinius' left eye. Searing smoke and blackened blood ran down the ruined opening as Gilthinius screeched for his life. Dugan ignored the gibbering cries, and slowly ran the sword in a path from the elf's eye, down his cheek and neck, to his chest and stomach.

As Dugan cut into the elf, a small flame erupted to chase the line the sword drew. Gilthinius' screams started to become louder, but less coherent.

"This is just the beginning," Dugan hissed with glee. "Come, let me show you to your death," Dugan picked up the convulsing mass of flesh.

"Release me...Guards...guards!" The wounded elf could barely speak through the pain.

"They won't help you. They're weak, like all elves!" Dugan's delight had become sadistic. He knew, though, he had lied, and reinforcements would be coming soon. There were nothing but distractions now from his real goal. He could die content knowing he sent Gilthinius to the pit before him.

Dugan hoisted the bleeding elf over his shoulder, and moved over to a window looking out over the arena floor two stories up. The night air was fresh and cool.

"This is the last night of your life, Gilthinius," Dugan barked as he flung the wounded elf off his shoulder, and through the window.

The elf landed in the sand with a thud.

Blood started to leak out of him in a thick pool, which the sand worked quickly to absorb. The Telborian could see the doomed elf struggle as he fought to stay alive, but all he could do was twitch; like a squashed bug in it's death throes.

Delighted, the Telborian leapt out of the window after the elf. Landing on his feet like a great cat, he quickly slithered up to the dying elf.

"How does it feel, Gilthinius, to be wounded and sore - knowing the end is near - and there is nothing you can do?"

Dugan growled as he kicked his former owner in the side. The action sent the elf into more violent spasms.

256

"Here is my gift to you, Gilthinius, for the long years of service to your family." Slowly Dugan lowered the blade into Gilthinius heart. He let it slide in inch by horrible inch so Gilthinius could feel the anguish of his life leaching out and away from him for as long as was physically possible amid his painfilled convulsions and anguished screams.

"You've trained me well," Dugan's delight was as sadistic as his grin. "I'm the best killer in your stables! I think you should regard your death as a compliment to my skill."

Finally, the sword plunged through the other side of Gilthinius, pinning him to the ground. The elf jerked wildly pushing out more sreams with the blood bubbling out of his lips and then lay silent, blood soaking into the sandy floor beneath him.

Suddenly, the blade began to heat up, becoming white hot, before bursting into a black flame. Dugan stood back from the sword and the elf's body as the sulfur-scented fire scorched Gilthinius' remains into a powdery ash before dying away into lifeless ash of it's own. It was at that moment, when the fire had subsided and the stench of the sulphur descending all around him that Dugan finally realized the gravity of what he had done - and what he now owed. As the price of his deed dawned on him, a clamoring of guards echoed from the tunnels and side corridors that hone-combed the coliseum.

They were coming his way.

He was free, but he would be hunted forever.

The sweetness of revenge had suddenly gone sour - and in that instant, Dugan saw the rest of his life unfolding before him; and it frightened him.

Chad Corrie

The Gladiator shook his head to clear out the cobwebs of the recent past. He stood before the temple of
Rheminas; one foot poised over the worn steps leading up to
the entrance. The smell of sulfur and heavy smoke became
more prominent as he ascended, and the air grew warmer
until he stood on the last step, dripping with sweat.

The atmosphere was so heavy as he neared the tall,
iron doors of the temple, he found it harder to breath. Even
the stones he walked upon seemed to send up wisps of
steam.

He stopped to catch his breath, slouching against the
doorframe as his body wilted before the heat. He pressed his
palms to his eyes. Who was he deluding? He'd never be free
of Rheminas' curse. For a moment, Dugan was about to head
back down the stairs, but a small voice inside of him encouraged him to continue. He had to go on, or he'd be tormented
until his death about having never even gotten an answer.

He had to try at least.

The Telborian gritted his teeth, and forced his legs
to move toward the heavy iron doors. Admiring the metal,
the warrior found certain areas had been highly polished to
reflect the sunlight, with the effect of making the door appear
as if it were white-hot iron, fresh from the forge. The con-
ceptual design of the temple gave him pause to think what
could lie inside. Consuming flames were not some of his first
ideas for art.

Tentatively, Dugan raised his hand to the door.
Instantly he withdrew it. The heat from the door had seared
him. The throbbing ache of his fingers was the only evidence
of damage; his hand remained unmarked by any blister or
wound. He quickly backed off, shocked by the experience.
He was hesitant to touch the door again, but knew he had to
try once more to force himself onward.

Building up his resolve, Dugan took a deep, ragged breath, and charged the doors like an enraged bull, ramming the entrance with his shoulder. The impact caused the doors to fling open noiselessly. The Telborian clenched his teeth as a burning sensation coursed throughout his veins, leaving him momentarily dazed and breathless, but otherwise unharmed.

The interior of the temple was hot and dark, dimly-lit by torches and small braziers of glowing ash affixed at random intervals on the walls. The gloomy hallway leading into the bowels of the temple radiated intense heat like a sunswept day. Dugan glanced into the hall, and found no one in sight. The entire building seemed like a crypt.

Moreso, the whole interior seemed very odd to him in some fashion. There was something there he couldn't put his finger on at the moment. The walls and floors of the temple were made of fieldstone. Years of soot and ash had covered them in a gray grime. The passage Dugan entered branched off toward the north from the entrance. It seemed to stretch on for what seemed like hours, before turning around a corner. The proceeding hallway was interspersed with a few darkened archways and doors. The ceiling barely rose above his head, trapping the heat around his body.

"Hello?" Dugan's voice echoed, bouncing of the walls and ceiling.

Nobody replied.

He needed to find a priest.

Dugan pressed on, exploring the many hallways and passages within the temple. Suddenly, he realized what was so odd about this place: it was larger inside than its outside structure would allow it to be. An unsettling feeling nestled in the gut of the gladiator, and he nearly made his way toward the doorway outside again when he caught himself and willed his body to keep moving forward. In an effort to help calm, his mind, he turned; looking at the decorations on the walls around him.

Many of the walls he passed were adorned with murals and frescoes whose bright paint had faded long ago, hidden under the layers of smoke. A few could be distinguished as depictions of the various rituals held to honor Rheminas. Each picture contained Remani, the given name for followers of Rheminas, circling the Lord of Flame in worship and praise.

One of the scenes depicted worshipers prostrating themselves before a large bonfire. Another showed them pointing up to the sky as the sun was lovingly cupped by two great flaming hands. Farther down the hallway, a picture, drawn rather crudely, illustrated tribal folk dancing around an erupting volcano.

The final picture was the most vivid, and the most striking. In the center of a field were two figures. One was standing with a bloodstained sword, gloating over the other who had fallen, clutching at his chest in the throes of death. Dugan felt gooseflesh rise over his body. It was the most frightening picture he had ever seen. The victorious figure was a massive Telborian male, with long, blond flowing hair. The victim was an older elf, wearing rich, silk clothing and many chains of gold.

Dugan's heart pounded heavily in his chest. He felt as though the heat had driven him to madness. Surely the picture was pure coincidence; nothing more.

"Admiring our walls eh? You can't see too much of them these days from all the soot collected over the years."

Dugan was startled at the husky voice, and his hand went instantly to one of the gladii at his side. Spinning around, Dugan caught sight of a middle-aged, deeply tanned, Telborian man, whose eyes smoldered beneath an expressionless brow. He wore an open outer robe of orange cotton, covering an inner robe of red silk. Both robes were embroidered in yellow and gold thread resembling tongues of fire.

"Greetings traveler, may I assist you with anything?" The priest's demeanor was disarming.

"I need to seek Rheminas' will and to make a petition." Dugan instantly refocused his attention to the priest and his environment. "Can you help me?"

"Yes, but it will cost you" the priest took in the Telborian with a rough gaze.

"I don't have anything of value."

"Well," the old priest spoke as he scratched his chin, "one of your swords will do." The priest pointed at Dugan's weapons, his fingertips dyed yellow and glowing dimly in the flickering light of the hall.

Dugan looked at his blades, pausing a moment in thought. His swords were the only things of any real use he possessed. He would need them if he had to defend himself during Clara's mission. He'd need them in the days after it too if he wanted to live…

After a moment, though, he came to the conclusion facing future danger reduced by one blade was worth the cost of freeing himself from Rheminas, and getting the answers he needed. Had he been worried about its loss causing any unwanted attention, he would soon find in the days to come none of the others noticed its absence at all, which seemed an odd favor of sorts in the midst of his struggles.

"All right," Dugan handed over a gladius to the older priest as he glanced back at the unsettling mural again. "Tell me what is this picture of before we go on?"

"Like all the pictures on the wall, it depicts one of the aspects of Rheminas. That particular image portrays him as the god of revenge."

"Is that how he is widely worshipped?" Dugan studied the image with greater interest.

"No, but more people do him honor each day by giving into revenge to solve their problems. It is even rumored Rheminas aided the great Aerotription with his rage; forging it into a mighty weapon... but you know of revenge already don't you?" The priest looked at the warrior with a smugness that Dugan found a bit unsettling.

"How...?" Amazement stole over the gladiator's face as he spun around to take in the priest once more.

"I saw it on your face, and saw the weight of the thing on your shoulders the moment you stepped in here. My lord has chosen you, laid claim to you already. What could you possibly want answers to when your future is already made so clear?" The priest mused.

"What do you mean?"

The old priest began to shuffle down the hallway into a more intense heat, admiring Dugan's sword as he did so. "Follow me. You obviously don't yet understand what fate holds to all those who accept Rheminas into their lives. It shall be my duty to explain to you what life with Rheminas means for you."

"So will you divine my fate as the followers of Saredhel do?" The gladiator started to follow the priest.

The priest stopped suddenly.

He turned back to Dugan with a deep scowl lining his face. "Never speak of another god in the temple of Rheminas. Here, he and he alone is supreme."

Dugan stood silent.

"I'm sorry if I've offended you. I-"

"Just follow me, we are almost there." A fire blazed hot in the priest's eyes. "While Rheminas is not interested in commanding fate, because you are already connected to him we will be able to petition him and foresee his answer for your petition…though I have a feeling I know it already."

Dugan noticed as they walked farther down the passageway the light became more intense, as did the heat. He began to feel faint from the high level of heat, yet he observed the older man hadn't even broken a sweat.

"Why is it so warm in here?" Dugan asked the priest. "And why is this place so large inside when it should be much smaller judging by the outside of it?"

"All will be explained in time." Replied the priest.

Why was it every priest he met made little sense when asked honest questions?

"Where are the other priests?" Dugan wheezed.

"I am all that is required today. The others are off performing other services this temple provides to those who seek it."

"What services are those?" Again the gladiator labored with his breath.

"Special services not involving you at the moment," the priest's statements pressed into the Telborian. "Though you would probably be no stranger to them."

The servant of Rheminas led Dugan to a massive stone entranceway carved to resemble an image of a great brazier, holding a mighty flame at its center. It was then Dugan began to feel lightheaded, and areas of blackness began to cloud his peripheral vision.

The old priest smiled at the warrior.

"All your answers are behind these doors. Only the most dedicated souls with wills of iron ever make it across. Though I doubt you'll be one of the weak-willed ones, hmm?

"However, if you continue to be so stubborn, you'll be dead from overheating. You have no need of your armor here, but if you feel the need to cling to it, I shall accommodate you" the priest placed his hand upon the swooning Dugan, and whispered a prayer over him.

Instantly, Dugan felt cooler, and his body began to shiver as his sweat was dried by the warm winds emanating from behind the doors.

"Whatever lies behind those doors, priest, I'm ready for it." Dugan's locked his jaw.

"I had little doubt, Dugan," a knowing smirk crossed the priest's face.

"How-" Dugan wondered aloud.

"All be answered later, remember?" The priest waved the thought away as he motioned Dugan inside.

Dugan sighed in exasperation at the strangeness of priests, and he leaned his weight into the colossal doors of rock. To his surprise, they swung open with ease, as if they were made of air. Behind them was a huge chamber out of which radiated intense light, as brilliant as sunshine, and the pungent aroma of sulfur. They hit the warrior hard in the face. He closed his eyes for a moment and gagged at the fumes.

"Come," the priest beckoned as he entered.

Dugan complied.

The roof of the grand chamber towered above Dugan. He noticed the brilliant light originated from a small opening in the domed ceiling. Light was also coming from a fire within a large brazier, which Dugan estimated was about thirty feet in diameter. It was crafted of bronze, and worked through with swirling designs and images, which Dugan assumed to be heroes of sort of their faith.

It was the only decorative item in the room. The ceiling and walls had been blackened by the giant flame, hiding any past adornment that might have once been there. The heat from the bonfire was so concentrated within the chamber, though Dugan could no longer feel it, waves of hot air distortied his vision.

"Go and sit on the chair," the priest motioned to a plain, bronze, high-backed chair stationed against one of the three legs of the great brazier.

Dugan sat down as the priest gathered up a smaller basin, also made of bronze. The old priest spoke a few strange, inaudible words over it, and a tongue of flame from the brazier shot out ,landing in the basin, igniting a fire all its own.

"Let us begin then," the priest spoke as he approached Dugan. He placed the warrior's sword beside the second leg of the brazier, the basin by the third leg, and began to pray:

"Oh, Flame Lord, great Mover of the Sun, hear your servant! Through the shared fire of your power, oh Lord of Volcanoes, grant me the insight into this man's fate. Though he has your mark already upon him, and his fate is already decreed, but yet he wishes to petition you great Rheminas. "Bless my eyes so they may see with the spiritual sight, oh god of revenge. Let me share with him your decrees."

The priest picked up to the burning basin, and stared deeply into its contents. His eyes became glassy, and his face lost all expression as flames of orange and yellow danced within the bowl. Wisps of smoke floated out of the basin, taking on strange forms as they waltzed through the warm air currents. Dugan found his eyes turning the amorphous clouds of smoke coming from the basin into images of friends and foes he had made during his years in the arena.

The fire was another matter entirely. It appeared the priest was intent upon his viewing of it as his eyes were as smooth as ice. They reflected the images he saw in their dark pools.

"What is this?" There was fear growing on the priest's face.

"What-"

"I can see your fate unfolding before my very eyes," the priest looked up at the Telborian, confused and a little worried by the development.

"I thought you said Remani can't peer into the future." Dugan was now growing concerned over the priest's anxious manner.

"We can't. This..." the priest peered again into the flames with vexed wonder...this is something all together different..."

After moments of tense silence, where the priest seemed hypnotized by the flame, Dugan spoke again. "What is happening?"

The priest looked up into the eyes of the gladiator with a wild expression made all the more unsettling by the flickering flame tossing shadow and light around his face.

"I don't know." The preist's voice was a low whisper.

"Well if you can see my fate can you tell me it at least?" Dugan pressed.

The priest nodded slowly, then hesitantly returned to his fire gazing.

"You shall live a life filled with passions and dangers; a warrior's life indeed." Though the priest's voice had gained some strength it was still shaken.

"Is it a long life?" Dugan moved to the edge of the bronze chair.

The preist shook his head. "That, I cannot see."

"Then what can you tell me will occur to me?" Dugan had moved to the very edge of the chair.

"I see you living as a free man. The mission you are on now...you shall survive. I see a powerful figure who brings death with him everywhere he goes. You and he are destined to meet twice before your end. Ah...Rheminas preserve me! How is it possible I can be seeing all this?" The priest peered more deeply into the basin, the flames wildly illuminated his face, harshly outlining his sharp features.

"I sense another presense here with us – oh, Rheminas preserve your servant.!" The priest tried to calm himself as best he could before he continued. "I now see your last moments. No matter the road you chose, they all lead to the same spot, just the dates change their form. You shall know suffering and sorrow - and feel the lash of indignity upon you once more, like splinters in your back."

"What of my spirit?" Dugan exclaimed as he nearly leapt off the chair.

"Your spirit goes to Rheminas' hand. There you will spend eternity." The priest looked up at Dugan, sweat now trickling down his brow.

"Is there no way out of that fate?" Dugan's heart sank.

"You have made a promise to a god; it cannot be broken," the priest sat back from the flames now, resting a bit as he did so from the ordeal.

"What if I were to seek out another divine patron higher than Rheminas?" Dugan tried his best at overpowering the disappointment in his voice. "Could they free me?" There had to be hope somewhere, he wouldn't give up just yet.

"Why do you insult the god in his own temple? Few, if any would touch the property of another god." The priest took a good, hard look into Dugan's eyes. "But you are a special case, aren't you? That wasn't the work of Rheminas, but some other power showing me your fate. What trickery are you trying to play?" The priest's eyes shrunk to slivers of slit flesh.

"I don't know what you're talking about!" Dugan had started to grow restless at the priest's accusations.

"Possibly…but possibly not either," the priest's brow wrinkled. "This whole matter is very vexing to me as are you and the presence I feel is still here polluting the temple of our great god.

"We have finished with your concerns, for I have a deep need to ponder this matter further in prayerful mediation." The priest was curt.

"Even if what you told me was true - what good is it if I am already fated to die in pain, and spend the afterlife with Rheminas? I traded one slavery for another."

"Some might think you blessed, Dugan. I included." The priest made a motion with his hand over the basin extinguishing the flame. "I believe the afterlife to be a paradise, and those who love Rheminas above all other gods."

"And what about those who don't love him?" the Telborian's words were crestfallen.

"Dugan," the priest replied, "You have been hand chosen by Rheminas himself. Surely you are more important than even you realize?"

Dugan now stood, making ready to leave as he could see he wasn't going to get much more from the priest and the recent episode he had just experienced did indeed leave him very troubled. "How did you known about my coming here?"

"Rheminas told me. Even though you reject him, he holds out his hand toward you. Truly you are destined to do great things in his service. I wish I could be as blessed as you. If you want peace, warrior, look to his hand. Fear not its warm embrace. Relish it and use it to nurture you and your ultimate goals. Learn to enjoy your freedom under his rays. Don't squander such a precious gift."

Dugan look at the great brazier behind him. "If this is being blessed, then I'm living in the Abyss."

"Our time really is now passed. I've beared this intolerable presence who came in with you long enough and can tell you no more for you have stopped listening to the truth." The priest motioned to the open door, "Please leave the same way you came."

Sullenly Dugan walked out of the inner chamber. He had come to the shrine looking for hope, and hadn't found it. Or had he? The priest never said the gods would not listen to his plea for release from the foolish pact he'd made with Rheminas. Perhaps there was still a way to get out of it, with another god's help.

Cadrissa had given him a brief introduction into the Tralodroen Pantheon. Maybe one of them might hold sympathy for his case, but who could he ask? And how? That was the question. He also wondered what power had made itself known through the priest of Rheminas to give him his fate. Was it Saredhel or someone else? Was this power an ally or neutral to the Telborian's plight though?

It was another matter to ponder when he could. For now he was certain he wouldn't accept his destiny. There had to be other ways - and with them…hope.

Dugan was so lost in this thoughts when he left the temple that he didn't notice a fair-looking apparition of a woman, cloaked in white light and wisps of fiery red hair. She watched him plod off back into the more congested areas of Elandor.

Chapter 16

Lecherous looking men smelling of oily sweat and manure belched loudly as they lustfully eyed Clara while she stood at the bar in the Sea Otter. She felt their eyes move over her body, like greasy palms touching her skin, and shuddered at their thoughts.

The Sea Otter was a good-size tavern and inn that served as a second home to many sea merchants and rogues of the waves. It had a fair selection of folks, most of them the lower class citizens of the area. They gathered for affordable food, and decent drinks. Mostly though, it was a port of landing for many nautical naves, traders and fishermen. As evening came, the room seemed to possess a greater collection of the uncouth members of the sailing community, and the atmosphere suffered for it.

Clara was beginning to think Gilban maliciously enjoyed sending her, and those they had gathered to colorful places, such as The Sea Otter. Thinking of him, she turned to view the old elf, who was leaning on the counter beside her. His face was tanned and haggard from their oversea journey, but his countenance was fierce and determined. Clara knew it would take a lot to push the priest of Saredhel into the wayside of exhaustion, though she also knew he was nearing its borders.

The two elves settled into the tavern after a brief walk around the city. They had wandered the busy areas of commerce and the bustling docks, keeping close to the shadows and watching for trouble. Clara wanted to be sure they were safe when they rested for the night.

It was a concern Gilban didn't share. His mind seemed elsewhere; his body was content and at ease. Clara wasn't so optimistic. When the sky started to darken, the two had headed for the Sea Otter to wait for the others, but with each passing hour their patience wore thin. Clara prayed the others hadn't wandered off, leaving her and Gilban high and dry. She had some faith in them, but not much. Most of her faith lay in Gilban. He was the glue holding everything together. She had a bit more confidence in Vinder and Cadrissa, but Dugan still could have changed his mind now that he was free of Colloni. Could have - but she doubted he would, given his recent actions following his healing with Gilban.

Clara thought herself a good judge of character, and believed Dugan, along with the others, would be walking into the Sea Otter shortly.

"Are they here yet?" Gilban asked.

"No. I don't see them," she looked around the room, and caught glimpses of some of the men sucking in their ale guts, doing their best to make themselves alluring. One obese mongrel with an inch of sea grit in his hair ran his tongue lustfully across his cracked lips at her. Clara wanted to gag.

Though Clara had taken down her hood in the freer land of Elandor, her looks were now attracting a different kind of attention, though it was just as unfavorable.

"I think I'll go get some air. Are you going to be okay?" She rose up from her seat, doing her best to ignore the jeers.

"Have no fear for me, enjoy your walk," suddenly Gilban's head twitched slightly, his eyes tightened, and his face scrunched into a maze of wrinkles.

What is it? Are you okay?" concern was thick in her voice.

"Perhaps I will go with you after all. It seems the atmosphere in here is not welcoming to those of better senses," the priest added in a dry, low tone.

Clara smiled, "Here, take my arm, it'll be faster."

"That it will," Gilban muttered to himself. "That it will."

As they exited the inn, two extremely drunk and cruel-looking ruffians, their eyes alight with dark mischief, wiped ale foam from their lips, and motioned to their comrades. A group of ten similar-looking men got up, and followed the first two out the door. As they left, the other patrons seemed to breathe a sigh of relief, and the mood of the tavern lightened.

Clara and Gilban walked down to the main street from the alley where the tavern faced. They found a bench they could rest on while Clara kept an eye on the road for the rest of the group. The sun was setting in the murky sky overhead, like a blazing coal in cold, gray ash.

"Do you see them yet?" The priest's eyes were lost amid the scenery.

"No. All I see are dock workers, ships' crew and townsfolk. They'd better get here soon. We have a lot to discuss tonight before they get rested for tomorrow." Clara's eyes were more purposed in their search.

"They will come back Clara, have faith. I thought you were a better judge of character than that." Gilban exuded a calm soothing her.

"I used to be fairly good, but these are different people from vastly different races and lands. It's one thing to judge a Patrious from a different region than my own, and another to try and make clear the machinations of a human or dwarf from as far east as the world permits," Clara brushed some of her silvery locks out of her eyes.

"Has the sun set yet?" Gilban asked as he leaned against the wooden backrest of the weathered bench.

"Almost," she replied.

"But not quite?" Gilban raised an eyebrow.

"No," Clara stated flatly.

"Then they will be here soon. You will have to learn patience and faith to weather the times ahead, Clara," Gilban grew more comfortable still in his chair.

Clara looked at him in bewilderment, "What do you see now?"

"Nothing. These are things we all must learn if we wish to succeed in life- if you wish to lead. Ah, I hear someone approaching now," he turned his gaze out toward the sound of approaching foot traffic.

Clara turned, ready to reprimand her tardy mercenaries, only to come face to face with the patrons from the Sea Otter Inn who had been leering over her earlier. She would never forget their evil, lined faces carved by sun, surf and notorious actions long molded by their visages into emblems of wickedness.

Clara knew them instantly to be pirates. They had the wild look of mixed blood speaking of Telborian and Celetoric, and even distant Napowese blending with still further foreign and odd mixtures of race. She didn't like the way the gang formed behind the larger men. She also didn't like their numbers. Silently, they stalked the two elves, forming a semi-circle of around them; a wall of muscle and violence.

"Well, what 'ave we 'ere boys?" The big man sneered, massaging his thick, black mustache. His companions laughed as he approached Clara. "Looks to me as if we 'ave a rather fine specimen o' womanhood, eh?"

"Who are you?" Gilban asked, his face suddenly blank.

"Well ol' man, if yer good, were da guys that are goin' ta letcha live," the mongrel man's eyes didn't move from their pawing over Clara with lusty delight.

"Clara, what's going on here?" Gilban inquired as he began to rise from the bench. Before he could fully stand though, he was pushed brutally back by one of the men.

"Sit down ol' man," the shove brought laughter from the drunken band as the elderly elf toppled back down onto the bench with a grunt.

"Gilban, are you okay?" Clara asked in a small and frightened voice.

"Tis you should be worried missy. If ye ain't up ta satisfaction, then ye getta feed the sharks." The lustly smile of whom Clara assumed was the leader of the others deepened. "Be a good girl and everything will be all right."

All Clara could do was play along with the drunken men, hoping she could win some time to think of a way out of the situation. She noticed that though they were armed with cutlass or daggers, half seemed too impaired by over-indulgence in drink to be able to defend themselves against a gnat, let alone a trained fighter.

She was glad she had kept her falchion at her side, not leaving it in her room with her bow in the inn. She doubted if she would ever go anywhere outside her homeland unarmed again too, if this was the way things were, or were going to be wherever she went. Still though, one sword against these odds were not the best to start out with, but there had to be a way out of this - and she could find it.

A plan started to form in her mind.

As she looked at the bench, she saw Gilban was mumbling a prayer to Saredhel, his lips moving silently in worship. She needed to lure the group's leader into a false sense of security, and then strike at him when he least expected it, gaining the advantage.

She waited with tensed muscles.

"That's right, me girl. Nice an' easy, and ya won't get hurt none now," the leader licked his cracked lips.

"She's a pretty one, Jake. I like them eyes," one of the men spoke up.

"Well you can look at 'em later after I finished with her," Jake, their leader, responded.

Clasping hold of Clara's wrist in a tight grip, Jake began to drag her toward him.

Clara looked back at Gilban, but the priest was still praying. Without a rescue in sight, she took the initiative and jabbed her knee into Jake's groin. The hairy man went to his knees groaning in deep-rooted cries of agony. As he wallowed on the ground, the others pulled their cutlasses out from their scabbards.

"Gilban, what are you doing?" Clara shouted as she drew her weapon, and readied herself for the coming attack.

"All has been prepared for, Clara - have faith, and you shall see," said the priest with as much peace and calm as if they were on the bank of some river in the height of summer rather then in the midst of a forthcoming confrontation.

Clara didn't have time to fully understand the priest's cryptic response as the first attacker ran toward her. She easily dodged the blows of his sharp sword, as the drunken swings sliced far from their mark.

"You're going to pay, wench!" The scrawny man cursed, as he took a step back, aiming his cutlass at her once more. He ran toward the elf with it, waving wildly overhead. Just as Clara was about to jump under the swing and knock the footing from him, she heard a loud crack followed by a splash of warmth across her shoulders.

Clara remained crouched on the stone pavement, ready to leap out of harm's way, and make her own swing when the opportunity arose. The attacker stood stiff as a pole, his face a mask of surprise, shock, and horror. A red pool formed beneath him, and a sword stuck through his chest; the point exiting out through the man's heart. The impaled man toppled to the ground like a felled tree as the sword was just as quickly withdrawn.

Surprised, Clara turned to Gilban, but his sightless eyes were directed elsewhere. Following their gaze, she saw a tall figure running up behind the mob. The pack of thugs turned to see where the blade had come from, just as a war cry erupted from behind them.

Those fortunate to turn around quickly saved themselves from certain death by blocking attacks with their weapons. The ones too drunk to move fast enough were either cleaved in two, or had their heads removed from their shoulders.

Dugan charged into the fray, his powerful body raging against the pirates. A bolt of lightning followed him, shooting down from the sky, charring the dock, and two sailors with it. The deafening thunderclap following it sent many of the remaining men to their knees. Cadrissa, her golden robes trailing behind her, came running down the street, a sphere of lightning dancing between her fingers.

Seeing these new arrivals, the pack of pirates broke up into smaller groups to deal with them. Splintered and drunk, the group was in their worst condition yet. They stood no chance against Dugan's heavy fists, and deadly thrusts. Nor did they fare well from Clara's kicks, jabs, and slashing steel - but Cadrissa was in need of aid.

The attackers came upon her as a pack of hyenas. Seeing another woman meeting their fancy, they took to her instantly, grabbing her legs and arms. With her body paralyzed, she was unable to make the proper gestures for most of her spells. Panic, the enemy of all mages, began to seize her. The drooling men began to stroke her golden robe, lust growing in their eyes. She could do little to fight back. She wasn't strong enough to retaliate with brute force, and what spells she could try to bring to mind wouldn't be effective against all of them.

"This one ain't half bad," one commented.

"Quit, you're pushing," a second said.

"I ain't pushing," another responded.

"Well, someone was kicking my leg, aieeee…," one of the men let go of Cadrissa's hand to place both of his own on his bloodied knee. The wounded man looked down saw his attacker. A grinning dwarf with one eye and a gleaming axe, now washed with a faint hint of red.

The others gathered around the mage, turning to see their wounded friend's attacker. Instantly they let go of Cadrissa as they raised their weapons to take on the small warrior.

Two swift swings carved one of Vinder's assailants into chunks of flesh. The second attacker tried to strike Vinder on the face, but the dwarf brought his axe up to block the blow, severing his enemy's sword in half in the process. The pirate, now weaponless, took off toward the docks. So intent was he on escaping with his life the ruffian ran unaware into another blade waiting for him.

The seaman's limp body fell to the ground as Rowan pulled his blade from the corpse. The Knight of Valkoria had been empowered by a cause and began charging into the brawl in the street before him.

Clara managed to clear a path for herself as she fought tooth and nail with the men who had surrounded her. Jake had gotten up several times again, only to have his groin explode in pain once more at the booted toe of the elven warrioress. Clara moved stealthy through the hole she crafted with strong swordplay and looked to Gilban momentarily. Amazingly, he still sat calmly on the bench, with no sign of attackers around him. She'd never understand the workings of his mind, nor of how his life was favored by his goddess. She couldn't dwell on such thoughts now as she needed her full strength of mind for the purpose at hand.

Clara backed up from the chaos of the fight right into Rowan, who was valiantly parrying the drunken swings of another thug.

He saw Clara, shook his head, then returned to the fight.

"Surrender or be slain," Rowan said.

The pirate Rowan had addressed looked around. Most of his comrades had been subdued or killed. Only two of the original band remained standing.

"Let's get out of here!" he shouted as they all dropped their weapons and ran off into the growing darkness.

Each of the mercenaries watched them run for a moment more, and then relaxed their guard content upon their victory.

"Gilban, you could have helped us," Clara panted as she dropped herself onto the bench beside the elf.

"Who's to say I didn't?" The old priest smiled. "Though I must say you all worked well as a team, and it seems like we picked up another traveler."

Clara looked at the person who had helped in the fight. He was a slender youth with well-developed muscles who, from the way he wielded his sword, obviously was skilled in its uses.

He was human, with a soft, yet commanding face and deep blue eyes. His reddish-brown hair was cut short, and his skin was pale, as though he was suffering from some sickness.

Instantly, Clara realized he was a Nordican-one of the fabled Ice Warriors. Tales told lived off snow and ice and fought for many strange causes, and for the simple out-pouring of blood.

Growing up, she had been told tales of the inhabitants of the Northlands, but never had she actually seen one in person, and never so far south as Talatheal. This young man was just a tiny bit shorter than Dugan, she noted, and he wore new-looking leather armor, imprinted with the design of a great cat about to pounce.

"Who are you?" Dugan made his way to the new-comer.

"Rowan Cortak, Knight of Valkoria," Rowan responded proudly in Telborous, staying with the tongue for the rest of the conversation.

"Valkorian Knight?" Dugan questioned. "Why did you join the fight?"

"It looked as if you needed my help, and I've sworn by Panthor to aid humans where I could."

"Panthor? Never heard of him," Dugan frowned slightly at the mention of the knight's diety.

"I have - and he's a she," Clara now joined them. "It's said in the frozen lands where you live, you sacrifice victims of past raids to her in dark and terrible ceremonies. She is a bitter and cruel goddess, demanding of her peoples, and never satisfied."

Gilban smiled to himself as he listened quietly to the conversation. Fate was taking root, the final pieces of his grand vision were becoming clear, and now he saw the way clearer than before.

"You describe some of the dark gods of the Nordic tribes well, elf," Rowan said the last word of the sentence coldly.

"Panthor, however, is a giving and powerful goddess. She has led us to countless victories, and blessed humanity with continued progress in all we do. Without her, there would be no human civilization, and humanity would be devoured by its enemies."

Clara blushed for no reason, and suddenly her hands were cold and clammy. Unable to think straight, she began to declare herself sick or suffering the aftereffects of the recent fight. After a moment, though, the feeling left, her body calming down once more.

"Forgive me, Rowan." Clara's tone was conciliatory, "I meant no disrespect. I must have been misinformed about your ways. I thank you for saving me and Gilban from those cutthroats."

"We would have had them in a few more moments," Vinder spoke up from the remains of a fallen victim he was picking over with all the delicacy of a vulture. He had already amassed a good handful of coins and odd trinkets and busied himself stuffing them into his pockets.

"A dwarf!" Rowan exclaimed. "I haven't seen your kind often enough here! In my homeland, they live among the frozen hills, and snow-capped mountains. They are hearty and strong, earning the respect of many of my brothers. To have fought alongside you, sir, is a great honor!"

"Well, that's a start, I suppose," the dwarf grumbled as he continued to rummage the slain pirates.

Rowan smiled widely, and laughed a deep, resounding laugh echoing in the street. "You speak as a true Nordican. Truly you have some Nordic blood somewhere in your line," the youth joked.

"It took you long enough to get here!" Gilban spoke up, turning his sightless eyes toward the youth, interrupting the conversation, and drawing all gathered to the blind priest.

"I didn't know how long we were going to have to wait here for you!"

"Who are you?" Rowan asked as he stared at the blind elf, an expression of pity and confusion played across his face.

"My name is Gilban. I am a priest of Saredhel. You have probably never heard of her, as her influence reaches only as far as the western lands, with a few temples to the east and south. You, Rowan, are the last person needed to complete our task."

"What are you talking about?" Clara asked Gilban.

"Yeah, Gilban, what are you talking about?" Dugan demanded. The others had similar faces of questioned understanding as they all listed to the seer.

"I have had a vision in which the Republic of Colloni shall once again become a vast empire." Gilban spoke with an authority that nonoe felt comfortable doubting. They shall come to power when they come across information long hidden in a long forgotten city. You, and the others gathered here, have been destined to work together to thwart the elves by getting to the information first."

Rowan bowed his head respectively to the elder elf, for he had been raised to show respect to his elders, even though he found parts of his mind mocking the frail elf's weak body and blindness.

"I must humbly decline, Gilban. I am already committed to a quest of my own. I have been sent to discover an ancient city jus-," Rowan stopped and looked at Clara, straight into her sapphire eyes. "You follow the same quest I do? How can this be? Are you enemies of humanity? Are you plotting with the Elven Republic to bring about humanity's destruction?"

"Calm down kid, you're starting to go berserk," Dugan laid his hand on Rowan's shoulder. "I'm not doing this task for the purpose of saving or destroying humanity, that's for sure."

"What for then?" Rowan wondered what could be more nobler a purpose.

"Freedom," came Dugan's hearty reply.

"So you're a slave of these elves then, and you have to do their bidding until they release you? Have no fear, I shall save you. Step behind me and I'll-" Rowan raised his sword, and moved closer to Dugan as if to defend him from the very folk who the knight had recently aided.

"Are you stupid, lad?" Vinder shouted as he walked closer to the gathering. His pockets and bags wider than when they first began the fight. "Haven't you been listening? We seek the same quest."

"Trust me, Rowan," Gilban grabbed the Nordican's attention once again. "You are destined to join us in our mission, for our two quests are one in the same. If humanity is to suffer, it will do so under the lash of the Elyelmic Empire."

"Panthor would never deceive me," Rowan started to mull over his thoughts with his mouth. "She only delegates tasks to her knights if she believes they can accomplish them - and I was sent alone for this mission. However, Panthor might have thought I needed help...but then she would have sent word to me..."

The confusion was intense in the knight's head. What should he do? Was this his goddess' will? Was this her way of adding him, even though he had lost his funding to undertake the mission he'd been given? Was this his second chance?

"Are you with us or not, lad?" Vinder's tone was gruff and hurried. "Make up your mind quickly as there is bound to be someone coming to investigate the commotion. And I, for one, don't want to spend the night in jail."

Rowan thought about the Code of Panthor. Listing its edicts in his mind, he pondered their implications on his current situation. If none of the rules were broken, he would be safe to assume it was Panthor's will he could go along with them. If one rule was broken, then he would set out on his own once more. It was a practical decision based on solid Nordic logic.

And so he went over the code: never attack, always defend; evil should be destroyed only if it cannot be saved; help your neighbors; strive to protect, not to control; be faithful to your causes, your word is your bond; practice control in all things; never be a braggart, humility is the finer strength. He didn't see any harm to the code, and took it as a favorable option.

"It would seem to be of mutual benefit if I joined you," Rowan vocalized his decision.

"Good!" Gilban smiled to himself. "We must be on our way. Time is fleeting, and the hour of Tralodren's darkness fast approaches."

Gilban took up a brisk walk, and trotted off down the road, the others were forced to run to keep up with him.

"Gilban!" Clara panted as she ran beside the prophet. "The vision you had on the boat, was he the one you just spoke of? Did you foresee Rowan joining our party then?"

"That, and much more. For a seed has been sown into the belly of present to later grow and develop into a strange, and beautiful plant of complex design."

The priest walked on as Clara slowed slightly, her head lost in thought. "Great," she said. Shaking her head with confusion, but faith in Gilban still intact, she darted after the priest.

The others were quickly on her heels as the procession traveled on toward the Sea Otter Inn.

Chapter 17

Kylor rubbed his tired eyes, and searched the timeworn tome before him. The book had been written long before the present day by strange and alien hands. The yellowed pages were scratched with a script of black hue long since been corrupted by time, and nearly forgotten - save by a select few. In their purest form, the words themselves had power enough to level cities or erect towers of staggering might from the earth itself, but over the eons they had fallen into disuse; pronunciation lost.

The dwindling power of those who knew how to read it had faded over time, only recently rediscovered by a small collection of people, of whom Kylor was a member. This archaic language, like any other ancient or modern tongue, didn't have the power to do much of anything but convey an expression or idea. When the Dranors had spoken such things, because of their very nature, the words held much power. Now, with the Ancients long-since faded from Tralodren, and only a fraction of that great lineage existing in a small percentage of mortalkind, it wasn't enough to have the nature of the Dranors, and to know the words to speak. Now, the modern-day mage required the loaned power of other items of rare and mysterious origins to act as supplemental components in spells.

This was the fate of magic in Tralodren. It was a constantly degrading art form needing to be propped up with each passing generation as more of its basic understanding was lost and forgotten. Further complicating matters was the Dranoric lineage which those who called themselves mages derived their abilities, further diluted with each new generation. If not for the efforts of the Tarsu, who had been reformed from centuries of absence, the ability to wield mystical power might be very well a totally forgotten thing left only in the books of legends and myths.

Many wizards had strived to master the corrupted tongue of the Ancients, to gain its powers for themselves, apart from the aid of Tarsu too. Kylor was not very different from these predecessors and peers. He studied the arcane arts in hope of a better insight into the workings of the world in seclusion. It was with this acquired insight he hoped to gain more power than was humanly possible - to be remembered for all time as the first Wizard King on Tralodren since their fall and destruction during the Wars of Magic and Divine Vindication almost a thousand years ago.

Kylor had become convinced, over the last year of studying the ancient blue column in the abandoned temple, it was the key to his glorious ascension. He knew if he could just properly decipher the runes, they would unleash their power for him. It was the waiting for him but the constant experimentation was taxing upon him, nearly driving him mad. This last attempt with that elf had been a vexing experience beyond compare, as that had been the last elf the hobgoblins had. Now he would have to revert back to the hobgoblins - and the dark mage knew that wouldn't be a winning position for very long. He had to be clever about his next move if he wanted to gain the secrets the blue column held.

"Relton, come here," Kylor snarled.

A large toad came out of the shadows. It had a bulbous body about one foot in diameter, and a wart-covered hide. It glistened a murky green in the torchlight, reflecting in the blood-red eyes of the creature.

What is it, master? Relton responded telepathically to the wizard.

"I must find out why my spell failed again."

Perhaps it was a simple miscasting. He hopped toward the podium where the dark mage stood in study.

"No. The words are too ingrained in my memory and heart to be fouled up by such a simple error as that. What have you discovered?"

I have found numerous references to the device in your collection of books. They call it the 'Transducer of Souls' He had neared the base of the podium and looked up at the tall spire of wood before him.

"That much I already knew, anything else?" The dark mage's annoyance churning over his words.

Relton ignored Kylor's anger as he began to climb up the Podium. *Yes. It seems it was constructed hastily during a great civil uprising toward the end of this city's existence. Apparently they were never really able to get all the flaws out before the inhabitants who created it were destroyed.* The toad's webbed feet stuck to the wood like a fly or small lizard's.

"So what are you telling me, Relton?" Kylor asked impatiently as he started to pace around the podium.

I am simply pointing out perhaps you know all that can be learned from the device, as it was never perfect to begin with. Relton rapidly climbed the podium to reach the large book on its flat shelf.

"But then what is it's true purpose? It speaks in riddles, and the books hint at it being a device granting immense power to its possessor. What is this granted power, and how can I attain it?" The mage stopped to peer over the text of the book as the toad hopped on top.

286

Of that, I am not certain. The authors seemed to assume the information they discussed was common knowledge to the reader. If it is the case, then maybe the answer is so simple it stares us right in the face.

"Perhaps," Kylor walked to the millennia-old stone desk littered with books of varying age and size. All of them were open to different pages of interest.

"Perhaps the answer is not in its mastery, but by what it granted a race who was powerful to begin with. The Ancients were akin to gods in legends. What would they then have to gain by such a device, eh Relton?" Kylor peered down at the bloated toad.

An interesting question master. Relton hopped across the large book on top the podium, taking a page with his sticky feet in the process so as to turn to a new section.

"Yes, and until we answer it, I am going to have to play up to those hobgoblins." A deep scowl marred the dark mage's face. "Already I grow sick of their faces and piggish language. I long to destroy them all out of sheer annoyance."

It would be your right, master. The red, unnatural eyes of the toad hungrily devoured the text before it.

"Still, I am not without my methods of protection, now am I?" He pulled a golden medallion out of the folds of his robes, and greedily ran his fingers over the raised scrollwork on its surface. It had the ability to hold back many a death blow in the past for its owner. Many men and fouler creatures had sought to introduce Kylor to Asorlok, and had failed, as their weapons had bounced off Kylor's flesh as if it were hardened iron.

Kylor had found the trinket in a ruin, not far from his homeland in Belda-thal. It had lain amongst the crumbled rubble of an archaic tower destroyed in the Divine Vindication. Rumors said it was once the tower of a Wizard King.

Kylor, drawn to the potential of power within the fallen tower as a moth to a flame, had discovered the golden item after hours of rigorous climbing over the ancient battlements and rocky terrain covering the site. How it had survived the centuries and years of looting from such bygone times as the Wars of Spoils, he didn't know. It took years of study and sacrifice, but in the end, he had found the secret of its charm and set up the pace by which he would live the rest of his life - on a quest for power.

"Relton, I shall be with the artifact again. Continue to look for information to aid me. I will be back shortly." Relton watched the power-crazed wizard leave. He continued to use his webbed feet to turn some more pages, stopping on an old diagram of the cylindrical artifact, maddening Kylor's thoughts.

The toad's face spread out into a disturbing, human-like grin.

Behind the toad, a shadowy, transparent form observed all that transpired.

Relton didn't notice this presence even as two twin blue flames shot up from the form's face to reveal a bare skull before the flickering figure faded away completely.

Chapter 18

"**I** think it would be much faster if we traveled around of the Marshes of Gondad. We could circle around them and cut our time in half, getting to Takta Lu Lama that much sooner. Time is of the essence," Rowan spoke as he drained his goblet of its hearty mead.

The old dwarf eyed him stoically. "For someone who just joined our company, ya sure have a low opinion of the leaders in this group who set this whole plan up. They've done better research about the location and terrain than any of us. I say we stick with the plan and go through the marshes."

"But we'd lose two, maybe three days if we -" Rowan was cut short by Cadrissa.

"Rowan, Gilban and Clara understand your need for speed, but we have to exercise caution if we wish to remain safe and undetected by other forces likely to be in competition with us, and discover the secrets of the ruins."

"You're right," Dugan spoke up as he wiped greasy meat drippings from his lips, waving a leg of lamb he had half-devoured as he did so for emphasis. "The marshes are the best bet if you want surprise as an ally. The elves will avoid them. They don't like 'em; draining them, and avoiding such places when they can. They'd never dream of going through them, and so we'll be able to get the drop on them in the end, should they beat us to the ruins."

Gilban sat solemnly as he had done for the last few hours. He'd quietly listened to the conversation around the table, which had stemmed from a discussion about travel arrangements, and had risen to full-fledged arguments. Clara spied at the old elf with a tired look.

This had gone on far too long.

Both Gilban and Clara had grown sick of the argument between the group members. After fighting off the seamen, they had returned to their lodgings at the Sea Otter, finding most of the darker element of the inn now gone, and sat around a large table to order food and drink. While they ate, they had discussed the upcoming journey into Takta Lu Lama. The conversation quickly turned into a dispute when Rowan proposed against the idea of traveling around the marshes to lessen the time to complete his mission. This idea had been opposed by Dugan, which had caused the others to quickly choose sides. It was a fruitless venture, wasting everyone's time.

"This is getting us nowhere, Gilban," Clara whispered to the priest.

"Don't be so sure, Clara," he returned in a whispered breath as well.

"But how will we get there? This arguing has lasted long enough. We have to be on the road by tomorrow morning if we want to make any progress," Clara had allowed some concern into her voice.

"Maybe it is time to start acting like a leader," Gilban turned his blank eyes to Clara. She cringed when he did so as his words hit her deeper than she expected.

"Maybe," she mumbled as she turned toward the bickering group. She knew the old elf was right though. Someone had to take charge. While Clara still assumed that

Gilban was the leader of this whole venture, and would have loved to have him step into a stronger leadership role, she knew he wasn't going to make that move. It was her time to step up to the task, or face the mob rule of her assembled mercenaries.

Taking a deep breath, she prepared herself for what needed to be done.

"Listen up!" Clara almost shouted. The table stopped their squabbling and turned toward her with startled looks upon their faces. "We don't have time for this childish behavior! The plan was to go through the marsh and that is what we will do. For those of you who don't like the idea; too bad! This arrangement was made before any of you signed on, and was not meant to be improved upon by those who were hired to do it, and who have little or no knowledge of the terrain.

"Tomorrow we're going to get the rest of our supplies and horses from one of our contacts, and then we set off to the jungle. Now finish your meals, and get some sleep. It'll be a long day on the trail."

The group had remained silent as Clara spoke, but she noticed during her speech, Rowan's left eye twitched spastically. She paid it little mind until the Nordican youth spoke up.

"You want us to waste so much time? I tell you the best way is around the swamp!" Rowan spoke with a mixture of a whine and irritated growl.

"The matter is closed, Rowan. Don't try my patience, and make me regret taking you into this group. Just make sure you're ready for tomorrow," Clara stood firm before the knight. "If you still wish to join us." Then, without another word, Clara got up from the table and headed for the flight of stairs to her room. The others sat in humiliated silence, eating the rest of their food. Gilban smiled.

"I say it's about time she took charge around here!" Vinder spoke up as his beard dripped malted ale onto his lap. "I once said the same thing to a fellow dwarf some fifty years ago. The men were pathetic without his leadership; only he didn't seem to have the spine for it 'til the end. It's good to see that Clara does."

"So you agree with her, then?" Rowan seemed a bit hurt by Vinder's declaration.

"Of course he does," Cadrissa answered. "None of us would be here if we didn't believe in her."

"Or her gold," The dwarf hefted the rest of his drink to his mouth.

"I think it's time for me to retire," Gilban groaned as he rose from the table, using his staff as a crutch for his stooping body.

"So who gives you your orders?" Rowan asked, his attention drawn to the wizened figure.

Gilban smiled serenely.

"Clara and I receive our orders from the Elucidator of the Republic of Rexatious. However, I grow tired and must rest for the journey that lies ahead of us tomorrow. Excuse me." Gilban left the table and ascended the stairs, stepping in rhythm to his staff strikes on the wooden planks amazingly making his way both to and up the flight of steps without any difficulty at all.

"So you're all going to follow a blind elf are you?" Rowan said as he rose from the table.

"That blind elf has more insight than ten able-bodied leaders," Vinder growled. "A boy should listen to the words of his elders; it might give him some much-needed wisdom."

"A boy? I will have you know, dwarf, I am a Knight of Valkoria, newly-pledged, but a Nordic man all the same!"

"Hmph," Vinder puffed through calloused lips.

Rowan shot up from the table, and stormed up the stairs.

Dugan watched him with a sideways glance. After the youth had stormed the stairs he too got up. "I've stuffed myself too full already. I guess I have to take this new freedom in stages till I get used to it. See you tomorrow."

Cadrissa and Vinder gave him a passing nod.

As the Telborian left, and after a long moment of silence, Vinder turned to Cadrissa. "So, what do you hope to gain from coming on this mission?"

"What do you mean?" Cadrissa's face was washed in innocence.

"It's a simple question," Vinder said with a slight twinkle in his eye.

"I could ask the same of you, Vinder. I thought we had a similar discussion on the boat.

"What makes you think by helping Clara and Gilban I'm fulfilling some secret goal? I simply seek knowledge" the innocence stayed about the mage's visage.

"Rubbish! We all took this task on to gain something," barked Vinder. "That kid, Rowan, he's on some mission for his knighthood. Probably wants to gain prestige and honor in the bargain; we're just a means to that end for him. Dugan joined the group for the purpose of getting safe passage out of Colloni, and freedom."

"Oh," Cadrissa's eyes fluttered about the table as she drank the rest of her wine, her silky black locks catching the lamplight as she tilted her head back to drain the last drops from the wooden goblet. "I suppose this is where I tell you about the marvelous scheme of mine to use this endeavor as a stepping stone to bigger and better things? Like becoming a Wizard Queen?"

"A civilized person would," Vinder gnawed on a heel of crusty bread.

"And you count me as civilized?" Cadrissa's eyebrows lifted with her heavy sarcasm.

"They found you in a civil enough place," retorted Vinder.

Cadrissa smirked. "Haven is far from civilized, Vinder. The people there may act enlightened and behave like refined people, but trust me, they are far from it."

"Then what were you doing there?" Vinder swallowed the dry bread and washed it down with a swig of ale he grabbed from Dugan's mug.

"Knowledge," Cadrissa replied curtly. "Haven, though it is rampant with criminals and degenerates, has a very large and well-admired academy of the arcane arts."

Vinder chuckled, spraying crumbs of bread onto his beard.

"You mean you were nothing more than a schoolgirl? Clara brought a lassie fresh out of school with us?"

"Dolt! Do you think wizards just understand their spells and abilities instantly?" Cadrissa frowned. "All wizards, no matter how great, are students first! The arcane arts require constant endeavor of feverish study. The simplest misunderstanding, or most minute of errors, can hinder mages for the rest of their lives."

"So you learned yer trade, eh? As a cooper or smith learns his," Vinder looked her over with his lone eye.

"I did, Cadrissa stated flatly. And still I am learning. It is a neverending process. It comes after hard work and study, much harder than the common thievery you practice."

Vinder's eye grew wide for a moment, like a frightened doe who knows its life was soon to end, then quickly squinted down hard in a surge of honor born rage.

"Are you calling me a thief?"

"If dwarves consider robbing the dead thievery," Cadrissa pertly replied, "then yes."

"How can you make such wild accusations?" Vinder's face became flustered.

"Oh come now Vinder, even Gilban could see you looting the dead of their possessions after we dispatched them. You accuse me of foolish ambition, and I could accuse you of taking this mission on to loot and pillage," Cadrissa spat back.

Vinder then sat silently for a moment. His eye dropped, and lost its fire. His head hung low, and his chest sunk inward. He took on the appearance of a slouching bag of flour.

The old dwarf smiled as his head raised slightly to look at her soft face. "My mercenary activities don't always pay so well, and... I have to make a living with the best I have. Being able to pay my tribute is all that is important to me."

"Tribute?" Cadrissa leaned forward slightly, her eyes dancing with curiosity.

"Yes, tribute. Mountain dwarves who have strayed from their clans are required to make amends to their brothers through tribute. To be welcomed back into Clan Diamant, I have to have a large enough tribute to be accepted by my Konig, or I'll never be able to return there again."

"If this is true Vinder, then why did you leave your clan in the first place? You obviously miss it greatly." A sense of concern was budding in the mage.

The dwarf went silent. His eye became distant, looking upon some far-away scene no one else could see. Even his gray-tinted skin developed a weaker, light gray pallor to it. After a few moments, Vinder turned to Cadrissa with a downcast face.

"Dwarves are really one race. Some dwarves and most of the rest of the world see us as two races. This is because some of us live in the hills, and others live in the mountains. Those who live in the hills are often more open to strangers, and other races. They typically are the dwarves who everyone has seen wandering the world.

"Those who live in the mountains, such as my clan, don't leave. Tradition demands us to be strong and self-reliant, with no need for the outside races in our lives. I, like some youths before me, grew curious of the outside world. I cared little for the beauty of the mountains in which we lived, or of our past history. I found a love for humans and their use of weapons. Warfare then caught my eye. I left my home, my clan, and my people, to learn the ways of a warrior, and the world outside my clan.

"I was branded an exile from the clan, and a disgrace to my heritage. They deemed me less than a dwarf, and forbade me to return."

"Yet you strive to return," Cadrissa countered.

At this the dwarf's eye lowered. "Aye. I wish to return, and do one last thing to regain my honor."

"What's that? The tribute? It sounds to me as though they will never take you back," Cadrissa's curiosity mixed with her growing sympathy for the dwarf.

Vinder raised his gaze. "The tribute is for the clan but the petition for forgiveness is for my god. If I succeed at both, then I will be welcomed back into the clan once more."

"Are you certain it will work?"

"No. If it doesn't, then I shall simply travel the world, a restless wanderer for the remainder of my life. There is no honor for me in self-sacrifice." The dwarf became sullen as he spoke of his possible fate.

"You mean suicide?" Cadrissa was taken back by such an idea.

"In some instances, it is an honorable way if one is killed through self-sacrifice. To kill oneself in self-pity, though, is considered effeminate, and disgraces not only the dead dwarf, but his entire family. I owe my family at least some honor," Vinder made his answer plainly.

Cadrissa sat back against her chair, and eyed the short figure sitting across from her. The dwarf had suddenly taken on more depth to her. He was no longer simply a hired thug, but another kindred soul trying to struggle with his past and future. More importantly, she could learn much more about the dwarven way of life, and such knowledge filled her with joy. Not only would she gain insight about a warrior, but a whole culture as well.

The one-eyed warrior she once thought was a troublesome, judgmental annoyance had now become something completely different, and very interesting.

"Truly," she said with a thoughtful stare, "you dwarves are fascinating."

Dugan had climbed the stairs quickly after he left his companions below in the dining hall. He wanted to reach Rowan before he had gone too far. He wanted to speak to him while they had some privacy before they took off into the journey the following day.

The young knight might be able to help him out, but he wasn't totally sure at the moment and had to check. Dugan grasped Rowan's leather-covered shoulder. Turning to face the Telborian, the youth's face changed from a scowl, to a pleasant countenance.

"I knew you had a sound enough mind to follow me, Dugan." Rowan smiled. "We're of the same kind, and cannot be lured into a weaker state of reasoning."

Dugan stopped for a second to wade through the knight's statement, and would have asked him for its meaning, had he not been driven by a more persistent need.

"Rowan, can you tell me more about this goddess you serve?" Dugan's manner was warm, even mildly inviting.

Rowan looked at Dugan with a puzzled expression. Had he made a convert already? He'd heard tales how often times the mere presence of someone who belonged to the Knighthood could convert another to his belief.

Before, Rowan had doubted the statement, but now he held it up to religious doctrine. Going back into his training for conversion, which was something he paid little attention to, he tried to work out the details of the question posed.

"So you have an interest in the Patroness of Humans do you? Well, I can speak about her for a short time in my quarters, but then I must get some rest; a well rested warrior is an alert and steadfast opponent." Rowan returned the warmth.

"It's my experience, it's the way the blade is played - not the matter of sleep acquired...but you were saying," the Telborian politely shared his view.

Rowan shook his head as the foreign thought entered his mind. Insight and learning would keep him safe and dutiful all the rest of his days if he remained loyal to Panthor.

"Yes, please come to my room," Rowan bide the Telborian to follow him, "and we can discuss any questions about my goddess, then when you are ready, I can introdu-"

"Hold on," Dugan caught Rowan on the shoulder again before he had resumed climbing the stairs. "You don't think I'm a new convert do you?"

"Well, I assu-" Doubt crept into the brow and corners of Rowan's eyes.

"Well you better stop thinking that. I just want to know about your goddess, that's all. So don't give me the missionary speech about trying to convert cause it just won't work." The warmth was fading fast as Dugan's internal battle began to spill outside himself.

Rowan's face calmed, and his eyes relaxed their vigilant stare.

"All right, but for someone who is so dead-set about knowing a god, you act as though you don't want to really come to know or understand them," Rowan calmed his Nordic blood.

The mighty beast-like claw rested heavily upon Rowan's shoulder.

"I have my reasons and they are my own." Dugan was curt. "All I want from you right now is to tell me of your goddess; I find her to be…interesting. No one down this far south pays her much heed."

Dugan started to climb the stairs with the knight.

Rowan smiled as the duo ascended the stairs as two strong warriors, mighty in battle and prowess. "You'd be surprised, Dugan, just how many do give her worship."

After entering Rowan's room, the two warriors seated themselves around a poorly-crafted table in one corner of the room. A bed of simple design rested against the far wall, underneath a tinted window, and a small chest with a broken lock rested at its foot. Rowan disarmed himself, tossing his sword and armor on the bed.

"Is that so?" Dugan asked Rowan. The two had been discussing Panthor in great depth for the better part of an hour.

"Yes, it's true: Knights of Valkoria are sworn to a code of conduct," answered Rowan.

"And this code makes you into a stronger fighting force?" The Telborian asked.

"It most certainly does. With it we are unified under one common goal, serving one common mistress, Panthor," Rowan took some pride in this feat, for few of his kinsmen could claim it.

"So what is this code then?" Dugan wondered aloud.

Rowan suddenly and unconsciously straightened, developing a greater air of pride and reverence.

"The code of a Knight of Valkoria is this: Never attack, always defend; evil should be destroyed only if it cannot be saved; help your neighbors; strive to protect, not to control; be faithful to your causes, your word is your bond; practice control in all things; never be a braggart, humility is the finer strength."

The Telborian dismissed the code with a chuckle. "It's a fine code for those who can uphold it, but I've found a stronger code is the law of survival. Kill or be killed. Live by this rule and you will live longer!"

"Panthor doesn't promote such things," the knight commented.

"She doesn't? Where then does she stand among the other gods?" Dugan crossed his strong arms over his chest.

Rowan's face grew confused. "What do you mean?"

"I mean, what is her rank in the pantheon? Is she as powerful as I am led to believe Ganatar is, or of lesser strength, as Khuthon or Asorlok? Perhaps she is of the rank of the least powerful gods as the hymns of other gods tell of Causilla, Perlosa and others." Dugan studied the youth's face. Here word be the meat of the answers he sought.

"Panthor is the mightiest goddess we humans have! I don't know the rank of her power or position in the heavenly courts, only she has the highest place reserved in my heart," Rowan struggled with the question and answer. What was the Telborian implying?

"Spoken like a devoted follower," Dugan sighed. "Obviously you can tell me about her history; the powers she has manifested."

"That I can do. It is said long ago, Panthor was a human woman with the skills and abilities of a mighty warrior. She was so strong, she united a fallen people, human beings, into one army to challenge the evils of her day in the Shadow Years. She led them to a great victory, but soon the Telborians forgot her, though we Nordicans honored her with each passing day.

"Because we held her in such esteem, the gods took notice of her, and showed her great favor, extending the right of godhood upon her. From then on, we have celebrated her ascension by spreading her message and love to every human we meet." The knight repeated his learned lessons perfectly.

"I thought I heard once that you believe Panthor created humanity."

"We do," Rowan cheerfully replied.

Dugan grinned. "Then how could she create humanity, when you said she was raised to godhood when she was a human?"

Rowan paused for a moment to reflect on the question.

Dugan simply waited trying to keep his amusement in check.

"That has been addressed by the Knighthood as well." He replied after a few breaths. "Our priests have put forth the idea she was a goddess before she was a human. They claim she formed humanity and then helped lead them before going back to divinity.

Dugan could do nothing but stare blankly at the knight before him. The humor had gone to a form of pity for the young Nordican.

"Dugan?" Rowan leaned forward in slight concern.

"That's a real interesting theory," the Telborian humored the youth.

Rowan didn't appreciate the Telborian's response. "It's not a theory Dugan, it's–"

Dugan leaned across the table to stare directly into the youth's face. "So what really brings you to these ruins? What do you plan to do once you get there?"

Rowan was a bit taken back but the Telborian's assult on his character. "I'm to stop this knowledge hidden in them from falling into elven hands. Same as you."

"Nothing else?" Dugan persisted.

"Nothing else." Rowan answered.

"You must excuse me now.Dugan," it was Rowan's turn to be curt. "It's getting late, and we have a long journey before us tomorrow."

Dugan had heard enough. Someone such as Rowan wouldn't give him the answers he needed. Any devout follower would raise their deity above any others; the Telborian had been told as much already. Passing the evening talk off as folly, he made his way to the door, maybe there were some others he could talk to. Others who were more open minded, and not so clouded by blind allegiance, and acceptance of a standard for all to follow.

"See you in the morning then," Dugan spoke as he halted in the doorway.

Dugan closed the door behind him, and proceeded down the hallway to his own room. Rowan undressed, and laid his clothes on the floor, being careful not to disturb them for the next day's interruption of events to unfold. After some brief prayers he climbed into bed, allowing sleep to overtake him.

Images of light and color played over Rowan's mind. Sounds and smells ushered into him places which could only exist in the world of dreams. Silently, he felt himself being whisked away by soft winds as tender as a lover's caress. Gently, the breezes cradled him across the great expanse of an unknown land laying beneath his floating body.

Suddenly, his eyes passed through a veil of misty clouds illuminated in sliver. His vision impaired, he continued to float peacefully through his dreamscape.

Gradually Rowan began to hear soft laughter drawing him forward in silent wonder. The noise was distant at first, but grew in volume as he drifted closer to his destination. In the universal understanding of dreams, he knew it was the sound of his love. Her voice was like the song of a bird - playful and musical. It also brought with it the gentle and alluring feminine tones Rowan enjoyed.

As the laughter drew nearer, the cloud began to part like a great curtain before him. The scene revealed to him was breath taking, and at the same time hauntingly familiar.

Before him stood Clara, though not as he knew her. As was often the case in dreams, she was something more fantastic than in the normal light of day. She wore a soft, flowing stolla and palla draped over her curves, its diaphanous material just barely covering her supple skin. Her silver hair gleamed in the light like fine strands of polished pewter.

She resided in a peaceful glade, with small, young saplings of trees, a gentle brook running beside her and soft flowing grass the color of emerald. All about her was a soft, silvery blue fog floating through the air, and all around like gauze.

He stepped into the sylvan setting with arms outstretched. Clara lovingly entered into his embrace as he crushed her to him.

Rowan felt compelled to touch the elf maiden - to kiss her and hold her until the days themselves ended. It was then Rowan felt a jab of fear enter his heart, a sense he was about to commit an unnatural act, but the illicitness of it made him crave it all the more. It fired within him a passion driving him to seek Clara's silken lips.

The thrill of battle, and the love for his goddess, was nothing compared to Clara's touch. The wanting grew within Rowan's gut, a strong longing to be with this woman whom he had a strange attachment for. However, a dark specter of doubt plagued him. It spoke of elven treachery, and evils to be worked upon him should he continue on his present course of action.

"My husband," Clara whispered as she ran her fingers across Rowan's face.

Thunderstruck, Rowan stared speechlessly at Clara, all the wind knocked out of him. Passionate thoughts, unknown to Rowan until this moment, flooded every inch of his mind and body. He felt his hands move to Clara's smooth, naked shoulders. He stroked them as though they were delicate gray porcelain washed with a soft gray tint.

He became intoxicated with her aroma, a sweet and fragrant tone of spring breezes and summer blossoms filling him with vigor. He reached out to remove the gauzy material covering her body, but before Rowan touched the fabric, the veil glided over his vision once more, and he was left alone with his troubled thoughts - thoughts telling him his love for an elf was unnatural, filthy. Yet he would never forget Clara's words to him, so strange, so loving: "My husband."

Then, just as swiftly as one dream had left him, another took its place and Rowan sank farther into the land of dreams; a panther's purring, lulling him into a deep sleep.

Chapter 19

ᴅugan pulled on the reigns of his cordovan steed to prevent it from running straight into one of the many pools of sucking mud covering the Marshes of Gondad.

"We're making less progress with the horses than we'd be if we were on foot," He grumbled to Clara who rode five paces ahead of him. The animals were constantly sinking into the muck, their slender legs forced into the mire by their heavy bodies and the weight of the group's supplies.

"We'll continue to use them until we reach more challenging terrain- where we will have to start traveling on foot. The mud will be too deep and dangerous by then, and the marshes will be harder to maneuver horses through," Clara responded.

"A few more hours?" Vinder said in his deep voice. "These beasts won't last a few more feet at the current rate of things." He had sat himself behind Dugan on the same brown horse. His feet barely made it to the middle of the horse's belly. He had almost fallen off twice since they started their journey, but failed to admit it to himself or anyone else, passing it off as a fault of the animal rather than his short legs.

In a normal situation, Vinder would have been given a smaller mount such as a pony or mule, but the animal would not have fared well at all in the marshes- the horses already were suffering challenges. So Vinder had to share Dugan's horse since the dwarf wouldn't be able to control the larger beast as easily as a human or elf could.

The group had been in the swamp for six days after their one week ride from Elandor. This gallop through the grasslands between Elandor and the Marshes of Gondad had been uneventful, but trying none the less on a minor level for many of the mercenaries who grew slightly restless with the endless prairie. To gain as much time as they could, each had pushed their mounts, allowing them very little rest, until the marshes came into view on the seventh day. Only then, did they allow the beasts to walk, knowing how galloping through the marsh, as it turned more soupy than solid, would prove disastrous for both rider and horse. Since then the marshes had grown more wild and expansive; growing stronger in suction and more fetid by the day.

Dugan looked down at the mud once more, and wrinkled his nose in disgust. The vulgar smells released whenever his horse stepped into the slurping mess reminded him of rotting flesh.

During the quiet nights of their camping the Telborian had taken it upon himself to get better acquainted with Gilban, the only one who possessed knowledge who might save him from his fate. Their conversations were often confusing and frustrating. It seemed Gilban didn't know how to speak in anything but riddles. He ran around Dugan's questions without answering a single one to his satisfaction, but rather than growing angry, the Telborian had learned to bide his time and try to listen and apply what the aged elf said.

"Is there a way out of this pact with Rheminas?" Dugan had asked Gilban on the fourth night as the rest were sleeping by the fires glow. The two had stayed awake into the evening, which had become usual in the past evenings that they had been traveling.

"There are doors to all possibilities, but first one must unlock them. Once done, then the choice is made. You have the key, but have yet to find the key hole." Gilban had responded with a flat tone. His white eyes caught the fire's glow and twisted it into a pale parody of itself.

"So what are you telling me? I have the answers right in front of me?" Dugan tried to clear up the priest's cryptic response.

"Often times, Dugan, one does not notice the stalk of corn from the whole field in which it resides," Gilban answered. "We confuse issues and beliefs with what is really possible, claiming it is impossible. You must find for yourself your own answers. Seeking advice is wise, but I cannot answer more than I should for that is the oath of my priesthood. One makes his own destiny, or a destiny is made for him. Those are the rules, Dugan, and that is all I can tell you."

Dugan recalled the conversation with a sore head. He'd made no sense of Gilban's riddles since they had spoken together the other evening. He was going to need more help than Gilban if he wanted to make sense of it all and save himself from his fate. It seemed the other gods wouldn't help, though, as he was already claimed property of Rheminas.

Still he held on tight to any last threads of hope.

"How are you holding up back there?" Dugan called to Vinder, who was managing to keep on his balance by catching himself from falling every other moment, as the horse used all its strength to free itself from the mud.

"Don't worry about me, I can handle myself," Vinder replied gruffly.

Dugan smiled at the dwarf's stubbornness. He could hear the small warrior grunt as he caught himself once more on the horse's haunches as it slipped into another pool of muck.

"Does it get any better than this?" Dugan asked Clara with a sardonic grin.

"Don't complain. When it's time to go on foot, you'll see what a godsend these horses were. We'll be reaching harsher ground soon; the horses won't even be able to safely walk through it," Clara looked on ahead, ducking underneath some vines dangling from a tree limb.

The marsh was littered with low, hanging trees dipping their branches and vines into the soupy soil beneath them. The dreary canopy also filtered out most of the light, preventing the sun from evaporating any rainfall, which was absorbed by the ground and turned into mud.

Rowan paid little mind to the surroundings he was riding through, or even to where his horse was stepping. The only thought racing through his head was his dream. He didn't know what it meant or why he had experienced it. It just felt like he had learned something from it, some kind of greater truth. The dream definitely put Clara in a new light and had awakened him to some powerful emotions increasing with each passing day. He now found himself drawn to the intelligent depths of Clara's sapphire eyes, where before he had only seen the look of veiled wickedness.

Each night, as they camped by the light of a glowing fire, huddled together against the cold of the night, Rowan longed to thread his fingers through Clara's flowing hair and run the back of his hand along her cheeks. He was desperate to tell her how he felt, but something held him back. However, his mannerisms toward her changed, and he found even simple conversation with the elf difficult. He began to sweat every time she was near him and feel unsure of himself around her, as if she were watching his every move judging his every action. Just as these feelings of admiration and attraction flowed through him, darker and baser thoughts and emotions seeped into his mind as well.

These dark thoughts sought to degrade the elven woman, to make her a mere beast, a savage creature beneath his time and interest. She was like all elves: a liar, a cheater and a savage beast. Elven woman were nothing when compared with the fair purity of human woman. So went the echoes in his head as he struggled with his conflicting inner emotions.

Throughout each morning as the party readied to continue the trek, Rowan also pondered his interruption in his clothing, as he was able to do it throughout this journey. It seemed to him, if he read the signs right, very soon something great and profound would occur. Though he couldn't place what it might be, each day brought him the message this event was getting closer. Needless to say, this message left him bewildered. He told no one, but kept it to himself instead.

Could the omen be pertaining to his feelings for Clara? Did she have similar experiences? Did the message mean he would get an answer to his feelings - a resolving of the turmoil inside him? Or was it pertaining to the mission he undertook himself? Were they about to have a powerful encounter or better yet meet with success very soon? The young knight didn't seem to be sure of anything anymore.

As Clara's horse trudged through the soupy mess, she began to wonder if she and Gilban had made the right decision in cutting through the marshes; whether the others weren't right instead. They had discussed the matter thoroughly in Rexatious before they left to pick up the first of their mercenaries, pouring over a map of the countryside.

The older elf had simply stated it was the path to travel, and left it at that. It was only when they began their trek to the ruins Clara was allowed an insight into just how much Gilban knew about the area.

It seemed to her as if Gilban already had intimate knowledge of the land they were to travel, like he'd been there before. He knew every turn to take and which route was the fastest and safest to take to Takta Lu Lama. However, when she questioned him about it, he gave her another cryptic response leaving her more confused about his familiarity with the terrain than when she had first asked him.

Clara looked behind herself to examine the progress of the others, and caught sight of Rowan, who instantly turned his head to the side when she looked at him. He had been acting strange of late, becoming so nervous and jumpy she began to think better of Gilban's decision allowing him to join the party.

He'd seemed good-natured at first, filled with some potential, but now was a little strange and self-absorbed, growing distant and cold. He had yet to speak to her since they had left the inn almost two weeks ago and his avoidance to comment on necessary matters troubled her. 'Often it is the silent traveler who poses the most danger,' an old Patrious saying went, and Clara couldn't agree more, especially since she began noticing him staring at her hauntingly from beneath veiled eyes. Maybe he still held a grudge for them not taking his preferred route.

"Gilban, are you sure we need Rowan?" Clara asked. "He's starting to act a little odd, and I'm concerned about what he might do."

The old elf smiled to himself as he sat behind the elf, his arms wrapped around her waist for balance.

"What concerns you about him? Is he not strong enough for the journey?"

"Yes, he's strong." Clara turned her head to partially take in the priest.

"Is he not well-trained in combat?" The priest continued.

Clara shook her head with her own assessment. "He's no stranger to the blade, no."

"Then what is it troubling you?"

Clara returned her full attention to the terrain before her. "I fear his mind, his intentions and character. It's nice to have another warrior for our cause, but what do we really know about him? And his Knighthood?" The maiden's face fell slightly with the introspection.

Gilban smiled deeply for a moment, exposing the age of his face with a myriad of wrinkles. "I understand your fears, Clara, but the only way to solve your dilemma is to ask him. Otherwise your worry will eat away at your judgment, making you mistrust all those around you. Any other way will lead us to disaster."

"Why can't you ask him? I'd feel safer, if you would," Clara pulled hard on the reigns to unstick her horse's hooves which had landed in a very muddy spot. "Besides, you're the leader of this group."

"Am I?" Gilban snorted in amusement.

Clara spun her head around then to take in a good hard look at the blind priest. "You're the one who got us all together, who had this vision in the first place. It's your lead that I'm following."

"But you are the one who leads them." Gilban's face became stoic again.

At this Clara turned around again in silence as Gilban continued to speak.

"Rowan wouldn't open up to me. He also has his fears about me. Remember, I am a priest of another god, who doesn't have the same view on things as he does. Not only that, I am of a different race. His order has taught him humans are his chief concern; we other races are secondary. No, it is far better if you converse with him. Besides, you are much more pleasing to look at."

Clara reacted with a sideways glance at the priest who quickly hid the grin piercing out behind a stoic face.

"What is that supposed to mean?"

"Nothing, unless you wish it to mean something," Gilban said innocently before his voice became more serious again. "If it will help, I can tell you how you and he have a destiny together, a future which will be made self evident soon. The choice is yours, Clara, but know what you do now will affect the outcome. Nothing in this world is free."

Clara frowned deeply in contemplation and then caught herself as she was about to fall off the horse, righted herself, looked ahead to make sure the way was clear enough for her to swing back around one last time to inquire of the seer.

"We have a destiny together beyond this journey, then you're saying?"

"Perhaps. If you so choose it." Gilban stared ahead of himself now. His words were taking root and would bear fruit soon enough.

Clara turned around again to see how the muddy waters had risen up to her horse's knees, then looked behind herself to Rowan. She hoped the sight of him would help her determine what it was she needed to say to him. As she did so, she noticed Cadrissa jump down off her mount in order to help it out of the muck in which it had become mired.

Clara noticed, as she looked farther on ahead, the terrain was getting much worse and it would be a good time to begin their trek on foot. The extra weight on the animals would be too much and they would sink down still deeper into the muck and become almost impossible to free.

"It looks like horse and rider part here. Take it slow, we don't want to waste time fishing you out of a sink hole," Clara addressed the group as she got down from her stead, then outstretched her hand to aid Gilban's descendent.

Vinder looked at Dugan with a sour face, his one eye scowling at the muscled Telborian who offered his hand to the dwarf.

"I can take care of myself thank you very much. I'm not a child." Vinder huffed.

"Have it your way then," Dugan turned to the front of the horse, his feet sunk into the mud just short of his knees, then picked up its reins. The Telborian gave the horse a pull on the reins to get the beast free of the consuming mud. The jolt rocked Vinder, who was proceeding to climb down the horse. Losing his balance from the jolt, he fell into the mud below with a loud splash.

"Are you all right?" Dugan rushed to the old dwarf's half-submerged body and mud smeared faced.

"Just fine." Came the dwarf's tight lipped reply.

"Did you need any help?" Dugan suppressed a belly laugh at the sight of the mud caked warrior.

Vinder brushed away the Telborian's offer with a muddy hand. "No-no-no. I can do it myself. Don't worry about me."

Dugan shook his head. The stubborn old dwarf proceeded to pull himself out of the sea of mud. Vinder placed his hands on the amorphous ground in front of him. Using them for leverage, he began to pull himself out of the muck, but discovered, much to his surprise, he was sinking face first into the brackish water instead as the marshy soil decided to pull his hands deeper the more Vinder tugged the opposite direction.

"Wo-" was all he could say before his head was swallowed up by the liquid dirt, in a covering of brown bubbles.

Dugan sped to the drowning dwarf and seized him from the mud with a powerful grip, then lifted up his sodden prize with a laugh.

The others in front turned to look at the commotion.

"Look what I caught." Dugan shouted with a snort.

Vinder spat out a mouthful of mud, and coughed hoarsely in reply. "Put me down!"

"I think it would be safer if you rode the horse until we got to drier ground," Dugan stated as he began to place the brown warrior on the horse once more, this time in the saddle.

"I will do no such thing! I'm a warrior, not a child! I deserve no special treatment," Vinder huffed as he crossed his arms in defiance.

"Vinder, it will be better for the group if you just stay on the horse," Clara added diplomatically.

"She's right," Cadrissa spoke up from behind the company, her golden robe held up over her pale knees.

"You all think I'm a worthless weakling, eh?" Vinder grumbled.

"No one thinks that at all," Rowan stated as he advanced through the slowing, fetid, waters toward the stationed dwarf. "We just want you fresh and ready to defend us from attackers. If such a time comes, we'll need a strong and fresh warrior to defend us should this marsh slogging wear us out. And from your vantage point you'll be better able to provide lookout for any dangers coming our way and keep from getting fatigued in these mud ponds."

"Well," Vinder smiled as he wiped the mud away from his embroidered patch and beard, "that makes sense, lad. You go on ahead, and I'll bail you out if ya need it."

"Very well then. Let's move on," Clara smiled at the young Nordican, who looked at her solemnly and blushed, then suddenly he grabbed his horse's reins and began to trudge through the muck, as did the others.

The others smiled to themselves at the simplicity in Rowan's plan. He had given the dwarf an excuse to stay on the horse- and save face. Where both he and Rowan knew where he belonged.

Cadrissa walked slowly through the thick brown water, the hem of her golden robes draped over her right arm in an effort to try and keep them somewhat clean as she heaved on the reins of her mare. The action to keep herself relatively clean had been in vain, though, as the lower section of the robes were caked in mud and sopping wet. Almost all of the golden fabric dripped discolored mud from their own shimmering surface into the sodden soil. The longer she walked, the more she began to come upon a foul odor. Though the whole marsh was full of the reek of decay, a much more potent aroma reached her, though she didn't know from exactly where this took place. The mage proceeded to lead her horse farther onward until it began to nigh and become hesitant.

"Come on you stupid beast!" Cadrissa cursed as she pulled on the leather straps.

"Something wrong?" Dugan asked, bringing his horse to a halt beside her.

"This nag doesn't want to cooperate." The wizardress wiped away a tangle of sweaty black locks from her head in frustration.

"Just tug on its reins; show it who's boss." Dugan replied.

"That's what I'm trying to do!" The mage muttered through gritted teeth. "Besides, it's easy for you to say, you're as strong as a giant!"

Cadrissa continued to pull vainly on the reins, dropping her robes into the murky waters once more to do so. "I'm pulling, so I'm the boss," she stated to the mud logged animal like it was a child. The horse whinnied in response and leaned back against Cadrissa's struggling attempts to gain control. The rest of the others waded onward as Cadrissa pretended to be winning the struggle with the beast.

"Look you," she said sternly as she looked her mount in the eye. "I am the master, and I say we move forward!" The troublesome black beast rebutted by giving a powerful yanking on the reins, causing Cadrissa to lose her footing and fall, landing backside first into the watery mud. The wizardress spit and spattered while eying the troublesome beast once more, this time with a hint of malice in her eyes.

"I don't want to hurt you, beast, but we can do this the hard way, or the easy way, the choice is up to you. I'm a wizardress you know." The horse seemed to pay her little heed as she pushed up her sleeves, preparing to cast a spell. By the gods, she would teach this beast some manners and respect, but first she needed to get the animal moving again.

She closed her eyes and stepped back, then began to chant strange words and phrases which never could have been invented by the human mind. As she progressed, she stepped still farther back from the animal and tripped.

Her spell was interrupted when she fell into the soup once more.

This time, something broke her fall. It felt like a slightly rotten log and kept her from sinking too far in the watery mess, but as she struggled to get up, she felt it move. It was buoyant and shot up after her as she struggled to stand.

Suddenly a pale, outstretched hand emerged from the mud, its fingers frozen into a rigid claw.

Cadrissa screamed.

Dugan drove through the grime to reach Cadrissa's side. The others came as fast as they could. Vinder turned on his saddle and Gilban held fast to the spurs of Clara's horse.

"What is it?" Dugan slid to a stop.

"Look!" She pointed to the hand which had now become a floating corpse.

It was slowly being joined by two more bodies.

The Telborian stepped closer to examine them.

"Be careful!" Rowan interjected. "You don't know anything about their deaths."

"I know these men died in the grip of fear," Dugan said, prodding them with his sword. "Look at their faces."

"They're elves!" Rowan declared in disbelief.

"Elves?" Vinder questioned in surprise.

"I thought you said elves don't like marshes." Cadrissa looked over at Dugan.

"I guess there's a first time for everything." The Telborian surrendered.

"Or they might have not wanted to be seen; keeping themselves hidden from everyone, and thing as long as possible," Vinder added from his horseback perch, having turned around a bit to get in a better view of the scene.

Clara came forward and looked at them, falchion in hand. "These are Elyellium, not Patrious. Gilban." She addressed the older elf who stayed beside their horse. "You were right, there were others sent after the information we're seeking. The Elyellium must know already about the ruins."

Cadrissa swallowed hard and took a deep, quivering breath.

"Then they might have the secrets already."

"Not if this is what is left of most of their force," Dugan mused as he moved a badly mutilated corpse with the tip of his weapon. The whole bottom portion of the elf had been ripped away as if it had been made of parchment.

Jagged edges of flesh and broken bone were covered in slime and maggots, who busied themselves inside the torn elf.

Cadrissa closed her eyes and shivered.

"Are those bite marks?" Rowan leaned in more for a closer look of the corpses.

"Yes- and big ones at that," Vinder stroked out some more mud from his beards.

"Well, that rules out the natives," Rowan stood tall once more. I learned from my training Celetors are fellow worshipers of Panthor and would never show this kind of disrespect to any sentient being. They're not a warlike race. "Besides, no human can make those marks. Those are the work of a beast for sure."

"My reading did speak of large reptiles that lived here." Cadrissa had found herself admiring Dugan as she spoke. She surmised she would feel safer if she had those strong arms around her...

"Do you think it's from a crocodile?" Clara moved to stand before the Telborian.

"If it was, then he carried a club as well," Dugan pointed with this gladius to a partially decayed skull staring out of its slushy grave with empty sockets. Its bone structure was normal, except for a large indention in the back of it, which had shattered inwards at the force of the blow. "If I'm right about how this adds up here, then we're in more danger than we thought."

"I'll get Gilban," Clara started to make her way to her horse but her arm was caught in Dugan's strong grip.

"A blind man can't help us here."

Clara stared down at the Telborians hand on her wrist.

"He can help us by divining their fate, and how it came about," then pulled free from the grip of the Telborian and walked off toward the old elf.

"What caused their death?" Cadrissa had overcome her initial fear and disgust of them to at least dare to turn her attention to the decomposing flesh without studying it in too great a detail. Though she was strangely fascinated with getting to see more details, whenever she caught sight of one her stomach tried to jump out her throat.

"The club marks and the bites remind me of a crea-ture I fought in the arena once. They have a name, but no one can pronounce it, so people just call them lizardmen. They could live in lands like this too, I'd imagine. I would imagine a swampy land would be paradise to these creatures."

"Lizardmen?" Rowan drew his sword. "How often do they attack?"

"I can't tell you, but in the arena they often ate what, or who, they killed. These elves have been dead for a while, but were only half eaten. The way I figure it, they left these out like marinating meat to get more foul in this mud until they came back after they ate their fill the first time around." The gladiator studied the bodies from a distance now, as his own senses were scouting the area around them cautious and observant for anything that might trigger his reflexes to danger.

"Either that, or they didn't like the taste of elf," Rowan peered through the jungle terrain, on his own lookout for a possible ambush.

"Do you think they'll come back soon?" Cadrissa's eyes grew wide.

"It's hard to say. Like I said, I'm no expert, but those things are damn hard to kill." Dugan continued his surveying.

"Dugan is correct in his assessment," Gilban spoke up as he was led to the investigating party by Clara's guiding hand. The color of his robes had long since changed to a dismal brown, and his white hair had lost its luster in the humidity.

"They were here, five days ago. Lizardmen hid in the mud, laying traps for their victims. They designed a sinkhole…it captured these elves…the elves were not aware of the attack…they were set upon by the beasts, and rendered limb by limb."

Gilban mumbled to himself.

"What is he doing?" Dugan rose and moved toward Clara.

"He is divining the murder of these men through the aid of Saredhel."

"Blessed Saredhel!" Gilban exclaimed. "They used these dead bodies as a lure!

"They are here and waiting for us!

"We have stepped into a trap!"

The others jumped around in fright as Gilban announced the news. Cadrissa cringed, Vinder hurried down from the horse ready to stand with his axe at any danger, and the others reading weapons and wills for an attack from an enemy they couldn't see, but only imagine.

"I don't see anything," Rowan scaned the marsh. "Are you sure the old elf is reliable?"

"I would stake my life on it," Clara replied.

"Ya just might do so, lass!" Vinder responded as he idly smacked the butt of his axe in the palm of his hand, a hint of irony in his voice.

"I have just the spell- ouch!" Cadrissa started to say, then fell silent.

She crumpled into the mushy ground below with a soft splash.

"What the-" Dugan growled as he felt a pinch on his neck, not unlike the mosquitoes which had been plaguing him throughout the trip. He felt dizzy, and blackness overcame him.

Rowan turned to see the big Telborian drop into the mud beside Cadrissa, before he too felt a pinch on his neck. The others were falling around him to the ground unconscious as well, but Rowan felt no desire to do the same.

What was going on?

All he knew was he was the only standing member of a party struck by what felt like darts. Indeed, as he brought the object that he'd felt lodge itself into his leather armor just below his neck before his face, he say it was a dart. A simple, bone tipped, white down fletched dart.

The thick protective leather had slowed the dart, and held back its tip from poking Rowan with what he could now see appeared to be some dark sap at the tip. This certainly was fortuitous- a blessing of Panthor for sure. He wasn't about to die in a swamp for a race he knew nothing about and whose favored meal seemed to be humanoid flesh.

He dropped the venomous dart into the mud, faking unconsciousness. He wanted to play along with his captures until such time as he had a chance to help the others and escape this danger. At the moment he didn't know how large the threat was and what, if anything, he could do against it either.

But he would wait, plan and try his best.

Silently he prayed to Panthor as he awaited the outcome of his action. He was a Knight of Valkoria, and he had a mission to complete.

Chapter 20

After a short while, Rowan heard the muddy wading of an approaching group of creatures, who seemed to stop every so often, possibly checking each of their victims. Moments later, he began to hear the guttural sounds of a throaty speech, which Rowan could only imagine was the lizardmen arguing over who was getting the choice kill. The splashes drew closer, and a large, scaly foot, webbed between long, sharp toes stepped in front of his partially submerged face.

Rowan quickly closed his eyes, but only enough to appear asleep and yet still be able to see out through tiny slits. In the small field of vision, he saw strong, broad reptilian legs and tails covered in the same thick scales as their claw-like feet. It was as if they were common lizards who had become not only the size of men but were able to stand upright like them as well.

The horses began to panic, whinnying nervously and prancing on the spot, but the mud held them fast, making escape impossible. Distracted by the commotion of the frightened mounts, the lizardmen turned and approached the animals and used their heavy clubs to shatter the horses' skulls. Rowan had to keep himself in check as his Nordic blood flared to life for the slaughter of such fine beasts. His training held him, though. He was thankful. He'd be no help to anybody dead.

The Nordican took advantage of the disturbance to catch a better glimpse of his attackers. Their torsos were those of well muscled men, covered in dark green scales, and their heads were similar to crocodiles.

Rowan closed his eye again and tried to calm himself, but all he could see was the intelligent malevolence behind the yellow eyes. Even when the lizardmen began ripping apart the horses and eating them as sloppy and savagely as they could, he held his ground. He needed to wait for an opportunity. He cleared his mind and continued in prayer to Panthor and for an answer.

After the lizardmen had devoured much of the horses, they proceeded to tie up their mercenary prey with crudely made rope. They bound every member of the group's hands and feet with the rough cord, and then trussed the unconscious companions to wooden poles about eight feet in length.

Rowan found himself dangling between two of the lizardmen as they braced the pole on their shoulders, leaving him to hang like a freshly killed deer. His sword had been taken from him, and was being held by what Rowan could only guess was their leader. The big scaly beast had fought off all his companions when Rowan's sword was discovered, claiming it for himself. The others' weapons were confiscated as well, and distributed among the remaining lizardmen.

Once their captors had the entire party hoisted onto poles, they started heading deeper into the lands. Rowan was surprised to see how little the murky ground hindered them. The lizardmen's webbed feet seemed to easily allow them to transverse the slushy ground. Only on one or two occasions did the walking become difficult for them, which Rowan attributed to the excess weight of their victims. As they walked, Rowan contemplated the group's situation and his ability to free them all, now he was weaponless.

His hope was dimmed further when he realized he didn't have any real plans at all. Even Panthor had remained silent in terms of coming to his aid. It seemed impossible to take them all on and now he had let them get his sword and tied him up his chances were even less than before. He knew he had little time to come to some means of action, but he also knew he had to be patient to bring it into fruition as well.

It was a tight and thin line he walked, and Rowan lost faith in it with each passing moment. His only hope was he could still keep faith in his goddess to come to his aid-believing her silence would be broken at any moment.

Daylight faded into twilight, and then night, cruel and black. The party halted when they came into a clearing where Rowan noticed the ground was dry, and covered in short grass. Crude huts made of thatch and mud were scattered about the clearing.

Tree limbs and vines enclosed the camp in a rough fence. Smaller fires dotted the growing darkness like giant fireflies, their smoke curling up toward the canopy like serpentine tongues. In the center of this gathering there appeared to be a large open pit.

The cargo carrying lizardmen joined others of their kind. Even though they were naked, Rowan couldn't tell if they were male, or female. Only a slight variance in physical size, such as height and girth. was noticeable by which Rowan assumed the females were the larger of the race, though he had nothing by Nordic logic to form such a deductive assumption.

The young knight found the whole camp eerie in the dancing darkness of night and at the same time fascinating.

The creatures seemed to live a life most Nordicans would understand. The lizardmen seemed a very tribal people, under the rule of who looked like a chieftain, whom Rowan could see standing near the lip of a great sunken pit some twenty feet from him.

The chieftain wore an elaborate coat of leather, bark, and feathers, and carried a large stone axe. His body was also covered in paints and dyes, which made for an interesting collection of shapes and images as he moved about the lip of the pit growling orders at the others carrying the mercenaries.

Slowly this hunting party moved toward their leader and the pit while the other lizardmen chanted and paraded around their victorious comrades with wild gestures and shouts. They flung cords of knotted vines around the heads of their captives, as those who wore crudely constructed masks tossed bone axes in the air, juggling them like street entertainers. The night sky did little to offer insight into much of the rest of the camp, only a few starlight areas were made visible. Added to the campfires were torches being juggled by masked lizardmen. Drum beats reverberated through Rowan's head, matching the rhythm of the dancing lizardmen.

The chieftain shouted something quite loudly when the company of lizardmen and captives reached him then motioned erratically with his arm, indicating the placement of the captives in the sunken pit.

Rowan tried to study more of his surroundings, in hopes of escape but his hope was fading fast. He noticed more lizardmen were pouring out of the sunken pit he and the others were being carried into, though he didn't know why.

One by one, Rowan and his companions were hoisted upright, their poles wedged into the floor of the hollow. Littered across the entire fifteen foot wide hole were broken branches, leaves and other combustible materials. The knight's mind began to race as he realized the fate awaiting him.

They were going to be roasted alive!

Panicked, he quickly looked toward the others, and found them still unconscious, heads sunken toward their chests.

"Dugan, Clara, Cadrissa," Rowan hissed.

If they heard him, none of them seem to acknowledge it. Rowan began to scan the area intensely. He looked for anything he could use to escape. It was pointless to continue the rouse of slumber. He had to take action or die. The chieftain looked at the fully conscious Rowan, and smiled, baring a long row of glistening, sharp teeth. Rowan cursed himself. He wished now he had taken his chances with the lizardmen when they had first attacked the party, instead of allowing them to take him and the others prisoner.

He flexed his wrists, and tried to stretch the ropes binding him to the post by his feet and hands, but to no avail, the bonds were stronger than they looked. As they hung on their posts, each captive was suspended five feet from the pit floor, which possessed an indiscernible depth as it was stacked with leaves and logs.

Rowan continued to struggle in a vain attempt to free himself. He refused to live his final moments as if he were some dumb animal to be roasted on a spit. The rope bindings held him fast as more lizardmen approached the rim of the pit, their clawed hands holding blazing torches, which sputtered and spat in the growing darkness like hungry asps.

The young Nordican prayed more fervently to his goddess.

The lizardmen then began to sing a savage, guttural song which filled the night with atmosphere of dread as the-mouths which sang were far from humanoid; the melody even more foreign and frightening. Upon the completion of their song, the reptilian horrors then threw their torches onto the trench. There was a scattered crackling, then smoke began to billow upward as small fires appeared across the kindling of the pit.

"Panthor!" Rowan pleaded at the top of his lungs. "Grant me aid. Don't let me die on my first mission serving you! The protection of the human race depends on my survival!"

The smoke thickened into a suffocating black wave. The acrid cloud chocked Dugan back into consciousness. He coughed repetitively, staring about him with burning, watery eyes.

"By the gods!" he shouted in panic. "Rheminas has found me!"

"Dugan?" Rowan shouted over the growing noise of the chanting lizardmen.

"Rowan? Where are you? Where are we?" Dugan coughed hard.

"We've been taken captive by some lizardmen, and we are about to be burnt to death. Can you break your bounds?"

Dugan strained against the rope that bound him to the post.

The tendons in his arms bulged as he pulled his wrists apart and clenched his teeth against the effort. The sleeping poison had weakened him slightly, but he would not be beaten. Not while he still lived. He pushed his body beyond its limits. He heard his muscles snap and crack with the strain, but he also heard the tell-tale creaking of the rope stretching away from his bloodied and bruised wrists.

"Rowan! I'm coming!" Dugan gritted his teeth.

"Hurry Dugan, the fire's growing!" The knight continued to fruitlessly struggle with his bounds.

Dugan wriggled out of his wrist restraints and quickly untied the rest of the rope holding him to the pole. He then slid down the pole into the burning pit beneath. The footing was unstable, and rapidly being consumed by the growing fire, but there were enough safe spots to run in order to reach Rowan.

Heat pulsated up the Telborian's legs. He felt his boots begin to smolder and melt with the rising fires. He had to be quick. He got to Rowan's side as rapidly as the flames would allow, and reached as high as he could.

He managed to grab Rowan's feet.

He wouldn't be able to get the young man's hands free unless he climbed the pole himself. If he did, then time surely would be wasted. The choice was easily and simply made. Scrambling up the pole, Dugan yanked on the young knight's knots, tearing the rope to pieces in his growing fury.

"You're going to have to untie the rest of your bonds yourself. I need to go look after the rest of the group. Once you've freed yourself, come help me."

The fire had increased in intensity, and over the roaring flames, Rowan could hear the angry cries of the lizardmen screaming at their captives' attempt at escape. Frantically, he struggled with his bonds. The fire sent sparks of burning ash into his eyes, causing him to lose his vision as he pulled against the crude ropes.

Anger poured into his soul, as he lifted his head toward the heavens in frustration and pain.

"Panthor, help me!"

With one final heave, of his young body, he heard a snap, then the burning ground rose up to meet him.

Dugan had freed Clara's limbs from their bindings. She was rapidly coming around from her drug-induced stupor with help from Dugan's repetitive slapping of her legs.

"Wake up! You're going to have to free your own hands," he shouted at her as he ran for Gilban, but changed direction toward Cadrissa when he noticed the older elf had already woken and somehow managed to untie the knots holding him to the stake. Dugan passed the priest right before he flopped to the smoldering earth like a sack of potatoes.

Cadrissa remained unconscious, drooping like a rag doll against the wooden pole. Dugan lifted her singed robes in order to get at the biting ropes around her ankles, all the while shouting at her to wake up.

"Wha?" Cadrissa awoke dazedly.

"Break the cords binding your arms, or you'll roast here like a stuck pig! I need to go help Vinder!" Dugan shouted up at the still sleepy mage.

Upon hearing this, Cadrissa became instantly alert, looking about her with frantic eyes The growing heat and smoke watered her eyes and toe at her throat like a dog pawing the earth. With renewed vigor she struggled with her bonds. She squirmed and pulled at them with great anxiety, and felt the flesh on her hands and wrists being rubbed away by the rough cord. Panic seized her and her fingers slipped and grasped at the knots to no avail. Frantically, Cadrissa raced through her mind for a spell she could use without hand gestures that might be of some use.

She needed to concentrate.

Slowly, a sense of calm washed over her and ancient words of power escaped from her lips and the ropes quickly dissolved into dust. Instantly, Cadrissa fell toward the inferno beneath her, but was stopped short by the embrace of strong masculine arms.

"I have you," Rowan said as she looked into his dark blue eyes.

Cadrissa was silent as the Nordican carried her away from the blaze, darting with sturdy strides across the burning, uneven thatch. Above the pit, dozens of lizardmen swarmed about the lip, gripping simple wooden spears in their fists and throwing them at the escaping prisoners in an attempt to keep them from leaving the fiery hole.

"What are those things?" Cadrissa dug into Rowan's leather sleeves with her nails.

"Those are our captors- Dugan's lizardmen."

"They're horrid!" She scowled.

"They have us pinned down. With the fire growing our options aren't that great at survival." Rowan dared a quick look back to the wizardress. "Do you have any magic that might be able to help us get out of here?"

"Yes, I think I have one that might do the trick." Cadrissa smiled as her eyes began to glow blue and a thin aura of cold surrounded her. "Oh yes, I can think of a great many spells with wonderful potential." She hissed in a frosty voice with both her own and of a stranger.

"Are you okay?" Rowan asked as he looked at her, his brow furrowed in concern. Even he could feel the shift in temperature about her frame amid the growing heat and could have swore he saw her green eyes becoming a bright blue... but the heat of life and death battle can do strange things to one's senses so he had been told.

"Perfectly fine!" She hissed again, looking at him through empty, azure stained eyes. "Now release me!" The snarl came out of her throat in a deep and powerful voice.

Rowan practically dropped the wizardress in his haste to have her out of his arms. His Nordic blood, the long lineage of being superstitious and intuitive on many a matter had taken hold. Something wasn't right about Cadrissa and he would be as far from her as he could at the moment. Perhaps the ordeal had been too much to take for the young mage.

Whatever the reason it would have to wait for later investigation as the rest of the group had now arrived at his side; Vinder moving along beside Dugan.

Before anyone could say anything, they all watched in astonishment as the golden robed beauty was enveloped in a glowing ball of azure light. Within moments, the heat from the flames abated, and the fire itself disappeared completely.

Smoke rose up from the remaining ashes and drifted away in a rising breeze. The lizardmen who were chanting around the edge of the pit began to cry out in frantic yips and yells as they ran back to their village in terror.

"I shall show them fear!" Cadrissa's voice echoed with a hollow tone which caused those around her to stare at the mage in slight concern. The voice she had used didn't sound totally like her normal self. Indeed, it sounded as if it were more masculine then it should be for her sex and past experience on hearing Cadrissa speak...

"Cona-laba Yulchere, Eqwese lghan spalow, spalow Niaka!" The strange voice resonating from Cadrissa's lips.

Dugan looked at Rowan in bewilderment, and then panic.

"Did she hit her head or something?"

"No." Then the knight added, "maybe it's part of the spell she's casting."

"Well, she's bought us some time, let's use it." Clara made her way to the edge of the pit.

Dugan shared Clara's sentiments as he hoisted Gilban up by his waist to Clara who had already risen to the top of the pit.

"Vinder, go get our weapons." He looked up at the dwarf whom he'd just pushed up toward the lip of the pit, he then turned back to Rowan. ."Bring Cadrissa,"

Dugan then scaled the height of the pit with one graceful move.

"I think you'll find Cadrissa can take care of herself," Gilban coughed as he pointed toward the pit.

"Feel my wrath, savages!" Cadrissa screeched from inside the crater. Suddenly the simple huts, where many of the frightened lizardmen had fled, burst into flame. The eruption of these tiny shacks sent smoldering pieces of thatch and lizardmen into the air.

The night was lit with the intense light, smothered with heat, and sundered by screams. The buildings burned fiercely, as did any lizardman who had been hiding inside the simple huts. Burnt flesh mingled with the aroma of choking smoke, as the companions scrambled out of the hollow.

Cadrissa walked toward Rowan, as if she was moving in a dream. Her footfalls were weak and misplaced, causing her to stumble and lose her balance. Rowan ran toward her, and helped support her weakened body, stopping it from falling.

"Can you walk?" Rowan peered into her eyes.

They were green once more.

Rowan suppressed the need to drop her right then and there in favor of doing what his training as a Knight of Valkoria had instructed he do: help a human in need.

"Yes." Cadrissa felt chilled, disoriented, and sick all at once. "What happened? Where am I?"

"Later," Rowan said, as he helped her out of the pit and toward the others.

Behind him, the lizardman village burned to the ground, along with every inhabitant. The screams and stench of cooked flesh were sickening.

Thick, greasy smoke traveled slowly skyward-a lazy serpent slithering through the night sky.

Cadrissa saw all this in fleeting glances but none of it made any sense to her. Like a drunk awakening after an night of wild debauchery, she didn't recall anything from the period when she grew dizzy in the swamp... there was something about a fire... she was tied to a post wasn't she? The details were murky and elusive and this drew even more concern to the mage who tried her best just to keep up with the others, believing that all things would be explained and make sense in time.

Chapter 21

The group of mercenaries ran into the thick jungle forest of Takta Lu Lama which had started to spring up around the outskirts of the marshes as they tried to distance themselves from the growing inferno.

The night was full of confusion and shadows. The village, and most of what surrounded it, was transformed into a monstrous bonfire spitting out sparks into the sky high above. The screams of the dying and suffering faded into the gloom as the group stumbled in fear from the chaos growing in the darkness around them.

Vinder had managed to retrieve their weapons with the aid of Clara, who also gathered up what rations she could that were also taken from them, and distributed them to the others as they ran beyond the burning ruins of what had been a lizardman village.

Clara hadn't been able to find her bow or arrows and didn't have the luxury to search for it either. She had found her sword and that would have to be enough. The meager rations she and Vinder had been able to take were pathetic by any standard.

Dugan and Rowan took the lead, directing their companions through the tangled trees and vines. Cadrissa lurched along behind the group like a drunk. Her mind whirled and her feet felt as though they were being held down by lead bars. She still had no idea how she ended up running for her life. She felt a deep throbbing fade away from her head;

the headache was so intense it had been clouding her vision, blurring the jungle into one big blob of green. As the pain was ripped from her skull, she thought she heard a distant frost laced voice scratch at the corner of her memory.

Soon we shall meet, the small voice whispered in her mind as it trailed away, leaving behind an echo of hideous laughter.

Cadrissa shuddered.

The lizardmen didn't pursue them. If any had survived the vicious attack, they had scrambled for their lives in the opposite direction from the events confronting them. Small pools of water began to form beneath their feet, and the smell of wet, decaying wood emanated from the soil as they ran across it.

"We're running back into the marshes again," Clara pointed out as they dashed over the soft soil, which had begun to suck their feet deeper into the mossy ground. Slowed by the terrain and deepening night, they stopped to catch their breath for a brief moment.

"So where are we going then?" Vinder grunted through some heavy breathing. "We lost our direction in that mad dash."

"Do you know where we are?" Cadrissa turned to Gilban as she bent over on her knees to catch her breath.

Gilban said nothing, merely closed his eyes and stroked his medallion. Though he too had ran with them, being dragged along by Clara, he didn't seem as worse for wear as the others did. Instead of heavy breathing, his lips mumbled a prayer.

"We are safe for now," he finally answered.

"Safe, but without direction," Vinder huffed. "I don't want to die here, so someone pick a direction and let's get moving again before anymore beasties find us in this overgrown tangle box."

As Vinder spoke, Rowan felt a stronger force calling him. Though it was faint, it still pulled at his mind. In a familiar woman's soft voice, it whispered: Come to me... come to me.

"So where would you have us go, Vinder?" Clara peered down at the dwarf.

"I didn't say I wanted to choose, just that someone should... like maybe the leader of this outfit." The dwarf's implication wasn't lost on Clara.

Clara's soft gray tinted face grew hard for a moment before Rowan's voice smoothed it out once more.

"I think I know where we are..." Rowan's voice trailed off as he was distracted by a sound seeming to be coming from the swamp toward his left. It was as if he could almost hear music that wasn't there, like a whispered conversation behind a closed door.

He stared intently toward the sound's location and thought he saw a female warrior beckon him onward through the marsh. He knew the form to be of Panthor, and he also knew the others couldn't see her. Just how he knew all this though he couldn't say.

The figure motioned Rowan toward her with soft gestures.

...come...come...the soft music called to him.

"Rowan?" Clara's questioning tone brought him back from the trance for a moment.

"Wha..."

"You said you thought you knew where we were?" the elf questioned again. The others present all had come to take in the youth with their eyes as well.

The youth felt a little uneasy under the scrutiny of so many gazes.

"Yes. Something looks familiar here and I think we can get back to the path if we travel through the marsh in this direction,"

He pointed toward his ghostly patron.

"How can it look familiar to you when you've never been here before?" Vinder's loan eye squinted.

"I don't know, it just seems familiar…like I know just how far we are from where we're supposed to be." The youth's eyes again grew dreamy with this statement as he found himself looking toward the woman who he knew to be Panthor by at the same time was unable to get any exact details of her person from his eyes to his brain.

"Really?" Vinder crossed his arms; axe still in his right hand ready for any more danger.

"Do you have any better ideas?" Dugan looked down at the dwarf.

None gave answer.

"I'm certain that I know the way," Rowan looked back at Clara now and felt his stomach flutter for a heart-beat.

"You all should trust him," Gilban interjected. "He will lead us to the right path. I have foreseen it."

"Have you now?" the dwarf chortled.

"Gilban hasn't been wrong yet." Cadrissa righted herself once more as she spoke.

"I just want to survive this mission," Vinder said. "I don't want to get lost in this cursed swamp with no horses or supplies."

"We all do." Dugan took a step toward Rowan. "If Gilban says we're to follow Rowan, then we follow Rowan."

Vinder shrugged. "I don't really care who leads, just so long as it eventually leads out of here and I get paid." The dwarf shook his head and uncrossed his arms.

"Personally, I just think this heat and humidity is getting to everyone. First it was Cadrissa and her wild behavior at the lizardmen camp, and now this sudden epiphany with Rowan."

"Yeah," Rowan turned to Cadrissa. "What happened back there? You okay?"

Cadrissa opened her mouth to speak but was cut short by Gilban.

"Now is not the time for discussion, but for action. We must be on our way."

"Agreed," Vinder nodded. "How are we going to complete this mission now without our supplies and equipment. We've just got our weapons- and a handful of trail rations.

"No more food or water, mounts or anything but the clothes and armor on our backs."

"He does have a point, Clara." Dugan turned to the elven maid.

"It will all work out," Gilban seemed hurried now, almost agitated in his speech and manner which was an odd thing for anyone of the others to see in the old elf and served to give extra weight to the priest's words.

"The situation isn't going to be improved any if we rested for the night or tried to retrace our steps," Clara finally spoke up. "We'd still be out of gear and supplies- and so we best make due with what we have. We're better off just following Rowan, if he says he knows the way, then trying to find another. If Gilban says it will be okay, then I believe it will be- if we get moving."

All fell silent at her reply at the simple logic and reality faced them.

"So let's get moving," Rowan's words moved them into action.

He had become bewitched once more by the ghostly music and began to make his way to the front of the group. His goddess beckoned, and he began to become lost in his thoughts, not caring whether his friends followed or not.

They traveled for one hour more in the humid gloom, until exhaustion got the best of them, then set up camp on a small island of dry land surrounded by ankle deep water and rotting trees resting half upright, half submerged- like bodies in a ruined graveyard.

Together they took turns at watch, as they had done every evening since entering the wilderness. However, for the rest of the evening nothing troubled them beyond the normal ambiance of the marshes.

Morning came with little conversation as the group devoured their meager rations. They ate their meal in silence, watching the strange creatures coming to life around them. Flying, rainbow colored lizards, like tiny dragons the size of a finger, flew overhead, hunting for food. They let out a chirping like a cricket and mingled with the bird calls that were themselves a symphony of wonder. Tentacles were also sighted in the marsh, feeling the surface of the swamp for their morning meal.

Marsh rats scurried back and forth amongst the underbrush, rustling leaves and splashing water as long tailed parrots, the color of brilliant jewels, screeched to one another high above the trees.

"We're back in the marsh again, when I thought we had to go to a jungle," Vinder watched in silence when another giant tentacle grabbed a large rat with lightning speed, then sucked it beneath the opaque water.

"Now that it's daylight, I'm even more certain the way can be found," Rowan hadn't taken his armor off the night before, preferring to be ready for any attack, and was suffering for it. His muscles were stiff and his joints creaked as he moved. Of course everyone else hadn't removed their armor either so he was in fairly good company.

"Relax, Vinder, it'll be okay," Clara comforted the dwarf, then strapped her sword to her belt and walked toward the Nordican.

"Are you feeling okay?" Clara inquired of Rowan.

"Yes," Rowan smiled nervously. "Why do you ask?"

"You just look flushed." Replied Clara.

"Oh. I'm just as healthy as any Nordican can be, must be the heat and sun on my flesh," The youth sucked in a great gust of air and inflated his chest. "I feel fine though, never better." He then took leave of the group.

Clara watched his hasty retreat with great interest and felt the same strange rush of emotions she had trouble identifying before flood her body and mind. She shook her head to clear it of the troubling thoughts. She didn't understand them and couldn't afford to study them at the moment. It was best to just bury and forget about them for the time being.

Cadrissa rubbed her left temple.

"I still can't believe I did all what you said I did-even casting that spell I can't remember any of it." Vinder had filled her in on the missing details of her life as they had made camp the night before. It was short and brief, but still fanciful to the mage who thought it sounded more like someone telling a story rather than a recounting of her actions.

"Well you did," The dwarf rose with the others, "and I'll be keeping my eye on you too in case you start doing anything strange again."

"How reassuring." Cadrissa muttered as she made a half-hearted attempt at smoothing out her ruined robes.

"So I guess we follow again," She felt better than she looked, though the mage had managed to get a good amount of rest, which allowed her mental capabilities to handle any fresh challenges placed before her. There was a slight headache to contend with but she could live with it. As long as she was able to keep herself from blacking out or whatever it was she had done before, she'd be content.

After packing up what minor items they had unloaded in their resting the mercenaries traveled farther into the vile region of mud, struggling to raise their feet from the sucking mire. From sunrise until midday, the sun watched their slow journey, like some cruel overseer laughing at their plight. With every passing hour, each person began to lose a bit of faith in their guide, who seemed to be leading them in circles. The first to grow frustrated and then lose hope was Vinder, followed by Cadrissa, and then Dugan.

Rowan didn't seem to care, or even notice his companions were lagging farther behind, slowing their pace as doubt began to eat at them. He walked along as though in a trance, his eyes constantly focused on the ghostly image of his goddess just out of reach, leading him onward.

Come…Come…the feminine voice filled his head.

Rowan couldn't help but obey his goddess' command. It pulled at him like an addiction, leaving him without care or worry, and he would have continued to follow without question, if not for the hand Clara placed upon his shoulder, breaking the trance.

"Rowan, are we lost?"

"What?" Rowan turned to the elf with eyes that were half aware of what they took in before them.

"We've been on this trek for hours, and we haven't seen one sign of our destination. Are you sure you know the way? I want to believe you do, but the others have begun to doubt you, and well... you don't seem to be yourself. You seem lost." Clara looked at the dazed youth through concerned eyes.

"So you don't trust me anymore, elf?" Rowan snapped suddenly, though he didn't know why. Clara was shocked for a brief moment, removing her hand from him as if she had been bitten by a poisonous snake.

"We trust you, lad," Vinder spoke as he hobbled through the mud toward Clara's side. "It's just you might not be the best guide right now. Perhaps in this heat you've gotten confused, and took a wrong step somewhere, that's all."

"Rowan..." Clara began.

"I'm telling you, I know the way! Gilban even told you all to follow me," the Nordican shouted. "Are you calling Gilban a liar then?"

Silence took hold over the others as each moved their vision to the silent seer who remained still and detached from the conversation and events. Clara locked her jaw in anger. What was she supposed to do? This was well outside the boundaries of the plan they both had set up to follow in Rexatious and grew more wild and organic with each passing hour.

Clara growled in frustration at these thoughts. She, like most Patrious, hated to make snap decisions. Time was an ally and uninformed decisions made in haste were the enemy of many a soul. Careful thought and deliberation was needed to best answer a question, and many elves would agree with Clara, only she was in the midst of a group comprised of mixed races who didn't share her philosophical view on the subject. Blast the old elf. The one time she needed his aid he chose to withhold it.

"Gilban did indeed support you, and for that I'm willing to give you another day to lead us to where you think the ruins are. If you don't get us there, then we move in a new direction.

"Agreed?" Clara peered into the Nordican's eyes which seemed to have grown more fascinating over the previous hours…

"Agreed," Rowan replied.

Cadrissa threw her hands in the air and stomped away through the muddy water. "He's insane, Clara. The heat and humidity must have done it to him. He's leading us farther into this godsforsaken land to die at the hands of its denizens."

"One more day." Her face had taken on the look of stone.

Cadrissa slumped forward. "Fine. I mean, what else have we got to lose right?"

"We'll have to keep moving toward the north." Rowan started off toward the path his goddess led him on.

Clara stormed off after the northern knight, pulling Gilban along behind her. Dugan shrugged his shoulders as Vinder let out a great sigh, limbering along the mud covered ground. Cadrissa simply muttered a curse under her breath and whipped her robes around her before chasing after Clara and the others.

Rowan traveled the soggy path as hours went by, but he scarcely acknowledged their passing as he spent most of his time living in his own little world. The others trailed behind him silently, observing all the shadows surrounding them, created by the new morning light filtering through the dew-draped trees. The knight was overwhelmed with the extreme need to reach his divinely appointed destination. Somehow, he knew his life depended on it.

The scenery flew by him, the colors of the jungle blurring together as if he were riding on the back of a galloping horse. He noticed the light dim before night was upon him once more with no better results in this trek than the day before. While the rest began to set up camp for the evening at the foot of a rather steep hill, they started to grumble yet again about the lack of purpose Rowan's meanderings seemed to have.

For the sake of unity, Clara had to call them all together and to stop Rowan for a brief moment so he could clear his dream laced eyes. The wasted exercise of foolishness had to stop with or without Gilban's words of insight.

"It's been a long day, Rowan," Clara started as she approached the youth who stood a little distance away from the others. "We haven't gotten any closer to our destination." She paused to let the weight of her words sink into the youth.

"Seeing how this is the case, tomorrow we'll go a new direction…as we agreed." Moonlight fell upon her hair which caused a soft aura to surround her head- a glow that made the elf seem appealing and brought Rowan back to his senses for the moment as he was drawn to her with renewed interest.

"Give up when we're so close?" Rowan couldn't believe what he was hearing. This was important, maybe more important than they knew. After all, didn't he have this experience already in his vision back on Valkoria? He couldn't turn back now.

344

"You're welcome to still stay with us, Rowan, if you so choose, or continue your trek on your own. We have our own missions here, and I understand if you want to go on your own rather than continuing to travel with us. "

Rowan listened with a blank face to Clara. She wasn't getting it, none of them were. This was vital for them, not just for him. How Rowan knew this he didn't completely understand yet, just trusting Panthor would make it all clear to him in time. How could he make Clara understand though?

Suddenly a compulsion, like that which came over him in his vision in the tower, came over him. His body was made to move on its own and he had little choice but to follow its lead.

"Come with me," Rowan heard himself as he grabbed Clara's arm in an iron vise and pulled her to the top of the rocky hill before them.

"Rowan, what are you doing?" was all she could get out on the rapid ascent of the hill. The youth was frantic in his climb and it took all her concentration to keep from stumbling.

At the crest of the hill, he stopped. His manner instantly became still, his vision again trance-like as it peered out and over the hill. After a few moments of looking at the youth and trying to wrench her wrist free of the knight's hold, she dared to speak to him again.

"Rowan? Rowan?"

"Look!" The knight let go of the elf to point out before him. "We've done it."

Clara followed the youth's gaze and gasped. Through the bright light of the moon, as it filtered through the thin canopy of clouds, she saw a ruined city below the hill. It spanned for miles. Here and there, blocks of rock would jut out of the green carpet slowly taking it over and crushing it to death. Tall towers, some fallen, some leaning on their last legs, shot up from the harder soil. Walls pitted and hollowed by the elements surrounded enormous temples and civic arenas. Most other structures were lost in the foliage of the encroaching jungle.

Chunks of marble lay scattered around dense brush like crushed bone. Split and tumbled pillars lay as fallen logs, disintegrated by the weight of tumbled statues which had long ago lost their images to the ravages of time. Moss, weeds and tree roots grew in the craters and crevices along broken battlements, storefronts and toppled walls. In the moonlight, the ruins looked diseased and dead, like some bloated carcass washed upon the shore, nibbled at by scores of hungry fish and carrion birds. But in Rowan's eyes, the city appeared as a celestial jewel. In his heart and soul, he knew where he stood and what he now saw.

He had experienced part of this place in his vision, but now he had a fuller appreciation for the setting as he looked down from the hill into the ruins.

"Everyone get up here!" Clara shouted to the others without turning from the sight before her.

"By the gods!" Dugan whispered as he moved closer to Clara after sprinting the hill, sword in hand.

"No dwarf quarried those stones," Vinder joined them in an amazed stare.

"We've found the ruins! We've made it!" Cadrissa shouted with joy. She was the last to make it up the hill; Gilban tying with her since she had to help the elder elf in his ascent. "What do we do now?" She spoke in an awed whisper.

"We camp," Gilban answered them from behind.

"Clara, lead me into the city, and help me find safe shelter for us tonight," Gilban reached for Clara's arm.

"Are you sure that's a wise idea?" She asked as they trekked down the hill toward the ruins.

"Positive," the seer tugged on her arm to get moving.

"Pack up what you've set up already, and meet us down there with it," she ordered.

The others obliged.

Chapter 22

Relforaz sat on his throne and watched Hoodwink perform minor displays of acrobatics. The hobgoblin chieftain was not amused by the small goblin's antics. Hoodwink had been trying to lighten his master's spirits, but it was to no avail. Relforaz's mood was far too foul. The chieftain scowled deeply as he stared beyond the goblin fool in the corner of the room where a fire smoldered in a hollow pit which once had supported a great pillar.

He watched the dwindling flames, and tried to decide how to solve the problem of the depletion of Kylor's test victims. Now that the last of the elven prisoners were gone, Kylor would surely have his way now with the rest of the tribe. Perhaps he could use the Celetors in the surrounding wilderness around their territory for the next victims. He just needed to find them, and capture enough alive, and that would take some time. They were harder to catch than panthers in the pitch of night. He prayed to Khuthon for guidance on the matter, but no reply came.

Sullenly he faced the destruction of his tribe on his own, desperate for any favorable omen or opportunity that would be exploited for his favor. Relforaz had tried to focus on the problem for so long his head pounded with the effort. The present jingling of Hoodwink's hat was just the added amount of pressure needed to drive him into a rage.

"Be silent fool!" he bellowed.

Hoodwink stopped and stared at him sheepishly. "Do you wish to hear a tale now?" The goblin smiled in a jovial manner. His lip had healed some in the recent weeks, but were still sore and a bit discolored from the chieftain's bootstrike. Hoodwink knew things were getting more tense the later the hour grew, and the small goblin dreaded the meaning to his person which would surly follow in time because of it.

"I wish your head upon a platter, but I will settle for absolute quiet right now!" Malice drooled out of the chieftain's lips.

Hoodwink swallowed hard, his face transformed into a ghastly mask of fright.

"Have I displeased you, my lord?" The jester became even more submissive than usual.

"Every day, you little worm, since the day you showed your true loyalty to this tribe by handing up one of your betters to Kylor instead of forfeiting your life for his experiments." Relforaz's gazestabbed Hoodwink through the heart.

"Forgive me my lord, but I value my life." Hoodwink blurted out and then instantly wished he hadn't. He'd been walking on egg shells already and now they had all been crushed beneath his heel.

Relforaz became further enraged. He erupted out of his chair and picked up a sharp sword leaning up against the cold throne. In one swift and deadly motion, he swung it at the smaller creature, missing by only a hair. Hoodwink cowered into a tiny ball in the corner of the room.

"The life of the Basilisk Tribe comes before one's own life! Even I suffered beneath Kylor to try and redeem our fate from that madman!"

Relforaz took a step closer to the cowering goblin. "He will continue his insane search, even though it has gotten him nothing. He refuses to see this and will never give up, though it may kill us all." Another step brought the strong hobgoblin nearly down on top of Hoodwink.

"Now, unless you can think of a way to get rid of the wizard, then I trust you will leave me to think in silence." Hoodwink shook under the shadow of the chieftain.

"Yes my lord,"

"Relforaz!" The chamber doors suddenly burst open as sub-chieftain Goth ran inside. His face was lined with fright and exhaustion. His hands, stained with blood as was the sword he still carried though it had been shattered to the hilt.

"What is it?" Relforaz moved toward the hobgoblin warrior.

"Kylor…He has begun…his experiments once more." The sub-chieftain panted.

"What?" Relforaz roared.

"He has killed many already, and still seeks out more for that blasted device of his. He…tortured them…their flesh is ruined…and they died. I could do little…his magic was too strong." Goth panted.

Relforaz grabbed Goth by the shoulder to support him. "You did all you could Goth. Rest here while I go to settle this issue. By Khuthon's Axe, he will die by my hand!"

Relforaz swung his sword in a mighty arc before running out of the room toward the mage's lair with murder on his heart.

Hoodwink peered up from his cowering position in the corner at Goth. "Would you care for a story while you wait?"

Goth snarled in reply.

The dismal light of Kylor's lab cast sickly shadows across the room. Surrounding the base of the shimmering column were heaps and puddles of ruined, smoldering flesh; their putrid fumes filled the chamber with oily smoke. Some of the blobs moved with sickening, twitching motions. Others still had their former hobgoblin visage, but little else. Contorted and charred faces stared emptily into the swirling air, their eyes reflecting the memory of abject pain and horror before they went on to Mortis.

Kylor danced about the carnage with glee. His eyes bulged with madness, as he ran about the bodies, yelling orders at two frightened hobgoblins who proceeded to shove another frightened victim into the gaping maw at the base of the artifact. Sweat poured down the mage's forehead. His mind had finally come unhinged when he realized he'd never come to understand the workings of the device if he had eons of study.

His drive for power, his quest for the ultimate prize still remained. Though he'd learned and mastered much, many things still eluded him as to the full control over the blue column- these very things causing his mind to conflict with itself for the past few months until the resolution of the mental battled ended in madness.

"It shall be mine, Relton! The secret shall be mine!" Kylor laughed insanely, the pitch of his cackling drowning out the moaning wails of his test subjects.

As the next hapless hobgoblin was shoved into the relic to be warped by its power, a heavy thud echoed across the room. The noise was followed by heavy running footsteps coming from the shadow of the stairs.

"Kylor!" Relforaz shouted. "You have gone too far, mage!"

Kylor ignored the enraged chieftain and began to chant the familiar incantation.

The two frightened hobgoblins ran for their lives, disappearing up the stairwell, taking their chance to flee from the insane wizard while they could.

"Thoth ron heen ackhleen lore uylchyre uylchyre...." The dark mage began his incantation.

"None of your magic will keep you from me!" Relforaz ran down the stairs, a mighty bull set to charge.

Kylor continued to disregard him. His chant rose the magical power in the room to a crackling charge. Red light emanated from the runes on the ancient pillar. The entire room was filled with a fiercesome heat.

This should be interesting, Relton thought to himself from his shadowed corner as he watched Relforaz charge toward the mage.

The massive hobgoblin chieftain lowered his head, and aimed his gleaming white horns at Kylor, hoping to impale the mage. Through it all, Kylor continued his incantation as the familiar, deafening hum of the azure artifact began to gain in volume.

There was a yell of rage from Relforaz; a flash of silver, and then the glowing light faded from the towering column, plunging the room into complete darkness. Relton lost sight of the two opponents when the light went out, but as his reddening pupils began to adjust to the shadows, he was met with an interesting scene.

Relforaz had run Kylor through with one horn, piercing the mage's midsection, forcing the mage's intestines out the other side.

"You shall regret your action, Relforaz!" Kylor grimaced, blood running from the corner of his mouth.

Kylor was shocked at being wounded.

What had gone wrong with his amulet?

Why had it failed?

It worked well enough against Goth and the others who had previously assaulted him. Perhaps he had used up all its magical energy in past encounters. No, he could still feel its power. It had not gone dry. Then why had it failed him? Why now? His vision was impaired from the wound, but the mage thought he saw something in the corner of his sight.

A skeletal outline robed in rags with blazing blue sockets appeared to be silently mocking him with laughter. The dark mage could feel the hindrance this protective amulet coming from it.

"What are you?" The nearly delusional mage asked of the flickering form. "Did this brutish pig enlist you to aid in my destruction?"

It did not answer; only stayed for only a moment, then faded from view, leaving Kylor to ponder his fate once more.

"Well it won't happen!" An insane fire burned in the mage's eyes. "Your previous tribesman couldn't succeed, and though you may have hit me, it still will be your doom not mine!"

Relforaz shook his head rapidly like a dog shaking out the water from his fur. The action cut deeper into the wizard's flesh as he sunk lower on the great white horn. Intestines and other inner organs began to spill out more as a gaping hole was increased in size. Then Relforaz placed his hands on the shivered Telborian. Violently he pulled the mage off his horn, and threw him onto the floor. Fierce and feral, he lifted up his head in a great, savage roar.

"Now I will crush you, like I should have done long ago. Your crumpled body will stand as mute testimony to those who wish to dominate Relforaz or his tribe!"

The hobgoblin raised his sword and grinned.

"Behold the testimony to your failure!" Kylor eyes began to glow silver; two angry beacons in the failed light.

Relforaz stopped dead as his bloodied horn glowed and then burst into flames. Wherever the blood of Kylor had been spilt, it turned into silvery drops, the same color as the mage's eyes, then erupted into fire. The miniature blazes wouldn't go out, no matter how much Relforaz pounded on his horn, head, shoulder and chest. Enraged and screaming from the searing agony, he dropped to the floor, and began to roll around in a frantic effort to relieve his suffering. This did nothing save spread the flames over his person. Through all the anguish, he cursed Kylor and his magic, cursed the gods above, below and in between, and even cursed the very ground he rolled over.

"Behold my testimony, Relforaz! You have tried to slay a wizard, but you have failed! I have mastered the artifact. Yes…I have developed the understanding of the words…and their workings…and the means to use them. This wound…you have…inflicted is nothing! I won't be beaten. Not while…success is still close at hand."

Relforaz could only respond with a futile grunt as he dropped to the floor, the last breath of life escaping from his burnt lips. Relton smiled and readied himself for the moment which he knew would be close at hand. Kylor was so desperate now he knew the mage would have little left to lose by using the column on himself.

Relton hoped to be right there beside it. He wished to overpower his master in his weakened state so he would gain the column's benefit without having to sacrifice himself. He planned to use his own limited understanding of magic to have the spell affect Kylor instead of himself should the spell go awry. He had believed it could be done from his secret studies from the ancient books Kylor had been pouring over, and at least saw an opportunity to bring it about.

What are you going to do? The toad hopped toward his master's side and shielded his eyes against the gleaming light of Kylor's silvery blood, which still flared in silver flames like puddles of dancing mercury.

Kylor fingered the magical amulet hanging about his neck, pondering the skeletal figure which had blocked its protection from the hobgoblin's death blow. He didn't have any time left to waste on wondering what or who it was. It was time for one last, desperate action. In disdain, he put the talisman back under his robes and focused his mind.

"Just as I had intended…when I first found the artifact, I was going to enter it and see what…befell me," he answered his familiar. "If I'm right…I'll have my wish and ascend to the ranks of the Ancients who built this…this monument of power."

Kylor groaned as he pushed himself up from the ground, gathered what organs he could in his hands, leaving the rest to dangle freely from his flesh and drip their silvery blood which flickered into tiny flame whenever a drop hit the floor. Grunting with the last bit of his life, he shuffled toward the cage and column, a simple hand motion moving the cage door open once more for him to enter.

Are you sure it will work? Are you positive the incantation is correct? Relton kept up beside the dark mage, hopping around the silver smears of blood on route to the column.

"Do you doubt me?" Kylor halted at the entrance to the cage, and peered down at the large toad with a half slurred smile.

Never master. The words were insincere at best. Relton didn't need to hide his true nature any longer. Now was the time of his ascendancy.

"Then come closer," Kylor held out his free hand to the familiar, holding back his guts with the other.

Why? Relton was hesitant.

"I have need of your help for the spell. I am not as strong as I once was after that insolent hobgoblin laid his horns into me."

Very well. Relton did his best to suppress his smile. He was so close to his own destiny, he could almost taste it.

The green mound of flesh hopped toward the dying mage, through the mounds of stinking, quivering flesh, with a cautious motion. When he was within a hand's reach, Kylor snatched up the toad to clutch him tight in his grip.

What...what are you doing? Relton struggled in the mage's fist.

"I know you plot against me. You thought you were so smart...trying to use me to...use the artifact. Now...I have a final use for you. The wild wickedness in his face was made even more fearsome by his desperation to live.

"You'll aid me in holding back Asorlok's hand for a few moments more so I can have time to use the artifact." Kylor crushed the toad in his hand, which caused a popping sound to burst into the air along with a eruption of purplish blood and innards. "You've served your purpose well Relton."

The mage chanted one last spell, a faint whisper on his lips. As he chanted, Relton's physical life flowed into the mage like a refreshing stream as he absorbed it into his own body.

He cackled to himself between coughing out a fine mist of silvery blood, then tossed Relton's body toward the corpse of Relforaz, and moved inside the great blue column itself, stepping over blobs of wasted mortality as he did so. His face had begun to lose its color, becoming an even paler white, as his breathing became even more labored.

Once inside, the column closed behind him. Instantly the red light of the column overwhelm and then merged into his being, shocking it with both heat and electrical energy. Though his wound and the effects of the column distracted him, he fought hard to focus his mind on the spell to begin the transformation.

"Thoth ron heen ackhleen lore uylchyre uylchyre…," the words whispered from his mouth.

Brilliant light blinded him and smashed into his head to twist and torment his brain as the mage cried out in pain, and he felt himself slip into unconsciousness.

After a moment of darkness, his eyes were open again. This time he felt different. Something had changed about him, and it was then he knew his one goal in life had become a success. The artifact had healed him! It had made him stronger - even greater than he was before! Every fiber of his being spoke of his healing.

As he stood up, the column opened to allow a well-muscled man to step out. His naked body stood well over six feet, and in many ways looked like the vandalized statues that populated the ruins, save it could be seen he now had pointed, elven ears and short, black hair. He flexed an arm and smiled as he watched his powder-blue flesh swell with newfound strength. His eyes sparkled triumphantly as he roared with joy.

"At last I am free! Free from death - and his war against me!" Kylor placed his hand upon the cooling artifact. "Oh yes. I can hear you, and I understand what has to be done. It's only a matter of time now before everything is in place then!" The newly-remade mage stepped from the wrought-iron cage with a grand stride.

"I shall be the first of many to come, and then the glory of the Dranors shall once again cover Tralodren!"

Chapter 23

Dugan walked over to a low-burning fire, and sat near the others who had gathered around it. They had moved their camp to the base of the ruins, hoping to get some rest in relative safety so they could go exploring the following day.

Around them, the sounds of the night came to life. Birds and predators of the land called out for their mates, or screamed out in desperation as their lives were cut short in the struggle for survival. Insects buzzed and hummed among the group as they stared into the light of the campfire. All had their own thoughts to ponder, and own fears to realize as the ruins overshadowed them and brought to light a whole new flood of questions and concerns.

With a sigh, Dugan took off his armor and threw it into a pile on the ground. He stretched out beside the fire and closed his eyes, relaxing and breathing deeply from the night air. No one would eat tonight, and they weren't able to hunt anything on their recent journey. Perhaps they would find some decent game in the morning, after soothing their minds and bodies for a while. Each probably knew this wasn't true. They wanted to get going, get this task done, and be out of this place as soon as possible.

Vinder polished his axe until it reflected the light of the flames. Cadrissa pulled out a small scroll she had managed to take with her on the trip, as she had left the rest of her books locked away in a storage area in Elandor. Clara

Seer's Quest

worked on her falchion, rubbing oil into metal, checking the grip and hilt.

Gilban simply stared into the blaze, and fingered his holy symbol.

Rowan stood a little ways outside the camp, looking into the city with a forlorn appearance.

"I don't see any evidence of elven activity," Dugan stated to the others. "Maybe they didn't get here then."

"No, they didn't," Gilban spoke. "These aren't the right ruins."

"What?" Vinder looked up from his axe with a sour expression.

"You mean after all we've been through, we're still lost?" Cadrissa asked.

"In part," Gilban solemnly nodded.

"Great," the dwarf sulked as he returned to his work.

"What do you mean in part?" Clara asked. "Where are we?"

"Gondad," said the older elf.

"Gondad?" Cadrissa's face exploded with excitement. "This is Gondad?"

"The very same," Gilban continued to stare into the fire.

"So what's Gondad then? Why such a big deal?" Dugan looked over to Cadrissa.

"You mean you really don't know?" She smiled in amusement.

"No, I don't," the Telborian shook his head.

"You're a human, and you don't know," the young mage persisted.

"I don't get out much," Dugan shot Cadrissa a sardonic barb.

"Oh…right," she smirked again, a soft, red fire played about the flesh of her cheeks and forehead.

"Well, about six thousand years ago," the mage continued, "during the Imperial Wars, when nation fought nation, this was once a great glen. Old stories, say Cirmelian, the ancient Gondadian king, died, cursing his land as it was taken by the elves of Colloni. The same legends say blood ran from his veins in great rivers of anger and sorrow - flooding his beautiful land with putrid water, and it was how the marshes were created. All the peoples of this territory had to move away in order to survive, including the elves. Thus Cirmelian was able to keep his land - but at a terrible cost. Gondad was destroyed, never to be rebuilt."

"So we've camped in a city cursed by a king," Vinder huffed as he put his axe down beside him, "how reassuring,"

"Don't worry, it's just a legend," Clara spoke up. "This city, and the land around it are safe from any curse. Legends often cover up the full truth. We Patrious have a more accurate recollection of past events than most races.

"Cirmelian didn't know Gondad was crafted by the Elder Race. It had an abundance of lush, fertile fields, due to the many tracks of irrigation running all over the countryside. This rich farming land made the city a prime target for invaders. In a desperate attempt to increase the city's defenses, Cirmelian decided to turn the irrigation canals into a maze of man-made moats.

"However, when he opened the floodgates to their fullest, he didn't take into account the force so much water would have on the canals. The torrent of water eroded the stone waterways, and flooded the land - destroying everything in its path. The floodgates could never again be closed; they were swept away, buried and ruined in the water. Since that day, the fields of Gondad became a great marsh, with the city itself becoming a ruined backwater, and then finally a desolate ruin."

"So the Ancients built Gondad then?" Dugan asked. "The same Elder Race whose secrets we're trying to keep out of anyone else's hands…at another set of ruins?"

Rowan didn't hear Dugan, nor Clara's answer. In truth, he hadn't heard any of what they had been saying. The dream-like vision had once again seized control of the Knight of Valkoria and refused to let go.

"Gondad, ancient Gondad. You still exist," Rowan whispered in awe as he stood before the diluvial ruins.

From the rocks, trees, buildings, and even Rowan's heart itself, a song of age-old melody and creation sprang up into being. It echoed through the walls and still stood in the night sky.

The ghostly anthem could only be heard by the young knight, whose eyes misted over as the others continued their talk around the fire. His spirit joined the hymn of praise for the old Origin City of humanity, even as his feet began to pull him deeper into its being.

> *Come into a great nation,*
> *Come into a great host.*
> *Blest from its first creation,*
> *And loved by gods the most.*
> *A nation of united, strong leaders of the land.*
> *Each day we hear our souls sing,*
> *And still our city stands.*

The melody and words welling up in him were as old as the Knighthood itself. It was the ancient Hymn of Gondad, and was taught to all knights and followers of Panthor for it was common knowledge how all humanity sprang up from the blessed city of Gondad. It was also common knowledge, at least to Rowan's mind, how Gondad was viciously destroyed by elven expansion.

His feet continued to pull him forward until they picked up speed, becoming a light trot, then jog and finally a mad run. He couldn't stop the compulsion, and had to follow where his goddess had led him. It was obviously for a purpose; a purpose he wanted to discover.

> *There are none who would shelter,*
> *Evil in our walls.*
> *Blest be the simple worker,*
> *And whom god calls.*
> *Our army is victorious,*
> *10,000 foes before them fall.*
> *Our nation will be forever*
> *For we are first of all.*

The others noticed the youth's sudden departure, but before they knew what happened Rowan had charged into the night.

"Rowan!" Dugan jumped up from his seat.

"That blasted fool!" Vinder cussed into the fire.

"Leave him, Dugan," Gilban advised. "He has come to find his destiny."

Dugan shook off the urge to pursue the youth. He wanted to keep the boy from being foolish, as he knew the rash behavior of the young knight might put everyone's life in jeopardy - not just his own. However, he also had come to trust Gilban's wisdom, and so let him run free.

"Let's just hope he doesn't rouse the natives here," Vinder echoed the Telborian's thoughts. "I'm not in the mood for a fight right now."

"Will he be truly all right?" Clara asked Gilban.

"Yes." Gilban stared off into the horizon. "He has to meet his destiny alone; only then will he return to us triumphant."

"If he returns," Vinder added beneath his breath.

"He will return Vinder, "Gilban turned his blind eyes toward the dwarf, "I have foreseen it,"

Rowan suddenly stopped in his run when a set of stairs caught his eye. They were the same stairs he'd seen in his vision during his dedication to Panthor. The exact same. What did that mean? Taking a breath, he sighed deeply. What was he supposed to do now? The compulsion left him for the moment, though he didn't know if it was a good or bad thing. After taking a moment to get adjusted to his current situation, the knight began to doubt the wisdom of his run into such a puzzling and potentially dangerous place.

"What I am supposed to do, Panthor?" Rowan raised his head to heaven, "Help me!"

Nothing.

Seeing he was already here, Nordic logic told him he might as well enter. Tentatively, the youth approached the dark opening of the doorway at the top of the stairs. He recalled from his vision a great panther had leapt upon him from the darkness, and didn't want to take any chances here. Silently Rowan drew his sword, as entered the black portal. As his feet crossed the threshold his body again shook. Rowan felt a compulsive impulse to continue as he entered the ruined building, and journeyed towards what he hoped would be answers to his questions.

In a heartbeat, his walk had accelerated to a run as he continue to sprint heedlessly through the darkness of yet another decrepit hallway, driven by his maddening quest to be in the heart of the ruins. The sour smell of decay and dust clogged his nose and mouth, but he paid it no mind. He felt the very presence of ancient Gondad call to him from the shadows all around him while the old hymn, sung by ghostly voices, whispered to him.

> *For our god-sent leaders,*
> *Kept us sore oppressed.*
> *Dreams crafted in marble,*
> *Lasted days at best.*
> *Sorrow long and weary,*
> *Tears freshly fell like rain.*
> *And only an elf named Aero*
> *Could take away our pain.*

Suddenly, the haunting murmurs grew silent, and the compulsion ended. Rowan stopped. His mind and body were now his own again. He looked around and realized, with a slight rush of fear, he was lost. He had no way of telling where he had come from, nor what lay beyond. Though the ruins were filled with holes, they provided very little light from the starry night skyoutside.

As the knight cautiously made his way across the debris-strewn floor, he heard the echo of purring from an animal. Instinct drove his head to his right just in time to witness a dark, gray panther appear out of broken shadows around him. The panther was of normal proportions, but there was something supernatural about it. The creature's bright, yellow eyes shined like lanterns when they turned to take in the young knight. Rowan readied his sword, and tensed his body as it drew closer to him for but a moment, then turned away to walk down another ruined corridor. To the knight's surprise, its eyes lit the path before it as if they were torches.

Rowan couldn't help but wonder about the significance of such an encounter. What was he supposed to do? Why did everything have to be so hard for him?

He decided to at least follow the panther since its eyes lit up a path for him.

Catching up with the creature was easy enough. It didn't seem to care about the human behind it, shadowing its every step. In time, the beast slowed, and then halted near a small wooden door which remarkably had managed to survive the assault of time, warfare, and rot. A beefy paw slashed at the wooden flesh of the door, then it crouched down, growling at the knight.

"I take it I'm to go in there then," Rowan pointed to the door.

The panther didn't answer, simply stared at the youth with its mystical, self-illuminating, yellow eyes.

"Okay," Rowan gingerly edged his way around the great cat until he was before the door, then gave it a little push. The structure fell down with a loud crash, scattering dust, spiders, rodents, and other vermin out of the way. The panther's unnatural eyes lit up the room beyond just enough to allow the knight to see it was quite small - no more than a ten by ten-foot room at best, the fallen door dominating most of the interior.

Rowan slowly proceeded into the room. He ground the door underfoot into splinters and chunks, which sounded like gravel as if the knight walked on it. His attention was drawn to an object ahead of him – a thick, stone spartan pillar, upon which a small, rusted iron chest rested. The chest was no larger than a hand's breath and width, but was the main focus of the room.

Rowan found himself drawn to it. His hands touched the cold metal, and he attempted to open the box, and the old, delicate locks crumbled away in showers of umber metal. Inside he found a strange, almost tribal-looking necklace crafted of leather straps and sporting a small, shriveled panther's paw, accompanied with beads, and a few small white and black feathers. The paw had to come from a baby panther, as it was much smaller than the adult-size Rowan had come to know growing up.

Rowan pulled it from the box to get a better look at the object. It was similar to something he'd seen growing up with the shamans of his tribe, but something seemed wrong - as if it were somehow out of place in this setting, like it had a greater place and purpose, but somehow wound up here. Why he felt this way, he didn't know. Something deep inside him just told him this was the case.

The young knight let the panther paw swing back and forth in front of him as he thought. Why had Panthor led him here? For what purpose? He'd come all this way, even had all those visions about an old necklace? What was going on? Why didn't any of this make any sense?

"The necklace is yours," the soft and familiar voice of Panthor came from behind the youth.

Rowan jumped and nearly dropped the necklace to the ground when he heard those words. Instantly the youth turned and knelt before the image of his goddess.

"Panthor, forgive me," Rowan hid his eyes from his goddess.

"For what?" Her voice was jovial. "I led you here to receive this gift."

"Thank you, great goddess. May I humbly ask why you did so? It seems as though you went to a great deal of effort to lead me to this rather simple necklace. I mean no disrespect; I simply wish to learn from your ways and grow better as your servant." He kept his eyes low to the ground as he spoke.

"Rowan, you have always pleased me," Panthor smiled. "The gift is given for another time to come. When you are ready, you will understand just what this token of my favor has to do with you and your calling into the Knighthood. You have a great future before you - that is yet to arise. A future where this gift I give you today will be needed.

"Until then, wear it as a pledge of my favor to you for the rest of your life."

"Thank you, " Rowan bowed to the floor. "I will do so always."

"I also understand your plight on this mission. I've been watching you. You've had a very difficult time about it, but things will soon turn around and when they do, you will begin to see your true calling, and your greater purpose. There are powerful and wonderful plans tied to you, Rowan, and one day soon you will understand all of what I speak." Her voice was as comforting as a mother.

"Until then, carry my gift with you and recall my disposition toward you."

"I will remember," Rowan rose from his prostration to return to his humbled kneeling.

"And don't doubt your heart. Listen to it, but don't be ruled by it - not yet!" The image of the goddess faded from sight as she spoke her last words to the youth.

"What does…" Rowan's question was cut short by a roar of a panther, and then silence. He dared a look around the room, and saw it was dark and empty once more. The knight stood up, and put the necklace around his neck, looked at it once more, then shoved it beneath his armor, close to his skin.

"Hello?" Rowan slowly felt his way out of the dark room. "Panthor?"

There was no response from the darkness. Rowan's heart sank as he looked around, then panic seized him as he thought he felt another presence in the gloom with him, though it wasn't comprised of the essence of his goddess. The grip on his blade tightened as he prepared to face the threat.

"Who are you speaking to?" A voice, no more than a whisper, floated to Rowan's ears.

The youth spun around ready to face his attacker, but he saw nothing but darkness. "Who are you?"

"I am a citizen of Gondad, but you are not. Yet you are human, how strange," the whisper continued.

"Where are you?" Rowan paced in a circle, his blade held in front of him. He strained his eyes looking for any movement outside his defenses.

"Do not fear me, young warrior, I mean you no harm," came the voice's reply.

"If that's true, then show yourself." Rowan steadied his nerves for anything that might come his way.

"Very well," a pale, translucent light shimmered into being. It took on the semblance of a human man, surrounded by a glowing white aura. He had obviously suffered a gruesome death: his torso was mangled by many open wounds - the result of being riddled with arrows and sliced through with swords. The worst, Rowan thought, was his face, which had a deep line cut diagonally through it, cutting the nose in half. The gash was so deep it exposed the bone underneath. Hideous in its incorporeal form,

Rowan had to avert his eyes from the sight.

"By Panthor! What manner of fiend are you?" Rowan took up a defensive position.

"I have already told you," the ghost said softly. "I am a citizen of Gondad."

"Gondad is dead. It was destroyed thousands of years ago," the knight held his stance.

"Yet I remain," the ghost hovered closer to the youth.

"Keep your ground..." Rowan leveled his sword before the ghostly figure.

"As I have said before, young warrior, I am not here to hurt you. Be at ease. I am here to guide you."

"Guide me to where?" Rowan scanned the darkness once more, fearing ambush. "Who sent you? Was it Panthor?" Rowan took a tentative step closer, for he thought the shattered face of the ghost looked familiar the longer he stared at it.

"No, I have no knowledge of this person you speak about." The ghost spoke the truth.

"You don't know the goddess of the human race?" Rowan was shocked.

"Yes, of course I do. Asora is the great creator of the human race," the ghost answered softly.

"No, you're wrong!" Rowan felt a sense of pride come over him. It twisted his mouth into a smirk of arrogance as he spoke words not solely his own, but still was fueled by the Nordic fire in his blood. "Maybe the elves who conquered you beat such thoughts into your head. Panthor is the only goddess of humanity, blessing us with her protection and prosperity. I am one of her knights, who see to it her will is carried out on the world."

"Forgive me, I have angered you. I forget I have not seen the world since my death. Much it seems has changed," the ghost bowed in respect. When he did so, a loose flap of skin on his scalp fell over his face, returning to its resting place when he rose up again.

"You still haven't told me who sent you," Rowan lowered his blade a bit, but remained ready for an attack.

"The ruler of this city, by divine right and by birth, and will be until the end of time. He wishes to meet all visitors to his city," said the ghost.

The realization finally came to Rowan;"You mean to say he's Cirmelian? That is who wishes to speak with me?"

"Yes," the ghost replied.

"Then take me too him- by all means. He is one of the foundations upon which the Knighthood is built!" Rowan was truly amazed at how highly he was favored by Panthor. The gift of the necklace was one thing - but an audience with Cirmelian himself? It was very humbling, and exciting indeed!

"Very well then - come with me," the ghost motioned the knight to follow as he turned and headed off.

Rowan sheathed his sword, and followed.

Chapter 24

*After Rowan's dash into the ruins, the others spoke about a few trivial matters, then grew silent. The long journey and present circumstances gained the better of them. Each simply stared into the firelight for a little while longer before they felt sleep clawing at their minds, and moved to rest for the night.

Cadrissa absently coiled a few black satin locks as she dared a quick peek at the Telborian, who was slightly across from the mage. Upon being noticed by the gladiator her eyes quickly darted away, a simple giddiness and smirk joined her flushed checks.

"I think she fancies you, Dugan!" Vinder whispered with a smirk on his face.

"I know," Dugan smiled. "She's had her eye on me ever since we met in Altorbia. She's a good enough woman, but I fear our nights would be consumed with dusting bookshelves and reciting histories. I'm a man who craves a woman with fire."

Vinder chuckled to himself. "They say wizards make incredible lovers. They have the ability to give their mate all they desire with just a touch of their hands."

"I don't have time for it right now. Besides, she's too young. She looks to have crawled out of her mother's legs not more than a few years ago. I have to keep my mind focused on the task at hand. There will be plenty of time for other activities once I'm free from this blasted jungle."

The Telborian arched his back to stretch from the day's long, hard trek.

"I'll drink to that," Vinder smiled. "That is, I would, if we had anything left to drink."

"Still though, she isn't so hard on the eye, and I haven't been with a woman in a long time," Dugan smirked. "Maybe after this little adventure is over I can learn a bit more about history."

Cadrissa peered at the Telborian again. Then both Dugan and Vinder erupted in laughter.

"What's so funny?" The mage's brow furrowing in uncertainty.

"Nothing lass, nothing at all," the dwarf chuckled.

"We should rest for the night," Clara strode to the trio, breaking up any further discourse. "It's getting awfully late, and we have a lot of ground to cover tomorrow. Vinder, you're on first watch."

The group said nothing, but within a few short moments, Vinder was on sentry duty while the others tried to get comfortable on the rocky ground.

Cadrissa was asleep as soon as she lay down, and though Vinder and Dugan wouldn't admit it, they too felt tired and sickly from the weather and terrain. Gilban and Clara laid next to each other, and watched the darkness for a while until their eyelids became weighed down by sleep's hand as well. All around them, the wilderness whispered its sweet lullaby as the fire shrank and cooled.

Hours later, Vinder woke Dugan to take over the second shift, but paused over the gladiator when he heard a noise. "Did you hear that, Dugan?" he whispered.

The Telborian had already tensed, his gladius ready. "I heard it. Sounds like its coming from the west."

Northwest, as I reckon it.might be Rowan, what do you think?" Vinder whispered.

"He wouldn't be trying to be so stealthy," came Dugan's soft reply. "Pretend you didn't hear it, and look like you're sleeping."

Dugan rose from his bed. "I'll pretend I have to empty the flagon. If it is Rowan, we'll give him a surprise."

Vinder smirked to himself as Dugan wandered to the stand of trees, slowly tearing up the cobblestone streets of Gondad with their corded roots like the rest of the jungle nibbling away at the ruins. The dwarf lay down on his blanket, his great axe in hand beside him. Both Dugan's and Vinder's nerves twitched as their muscles bunched; each could taste the keen tang of steel in their mouths.

Dugan went further into the bushes, and scanned through the dense growth as best he could in the limited light, while he pretended to be preoccupied with emptying his bladder.

He found nothing.

Heard nothing.

Convinced it was the movements of an animal, or even the wind, he left the area. As he turned to leave, he felt a blade pressed up against his neck. The blade itself was rough and uneven. Though it was crudely fashioned, Dugan knew it was sharp enough to cause grievous injury if drawn across the throat of its victim. He struggled to see his attacker, but could only make out a tight iron arm of dark skin.

At least he knew it wasn't Rowan who held him.

"Obja nemoa keinke!" Dugan's captor shouted next to his ear.

The wilderness became alive with dark forms of Celetor warriors who quickly encircled the camp in a mob of men too thick to count. Celetors were a type of human who possessed darker skin and hair, preferring to live in the jungles and deserts of the Tralodren, where other lines of humanity tended not to go.

Vinder jumped up from his bed, ready to fight. "To arms, we are under attack!" the dwarf shouted, as a fierce black warrior came toward him.

Chapter 25

Together, Rowan and the spirit traveled down endless corridors and dark rooms full of pitfalls and traps which could easily have killed an unwary explorer if they didn't have a guide to help them. The ghost's illumination was almost equal to a torch, and easily led the knight through the broken and twisted halls.

They were the dim rooms of yesteryear, covered with thick carpets of dust and cobwebs. Any former glory they once held had long since faded.

Rowan had been taught, like the rest of the human race, it was from behind the archaic walls of Gondad that humanity ushered out of to cover Tralodren. They lived in the city for hundreds of years in peace and prosperity, increasing in knowledge and size until war-hungry elves came down upon them. Cirmelian fought them with the righteous power of the gods on his side, holding them at bay until he died of a wasting disease which came with old age.

Rowan walked through the halls with a sense of awe. He was traveling down the very halls the mightiest human kings had walked. He was in the presence of history! Though his surroundings were drab and decrepit, Rowan's very soul felt as though it was soaring in the heavens. No one in his Order had ever found this ancient city - and now here he was; inside it - and about to speak with the last great ruler of the city as well...

"We are here," the ghost sighed as it stopped at an old cobweb-layered wooden door. Rowan placed his hand reverently on the large door. It was about seven feet tall, and ten feet wide, with a carved image depicting a lion and a rabbit standing on either side of a great cauldron.

"What's this crest on the door?" the knight asked. "I'm not familiar with it."

"Strange you are not," the ghost's words were dry. "It is the crest of Gondad. It tells of our belief in creation by Asora, which you also do not seem to share."

The youth cleared off the old cobwebs, and used his fingers to dig the grime of ages out of the deep grooves. "A rabbit and a lion?"

"Long ago, these were the two animals Asora put into a great cooking pot. She stirred them around so fast what came out was a human being. It is because of this creation we have the heart, strength, and willpower of a lion, and the gentle, loving, peaceful traits of the rabbit."

"A good myth, but nothing true rests in it," the youth pushed the doors open. They creaked and moaned after years of neglect.

"Cirmelian is in here then?" Rowan peered with hesitant wonder into the opening beyond.

"Yes," the ghost's voice grew fainter, but Rowan paid it no mind. He stepped into the pitch-black room without a second thought.

"How can I see if I have no torch?" Rowan tried to search about the darkness of the interior.

Suddenly the room was lit up with a burst of flames from a row of empty sconces lining the side walls. Like spectral torches from long ago, the light sources illuminated the room's interior.

It too, like the rest of the building, hadn't been treated well by time's ravages. Only a rotten wooden throne remained with a skeletal form resting upon it.

This skeleton was draped in a few scraps of robe, and some dull jewelry. Wisps of hair no more visible than strands of spiderwebbing draped down from the skull's crest. A crusty green-colored crown sat on his head, and a scepter of tarnished iron was in his left hand, which lay across his empty chest.

"Cirmelian..." Rowan whispered in awe, breaking the silence.

"Rowan," a faint voice called from a great distance away.

"Is it you, Cirmelian?" Rowan checked around the room. All he could see was the ghost who had led him to the chamber, though the specter wavered in and out of sight more frequently than before.

"It is I," the shadow seemed to shift slightly, then a figure emerged from beside the throne. Like Rowan's guide, it was translucent and pale white. He wore a death shroud as a cloak, which hid a great deal of his features as it twisted in an unseen wind that sent waves of cold, frosty air into the warm room.

Rowan bowed.

"Rise, sir knight. Though I was once a king, I come now to bring you a message to aid you on your quest," the spectral figure motioned for the knight to come closer.

"You know of my quest?" Rowan cautiously drew closer.

"Yes. You seek the ruined city of Groledron, in the misty land of Takta Lu Lama, not far from here. There, you wish to meet with the dark inhabitants of that city in order to bring honor to your knighthood by finding out what can make a nation great," the figure watched Rowan stop a few feet from his throne.

"That is true, but you said you were a messenger. What is this message you bring me?" Questioned the youth.

Before Rowan could react, the spirit's translucent hand shot out, and gripped his head. Icy bursts of pain washed over the youth for a moment as he tried to struggle, but failed in his attempts to become a receptive thrall of a man instead.

Content with the condition of his victim, the ghost's form shifted toward that of The Master. His cold, empty, bony grin peered across at the youth triumphantly.

"Now listen, whelp. You are going to locate a tall blue cylinder in the ruins. Don't touch it, but instead, after the mage has cast her spell, you are to kill the demon who comes through the gate.

"Do you understand?" The command came as a frigid snarl.

Rowan nodded.

"Good. I've given your sword the ability to destroy the demon, so don't have any fear when you confront him - he's a threat to your Knighthood, and has to be destroyed.

"After you've destroyed him, your mind will be your own once more, and you will remember nothing of what was spoken to you here by me. You also won't recall anything more than speaking with the ghost of Cirmelian who told you how your service to humanity is a matter of seeking out these lost ruins, and hindering such knowledge from being used against the world again.

"Do you understand?"

Rowan again silently nodded.

"Good. Now go!" The Master ordered.

The Master lifted his hand from Rowan's head, which caused him to rise to his feet as the room faded from existence, replaced by the campsite where he had left the others resting before he was drawn inside the ruins. The fire had grown low, and the others were nowhere to be seen.

Rowan stood still as he figured out what he needed to do. This moment of deliberation passed quickly, however, as he felt a familiar twinge, making the hairs on the back of his neck stand up. There was the presence of other beings close at hand. He could almost feel their breath upon his skin.

He looked from side to side, trying to make out shapes in the gloom, and caught sight of a dark silhouette. It appeared to be a man of normal height and weight, yet the being was so swift Rowan could barely make it out. The youth found he was incapable of sensing where the stranger might appear next. From what he had just experienced with Cirmelian, he wasn't about to rule out whether the creature was supernatural. The knight didn't know if the man-thing in the darkness was harmful or benevolent. He would find out soon enough, however.

"Who goes there?" Rowan called out in Telborous into the shadows. "Identify yourself!"

No sooner had he spoken when he was surrounded by dark-skinned warriors who wore nothing more than loin-cloths, and carried spears of roughly-hewn wood. One of the more spindly men approached Rowan with his spear out-stretched.

"I mean you no harm," Rowan said in Abjula, the language of the Celetors.

The ebony men halted for a moment to whisper among themselves. Rowan waited as their conversation drew on for a few more moments, then allowed another Celetor to pass toward the Nordican.

This Celetor was dressed like the others: a simple loincloth, bare feet and short-cropped, tightly-curled, black hair. However, he wore a green and blue feathered necklace as well as a simple bone bracelet about his left wrist. Like the others, he carried a bone-tipped wooden spear, but his was of a higher quality from what Rowan could gather – and newer too.

"Why do you come here, white man?" The young Celetor asked in the same tongue Rowan spoke. "How does a pale-face know the words of my people?"

"I'm Rowan Cortak, a knight of Panthor, and I am here with some other people on a mission for my goddess."

"You honor Panthor?" The Celetors lowered their spears, and took up a more relaxed stance, as the lead Celetor took a step toward Rowan.

"Yes. All the Knighthood to which I belong does... you haven't seen any other people here have you? They were right here by this fire, and now they're gone."

"Ah, you mean them," the lead Celetor pointed to a dark corner of the wood where slumped, tied bodies could be seen just out of the firelight. "We thought they were coming to attack us, like the others did."

"No, these are the people I traveled here with... they're not here to attack you, or your tribe," Rowan moved to look over at the bodies. The nearby Celetors tensed at first, but with a wave of the lead Celetor's hand, their bodies relaxed at the Nordican's passing. Only their eyes followed him.

"What did you do to them?" Rowan asked.

"Sleep dart. We didn't want to kill. Just question them," the Celetor replied.

"Why did you think they were here to do you harm?" Rowan turned toward the lead Celetor.

"Those two," the Celetor motioned to Clara and Gilban. "They look like the same people who came to this land a short time ago, and attacked us before we drove them off into the jungle."

"Elves?" Rowan said flatly. "People like this attacked you?"

"Yes, one moon ago they came out of the jungle to slaughter us after we caught them trying to steal some of our food. My own brother, Ekube, was killed in the attack."

Rowan shook his head in sympathy.

"What's your name?" Asked the knight.

"I am called Nabu, son of Kabawa."

He held out his hand. Nabu looked at it, uncertain of what to do. Rowan laughed. "Like this." Rowan took Nabu's hand and clasped it tight at the wrist. "This is how my people show friendship."

Rowan grinned at the cautious look crossing Nabu's face. Nabu suddenly gave him a toothy grin. "I am also glad to call you friend."

"You have nothing to fear from the others either." Rowan motioned to the unconscious elves. "They mean you no harm. They aren't the same people who attacked your village."

Nabu peered into Rowan's eyes for a long moment "Your words have the weight of truth, and I can sense you do hold a reverence to the great Panthor."

Nabu motioned to the other Celetors standing by their sleeping captives, and they began to cut the rough bindings holding them.

"They seem to respect and trust you. Are you their leader?" Rowan asked Nabu.

Nabu turned back to Rowan with a twinkle in his eye, "You may say so."

"You answer like some priests I know," Rowan grinned.

"I am not as wise or gifted to be a priest," Nabu stated flatly, obviously not understanding the private jest.

"How long will the sleep poison last?" Rowan turned again to where the others were. The Celetors had managed to free them, and lay them on the ground.

"Not that long," Nabu assured the knight. "We just wanted them to sleep long enough to get to our village and question them there."

"So they should be awake by morning then?" Rowan asked.

"If not sooner," Nabu looked down at the slumbering figures.

"How far away is your village?" Rowan took a look at the night sky.

"Not far from here," Nabu answered.

"Could you lead us back there?" Rowan took a few steps closer to the sleeping mercenaries.

"Why?" Nabu looked the young knight up and down.

"We need some food and supplies for our journey," Rowan held up his hand to calm Nabu. "However, we would pay or trade for what we needed. You have my word on it."

Nabu looked at him for a moment, his brown eyes shimmering in the starlight. "Where are you traveling to?"

"To the ruins of Groledron. We thought these ruins were the right ones, but it turns out they're some ways off yet," the knight answered truthfully.

"Why are you going there?" Nabu's face wrinkled in wonder.

"We are looking to protect some knowledge hidden in them from the people who attacked you."

"That is a worthy cause, friend Rowan, and I know those ruins well."

"You do?" Rowan's eyes widened.

Nabu nodded. "Yes, they are not far from our lands."

"Really? Would you be able to guide us to them?" Rowan's face lit up with hope.

"I trust you, because you share the same faith, and are human- but the others...they are not human, save for two," Nabu pointed them out among the slumbering group.

"If you trust me, Nabu, then believe me when I say the others are worthy of the same trust," Rowan peered deep into Nabu's eyes, trying to impress his honest intentions as he could since, this was how Nabu and his people seemed to measure the validity of each other's word. "We mean you no harm, and share the same enemy. We just want to resume our mission, and get some food, water and supplies for our journey ahead."

Nabu pondered this before he walked to a group of his people to discuss the matter. Rowan waited patiently until Nabu returned.

"The others have agreed to take you back with us to our village. If they are trouble, we can easily deal with them there. Once there, the chieftain will make the decisions to your requests."

"That sounds fair," Rowan smiled. "When do we leave."

"Now. The others will carry your friends. You will follow me." Nabu started off for the dark jungle as the others picked up the slumbering mercenaries.

"Are you sure you can carry them all?" the youth asked.

The other Celetors erupted in laughter.

"I'll take that as a yes then," the knight quickened his pace. Nabu had already been swallowed by the jungle.

Chapter 26

The Master hurried at his task, the dismal light glowing from his scrying skull; casting haunting shadows across his fleshless face. He piled old tomes and other mystical objects into a chest made entirely of bones. The horrid construct glowed a soft amber as its insides became more congested. When the trunk was full, he spoke a few mystical words over it: "Sop-Yek." The magical chest closed, and a tongue of red flame ran along the seam of the lid, sealing the container.

"And now I wait," his dry voice rasped.

We wait, mage. The shadows swelled behind The Master. They pulsated like human breath before thickening in form. Balon materialized out of the darkness behind The Master, his fiery eyes scorching The Master with their malevolence. His evil presence was like syrup as the demon poured himself closer to the lich.

He knew Balon would be along soon, and so was glad he had been able to finish up the other matter with Rowan and the other pieces of his plan before the demon had arrived. Now he just had to put up with his presence a little while longe, and he'd be free to complete his goals.

It seems all is in preparation, Balon's words hissed in The Master's mind. *When do we leave?*

"Soon," The Master replied, piling three rat-colored bags filled with his remaining possessions on top of the skeletal chest. "It is best not to get impatient. Rest, the time will come."

I am not leaving your side for a moment. Deceit runs through your bones as deep as your magic. Balon stared into the vacant eye sockets of the wizard.

The Master ignored the veiled threat, and sprinkled some dust from a small pouch over his stacked belongings. The chest and bags glowed with an unnatural, yellow light, then began to shrink. The chest had once been the size of half a man, but became equal to a hand in width. The bags on top, changed into a size likened unto fingernails.

"Very well," The Master sighed reluctantly, "but your presence here could disrupt my spells. Don't get in my way."

I think your lack of respect for my station is a great error. Balon floated behind The Master. Chilling waves of cold hate washed out from him, enveloping The Master's own frigid aura with its intensity. *I am royalty, one of the most powerful dukes in the Abyss. It is I who out rank you.*

The Master stopped in the middle of an incantation. His disheveled robes rustled up a puff of dust as he turned to face the demon, eye sockets as empty as his heart.

"Order me? It seems, sweet duke, you're at a loss. What gives you your station? Whom do you rule? I see no subjects!" The Master looked around the room mockingly. "Where are they, Balon? Come on out!" The Master feigned a distressed tone as he addressed the gloom around them. "Do duty by your duke!"

Had the undead wizard still had flesh about his face, the sarcastic sneer which followed would have been more evident. As it was, only a slight angle of the lich's head showed to give any evidence away of this mannerism.

"If you are a duke, then it is one of dust and emptiness. I found you wounded, and gave you shelter from your enemies. It was I who told you of my plan to escape this realm and allowed you to come along with me. Do not be confused!"

Balon fell silent for a moment, his eyes flickering with hot wrath.

You assume much, wizard, he said in a quiet, hostile tone. *I have had to suffer much for the benefit of my subjects. These trails though, will all be worth it if I lay claim to Tralodren where I will regain my strength and raise an army to take back my domain.*

The Master wandered gingerly, placing his miniaturized possessions in a timeworn pouch hanging from his belt. "Don't delude yourself, Balon. Tralodren is a world of mortals. They would make poor subjects and even poorer soldiers. Why would you want to aid your people at all? A people who willingly expelled you, I might add. I would just let them rot in their own suffering."

They were deceived into thinking unjustly. When I return, I will show them the error of their ways. Balon's eyes flared with a deep red glare.

"If you return," The Master muttered dustily.

What are you implying, treacherous mage? Balon growled as The Master wandered away from him toward the glowing skull perched on a pedestal across the room. The lich ignored the question, and began to peer into the bone sphere.

He hated the long years of torment he had endured since his expulsion from Tralodren a thousand - years ago. At first, Balon had been a useful pawn, but he had outlasted his potential many centuries ago. The lich began to see him as an incessant child, always demanding more with each passing year. He would be free of the fool soon enough.

In the beginning, when The Master had first come to this hell to escape the Divine Vindication, where all the magic of Tralodren was revoked by divine decree, Balon had been a good ally. Freshly dethroned from his rulership over his demonic territory, his will was strong and he still managed to hang onto life, albeit a shadow of his former existence even after his body had been ripped into it's three separate natures; body, soul and spirit.

The Master taught the demon the will needed to keep himself together, and Balon allowed him to gain an insight into the politics and landscape of the Abyss. Keen among his aid to The Master was steering him clear of the Lords of Evil, who were the ultimate authority of the Abyss and would have liked nothing better than to add The Master to their collection of tortured slaves. Here the lich would spend many centuries until Tralodren again was allowed magic and mages. The lessons had helped Balon, but he grew impatient with The Master as he began to look for a way to return home. Thankfully Balon didn't know how much of The Master's power was fading.

Most of his magical arts were dwindling; it seemed even the decree of the gods hindered him on another plane. In the end, all he had left to use were a few enchanted items - chief among them, his staff. In time these, too, were used up and the lich had to begin to conserve his power. He didn't tell Balon this - he wanted to keep the slight edge he had - but he knew if he didn't get out of the realm soon, and back to Tralodren where he could recharge his power and form, then he would dwindle away on the realm he now abided, his one-time haven would become his prison.

He had to bide his time carefully. He'd laid his plans, and sought out his players; now he just had to be ready and wait. It would happen soon enough. He had to conserve his mystical powers long enough to survive the journey and task at hand. Balon would be finished soon enough. However, it seemed of late the demon was more crafty than The Master had supposed. He'd been growing bolder of late, making more innuendoes about his suspicious the lich wasn't as great in mystical might as he once might have been. Once they got to Tralodren again, though, things would take a dramatic upswing for the lich.

The fiend's death had been arranged by The Master. He had fooled Balon into thinking once he got to Tralodren he would be made a god. What he knew instead was when Balon stepped forth onto the world, he would be made flesh - mortal flesh - and could be killed in finality - ending his perpetual prattling, and schemes of returning to glory. The Master now just had to be patient as his plans came together. Patient and entertaining for a little while longer…

I said: what are you implying? Balon spat.

The Master turned toward the hunched, shadowy demon and sighed. "Why must we always have this conversation?" How he would relish his absence.

"You are not as powerful as you think you are. Need I remind you how your corporeal form is hardly able to maintain itself? You exist only as a shadowy outline. You are weaker than the subjects you ruled over. Now, for the final time, will you let this tiresome conversation end?"

Balon's shadow shifted, and changed for a long time, as if he were trying to wrestle himself back into a solid shape.

We shall see who comes out on top, Balon coldly snapped as he floated off to a corner to stand watch over the mage. Balon wasn't going anywhere. Not yet. The Master couldn't be trusted any more, and the demon wasn't going to take a chance at being betrayed when he was so close to getting free, and being given a chance to reclaim his lost glory.

Satisfied with the result, the old mage continued to recast his interrupted spell.

Chapter 27

So they will take us to the ruins then?" Clara asked Rowan, who looked at her face with a pleasant air about himself. A strange, almost childlike excitement had claimed his stomach and heart when Clara looked into his eyes.

"Yes," Rowan said softly to the elf. "I'm still waiting to hear if they will allow us to get some supplies,"

The sun rose higher in the sky as the early morning grew old. Rowan had just finished explaining what had happened to them since they were camping the night before as they had finally awakened and were coherent enough to understand what he told them. He shared with them how the Ghin, Nabu's tribe, originally thought they were enemies, and drugged them for questioning. He explained how the Celetors carried them back to the village where they had rested through what remained of the night.

The village was crafted from simple, natural materials, sprawled out across the forest floor. Although they were crafted to be temporary structures, ready to fold at a moment's notice, they were sturdy, and made to blend in with the leafy surroundings.

The houses were simple huts with frames of thick branches wrapped in animal hide with conical thatch roofs. Small fire pits were dug about the area every so often as communal hearths, each with a spit for roasting and smoking game, some of them already in use for the morning. Only a few of the villagers were moving about at this early hour.

It took some convincing by the knight, but he got the others their freedom and possessions once more. Once they understood the mercenaries were not a threat, they agreed. Rowan, however, still had to wait for the chieftain's decision before they could get supplies for their journey. Nabu had left to take up their cause with the chieftain.

It was also decided a group of Celetors would lead them to the ruins they sought, partly to make sure they leave their territory, and partly to help Rowan. Nabu seemed to like the Nordican for some reason. Rowan assumed it was partly from their shared faith, but the knight thought it was more, and wondered if the necklace near his chest had something to do with it. If it had caused something to occur between them... he was unsure; his mind tended to wander to Clara's sapphire eyes as he spoke.

"I still can't believe they drugged us, and didn't kill us. I know I would have," Dugan sat on an old, toppled log among the others in a semicircle. Rowan crouched in the middle of them.

"That's not their way," Rowan answered.

"I still can't believe they fed us and took us back here, too," added Vinder.

"We should be able to get those supplies. I have a good feeling about it," Rowan added some more optimism.

"Well, what do we do until we have the verdict then?" Dugan asked the knight.

"Nabu said it was all right for us to wander around freely, and explore the village." Rowan answered the Telborian.

"Really?" Cadrissa's eyebrows raised.

"Yes," Rowan continued. "In fact, some of them can speak Telborous. They learned it from a Nordic missionary of Panthor who came here about 300 years ago. While it's not always good, it can be understood most of the time, and you all should be able to look around and ask questions without trouble."

"Beats sitting on this log all day," the Telborian rose, the others around him following his cue.

"I should have the answer soon," Rowan said to them as they began to leave. "Don't wander far - I'll send word when I hear it."

The group spent the remainder of the day watching the tribe in wonder. They saw topless women carrying baskets on their heads filled with all manner of food, clothing, and other supplies, while children of all ages ran about their heels. Men sharpened spear points, and basked near outdoor cooking fires, talking and bragging about days long past. It was a tightly-knit community with at least 400 members.

Eventually, Cadrissa went to speak to some wise men, hoping to learn their native tongue, and some of their history. Gilban left also, to speak to the village priest about his views on religious matters. Vinder surveyed the various tools and art objects the tribe made and collected over the years, watchful of anything that might be worthwhile to add to his tribute. Dugan looked around the village with a disinterested eye, and returned back to the log. He was content to simply sit around, and look deep into a nearby fire in contemplation. Rowan did the same, as he was lost in his thoughts. Clara joined them, watching the young knight and the fire.

The strange feeling troubling her before returned once again: a knot of sorts, which had been growing stronger since she met him It tied itself firmer in her stomach. She felt sick, but at the same time wonderful, as though she was fully alive. Looking at the self-reflective knight filled her with a powerful tingle running up her legs and chest. What was going on?

Then, it hit her square between the eyes. She was falling in love with the Nordic youth. How could she be seriously falling in love with this child? She was old enough to be his grandmother! It was insane - and she tried to pass it off with all the excuses she could come up with; from the heat, humidity, the stress of the trip - and any other probable cause. Still, the feelings wouldn't go away, and her body continued to tell her what she didn't want to believe.

She dreaded the feeling - as it wasn't good for elves and humans to become lovers. Though they were compatible - the only compatible coupling of two different species on Tralodren who could successfully reproduce - their offspring and strain on the relationship was often more a curse than a blessing.

Elves lived for hundreds of years, whereas humans lived barely beyond a mere century. Ultimately, she would be an elven widow, living with grief for the rest of her life should she not seek out a new companion.

Offspring was another matter. Elven and human unions produced children who were neither elf, nor human, but somewhere in between. They were half-breeds; half-elves, or half-humans - depending to whom one spoke. They could look like elven children with slight human attributes to strange and exceptionally handsome humans - or perhaps, a frightening combination of both parents. So few were born, though, that most reports of such children were legends. Myths and folklore weren't the best source of what to expect from such a union.

What could be said to be undeniably true was that often the mother was left alone to raise the baby, deserted by her mate of either race, who usually couldn't handle what he'd sired.

These, and other grim thoughts ran through Clara's mind as she watched Rowan through veiled eyes. A quick shift in his sitting position though, and her heart was a flutter, her dark thoughts put to rest. At the same time she thought of these things, she was repulsed by a deep, inner voice. A voice told her to temper her emotions, and keep to the task at hand.

She didn't have time to be a moonstruck fool. Countless lives depended upon her, and this mission's success. She had a higher duty - a goal to succeed at any cost. She grew angry at the turmoil inside herself, and so left the fire's edge as the smells of freshly-cooked meat wafted through the village, heading for the forest's interior.

The anger was not only about her feelings, but also at having finally been able to figure out Rowan's mood and mannerisms since they met. He felt an attraction to the elf as well, she was sure of it! The weight of her recent discovery sat hard upon her shoulders. Everything had suddenly become all the more complicated.

Rowan looked up at her for a moment as she left. He too, had been fighting an internal battle, and trying to win over his emotions. He was actually about to join the elf, to explain his feelings to her - and be done with it, when Nabu's hand rested on his shoulder.

"Hello friend, Rowan," Nabu smiled and sat down next to the youth, across from Dugan. He spoke in Abjula.

"What did they decide?" Dugan asked Rowan.

After a few moments of discussion in the Celetoric tongue, the knight gave the Telborian his answer in Telborous. "He's convinced them to let us have the supplies we need, and they will lead us to the outskirts of the ruins, but no farther."

"I'll go tell the others," Dugan left.

"I'll find Gilban," Clara joined him.

"Thank you Nabu," the youth patted the Celetor's shoulder in appreciation as they continued to talk in Abjula. "I hope our coming here didn't put you in bad position."

"No, I know the chieftain well, and he respects my judgment," Nabu smiled.

"Really?" Rowan smiled back. "Then thank Panthor we met as we did. I'd hate to make an enemy of... what are you then? Sub-chieftain?"

"I am his son," Nabu poked a nearby stick into the fire.

"His son?" Rowan spouted out in Telborous as he braced himself from nearly toppling off the log where he sat.

"Yes," Nabu remained calm throughout Rowan's excitement, switching to Telborous now that they were alone. "I will be replacing him soon as he is getting older and sick. Until then, he is chieftain of the Ghin, and a wise father as well."

"You speak Telborous very well." Rowan was amazed..

"I learned it almost as well as I did my lessons on Panthor," Nabu's grin widened. "I had a good teacher."

"Thank you for trusting us," Rowan's face became a bit more serious.

"You convinced me of the others' good faith, Rowan. True friends do this. There is nothing to be thanked for." It was Nabu's turn to clap his hand on Rowan's shoulder.

"I'm just amazed with how the grace of Panthor moved in this affair. I never would have guessed a missionary from my Knighthood so long ago would seed the faith and fate."

"Yes, Panthor is a wonderful worker of miracles," Nabu was then concerned."Before I came here, I saw your face was long and thoughts and wondered why you had such pain on such a beautiful day?

"Panthor has given us much to be thankful for. What troubles your thoughts, my friend?" Nabu's inquisitive eyes locked onto Rowan's.

"Life," the young knight released a deep sigh.

"Ah, then you will never find the end to those murky waters. Living is full of them. Like my father's father said: Any man can look at his life, but only a true warrior can change its outcome." Rowan noticed Nabu made himself straighter when he spoke of his father – his chest puffed out with pride as he did so.

"He was very wise," Rowan looked back to the vacant spot where Clara had been moments before.

"You, my friend, are troubled by more than life. A woman has gotten a hold of you." The Celetor laughed a deep belly chuckle, making feelings of rage swell in Rowan.

"What woman?" The youth eyed the Celetor coldly. He was afraid to admit his weakness. Though why he thought of his growing love of Clara as a weakness, he didn't know. He was supposed to be a loyal and dedicated knight, and not be given to such flights of fantasy. However, if Nabu could see his affection for her, the others must as well - and that wasn't good at all. He wrestled with the emotions, at war with his very soul, yet he couldn't stop the battle in his heart, no matter how hard he tried and prayed.

"The elf woman is quite beautiful, my brother. You shouldn't be blamed for your feelings for her," Nabu counseled.

"But she's an elf!" Rowan shook his head as he turned his gaze toward the fire.

"Yes, she is. It is not unheard of for human and elf to marry. Such tales were passed on to us by the same priest who showed us the truth of Panthor. Why does this trouble you, Rowan?" Nabu asked the youth.

"You, of all people should know, Nabu. She is an elf, and we are humans." Rowan looked desperately at the dark-skinned warrior, hoping for some understanding of his point, some guidance along this path he was walking.

"Do you think, then, I have a problem with elves?" Nabu studied his face with care.

"Don't you?" It was Rowan's turn to study Nabu. "They raided your food supply, and killed you brother,"

"Not her, not Gilban" Nabu corrected the youth. "You told me that much already. While some elves might have attacked us, I don't hate them all. The few do not speak for the many, and the many are not the individual."

"What?" Rowan stood up from his seat with a bolt of energy. His face filled with anger. "How can you bear good feelings to a race of cruel and greedy rodents who seek to pillage and destroy the good and righteous in this world? Their kind wished to eradicate all humanity from existence! You cannot truly worship Panthor unless you only love humanity. You have sold yourself out to the enemy!"

Nabu remained calm throughout Rowan's tantrum. He had found a deeper problem troubling the youth. The missionary came to his tribe long ago speaking of the Valkorian knights having such views. Views remaining alive and well in force to the present day, it seemed.

"It is not I who have cowed to the enemy, it is you." Nabu spoke his words with care.

"Hold your tongue, Nabu! I would slay any other man who slighted the Knighthood - I..." Rowan stopped himself with his hand firmly grasping his sword. What was he doing? Where had he gotten these ideas - and such a strong conviction in them? Furthermore, what was he doing to his new friend, a person who meant him no harm, someone who paid him no ill will? He had done everything he could, and gone out of his way to help him on his quest.

"What have I been saying?" Rowan collapsed back into a sitting position.

"This was just what I was wondering," Nabu put his hand on the knight's shoulder. "The elves have never been seen as evil by my tribesmen, nor myself. So why would I bid them ill will now?"

Rowan clasped his head in his hands. "I wish I had just stayed at home. I should have never joined the Knighthood, or come on this mission. Life was much easier before all this."

"Your Knighthood must have taught you these ideals," Nabu enlightened Rowan with his belief.

"I don't see how they could have taught me them. I was trained and taught in the glory, honor, and dedication to the goddess. I would have remembered messages of hatred toward the elven race." Rowan was struck by the weight of the Celetor's words struck hard, because a part of him thought what Nabu said was true.

"Maybe they were taught to you in secret," Nabu said.

"In secret? I can't believe they'd do such a thing," Rowan looked up to the sky. "They're too holy. No. There must be another explanation."

"Perhaps," Nabu said no more, though he knew the truth.

But Rowan wasn't ready for the truth.

A commotion behind the pair alerted them the others had arrived. Dugan was able to round them up from all over the village.

"Dugan said they agreed to lead us to the ruins, and give us supplies," Clara stood next to the youth.

"Ask him when he is ready to leave," the elf sat down on the log beside Rowan.

"Ask him yourself," said the knight, "he understands Telborous."

"Vao, our priest, has said tomorrow has more favorable omens for travel." Nabu addressed Clara in Telborous.

"Forgive me Nabu," Clara bowed her head to the Celetor, "I didn't know you spoke Telborous so fluently."

"There is nothing to forgive," Nabu smiled. "You didn't know because I didn't tell you - not even Rowan until just recently."

"Making sure you knew our true intentions first then, eh?" Vinder studied the Celetor with a cautious eye.

"Something like that." Nabu returned the dwarf's stare with a smile.

"Well, if we are going to enjoy another night of your generous hospitality, could you tell us more about these ruins?" Clara asked.

"They are dark and ancient, filled with much evil. Often my fellow tribesmen left to look around the area to find food and animals to hunt, but many didn't return. Those who did said demons now live there, and take men for food,"

"What do these demons look like?" Clara was intrigued.

"They come out at dusk, when the sun is just vanishing into the night sky to catch my brothers unaware. They are slightly larger than a man, have yellowish skin... like the skin of a gourd, and monkey-like faces. They take those who fall prey to them away with little fight, leaving others alive to carry off the wounded." Nabu held the group captive with this tale.

"Hobgoblins," Dugan said as he listened.

The others looked at Gilban, but the old elf remained silent, and sat looking into the fire as though he were in a trance.

How long have they been living in the city?" Clara continued.

"Since at least ten moons ago, when they first decided to travel closer to the ruins in search of food." Nabu informed them.

"But they have never attacked you here, in your village?" Dugan asked.

"No…they have never attacked us here. They seem to stay near the ruins." Nabu's brow furrowed in thought. " I haven't figured out why, though."

"How far away are the ruins?" Clara took a step on the log, resting her shapely leg just beside Rowan, who spied it for a moment with an emotional jiggle in his stomach, as she leaned closer to the Celetor, waiting for answers.

"They're just a few hours travel through the thick forest - toward the west, if all is favorable for us." Nabu pointed out the way with his hand.

"Not so bad then, eh?" Vinder nodded. "I suppose we can rest up here one more night then, and get outfitted for the journey tomorrow before we head out."

"Agreed," said Clara.

The rest of the day saw the mercenaries lounge about the village in relative comfort. They ate well from a stew of fresh meat and vegetables the Celetors gathered from the jungle. Then at nightfall, at Nabu's request, the tribe entertained them with singing, dancing, and storytelling. It wasn't until the late evening, when the fires barely kept the darkness at bay, the group gathered around their own fire to rest.

Rowan and Clara could hardly sleep. They both tossed and turned. Thoughts of the other plagued their minds, and they were filled with an unquenchable fire.

Clara was able to contain herself with thoughts of her duty to the mission, Gilban, and her nation. Rowan was different. The more he thought about Clara, the more he heard a voice in the back of his head telling him tales of the evil elves who used people for their own ends, and how Panthor didn't support such feelings toward the elven race. The words conflicted with his heart, which burned in deep desire for the elven maid.

Nabu's words came back to him: Maybe they taught them to you in secret.

Trying to forget his troubled mind and heart, he closed his eyes and tried to let sleep overtake him.

Eventually it did.

Chapter 28

The sun had just risen over the thick canopy of Takta Lu Lama when the group finished readying the equipment they had been given by the Ghin. Though they wouldn't admit it, everyone was happy to finally be close to completing their task. The jungle was beginning to take its toll on them. Once they had all slung their gear over their shoulders, they headed into the forest.

Nabu was a strong and knowledgeable guide. Under his leadership, they managed to avoid many potential dangers and make good time.

Behind Nabu, Dugan cleared the way for the party, slashing through the thick undergrowth. Behind him, swatting away flies, gnats, and mosquitoes, was Clara, guiding Gilban through the twisting vines and roots constantly threatening to trip him. Cadrissa and Rowan followed suit, with Vinder taking up the rear.

"Where is that blasted Celetor?" Dugan grumbled as he swung again and again at the dense greenery of the forest. Nabu had vanished from his sight.

"He said he'd scout ahead for us, and then come back with the best route," Rowan kept his eyes looking around them, careful to note anything that might signal approaching danger.

"More likely he's been captured by some other band of savage brutes who seem to plague this place, and is lying dead somewhere," Vinder huffed.

"No," Gilban solemnly spoke. "He's alive, and he'll return."

Silence instantly fell over the group when the elder gave his answer.

Only Clara dared to speak. "Can you see anything up ahead, Dugan?"

"Nothing but more trees and vines," the Telborian continued to hack away; sweat running from his forehead, down his neck, and under his armor.

"Well, keep moving. We're bound to meet up with him sooner or later," Clara wiped her sweaty brow with her sleeve.

They traveled a while farther before Nabu emerged from the surrounding scenery without any noise to mark his arrival, startling them with his unique dialect.

"The way is not much farther, and clear of all danger."

Dugan and Vinder began to worry, based upon the ease in which Nabu had reappeared without a sound being heard. They realized they could be caught unaware of a potential onslaught of a whole host of silent dangers. Anything could be waiting for them... Now, they could almost feel hidden eyes searching them out; spearpoints leveled at them.

"Good," Dugan grumbled. "I'm getting tired of this infernal jungle."

"But are you ready for what may be ahead of us?" Cadrissa looked at him with an inquisitive smile. A small, girlish part of her was enjoying watching the Telborian work up a sweat.

"What are you saying?" the Telborian grunted through his rthymic swings.

"These ruins have been deserted for thousands of years, and now are inhabited by hobgoblins. It stands to reason it will be a trying task to even get inside them in the first place." Cadrissa voiced her thoughts to the others.

"Dangers I have faced before, in the arena no doubt," Dugan grunted.

"Have you now?" Cadrissa toyed with the Telborian. "Legends say many of these ruins are haunted by the past failures of the Ancients, a testimony to their ambition and pride."

"In my experience, lass," Vinder spoke up from the back of the line, his shorter strides keeping him equal with the others. "a quick slash with an axe renders anything less a danger,"

"Before you begin speculating about what may or may not lie in the ruins, let's get there first," Clara interjected. "The more you hypothesize, the more likely you'll get yourself into a panic over nothing."

Clara took charge of the conversation as she aided Gilban over an unevenly cleared section of ground Dugan had provided. "For now, let's just concentrate upon the matters at hand we do know about, and save our energy for any challenges as we face them."

Upon the heels of Clara's rebuke, they all fell silent. Left with their thoughts, they trudged through the jungle, following Nabu's lead. A little while later, as the group was beginning to think there was no end to the choking greenery around them, they suddenly came upon a large, hacked-out clearing of jungle. It was a strange contrast; as there were burn marks everywhere -, scorching their way up to a great towering mass of pitted stones and mortar.

"There is the city," Nabu pointed to the walls in a hushed tone.

The man-made clearing snaked around the whole outer city's old,half-crumbled walls, and away from the deep forest. The sun was just falling below high noon, and bled

liquid gold down behind the monolithic walls, adding a resonating aura to the scene before them.

It seemed as if the city had existed long before the
forest had come into being. Hardy ferns and creeping vines
were winning their slow invasion, however, making the walls
seem more like a lush waterfall of green than ancient stone.
Like ageless rock sentinels, they stood silent watch over a
jungle of life and death.

"Everyone, be on your guard," Clara ordered.

"Gilban?" Clara turned to the old elf, who had closed
his eyes, and stood in silent concentration.

"It is still here," his voice was barely a whisper.

"Then we have little time to waste," Clara focused
her eyes on the walls - partially rebuilt walls she noticed in
certain areas.

Vinder trundled forwards on his stunted legs to stand
next to Clara. "Look smoke," he pointed to the city skyline.

Everyone craned their necks skyward to see thin
trails of smoke float up from the interior of the city.

"Too soon to tell if they're elven or goblinoid," Clara
searched the horizon.

"I sense some powerful energy beyond the walls
also," Cadrissa spoke up. "It might be wise to be as secretive
as possible, until we have assessed the whole situation."

"Agreed," Clara looked toward Nabu. "Do you know
of a way into the city that might not be guarded by these
demons."

Nabu nodded. "I will take you to an area of clustered
ruins, just behind the wall, but will guide you no farther.
Once I've taken you beyond, your lives are no longer in my
hands, and I'll return to my tribe."

"It will be enough," Gilban said, and motioned to
Clara for her help. She went to him, and together they walked
toward the city. Nabu scampered before them, silently ges-

turing to a great hole in the wall leading into the ruins. The others followed behind them, keeping a constant vigil for danger on all sides. .Only Cadrissa took the time to fully enjoy the view the old city provided.

To the untrained eye, it seemed to be nothing more than a ruined wall, but to her, it was a treasure trove of stories from long ago, when a different people lived on Tralodren - a people whose very commands brought forth rock and flame; demons and angels. A race who crafted a mighty nation with their willpower and mystical might - but were not - it seemed, immune to the power of Asorlok and time.

She couldn't believe she was finally inside a Dranor city! She wanted to stop, search and catalog it all - but she knew the moment was against her. Quickly, the mage studied the old rock in earnest, lightly running a hand along pitted and worn stones as she hurried behind the rest of the group. She could feel so much knowledge dripping from the walls, through her fingers, and into her mind.

It was intoxicating.

Together they approached the hole in the ten-foot-high wall and peered into an opening stretching through fifteen feet of thick rock and mortar. Nabu softly chattered away with Rowan as the group stopped to look beyond the gaping opening. Beyond it, they could see nothing but fallen rock and ruined shells of buildings with the beginnings of structures appearing more sound beyond it. To the north, they could see black obelisks rising from the fertile jungle soil, each one that followed becoming more whole than the preceededing dark pillar.

The fourth and final obelisk stretched twenty feet into the air. From where they were, it looked like a burnt cinder of some old tree polished to a dull shine. The east was littered with rough tent-like dwellings interspersed with rougher stone houses made out of debris. They could see small fires with meat and other victuals roasting on low, smoky flames. The fires though, were too far away to see who tended them.

"What do we do now?" Dugan asked Clara.

"Be as silent as we can, and hope to get around the dwellings into the center of the city." Clara pointed their destination to the others. "Gilban believes the center of the city is where we will find the information we seek."

"And our deaths, from the high concentration of activity there," Dugan scoffed at the notion of being so reckless, so soon. "I think it will be safer to split up into smaller groups, and meet up at the center. Smaller numbers are easier to hide."

"I agree," Vinder stepped up to the conversation.

"I don't," Clara spoke softly. "We stick together. That is the plan,"

"I must go, my friend," Nabu clasped Rowan's hand as the others talked.

"I understand," Rowan replied. "You've helped us as best you could. Thank you. May Panthor eternally smile upon you."

"It wasn't a choice, but a sacred duty. I will pray to Panthor to grant you success in your quest." Nabu waved goodbye with a smile. "Farewell." .

"Farewell," Rowan returned the gesture.

Rowan watched the Celetor leave before he returned to the others. He would never forget Nabu's sacrifice, or his words, which still rang true to him at the moment: Maybe they taught it to you in secret.

After the dark-skinned son of Kabawa had merged into the woods around the ruins, Rowan returned to the others, who seemed ready for action. After filling him in they quietly moved through the ancient city.

They skittered past decaying dwellings, and discovered the number of opposition they faced.

"Hobgoblins!" Vinder hissed - just a hair above a whisper as they passed. "There must be well over fifty there alone."

"Shut up!" Cadrissa whispered. "Do you want to get us killed?"

None of the hobgoblins seemed to hear him, as they ravenously devoured their cooked flesh.

The mercenaries trekked farther inward, pausing only when a strange, eerie darkness fought for ownership of the afternoon sky. The thick blanket of blackness fell fast upon them, absorbing all light, melting it away into the ebony sheen.

Unable to see clearly, the party had to move more cautiously.

"This darkness isn't natural," Cadrissa whispered from behind Dugan.

"No, it isn't," Gilban agreed.

"Really?" Dugan flung out a sarcastic barb.

"What's causing it?" Vinder looked above him into the darkening heavens.

"Nothing good, I'm sure," Dugan kept his eyes on the hobgoblins, who seemed to be troubled by the sudden coming of night as well.

Vinder drew in a sharp breath as he took in a strange sight in the darkness above him. He thought he saw a humanoid face in it The image merged back into the colorless canopy, and Vinder shook the thought out of his head as so much foolishness.

"We must hurry - I don't like the feeling I am getting." Cadrissa shivered slightly.

"Nor I," Gilban concurred.

Sneaking and snaking about the deep darkness under Clara's lead, they managed to reach the interior of the complex using the small puddles of campfires and torches the hobgoblins had placed at various intervals. They were further aided by the darkness and the unease it continued to case the hobgoblins they passed.

The group came to stop in front of two large buildings., One had been rebuilt to look as though it could withstand any attack, the other seemed only partially rebuilt.. Both dominated the area, like giants crouched for an attack, overwhelming everything with their cold facades. A few hobgoblin guards - also distracted by the growing darkness as they patrolled the perimeter - were followed by leashed reptilian beasts surveying the area with sluggish glances.

The beasts had long lizard-like snouts, and bodies like dogs. Their tails were like snakes and their feet ended in deadly-looking claws. Their flesh were covered in thick, dark green scales; the hard form of their frames looked alien and diabolic in the unnatural night.

"Those are basilisks," Cadrissa whispered as they cautiously approached the buildings. "Don't let them bite you. Their saliva carries a toxin causing paralysis leading to death.

"It's led to legends of them being able to turn people to stone."

"Pleasant thought," Vinder whispered as he watched the beasts pass.

"They have poor eyesight, however," Cadrissa continued her short lesson, "so as long as we stay a fair distance from them we should be fine."

"We're up wind of them too," Dugan added in a low voice. "That should keep us from being noticed for a little while longer. Your worse enemy with beasts is their ability to smell you coming before you can take them out."

Dugan turned to Cadrissa. "How well do they hear?"

"Fair," she replied, "but their strongest sense is smell- which they taste from their air."

"Then let's get moving while the wind is in our favor rather than wasting what advantadge we have running of our mouths." Vinder grumbled.

"I agree," said Clara.

"These buildings are heavily guarded; the information we're looking for must be in one of them," Dugan grunted. "How are we to get past them though? We'd be spotted in a moment - even with this darkness."

Clara turned to Gilban, who said nothing, only stared ahead.

"Attacking them would just be stupid. The whole camp, not to mention the troops inside the building - if there were any - would have us skewered in moments. We must use stealth," Clara addressed herself more than the others, but they all shared her train of thought.

Suddenly Cadrissa recalled the powders she'd bought in the shop in Elandor.

"I may have just the thing," Cadrissa dug around her belt pouches and pulled out a handful of dust - she threw at the gathered group without warning.

"What are you doing?" Rowan's hoarse whisper echoed everyone's concerns as each began to fade and grow transparent.

"This dust makes anything it touches invisible," she told the knight as she threw a small handful on herself.

"I can't see anyone! I can't even see myself!" Rowan's concern rose above a whisper.

"Keep your voice down! It makes us invisible, not deaf!" Cadrissa cautioned. "Just as the powder makes us invisible to the hobgoblins, it also makes us invisible to each other."

"How will we be able to follow each other if we can't see ourselves?" Clara pointed out. "We could inadvertently get separated, and not even know."

"Don't worry," Cadrissa said with an edge of pride. "I have a spell to solve that problem!

"Golroth keen. Ulth von uth. Relto orath," the mage chanted.

Suddenly, they could all see their hands, limbs and each other once more, though each one appeared slightly transparent, like ghosts haunting the old ruins.

"How long will we be invisible?" Vinder look at his hands, waving them madly in front of his face, glad to have his body back.

"Unfortunately, the powder doesn't last long. Only a few hours, but it should give us enough time to locate the information we seek."

"Then we haven't much time to lose," Dugan contemplated his own transparent hands.

"We must hurry," Clara moved to the first of the reconstructed buildings. The invisible travelers stopped behind Clara, who had suddenly come to a halt, and was looking back and forth between the two buildings.

"The item we search for has no supernatural or mystical properties; they are just scrolls and tomes of rare knowledge," Gilban whispered, "but they might be guarded by some powerful enchantments."

"Can you discern where the magic is strongest?" Clara asked.

Both structures appeared to have been well repaired, except for a crumbled section of masonry on the southwest corner of the closest building. Two double stone doors appeared to be the only entrance, and two rather mean and vigilant hobgoblins stood guard there.

The other building was a semi-preserved structure, with the original stained glass windows on the north and south sides, it and appeared to be some kind of temple. Frescoes of long-ago days still managed to cling to the walls, while others littered the ground in crumbled shards. The temple also had a set of double doors. However, these were unguarded.

"What's the matter?" Clara whispered.

"I can't tell which building has the strongest amount of mystical energy in it. It could be either one," Cadrissa shook her head. The area was thick with mystical energy. For a short time, she had been lost to it. This was such an amazing place that she wanted to stand there forever, absorbing energy through her body, but knew she had to fight the urge.

"Can you make a guess?" Clara pressed. "This darkness will make it impossible to see much of anything pretty soon."

Something now pulled at the back of Cadrissa's mind.

She felt cold claws of thought dig into her. It burned her mind with its arctic touch, but only for a moment. Somehow, she managed to shake it free, and regain her thoughts once more.

"I feel more energy coming from that direction," she pointed to the temple.

"Then we go into the other one, like Gilban said," Dugan smiled. "I have the two hobgoblins."

"It looks much easier if we slip into the building through that hole in the corner," Clara whispered. "Vinder, you cover our backs. Dugan and Rowan will lead us in, and the rest of us will follow in the middle."

Rowan prayed to his goddess for safe passage.

Dugan's smile faded into a stoic visage upon Clara's declaration, but slowly crept up to the hole. The opening appeared to have been caused by faulty masonry. Fresh stone and mortar were stacked near the damaged wall, a sign repairs were underway, although there was no sign of the construction crew. Dugan risked a look inside the hole.

"All clear," he waved the others forward as he and Rowan leapt inside. The interior was of good size, perhaps as large as the colosseum he'd left behind and empty.. The only change that had been made to the bleak, stone walls was a door at the north end of the room made of new wood.

Inside, the air had become clammy and sticky, though most of the heat from the wilderness outside followed them in as well to make it feel like they were climbing into the carcass of some freshly-slaughtered beast. The light outside was nearly almost gone, making it like a starless night, hindering any chance at looking around the area in much detail.

"I'll check the door," Rowan crept up to the newly-replaced door, and put his ear against it. "Nothing. I'm going to open it a crack. Everyone be ready."

The young Knight of Valkoria slowly opened the door. The hinges were new and well-oiled, so they didn't squeal.

"It looks like a hallway beyond here. There's a little light from some sconces, and it smells really bad. I think it branches off in two directions: northwest and northeast. Which way should we go?" Rowan reported back to the group.

Clara looked at Gilban. "Well?"

"I'm not the one to ask, for here my goddess's insight ebbs," said the priest. "This is where each of you now must rise to your strengths - this was why you were chosen for this mission. Here is where you will shine."

Gilban pointed to Cadrissa, which the mage found eerie, given the priest's lack of sight. "Try asking the mage; she knows far more right now than do I."

Clara turned toward Cadrissa with a questioning look.

Cadrissa closed her eyes to help her stay focused on locating the lost knowledge. The excitement of all the other potential knowledge surrounding her nearly overwhelming her senses and concentration.

She saw two paths...yes...one was more dangerous...

Which one?

Cadrissa couldn't see. It was as if something blocked her attempts to read the path's outcome. She had to choose quickly - she knew they could be discovered at any minute. A hobgoblin's nose was more sensitive than his eyes, and although they were invisible, she knew her spell hadn't rendered them undetectable to smell. Unlike the basilisks and guard dogs the hobgoblins kept about them their sense of smell wasn't anything special - being equal with the human or elf in nature.

"The path to the northwest looks the best, as far as safety is concerned," she opened her eyes, and walked softly forward.

The group followed her.

Chapter 29

The mercenaries walked through the near darkness of the filthy hall. Roaches, worms, and other strange denizens of refuse crawled over the floor. Dotted here and there were rough-hewn clay plate oil lamps forced into crevices and. The sporadic light did little to ease the mind of the travelers who gently treaded upon the questionable ground covered with silent and foreplanned steps.

The area showed signs of infrequent use: some scattered debris that marked out a simple trail down the more soild areas of the floor and a small collection of graffito, written in Goblin, in various locations. Scattered around in small clumps as well were dog and what could probally be convieced of as basilisk scat. Some of these small mounds had seemily petrified, others appeared to be recently deposited. Despite these signs though, the entire area was silent and still.

They took the hallway to the northwest. It led them to another door set into the wall . It too was new, like the first door they had encountered. This was a clear sign the old ruin was being remodeled thoroughly.

"I don't like this," Vinder whispered. "Where are the guards? If this is such precious treasure, why haven't we run into anyone yet?"

"Keep your voice down," Dugan grunted. "The less we have to deal with the better. Besides, you saw how many of them were in those camps when we came in. I don't know about you, but even I can figure out the outcome of those odds, should we have to face this whole group."

"Just doesn't seem right though…" Vinder trailed off.

"Well, it does to me," grunted Dugan.

They moved onward, and came to a ruined hallway littered with fallen masonry. They silently moved around the debris to a set of stairs in the wall to their right. They climbed the stairs cautiously. No one wished to take a wrong step and fall, or attract unwanted attention by kicking a small stone down the steps.

At the top of the stairs, the group found a sturdy wooden door. Behind its thick mass was another hallway. This one was marred with gaping holes. The walls had been repaired, but only in part. The party froze, however, when they heard the sound of barking dogs echo from a lesser hallway to the left of their current position.

They quickly left the landing into the damaged hallway. As they walked by the holes, the party was able to see beneath them to the littered floor they had just passed through to get to the stairs. Uneasily, they walked sixty feet through the long hallway where it connected with a solid wall.

"Where do we go now?" Clara asked.

Vinder eyed the walls around them; his lone eye searching diligently.

"There was a smaller hallway I saw as we walked into this one branching off to the south. It looks like the only way," said the Telborian.

"It looks like the only way, but I've found another," Vinder grinned.

"What do you mean?" Wondered Cadrissa.

"Look here, on this part of the wall. This stone doesn't seem to fit right, and when I push it…"

Vinder pushed on the wall to demonstrate his point, and as he did so, a whole panel of the wall gave way to become an opening. "We have another way."

"How did you find this?" Rowan was awestruck.

"I saw the different patterns in the rock," the dwarf shrugged his shoulders. "It's easy to see if you have the eye for it."

"What do you think, Gilban?" Clara asked.

"I will do what I can, but my goddess has remained oddly silent on some matters of these ruins. The old elf put his palms against the stone and stood perfectly still, like one of the many dilapidated statues inhabiting the city. "The way is filled with blessings and curses."

"That's not an answer." Dugan scoffed. "Is it safe?" "As safe as it is going to be!" Vinder pushed ahead of the milling crowd. "Standing around isn't going to accomplish anything, and although nothing can see us standing about, I fear those dogs have a nose that can find anything."

As if to emphase Vinder's point, the barking dogs grew louder, forcing them into the passage. Dugan protected their rear until they had all passed by, then he moved into the passage as well. The narrow walls forced them to snake in single file, like rats scurrying inside a wall. They continued on like that until they came to a massive crater in the floor where the hallway curved off to the east. It would have been where the building's corner jutted out and the party had first entered in the ruins, through the hole in the wall.

"You'd never find such mess and ill-mannered workmanship in a dwarven city," Vinder cautiously looked over the hole in disgust. It was a chasm of sorts which would definitely hinder their progress, if not cause them to stop completely.

"How do we get across?" Rowan peered down into the hole.

"There," Dugan pointed to a shadowy ridge of rock hugging the wall like old flesh clinging to bones. "That ledge looks solid enough."

"Oh no!" Cadrissa objected. "I'm not going to travel across that. You've already got me crawling around this tunnel like a rat, I don't want to die like one."

"Do you believe this is the area in which you feel the information to be? " Clara asked Gilban.

"Yes," the old elf responded.

"Then we travel across it," she began to unwind some rope from her back pack, looping it into big knots every few feet, and then fixing it to an iron arrow she had in her quiver. Clara took her bow, and fired the arrow at the far wall, where it bit deeply into the stone. She took the remaining rope laying at her feet, and fastened it to a large rock she had Dugan dislodge from the floor's edge.

"Now we have a guide rail," she said smugly as she dusted off her hands.

"I'm still not going on that," Cadrissa protested.

"Yes, you are," Dugan picked her up over his shoulder, and proceeded to carry her toward the ridge, while she kicked and protested loudly. Although, in truth, the young mage didn't mind being manhandled by Dugan, she didn't want him to think she enjoyed being treated like fresh kill. The principle of the matter was at stake.

"Shut up! Do you want the whole city to know we're here?" Dugan grunted under her weight. "The less you struggle, the more chance I have to keep you on my shoulders."

Cadrissa complied with the Telborian's wishes. She didn't want to fall either. Dugan wasted no time, but shot into action - and with Cadrissa in tow, skimmed across the ridge. Then he set her down safely on the other side. He tried, unsuccessfully, to suppress a smirk bubbling to his lips after the episode had passed.

It was the first time Cadrissa had seen any kind of emotion toward her from Dugan. Though it was a bit of mischievous levity at her expense; it was still something…

The others followed.

Gilban was slower, as he was led every inch of the way by Clara's gentle hands. After they left the ridge, they came to a spot where the hallway ended again, but there was a door to the north. It was a very old and solid form carved with strange faces no one in the group could understand or trace to any kind of origin. They seemed to be a mixture of all the known races: dwarf, elf, human even a bit of gnome and halfling all mixed into one.

After they had briefly looked them over, Dugan pushed hard against one of the doors.

It didn't give.

He tried again.

Though he pushed with all his might, it wouldn't yield to his strength.

"Locked," he grunted. "Stand back."

With muscles tensed, he ran into the center of the doors colliding with them in a thunderous echo of destruction. The doors couldn't stand up against such a force, and the old wood exploded into splinters, chunks and dust. The mercenaries waited with baited breath in the silence which followed. After a fine cloud of dust settled, the interior was displayed in all its glory.

"I think they know we're here now," Vinder coughed as he entered into the room beyond. "If they don't find that hidden passage, then they just got a clue where to find it."

"All the more reason to hurry," Clara, Gilban at her side, made her way into the darkness of the room.

The others followed.

Inside the mercenary band found a place none would forget as long as they drew breath.

Over all, with all it contained (or maybe because of it) the room seemed rather small, but contained many riches and wonders, making Vinder's head spin, and Dugan's thoughts of freedom reach even greater heights when he saw just what a free person could attain in life. Cadrissa was equally amazed to the point of growing faint-headed from the onslaught of so many things calling out to be studied, possessed and collected. Rowan, too, was overwhelmed by what he saw around him, but did his best to keep his mind grounded in the task at hand - completing his mission for the Knighthood, and his goddess. Clara and Gilban had similar goals as they scanned the room's interior.

In the center there were iron chests; lids open, with the glimmer of copper, silver, gold, and platinum coins. Nestled amid these coins of ancient make were gems of all sizes and shapes. Amethysts, moss agates, black opals, and rubies were but a few visible in the dim shadows of eldritch flickering light shining from the walls and ceiling itself, as if bathed in starlight.

Dominating the rest of the room were nine lifelike jewel-encrusted, gold forged, statutes. The statues themselves seemed to possess faces similar to those found on the door to the chamber, though of higher quality than those carvings with curled strands of beard made out of pure onyx. The more each of the mercenaries looked at the statues, the more they grew alien - and at the same time similar to them, as if there were some shreds of bizarre unity between the viewer and the viewed.

"These beings must have been gods," Rowan said in a hushed tone when he had managed to regain his senses after peering up at one of them.

"They weren't," Gilban's blind eyes continued to scan the interior, "but they thought they were."

420

"Drued's sweet beard!" Vinder's eye spied other treasures in the room as well. Two short swords, a broad sword, and a shield lay next to the statutes along the far wall. It would be a mighty shame to leave such fine weapons behind. He could tell they had a great value as well - enough to put him over his presupposed limit on the tribute he'd collected. However, they might also be harder to move in the jungle, and the ruins when compared with the ready coin presented to him, which could easily be stuffed into a sack and slung over a shoulder or hip.

"Take what you wish, as long as you can carry it without slowing you down," Clara said to the group as each member eyed some part of the treasure which happened to catch their eye. "This is your payment for this mission. As was our agreement. Be quick about it though, Cadrissa's powder will be wearing off soon." Clara then gave the room a quick look before turning her attention back to the exit.

"So where is this information, then?" Dugan asked Clara. "I don't see anything here but gold and jewels and a few weapons."

"That is what we sought," Gilban said as he pointed to a small chest no one had noticed before. It was made of simple dust-covered and aged-worn oak. It appeared to be without a lock of any kind. Between one and two feet in length, half that in width and height, it appeared fairly humble among the other more splendid riches of the room. Amid such grandeur, it was practically invisible.

"Chose your spoils well, for you may have need of them in the time ahead of you," the priest added.

"What does that mean?" Rowan looked back toward Gilban, stopping midway toward the collection of weapons that had earlier caught Vinder's eye.

Gilban said nothing.

Clara walked over to the small chest, and touched a section of the wood with one finger. It had a dry and worn feeling - like weathered bone. Cautiously, while the others searched for their rewards, Clara lifted the lid. Dust flew up into her face, which she managed to duck out of the way, and avoid. When the dust had cleared, and her eyes had stopped watering, she peered inside. She saw three tightly-rolled scrolls, and two leather-bound tomes no larger than her hand, nor thicker than two of her fingers combined.

Gently, she pulled out one of the tomes and opened it to a page at random. More dust fluttered into her face, which she again mostly managed to avoid. The language was familiar to her, but she couldn't read it. Familiar because she had been trained what she would be looking for before she left Rexatious.

The book was written in the Dranoric language.

"This is it Gilban!" Clara nearly shouted in her excitement.

"Then things go well indeed." the priest stood his ground as the others dug through the contents of the room for their own treasures.

She smiled excitedly as she carefully packed the book back into the chest, closed the lid and brought it back to the elder elf. "I thought the Ancients would have hidden it a bit better than this, though, and that it would be a larger collection as well."

"Sometimes the most effective hiding spot is in plain sight," Gilban sighed as he touched the plain wooden chest as Clara held it out to him to receive. "It is finished then. The Elyellium shall never rebuild their empire now. Peace shall be preserved," Gilban smiled.

Chapter 30

While the two elves spoke, the rest of the group still was absorbed in their exploratory appropriation. Rowan found his way to the cache of weapons, and other equipment Vinder first noticed. The weapons really didn't catch his eye, he still felt safer with his own sword than what was present, and really didn't feel right about taking things from the ruins anyway. It smacked of grave robbery to him, and didn't sit well with the new sensibilities he had learned through the Knighthood. Though some of his kin were more inclined to plunder and pillage, the youth never found a taste for it.

Despite this, something caught his eye.

It was a shield.

Round and large enough to cover most of his upper body should he wield it in battle, it was emblazed in gold, a two-headed dragon upon its black background. Fire blasted out from both of its mouths, drawn in bronze in molten coils of burnished metal.

Something about it called him to it, told him to pick it up, and examine it closer…

So he did.

Meanwhile, Dugan picked up two short swords resting nearby the shield. One was crafted with a skull on an emerald bejeweled pommel. The other had a black opal set in the center of a cross hilt. He slashed the air with them to get a feel for their weight, and was impressed with their balance and excellent craftsmanship. He could use the gems and coins to live a better, freer life, but he needed to be practical too - and knew how a decent set of blades would go a long way to help secure the path he could not walk since being freed from Colloni. With grim satisfaction he took in a closer look at the weapons.

Cadrissa looked into the spoils bubbling over from one of open chests, and took out some gems. When she did, a golden medallion was revealed. It glowed with a mystical energy all its own, and she couldn't help but pick it up. Her schooling at the academy had aided her in being able to gauge the nature of such treasures, and she felt perhaps this item was enchanted. To what degree, and with what abilities, if any, she was uncertain - but it was a curiosity none the less. It would certainly warrant further study to unlock any secrets it might hold.

The mage quietly put it into in one of the secret compartments cluttering the folds of her robes. Following that, she flushed more of her secret pockets with handfuls of the plentiful coins. She would need to be able to pay for more schooling at the academy. If she wouldn't be able to stay and study this place, then at least she could gain the ability to advance in some level of knowledge under tutelage.

"Let's go!" Clara's voice roused each of them from their scavenging.

Vinder didn't really hear her, though. He had become transfixed by the large statues lining the far wall. He had already taken more than his fair share of the coins and gems, and they would be enough for his tribute…he hoped. To have the time though to take one of the statues, though…it would be wonderful. He became lost in what would happen should he be able to bring such a wonderful work of art to his clan…

"It's a shame we have to leave them here." the dwarf softly spoke at the foot of one of the golden statues, which oddly made him think them to be a type of giant, regal dwarves.

"How would you carry it out of here, though?" Rowan laughed as he examined his new shield. He had placed it over his left arm and seemed to be getting used to its weight. It did indeed cover a good portion of his upper body as well when he raised it up to his chest.

"I know," the dwarf sighed in resignation.

"We must hurry," Clara's concern had grown with the others' lack of raid response. "We've already spent too much time here as it is. Let's get as far from this place as we can before we lose our advantage."

"But we need to go back to the source of magic in the other building," Cadrissa turned to Clara.

"Why?" Dugan sheathed his two new weapons in his belt, which kept his gladius there company.

"We should make sure we don't leave any loose ends here. Anything for others to salvage," Rowan joined the others at the door where they have congregated. He wore the shield now, ready to use it in case things should take a turn. "We're here already anyway, so we might as well make sure nothing of any aid to the elves could get into their hands."

"Good point," Clara looked toward Gilban, who said nothing. He merely held the chest she had given him. "It wouldn't hurt to be thorough.

Clara then turned to the mage. "Can you lead us back there, Cadrissa?"

"Sure," the mage nodded.

Following the wizard, they backtracked until they came to the corridor they had passed Upon first entering the upper level, they traveled down its long expanse. However, Cadrissa's fears were brought to life.

"We've been invisible for too long!" She cried as she watched her hands become solid. "We are becoming visible once more!"

"What?" Dugan growled.

"I told you, the powder only lasts for so long, and then fades away. We will have to be careful. The handful I used on myself was the last." There was panic in Cadrissa's speech.

"From here on out, we must rely on stealth and speed," Clara told the others.

"That's just great," Vinder scowled. "How am I to get my treasures and still survive this place once my disguise is gone? We should leave now. To the Abyss with the rest of these, Clara! We've risked enough as it is - you got your information! Let's just go!"

"We will manage," Clara replied. "The other building is right across from this one. We have yet to meet any opposition - and if we do, I'm confident we can handle it."

The dwarf continued to mutter under his breath until the group heard noises from the end of the hallway – - growling dogs. They all stopped at a break in the passageway where it bent suddenly to the east and formed a narrow strip of floor, snaking around another hole in the floor where the ceiling had collapsed onto the ground below, leaving a small chasm in the level above.

"The dogs again," Dugan grunted and drew out his new blades.

"Quickly! Hide!" Clara whispered as the group tried to find pockets of shadow to disappear into. Just as Vinder dove into a crevice in the wall, two large hobgoblins dressed in chain mail and carrying jagged short swords turned the corner. Each had five vicious dogs with them, all leashed to wrought iron chains. The five chains were attached to two thick steel rings held tightly by the muscled forearms of hobgoblin sentries. The dogs slobbered and barked as they turned the corner. They smelled the intruders, and hungered for their flesh.

The animals appeared to be a mixture of wild wolf, and common hound. Their sleek brown and black bodies were covered in short hair, bristling around the muzzles and necks of four-foot-tall frames. Their bodies were at least five feet long, and their teeth and claws shimmered a deathly white in the limited illumination of the hall.

"They sense something, Moab," one hobgoblin growled harshly to the other in their native language.

"Be ready, maybe it's Kylor again," the one called Moab replied as he drew his sword. "He's gone insane, they say - and looking for more victims."

A set of the hounds clamored their keeper over to a shadow, hiding Dugan.

"What is it?" The hobgoblin asked his dogs. "Do you smell something?"

The hobgoblin peered closer into the darkness, covering the Telborian, allowing Dugan to smell his jaundiced, leathery flesh. The Telborian could take no more; he needed to act while he had the advantage.

Without much thought, just fluid motion, the Telborian stepped from the shadows, shouting a challenge at the hobgoblins.

"Dugan, are you mad?" Clara shouted as he did so, realizing as she did so her own cover was wasted - her presence revealed.

Moab and his comrade jumped in surprise at the sudden appearance of an assailant and released the hounds. The dogs scattered in every direction, heading for the scent of the concealed intruders. Moab charged Dugan, while his partner went after Clara, whose voice he had heard coming from a dark recess in the hall ahead of him.

Moab swung at Dugan, who ducked, and hit the hobgoblin's arm with a return blow, causing the creature to lose his weapon. Spinning about, Dugan followed through with an arcing swing, and plunged his sword into the hobgoblin's heart. Moab staggered, coughed up blood, and fell to the floor. Before Dugan could react, three of the vicious dogs attacked him.

The remaining hobgoblin grinned wickedly as he spied Clara pressed to the edge of the hallway. He spun his weapons in his hands as he passed them back and forth, trying to intimidate the elf. Clara stood her ground, and studied his posture, looking for a weak spot. She feigned a run to the left, and the hobgoblin swung in anticipation of her movement, and missed as she danced away to the right.

The swing left the hobgoblin unbalanced, and Clara took advantage of the situation - stabbing her opponent in the back; slicing through his chain mail as though it were leather. The hobgoblin collapsed to the floor, joining his partner in death. Clara pulled her weapon out of her foe just as two dogs ran her way.

Cadrissa watched the battle from a safe point. She hoped for the best, but began to think of ways to better the outcome of the situation. She didn't travel so far and see such wonder to die at the tooth and claw of dogs.

Determined at self-preservation, the wizardress cast a brief spell upon herself. She glowed a soft azure for a moment, then faded like a soft mist from her frame. At least she would be a little better protected with the arcane energies of the spell absorbing the brunt of an attack. She turned her eyes to watch from another distant corner. Gilban sat silently against the wall, and looked as if he had no care whatsoever. The whole battle was not even his concern. She would have pondered this more, but made another list of spells that might give her some aid against the current threat.

Vinder growled ferociously as he was set upon by two snarling dogs. Though the dwarf defended himself well, the faster beasts managed to gnaw through his armor and draw blood, which further angered the battle-worn dwarf. He cursed them and gave a great shout. His great axe shown brightly as it fell upon the first dog. The swing lopped off its head as if it were a flower. On the upward stroke, the blade connected with the body of the second dog and cleaved it into two sections, leaving it to wiggle back and forth like a dissected worm, emptying its internal contents upon the floor as it died.

All three of the dogs viciously attacking Dugan dug into his tanned flesh, ripping leather and flesh from his legs and hands as he fought them off as best he could. He drove back the snarling faces as they tried to bite off his face with deadly leaps and bounds. Through the chaos though, the Telborian managed to get his hands around the chain collars of two of the dogs. He twisted it tighter by doubling the chain, and used his immense strength to ram their heads together. The dogs collided with a wet thud and crack, then were silent.

Dugan let them lay motionless to the floor.

The third one saw what had become of his comrades, and retreated from the battle with a whimper, his tail between his legs.

Rowan dealt with three dogs of his own. They nipped, snarled, and gouged his flesh with their terrible teeth. His newly-acquired shield blocked some of the strikes, but others still managed to get over and around the reptilian-crested shield.

The youth put off the harsh stinging of their bites, and turned to the matter at hand. His Nordic blood wanted nothing more than rampage and violence and the youth was happy to comply. Rowan shouted a Nordic chant as he let loose a downstroke, then up stroke, then down stroke again. Each time he cleft the skull and brain of a dog.

In the short time since it began, the bloody din of warfare died away and left the messy remnant of their work. Sloppy and cruel, it had been anything but quiet. They all knew it was only a matter of time until the whole complex would be after them, if it wasn't already.

"Let's get moving before any more show up," Clara warned.

"Kill them!" Came a new cry from hobgoblin lips.

Suddenly, from around the corner, twenty hobgoblins rushed into view, weapons at the ready. They ran over the ledge near the hole and balanced over its deadly gap even as they ran to slay their enemies. They were better trained than the two who had just been dispatched - and seemed hungry for bloodletting. However, as they drew closer, Cadrissa took charge.

"Grab on to something tightly,"

The others wasted no time in complying, as the mage chanted a spell. For a moment she closed her eyes and drew forth energy from the 'well' within her. There was a faint, muffled clamor of voices, and then silence. Oddly, she felt slightly more powerful than usual, and the feeling of the words of the spell simply slid off her lips.

"Darin lacara elhieem! Soreen. Soreen."

The chasm began to glow bright orange, then a gust of wind emitted from it. Then, before the hobgoblins had time to react, a great whirlwind emerged from the jagged stone opening, and pulled all it could into it.

It sucked in a few hobgoblins, then more, all the while swallowing them in great gulps like some gluttonous beast. The others held on for their lives as the once-proud gang of hobgoblins dwindled from twenty to ten, to five - and then finally none. They fell to the floor below, lifeless and cold.

When they were all gone, the orange wind subsided.

Cadrissa leaned against the wall, steadying herself on weak legs, and panting for breath. She knew she had taken a lot out of herself with such a casting, and would need some time to recover if she was going to do anything quite as strong again anytime soon. She prayed it wouldn't be needed.

"Very impressive," Vinder surveyed the littered floor below.

"Yes, well done," Clara agreed as she dusted bits of leaves and dust from her clothes.

"You didn't get them all, though," Dugan pointed to a dark corner where the pit and hallway met. Everybody looked as a small, squat, cowering goblin came out into view.

It was a repulsive enough beast, but this one dressed in a bright orange shirt, torn purple pants, and a forest green jester's hat with gold and silver bells that jingled when it moved.

Hoodwink had decided to put on his best clothes. If he was to be to be sacrificed by Kylor he wanted to look his best. Since Relforaz hadn't returned, and as he wasn't the stupid creature everyone believed him to be, he decided to escape at this earliest opportunity. Goth had tried to stop him, but he was too weak from his battle with Kylor to do much damage to the small goblin. He would've made it out of the building, too, if not for the guards, who while out looking for Relforaz, had detained him - and were going to bring him back to the throne room when they were sidetracked with the most recent conflict.

It seemed he'd been given a second chance at escape by the mage, and wasn't going to see his chance taken from him again. If he could just play the part right. Fate could not be tempted too much he understood, and he thanked the gods he had at least one last chance at freedom. He couldn't let it slip through his fingers.

"Please spare me, mighty mistress," Hoodwink fell to his knees to grovel in grating Telborous.

"Who are you?" Vinder demanded of the sniveling goblin.

"I am Hoodwink, and mean you no harm - please don't hurt me," his bell-covered hat jingled as he crawled closer to them.

Rowan raised his sword, "Goblins are crafty - and he might be playing us for fools. He could be stalling for reinforcements."

"No fools. No fools," Hoodwink recoiled from the knight.

"Hold Rowan," Gilban held up a warding hand. "This one too has a fate intertwined with ours."

"You must be joking," Dugan snorted. "Let's just kill it or leave it - and get going while we can. They're bound to be more hobgoblins where those came from."

Gilban's face took on a serious tone. "I mean no jest. I have foreseen this. He is a help to our cause not a hinderance."

"I think Gilban's right; anyone who dresses this garishly can't possibly mean us any harm," Cadrissa snorted sarcastically.

"Listen to her," Hoodwink jumped, and pointed at Cadrissa.

"All right," Clara eyed the small creature. "I'm in no mood to argue at the moment, so I will just have to agree for now on Gilban's word. Show us the quickest way out of here and we'll let you live."

"I will do so most humbly, mistress," Hoodwink rose to his knees. He bowed politely to the elven maid. "I was just on my way there myself.

The goblin rubbed his still sore jaw and lip as he thought a moment. "We should be able to get out of here before any more guards show up."

"What about checking out that ruined temple?" Rowan's eyes met Clara's.

"It's too dangerous now," Clara felt a slight flutter in her stomach, but it just quickly passed. "We've already been in some tough fights, and I don't relish any more. We got what we came for - and I don't want to risk losing it on something even more dangerous."

"But there could be more hidden knowledge in there, Gilban even agreed," Rowan pleaded.

Clara looked at the blind seer for answers. Chest clutched under one arm, walking stick in the other and all the while silent. A habit the elf liked less and less. She was truly on her own then.

"It would be foolish to not check and see if anything was left as long as we are here," Cadrissa repeated the plea.

Dugan had grown tense as he kept watch over the gloomy hallway. "Someone just decide, and let's move. We wasted enough time as it is."

"Ruined temple?" Hoodwink's yellow eyes grew large.

"Yes," Cadrissa peered down at the small creature. "Do you know of any place here where some knowledge or artifacts of the Ancients may be hidden away?"

"There once was a great library where the priests of the tribe once sat, but it was taken by Kylor," Hoodwink was sheepish in his reply. "Now it is in his possession. There is a big great column there which Kylor claims is an artifact from the builders of this city."

"Who is this Kylor?" Clara asked.

"He is a cruel human - an evil wizard. He has taken many hobgoblins of to use us for tests. He uses the books in the library to make his column work," the goblin answered.

"Tell me more about this column," Cadrissa's eyes flashed a soft azure blue for a moment - Hoodwink was sure of it, before returning to their previous green hue. He barely managed to suppress a shiver.

"There is a great blue cylinder which he believes can grant him a great secret if he is able to master it. My own lord himself was cast into the cylinder, but he managed to live. Many never came out alive again." Hoodwink cautiously looked up at the mage. He was relieved to see her eyes were still green though now they seemed slightly lost - as if in deep thought.

"How many books are in this library?" Clara's question pulled the goblin away from his observation of Cadrissa.

"Many. They line the walls to the ceiling." Hoodwink rose his hand high above his head.

Clara sighed, "We had better check to make sure nothing beneficial will be left for the Elyellium to discover, or any others, should they come seeking. It will be more dangerous, but at least we'll be thorough."

"I agree," Gilban nodded.

"You don't want to go to Kylor's library," Hoodwink took on more of the servile tone. "You want to get out of here, remember. I can show you the way out of here."

"How many guards are there?" Clara asked the goblin.

"Please, it is too dangerous; like you said. I can get you safely to the jungle, and then we can all be free," the goblin pleaded.

"How many guards?" Clara repeated firmly.

"None, now since Kylor's attacks," Hoodwink bowed his head in defeat.

"Attacks?" Dugan peered over at the goblin.

"He has started to take the hobgoblins, and use them in his experiments once more. My own master, the chieftain of this tribe, has gone to kill the mage. He fears Kylor will never reach his true goal, and will slaughter the tribe on his mad quest," Hoodwink's voice had shrunk in hope of convincing them to get out while the going was good.

"So he'll be distracted a bit perhaps," Dugan looked over to Vinder who simply shook his head. "Foolish, but we're only going to get out of this place in numbers…"

Dugan and Vinder both shifted their gaze toward Rowan.

The youth merely stoically nodded.

"It's still very dangerous," Hoodwink pleaded. "Kylor is very deadly, and the room has no escape either." Maybe there was still hope to get them to see the potential danger if they went ahead with this idea, taking him along with them.

"No escape?" Rowan lowered his sword point to the goblin's chest, which caused him to swallow hard. "This won't be a trap now, will it?"

"No trap." The words jumped out of Hoodwink's mouth. "I guess there is the portal…"

"Portal?" Cadrissa's eyes widened, and thankfully for the goblin's comfort, stayed green.

"There is a mystical portal on the wall allowing people to travel from place to place - at least that's what the priest said was how Kylor got here in the first place." The goblin sighed.

"I suppose, if you could figure it out," Hoodwink looked up at the Cadrissa, "then you could use it to escape."

Clara turned to Gilban "We need to check it out. I only fear we could be walking into a trap."

"All the more reason to avoid the library and let me show you the way out of here," Hoodwink tried one last attempt at subtle, persistent pleading.

"I say you can trust a goblin or his kin as far as you can throw them, and even then half that distance," Vinder interjected.

"I could handle the mage, Clara. I may not be as powerful, but I could keep him occupied while you looked for what you needed," Cadrissa had regained her composure, and stood normally once more. "I could even try my hand at the magical portal as well. I can't guarantee anything though."

"I understand," the elf nodded.

"Time's up," Dugan's eyes narrowed as he took in Clara's sapphire orbs. "What is it going to be? We've wasted all the time we can standing here talking."

Clara agreed.

For a Patrious this was too rapid of a debate, but they weren't on Rexatious, and they didn't have the luxury of greater thought on the matter.

"Whether or not the goblin is telling the truth is still up for debate, but we cannot risk the chance of this information falling into the wrong hands or getting overrun by more hobgoblins." Clara wiped her sword on her cloak. She then turned to Hoodwink, who had changed his posture to that of a subservient lackey. "Tell us then, the best way to reach this Kylor."

"Are you sure?" The yellow eyes of the goblin shined with a brief gleam of optimism.

"Positive," Clara replied.

"Oh." Hoodwink's fleeting optimism melted away.

Chapter 31

In short order Hoodwink led them outside to the adjacent temple without further incident. They were cautious as they approached; armed and ready for anything that might come at them.

"Where are the guards?" Vinder studied the entrance.

"Gone. Nobody wants to be anywhere near Kylor now," Hoodwink turned toward Clara. "You don't have to go inside - well you can," Hoodwink started to walk off away from them. "You don't need me."

"Keep going," Clara prodded the short green figure away from his present action with her falchion.

Hoodwink huffed his displeasure, then led the group silently onward. From time to time, he would wave up his hand to hurry when they lagged behind. Hoodwink wanted to be done with this as quickly as possible. He led them through a set of heavy wooden doors carved with a worn image of a great being similar in appearance to the statures they'd seen earlier, save its face and head had been all carved away, scraped from the wood, like wounded skin. The figure held a sword in one hand, and what looked like a holy symbol in the other. The symbol was strange. None could say for sure what god it was meant to honor. Beyond the door, they traveled ruined hallways lined with the bodies of dead dogs, and butchered hobgoblins sprawled out and slaughtered like helpless beasts.

"This doesn't look good," Vinder clenched his axe tighter.

"Not at all," Cadrissa echoed the concern.

"Look sharp" Clara took decisive steps around the body and debris. We don't know what we are getting into here,"

"We're almost there, hurry," Hoodwink jiggled over the fallen mounds of flesh, nearly tripping over the cold arm of a larger hobgoblin as he did so.

The hallway turned to the right, and also kept going straight ahead. After they had traveled a moment more, they came to a great, decapitated statue. It was similar to the ones dominating the ruins, and the golden statues in the other building, as well as the door to the treasure room. Its body was nearly intact, though pitted and slashed around various spots. Its head had been completely severed from its neck.

"Push it open," Hoodwink gestured with an outward rowing motion.

"What open?" Dugan asked.

"The door. Push it open," Hoodwink motioned again.

"I think I know what he means," Clara motioned with her hand. "Just push the statue aside."

Dugan grunted as he moved to the side indicated by Hoodwink, took a deep breath, then began to push the statue aside. His muscles flared for a moment as the statute scraped against stone to reveal a hidden doorway behind the stone image.

It was as tall as the statue covering it, and just as wide. Behind it was a strange, eerily silent, black opening wafting the smell of decay and death into the air like a foul, plague-ridden wind.

"Down there," Hoodwink pointed.

"This better not be a trick, goblin," Vinder growled.

"No trick. Below is Kylor and the library," Hood-wink's face grew paler.

"Everyone, be on your guard." Clara ordered.

"Cadrissa, I want you to tell us the moment you feel any presence of this mage, or his magic. We have to make sure we're not surprised by him. Rowan and Dugan, I want you up front. Vinder, you can cover the back. Hoodwink - you're going first to ensure a safe descent." The group assembled to Clara's lineup.

Silently they descended the stairs.

Each step they took made the smell from the lower chambers grow stronger. Light, though dimly red, began to shine also and dusted everything in a gentle film of seemingly bloody incandescence. After a brief journey, they reached the bottom of the solid stairs. It was here they were made aware of what could befall them.

Red light glowed from a tall column in the center of a square cage standing guard over the object. The cage went up to about twelve feet, which left the column free to advance another five feet above that. Littered all around the structure, between books and scrolls, were piles of flesh that had once been hobgoblins. Some more foul liquid also trickled through the small cracks in the rocky floor, touching the books.

"What a horrid end," Clara spoke softly.

"What a horrid smell!" Vinder's nose wrinkled at the rancid order of the chamber.

"What caused this, Hoodwink?" Rowan asked the small goblin from behind his shield, which he carried before him, prepared to deflect anything that might assail him from the gloom, who now cowered more so than normal behind the Telborian.

"The blue column," the tiny goblin quaked. His voice had become incredibly weak.

"Cadrissa?" Clara whispered.

"There's a great amount of energy from that column, and..." Cadrissa trailed off. She felt her body shiver with a deep numbing cold. She fought it off, but it flowed through her more steadily than ever. It seemed to want her to notice a great circular mosaic dominating a far wall in the room. In a dreamlike state, she turned her head to see the object.

The mosaic was made up of a vast array of colorful tiles making the viewer grow dizzy just looking at the patterns, and trying to comprehend the design. The greens, purples, blues, and whites all blended together, and seemed to swirl like the vortex of a whirlpool.

"There seems to be arcane energies coming from this wall as well. I don't sense anything else at the moment," Cadrissa reported.

"That's the portal," said Hoodwink.

"What about your chieftain?" Rowan asked. "He's not here, is he?"

"No," Hoodwink answered.

"Are you sure your master was even here?" Clara studied Hoodwink carefully.

Master...master...master...the thoughts lingered in Cadrissa's mind and were like the blows of a sledge hammer upon her head. She shrugged off the near-smothering frigid air accompanying the thought, and had begun to fight with her neck now too as it kept turning toward the portal. No matter the strength of her will, her body still disobeyed her. It took all her strength just to get her eyes to focus on what she wanted them to view.

She was quickly losing this war inside her, and it frightened her, for she didn't know what was happening or why. Was it an attack by Kylor? Was it being in the presence of such a room laden with so many books, scrolls, and that strange blue stone column?

"Yes, and he must have won if Kylor isn't here. I can't see Relforaz anywhere, though. He had a very strong set of legs and arms. The mage is very small and scrawny," Hoodwink nervously chuckled.

"Then I guess this whole thing was easier than we thought," Vinder began to scan the gruesome floor. "What are we looking for then?"

"Ancient knowledge on the Dranoric Empire. The same as the material we have in our possession," said Gilban.

"You mean like all those books then?" Vinder pointed with this ax to the top series of bookcases jammed full of scrolls and tomes.

"If what we seek is in there, yes," Gilban flatly answered.

"You're nuts," Vinder scoffed, "I'm not going to go through all those books to find anything."

"Agreed," Dugan added from behind Clara. "Let's just get out of here."

Suddenly a solid mass dropped into the midst of them, making a sloshing sound similar to when a foot steps into melted snow. The flesh of the being skinned away, exposing muscles, and grievous, injurious ebbing, a blackish blood, like melted chocolate, all around it. The skull of the great head was exposed as well, which appeared to be of a darker tint of bone than the set of bull-like horns which protruded out of it.

Rowan, Dugan, Vinder and Clara were immediately alert. Their eyes darted everywhere seeking out any threats; Rowan rose his new shield close to himself.

"Back up the stairs!" Dugan started to back toward them.

"Way ahead of you!" Vinder followed as Rowan and Clara still held their ground.

"Relforaz?" Hoodwink cocked his head.

"This is your chieftain? You mean he's dead? If the wizard isn't here then…who killed him?" Cadrissa spoke up from her dreamy world view.

"You were right, goblin," a strong voice thundered throughout the chamber. "The mage was weak and scrawny, but so, too, was your Relforaz. I had to revive his corpse just to have any fun with him."

An unnatural light source exploded the whole chamber into light, revealing a flesh and blood figure mirroring the statues they had all been seeing all over the ruins, save this one whole and impressive and in their midst.

"The cold…" Cadrissa grabbed her head with her hands, a chill so intense she felt she might have frozen solid took over her heart, even as her green eyes turned a glowing azure.

"He's a Dranor! Saredhel preserve us!" Gilban shouted in fear. "How could such a thing be?"

"Yes I am and I'm very happy you've shown up to entertain and enlighten me," Kylor said as he let loose a flashing line of cackling energy from his hand to collide into Cadrissa.

The wizardress shook violently from the impact,then fell.

Gilban beseeched his goddess for aid, then vanished from sight.

Clara swung twice, gaining the advantage of surprise to lightly wound him from the strikes. Kylor screamed curses in a strange language, then turned to the elf maiden; golden blood seeping from his wounds.

"You shall pay for harming me," Kylor's eyes glowed a brilliant silver.

Before he could act, however, he was attacked by the three warriors. Rowan swung high, Dugan swung low, and

Vinder charged in. Dugan's new enchanted blades dug deep into the flesh of their victim, cutting into his ribs and thigh, exposing more golden blood, which splattered everywhere.

Rowan's first swing was brushed aside by the Dranor's arm, but the second one swung true. Kylor cried out in agony as Rowan's blade returned from the strike washed in liquid gold. The being seemed to move just in time to avoid the swings of Vinder, however, adding frustration to older warrior's drive.

"Insolent worms!" Kylor punched Dugan in the stomach with such force he traveled through the air for about ten feet, landing with a thud near the column's outer cage. Unconscious and dying, he joined the other mangled bodies nearby in a slow, painful death.

Taking advantage of the situation, Clara swung twice more into Kylor. "You shall die yet, monster!"

"Monster? You have yet to see me at my full strength!" Kylor kicked the dwarf, and sent him flying into the opposite wall so hard dust fell on top of him from the ceiling. His body slid down the wall to slump at its base as pain beyond all words wracked Vinder's frame.

"By Panthor's might you shall not live beyond this day, fiend!" Rowan sunk his blade deep into the being's side, skewering the muscle over Kylor's left hip. Kylor retaliated with a strong strike of his own but was buffeted by Rowan's shield. Kylor growled in anger as a cracking sound - like a falling tree came from the former mage's hand when it connected with the golden disc.

Through the battle, Cadrissa barely held onto consciousness. She drifted in a land halfway between death and life. In this cold void, she heard a voice call out to her. The voice came with a frosty grip -the soul-numbing cold taking her over completely.

443

Cadrissa…you are my life, you will remember the words I spoke to you. I am now you. Arise and cast the spell. I will give you the strength. Hurry!

Cadrissa's azure eyes parted.

She felt the cold numbness about her, but she really wasn't her own anymore- she was now the property of another. The Master now gripped her with his hand, and used his brief hold to open and recite the necessary passage to free himself from his prison. Forcing her to sit up, she turned to the mosaic portal on the far wall opposite her. He moved Cadrissa closer toward the portal itself, then had her recite the passage.

"Torne acana yiglar ack'braha talzeen!" the cold voice of The Master spoke through the body of Cadrissa.

The column glowed a bright silvery white, and blinded all who were in the chamber as the air became thick with mystical energy. Kylor screamed in true pain as his very spirit was sucked into the cylinder, leaving the dead form of the mage's former guise in its place, after the light subsided, where once the Dranor has stood. This light then shot out from the cylinder to the portal then vanished, leaving only a dim red outline amid the circle of mosaic tiles as the entire chamber was plunged into red tinted gloom once more.

"Panthor keep us, what was that?" Rowan rubbed his eyes with this sword hand against the brilliant flash. "Is the battle won? What did you do, Cadrissa?"

It was at this time that Gilban materialized beside the dying Dugan. The Telborian's blood-filled mouth bubbled out his last few breaths in futile defiance at the hand of Asorlok who came to claim him. "You cannot die yet, Dugan. The path ahead of you is still in need of your tread," the priest laid his hands upon Dugan.

"Saredhel, I see your hand upon this man and know his destiny is far greater than what he might even believe.

Keep him here to fulfill that calling - convince Asora he is worthy of life - that this hand of destiny upon him is to their benefit as well." The priest feel silent then to await the response to his prayer. He didn't have to wait long. Dugan's injuries were healing beneath his hands.

Gilban quickly left the Telborian's side to attend Vinder's wounds, and sent him to a state of healing rest as well. His injuries weren't as great as Dugan's, but his goddess was able to convince Asora to heal them none-the-less.

It seemed both had much more to do of some importance in the days ahead.

As this all went on, Cadrissa shuddered, and then collapsed to the ground. She was too tired to move or even speak; her own wounds, though mostly internal, ached as well. The cold was gone, but she was still not totally in control of her mind and senses yet.

Clara was speechless. Even as she tried to make sense of the whole affair, her eyes were drawn to the mosaic circle. It had begun to spin in a great whirlpool of color and light.

"What's happening, Gilban?" Clara shouted. "The wall is spinning." She felt her heart race in her chest, and knew the others shared in her experience. The portal spun out of control in faster and faster circles as the echo of screams, and the smell of sulfur and blood flew toward her with hot, gusty gales. With a violent belch of power, the portal burst outward in great silvery light. Clara almost fainted from the fear flowing into her soul upon viewing two new forms stepping out of the shimmering illumination.

From the silver outlined, circular doorway, stood the form of The Master. Beside him, Balon took in the whole chamber. His shadowy substance had been replaced by fiery red skin over an eleven-foot tall body pulsating with muscles. A black silk loin cloth swayed in the slight breeze the portal had created as small serpentine veins of flame slithered over his frame. His back held two bat-like wings, his feet were cloven hooves, and his hands were deadly claws sent to render all things coming his way.

But his most horrid addition to his frame was his head. For here rested two sets of horns. One set of horns was like a bull, jutting out about one-foot from both sides of his head above his pointed ears. The other set were goat-like and curved up from his forehead. From the top of the demon's bald head fire danced about instead of hair, flickering and swaying with a seeming mind of its own.

The most frightening part of the demonic visage, however, was Balon's bright yellow eyes. The sockets were filled with a glowing set of neon yellow orbs that sputtered out a collection of flame around the sockets, curling under the demon's thick brow. So monstrous was the face, it froze Clara where she stood. The others who were still alert couldn't move as well. The scene was just too amazing. The bright yellow eyes of the fiend called all who saw them to acknowledge fright incarnate. His mouth was a toothy maw of destruction, glistening with yellowed teeth like those of a great beast used to render limbs for meals.

"We are here at last, mage," Balon was fat with satisfaction.

"Yes, and now I must leave you, for I have things to be off to, and I trust you do as well." The Master stepped back from the fiend, and looked deep into Rowan's eyes - who was still awed by the demon. Suddenly the knight felt another presence in his mind as the Master spied him with his azure flaming sockets. The youth now saw his goddess beside the fiend, calling out for its destruction.

"That I do, mage, for I shall conquer the world!" Balon surveyed the room with pride. "Now that I am free from the Abyss. I shall raise an army and lead them to victory. I shall at last be hallowed as the great being I know I am."

"That was our agreement. You would aid me in my needs, and I yours. We are now through with the deed then, and I must be off. Enjoy your brief stay on Tralodren," The Master walked over to the fallen Cadrissa, as Gilban listened to the whole conversation. His sightless eyes peered at the combatants.

"What do you mean brief stay?" Balon growled in suspicion.

"Now," The Master shouted. Rowan charged through Balon's confused state, and rammed his sword deep into the bowels of the demon; a webbing of firey veins climbing up the blade. Balon emitted a cry so powerful it shook the whole chamber, and threatened to collapse the antique structure on top of them.

"How can this be?" He grimaced in agony. "No mere blade can pierce my hide!" Balon slapped Rowan across the room like an insect; his shield unable to defend him from such an attack "You have betrayed me, mage."

The blade still stuck in his gut as he charged The Master.

"Careful, Balon," The Master delighted in the demon's sufferings. "That blade is more than enchanted to harm you; it is poisoned as well,".

Balon suddenly fell to his knees in agony. The demon convulsed on the ground like an overturned tortoise. "I shall have my revenge, mage! I will hunt you down and destroy you!"

"Fool!" The Master chided the dying fiend. "Did you think I would let you take over the world I will govern over? I used you to get what I wanted. I cannot have you now enacting your own asinine plans when mine are so near completion. Just as I used you, I used the youth to carry the weapon I so wanted to use against you myself. The magical poison will slay you in moments and send your spirit back to the Abyss.

"You will never find me again, Balon. You are doomed.

"You will never be free again," The Master laughed a hollow laughter, as he picked up the slumped form of Cadrissa who lay at his feet in one smooth gesture. With the wizardress in hand, his skull-topped staff began to glow a bright gold.

Then the two wizards did.

Then they were no more.

Balon screamed revenge as they passed out of the ruined library. The foul fiend faded from Tralodren and back to the nightmare of the Abyss. His passing closed the gate from whence he'd come with a massive explosion of light, color, thick columns of flames, and thunderous clamor. The flames belched outward toward the massive quantities of books lining the walls, setting them on fire.

Within moments, the whole room was ablaze.

"This place will collapse on us if we don't get out of here!" Clara shouted through the hazy film of dark, gloomy clouds.

Rowan was able to quickly recover from Balon's strike; shaking his head to clear it from any clutter that might have remained. The motivation to action was even more quickly sparked by the realization of the burning room around him.

"I'll take Dugan, you get Vinder!" Rowan shouted over the roar and crackle of the flames as he jumped to his feet. He went to retrieve his sword first where it lay on the ground before the mosaic portal. Snatching this up, he made his way to Dugan, seeing Clara has already come to the aid of Vinder, and was helping guide Gilban (with Hoodwink's additional aid) outside the room as well.

Rowan reached Dugan, sheathed his sword and-helped lift the Telborian as the chamber began to moan and quake. Dugan became conscious and started to understand what was going on around him.

"We have get out of here!" Rowan told Dugan, who defiantly stooped to pick up, and then sheath both weapons, even though the knight could see it caused Dugan some discomfort.

He then looked into Rowan's face with his hard, blue eyes, and even harder face. "No - we go."

Together both Rowan and Clara moved as fast as they could under their burdens as the roof started to crumble, and the rest of the room began to fall in upon itself. They had just made it to the top of the stairs and reached the doorway hidden behind the defaced statue, when a large chunk of masonry landed on the column, and cracked it from top to bottom. A moment later, the ancient relic exploded with a great whoosh of heat and red light, further destroying the ancient temple complex and surrounding area with fiery debris raining down like meteorites.

Chapter 32

The towering fires burned bright and warm in the tropical late afternoon of Takta Lu Lama. The uneasy darkness that had arisen when they entered the ruins faded, but the sky was darkening again under the thick smoke. The remaining mercenaries looked on at the high flames the ruined city emitted. The yellow claws tore a whole echo of a faded civilization to dust, ash, and cindery rock.

The group had barely managed to escape with their lives. Hoodwink led them out of the smoky halls past a handful of fleeing Hobgoblins, who ignored them to save their own lives, by fleeing for the safety of the jungle beyond where they now stood - just outside the clearing around the ruins. Though even near the beginnings of the jungle, as they now were, they could feel the heat.

They had managed to get Vinder and Dugan to safety, though they still had a few minor wounds, beyond the healing touch of Gilban's goddess. They would live and be able to recover quite well as the days progressed. The wounded warriors stood tall, watching the flames take their fill of the past.

After being told what had happened while they were incapacitated by Kylor, both Vinder and Dugan were relieved to see they had not lost any of their valuables. In that, they were able to see the whole affair as a success - even if they would be in pain for a little while longer with their wounds. It had been worth it.

For a few moments, each watched billows of thick, greasy serpentine strands of smoke ascend into the sky in silence. Their task had been completed and they had won. Though not totally, as Gilban and Clara had wanted, they had achieved their objective. Gilban squeezed the small chest containing the lost information under his arm as he observed the blaze.

"Is it over, then?" Clara turned to the blind elf.

"Our task is done, and we need only to report it to those who sent us," the fire danced across his mirror-like eyes.

"What of Cadrissa?" Rowan had placed his newly-found shield over his back. He believed he wouldn't be needing it for a while, and he had more pressing matters to contend with. His mind raced with questions, and a drive to find Cadrissa; a human wizard. Leaving her to her fate would be an injustice of the highest order.

"She cannot be helped by us. She could be anywhere and nowhere," Gilban responded dryly.

"That's it?" The knight was indigent. "We risk our lives together to get this information, and lose one of our band in the process - and now treat her as dirt?" Rowan pleaded with Clara. "Something must be done."

"Rowan…" Clara's eyes melted when her eyes met his. For the first time, each saw the unguarded emotions and thoughts of the other. Each set of eyes spoke the same silent words, and felt the secret joy in realizing how the other felt the same inside. "You're mercenaries hired to do a job. A job with risks…"

"I'm not a mercenary. I'm a knight - and I won't have a human woman be held captive by that…thing that took her." Rowan's Nordic blood boiled.

"I understand, Rowan," Clara replied, "but we have to get this knowledge back to the Republic of Rexatious, or be faced with the possibility of having it taken still by outside hands. It isn't safe yet."

"You too must have obligations to your superiors," Gilban cocked his head to the knight.

The youth realized the elf was right. He had almost forgotten why he'd come to Talatheal in the first place. His mind raced with freeing Cadrissa from her abduction. However, his superiors would want to know what had occurred here - be briefed on his mission. He was bound by duty to return.

"You're right," Rowan bowed his head sadly. "It just doesn't seem right."

"Well everything seems right to me," Dugan grinned. "My obligation here is over, and I'm a free man now with enough money to begin a new life." He turned toward Clara. "And it was worth the sludge and battles to get it."

"I agree," Vinder looked up from counting the coins in one of the handful of purses which rested near his feet. "The times have never been better."

"Is that all you care for?" Rowan scolded the two warriors. "A human woman has been abducted on the same mission we took part. We owe it to her to rescue her."

"Go right ahead, Nordican," Dugan invited the knight to move on with a gesture. "I have what I wanted. I'm not about to go risking my new life after I was just handed it. She had a fair choice, like we all did." Dugan then stepped closer to put his hand on Rowan's shoulder. "Clara's right. Fate is fate."

"Nor I lad. Home has never looked brighter as it does now," the dwarf pulled the purse he had been eyeing in close, then attached it to his belt to join a collection of others.

Rowan turned back toward the ruins in silence, disgusted with their attitudes on the matter.

Hoodwink eyed the whole situation, and was fearful of what might befall him. He had escaped with the others to flee the fire, and so far they hadn't spoken to him or of him. He knew things would change in time, though. He also knew he should probably make a run for it before the others were made aware of his presence again.

However, he didn't want to go into the jungle. Alone, undersupplied, and unarmed he was just inviting death. He didn't have anywhere else to go either. The tribe was gone now, either split up or destroyed by Kylor and flame - and even if he could find a small pocket of survivors he wouldn't be welcomed with open arms, that was for sure. As much as he hated to admit it this very group of mercenaries, who might just as well cut him down in the next breath, were his only real option of getting out of the jungle and possibly living long enough to enjoy it.

Swallowing hard, he prayed some god would show him favor, then made his presence known.

"What do you do now?" The goblin asked, looking toward Clara and Gilban.

"You're still here?" Vinder turned his gaze toward the goblin. "I'd thought you'd scurry away like the other cockroaches."

"Vinder," Clara reprimanded the dwarf. "He helped save your life. You should at least try to be civil."

Vinder snorted as he tied the rest of his purses around his belt.

"Clara and myself travel back to Rexatious, to give a report of the mission we undertook. Speaking of such, are you ready Clara?" Gilban's sightless eyes moved to the elven maid.

She looked at Rowan for a moment, and in that instant felt a thousand daggers jab her heart. "In a moment, Gilban.

"Rowan, what were your plans on discovering the whereabouts of Cadrissa once you have reported to your superiors?"

Rowan looked at her for a moment and blushed. He too felt the grip of loss and fear take his heart. He didn't want to see the elf leave him. "I will seek out the lair of a powerful wizard who lives in the snowy wastes of northern Frigia, and ask him if he can help. It is said he knows all that transpires. He should know of a way to help since it was magic taking her in the first place."

Clara thought for a moment, then returned to Gilban. "Gilban, I feel partly obligated in this task as well, since it was I who asked her to help us in the first place - but I don't want to desert my obligation in taking you back to Rexatious."

"Obligation is but one of the many things you feel," the old elf muttered with a smile. "If you feel your call to such a place, then go. I have an eager pair of eyes awaiting to take your place." Gilban's sightless gaze fell down toward Hoodwink.

"Come here, goblin. You shall be my eyes until we resolve matters in Rexatious."

"You're trusting a goblin?" Vinder was dumbfounded. "Worse still, you're taking him with you?"

"Great gifts sometimes come in strange packages," Gilban's white eyes washed over all of them as he spoke. "His fate is still intertwined with all of us, remember that as well.

"In fact, I sense he has a larger role to play in the days to come than what we now realize. There is as heavy weight upon him…a heavy hand that is-" Gilban stopped his musings, turning towards Clara. "I must be off though, as the Elucidator will wish a prompt and accurate report."

Gilban held out his hand to Clara in blessing. "May Saredhel watch over you Clara."

"Hoodwink," Gilban looked at him as he headed toward the small goblin. The jester moved near the priest with steady, but hesitant steps, then rested at his feet.

"You sure about wanting me to join you?" The goblin asked.

"You can always stay here," the seer responded.

A quick look around him made up Hoodwink's mind. "I think I'll take my chances with you."

Gilban smiled.

"Farewell all of you, and may you find joy in all that you do. The Queen of Fate shall wind our roads together again I'm sure." With that, Gilban raised up the symbol of his goddess which he wore around his neck, said an old prayer, pointed to where Hoodwink was, then both vanished from sight - their bodies evaporating into a silvery mist.

"We're you headed Vinder?" Dugan asked the dwarf after the priestly spectacle had passed.

"The Diamant Mountains," the dwarf replied.

"Sounds fine by me," Dugan drew closer to the dwarf. "Mind if I tag along ''til we get to a city again?"

"I suppose you can. I won't be much for conversation, but the extra sword arm could help 'til we get into more civilized lands," Vinder looked up at the tall Telborian with a tolerant eye.

"Don't worry," the Telborian grinned. "I'm not up for any conversations either."

"Then we better be off as well. The sun will keep for a while, and guide us out of this mess." Dugan asked Rowan and Clara. "Are you going to come with us?"

"No," Rowan said. "Go on ahead. We'll have to go to Elandor to get to my ship.

"Take care."

"Yeah," Dugan smirked at Rowan with a mischievous twinkle in his eye. "You too, kid. You two have a safe time together now, and don't do anything I wouldn't do."

Dugan turned to Clara with a wide grin before the knight could ask him what he meant. "I guess I was wrong about you. You do your elven heritage proud by allowing another man to live in freedom as he was meant to. Thank you for doing what you promised. The only elf I have ever met who was true to their word."

"I pray there are others. Enjoy your freedom, Dugan," Clara bowed her head in farewell.

"May a benevolent and caring god aid you then on this foolish quest for that mage," Dugan turned and walked past them into the jungle. "Who knows, you might actually get lucky, and find her.

"Vinder?" The Telborian cocked his head toward the dwarf.

"I'm ready," Vinder shuffled back to the elf maid for a moment as Dugan started to trek through the jungle growth. "It was a pleasure meeting you, lass. You too, lad. Keep your heads above water now." Vinder trotted off to join Dugan.

"Money-hungry warriors, but they are good men," Rowan commented after the jungle had swallowed them whole.

"Yes, good men at heart," Clara turned to Rowan and smiled.

"I suppose we should be off as well then, as long as we have some light to aid us." Clara made ready to depart.

"That is what I propose," said Rowan. "We won't make it out of here as quickly as horses would aid us, but we should be able to get some at Nabu's village and maybe some others along the way. That should help cut down some time."

"How far is it to your homeland?" Clara started to move out of the jungle.

"Farther than you can think," Rowan joined her. "It will take some time, but the travel arrangements have already been made. Like I said already, by the time we get back to Elandor, a boat will be waiting to take me home."

"Clara," Rowan gently gripped her arm, "why are you doing this?"

"I feel responsible for the whole affair, and that foul creature Cadrissa released must be up to little good as well."

"No other reason?" Rowan looked into her eyes and felt his stomach flutter.

"I also see this as a chance to be a diplomat to your nation from the Republic. There is much we have to discuss," Clara drew herself a little closer to Rowan, and felt herself become weak in the knees.

"The last such convoy was killed, their women raped, and sent to the high seas once more," Rowan's face grew stoic. "That was a few thousand years ago though. I'm sure we've changed since then," Rowan grinned a sardonic expression.

"I'm sure you have, too," Clara returned the grin. "So you have no problem with me coming along?"

"Sounds fine by me." Rowan's smile deepened.

"Good."

"Good," Rowan repeated the elf's words.

Clara quickly planted a small kiss on the youth's cheek, where it turned his whole face red.

"For luck," she giggled, and they entered the jungle.

Rowan gingerly touched his cheek with his hand as he watched the green absorb her with ease.

"For luck," he repeated with a large, toothy smile.

Chapter 33

The empty, black chamber was silent as two dark forms shifted in the ethereal shadow about its walls. These dark forms drew closer to the center of the chamber with solemn steps. Each of equal bearing were Telborians, and were well-schooled in the ways of ceremonies and rituals. They approached the center of the circular the room with great care.

The room was the chamber of the high priest of Asorlok, whose temple was hidden away on a remote corner of Tralodren. Fear and mistrust of the religion by most people of the world caused its practitioners to hide away and seek secret solitude to practice their faith. Needless to say, such actions added to the mistrust and fear of the faith like a great wheel feeding back on itself.

The temple of Asorlok chamber was small, but effective. It had about fifty odd persons serving in the faith as priests and laymen. It was enough to service the temple and enable the theological sect it called home to thrive.

The faith of Asorlok, like all global faiths on Tralodren, had different sects. Some, who followed Asorlok, dedicated their duties to the burial and protection of the dead and their resting places. Others made the temples into houses of rest for travelers, or opened up small inns and lodgings to take care of travelers on their journeys. Still another sect looked to protect and learn more about the afterlife. A fringe cult had even developed over the years sought to actually kill all living beings in homage to their god.

Faith and religion were often two different matters on Tralodren. Many people of the world were faithful to the gods, however, there were often just as many ways to express faith as their were races. Over the years, a generally-held theology had come to be accepted by most. It believed the gods allow the various sects in their faithful because, in some way, all of them brought greater glory to their godhead by existing. The followers of Asorlok, called Asorlins, was one of the first faiths to agree with this theology. Since each sect was usually centered around one aspect of the god, then they held each worked to promote or honor side of the god above all else.

Most sects were left alone by the universal faith of the god and other sects, unless the divergence of dogma was so extreme as to border on the heretical. This was what many of the Asorlins felt about the death cult.

Most Asorlins hated the bad images and stories generated about them through the death worshiping cult of Asorlok. Like most things in life, the followers of Asorlok were allowed to voice their concern to the priestly hierarchy. Though they hated the cult as well, the main bodies of beleivers learned to live with it over the years. They had tried to stamp it out on so many different occasions, only to have it return once again in a new location some time later. Since the cult was seen as being a minor thing among all the other workings of their religion and god, they turned their focus toward more important matters instead, dealing with the negative stigma the cult dealt the faith and followers as it came.

Such were the workings of the hidden temple of the Sovereign Lord of the Silent Slumber, as Asorlok was called in their temple. Though not a death cult, the temple housed a sect of priests who were dedicated to finding and purging the undead hidden on Tralodren, as well as those who would cheat Asorlok's claim upon them through various means.

Over the years, they had dealt with many such beings but they'd never had to deal with a lich before.

With the return of the Master to Tralodren, however, they were given their opportunity. The god of the dead wanted him very badly. He had eluded his power for many years. Since that time, he'd caused much damage, and perverted the natural cycle by being alive when he should have been dead. It was the call to every follower of the sect to seek out and destroy the abomination at any cost should he appear again. So it was that the first to notice his return was the hidden temple, and two priests were summoned to meet the task at hand.

The two dark forms stopped when they reached the center of the room. When they did, a blinding light exploded before them, centered on a stone dais in the heart of the chamber itself, like a tall column of grayish-white illumination. The immediate sensation of light allowed the chamber to emerge from the darkness.

The room itself was crafted from simple stone formed into tight, smooth walls, a floor, and ceiling. All along those walls, empty eye sockets stared at the duo. They peered out from the skeletal faces carved into the very rock where the ceiling met the wall, fifteen feet above them, lining the entire room in a macabre parade. Their closed jaws seemed to be formed into a sneer. Had they been covered in flesh, their eyes would have burned with contempt. Below them though, the two priests paid them no mind as they knelt before the pillar of light.

The priests were dressed in simple garb. Parchment-shaded robes draped their frames tied at their waist with a blood-red sash and ending with common leather sandals. Around their necks each wore the medallion of their faith, the symbol of Asorlok. The silver object depicted two crossed sickles in simple relief.

"You have sent for us Denri?" one of them asked. He was clean-shaven and young. His red hair was cropped close to his head. Soft, white flesh and dark, brown eyes spoke of a dedication and understanding far beyond his young appearance.

The dun-shaded light present in the pillar separated itself from the soft gray hue, much like that of oil parting from water, as it merged together into a sketchy version of a humanoid face.

"The time has come," the image in the pillar spoke with a voice filling the chamber.

"Tell us what we must do," the other asked. He was older, but seemed not as wise as the younger priest. He possessed dark brown hair with a stripe of gray on the sides. His face was covered in stubble, and his flesh was tan and rugged, like a woodsman or farmer.

"I sense his arrival once more. We cannot suffer his return. His very nature is a blasphemy against our god and his edicts. Go find him. Return him - soul and spirit to Asorlok," the command from the column was lifeless as the dead.

"Yes, High Priest," the older Telborian replied.

"We shall obey," the younger priest returned.

"We have waited a long time for this day, but now we can do the greatest service to our god. His ultimate death will please Asorlok to no end. With its completion we shall rest in his favor," the gray face smiled.

"Go. Prepare yourself with whatever armaments you shall need - they shall not be denied you. I will arrange divinely-touched items to be made available to you so the task may be accomplished."

The two priests bowed and left the chamber swiftly.

"Hurry, we must not waste anytime," the luminous pillar echoed behind them. "The Master must die."

Chapter 34

adrissa's eyes adjusted to the dimness, then she felt herself materialize in a different spot. She felt the numbing cold the undead mage released beside her from his skeletal frame. She wasn't inside the dark and grisly room anymore. The bodies of the corrupted hobgoblins and the stench of death about her had fled. She saw tall trees of a millennia of growth loom over the green fields of rolling country instead.

Sun stroked and covered the gentle rolling grassy hills. The scene was the most beautiful she had ever seen. She would have begun to explore the area at once, if her arrival hadn't limited her freedom on the land itself.

"What is this place?" She whispered aloud to herself.

The Master heard her words.

"This is my island. I claimed it when your greatest grand sire was but a faint glimmer of hope in the eye of two young lovers," The Master replied coldly.

"But it is so beauti-"

"Beautiful?" Cadrissa was cut short by The Master's cold words. "You think I cannot make such things and enjoy them? You see me as some dark being bent on destruction, as all the others did, and still do. It shall be you who is surprised with them when I prove them all wrong." He pulled on her arm. "Come. There is much to do."

"And if I refuse?" She looked at him in the empty sockets of his fleshless skull for a heart beat. It was all she could bear.

"Best not to think of it my dear; it would be far worse than you could imagine. If you cooperate with me, then your life will be spared, and you can go about your way. You might even learn a thing or two about the arcane arts, but you shall not have them taught to you through me. You are a tool I need to use right now, nothing more."

"I see I have little choice," Cadrissa said flatly.

"There is always a choice; you will just make the more intelligent one. Now come, I haven't a moment to waste," he pulled her along.

"Where are we going?" She braved a question as she trekked behind the rotten wizard.

"To my tower. Now hurry," he gave her another tug. "I wish to get there as soon as possible."

Cadrissa stopped a moment and thought. Perhaps the tower would be a way to revive him and, without it, he was weak. Perhaps even growing weaker. If she could muster up enough courage to stay outside the tower, she could even weaken him enough to escape. It was an uncertain thought, as she didn't know exactly if it was true or not in the first place; but did she have any other options than to comply with the wishes of this lich? The vise-like grip of The Master crushed deeper into her flesh-like chilling daggers.

"You would not wish to anger me further. None have lived through my wrath," his skeletal hand clenched harder and bruised her bone itself with a throbbing cold.

"Very well," Cadrissa gave up on her plan. It was foolish to try anything now, and somehow, deep inside, she knew it too. Best to live a while longer, and then look to flee when she could. "I shall obey, but first I must remain uninhibited."

"But of course you must. I must keep you in good condition." He released her arm.

"Why? What do you need me for?" Cadrissa pleaded.

The Master moved along with measured, bony steps.

"Come!"

Cadrissa obeyed.

They walked through a soft meadow, fragrant with flowers of every color imaginable. Green leaves and grass that was low and well-manicured, looked more like temple grounds than wild countryside. The sun was out, and all was clean and fresh, as if it had recently rained, but no water was about. The further she traveled, the more Cadrissa realized the land was silent. No birds or animals of any kind rustled, tweeted, or growled. Not a leaf stirred or blade of grass swayed, though a soft wind flew through Cadrissa's hair. Something wasn't right about the island. It seemed alive - and at the same time, dead.

The Master didn't care, and continued to trek upward - further into the interior of his land with rapid speed. It was as though his life depended upon reaching his tower. His tattered rags of beige cloth fluttered on his skeletal frame. Cadrissa found it hard to look upon the dead wizard and not become sick with fear, but at the same time she was drawn to him for his mastery of knowledge and power. Knowledge which had kept him from the grave.

He came to the top of a tall hill they had been climbing,, and rested in silence as his skull surveyed the countryside. Cadrissa did as well. She found a clear view over the treeline of the island, and there was nothing but a greenish-blue sea all around them. For miles unto the horizon, nothing else, save the island and water could be seen. Far off in the distance, she thought she heard a thunderclap.

"Hah. They sense me at last, but I shall outsmart them. My land knows me - and I it, but my absence has left it confused!" The Master turned to her. "Quickly, come here!"

Cadrissa approached the lich and waited.

"Close your eyes and open your mind to me girl." He ordered.

"What do you plan?" Cadrissa then looked at him in fear, for she knew she should not have asked, but her inquisitive nature got the better of her.

"This is my final warning. Questions stop now, or your life stops forever. Now do as I say!" Cadrissa saw a shimmer of evil so horrible in the lich's eyes as to freeze her soul.She quickly closed her eyes and opened her mind though her body trembled, and her mind raced. The Master whispered something, and she felt him inside her head once more.

"You cannot stop me now. I've waited too long for this day to occur, and your wrath shall never match mine!" The Master shouted into the sky, which had begun to grow thick with thunderheads that seemed to run together, and then collide overhead like a pack of rabid dogs racing toward their kill.

"Ka'lah noreen, ashul exgrai. Exzombrie seke Exzombrie Crestus!" the Master chanted.

The mystical energy ebbed from the connection between the two wizards, Cadrissa jerking as she felt it ripped out from inside her by The Master, and into the hill itself. The grassy mound began to shake and tremble with great force. The Master laughed with maniacal glee. Out of the solid and green growth shot up a thick, black, stone tower.

It erupted with such vigor Cadrissa was thrown down from the hill, but The Master seemed to remain sure-footed where he stood. The tower was at least four hundred feet high, and crafted from black marble. It shined with a force of radiance seemingly holy in and of itself. It had few windows, those being on the higher levels of the tower - all dark and empty like the sockets of a skull.

The ramparts were crowned in highly-worked gems and gold of the highest caliber. A ten-foot wide golden door, carved to represent two demonic beings holding it in side profile, stood at the tower's base. Overall, the tower was truly beautiful, but even from its root, where Cadrissa had fallen, she felt the evil of its magic radiate outward like some throbbing infection upon the land.

"Hurry up, wench, and get up here," The Master snarled as he approached the golden door.

"Open," he whispered through absent lips.

The great demons, whose hands clasped the doors shut, released their grip - and the doors opened with a will all their own.

The storm clouds had grown closer, and Cadrissa felt the wind pick up as she neared the evil tower. The storm would be the very fiercest she'd ever experience.

The Master entered the dark portal of his tower.

Cadrissa ran inside after him.

Outside, the storm raged closer as the gap between the dark canopy and blue sky narrowed to a fine line. As soon as she entered, the doors closed, and she was left in utter darkness. All she could see for illumination were the blue flaming sockets of The Master.

"At last I am ready to begin my plans," The Master cackled a hollow laughter that echoed upward inside the tower. Light then illuminated the tower's interior, flooding the ancient furniture and relics with a cold fire-like light which seemed to come from the very walls.

Cadrissa saw the inside flooring, plush rugs of an ancient make snaking along the ground for a great distance before stopping at ascending, black, marble stairs. The walls were covered with countless tapestries older than the rugs themselves. Sculptures of figures and forms from various races and times also dotted the interior. It was as if they were carved from their varied substances by the hands of the gods themselves.

Suddenly, the storm was upon them in the middle of her observation and the tower shook like some strong hand was striking against it.

"This is not a normal storm," Cadrissa shouted over the gale.

"It is Endarien's wrath, by will of the god. He will fail in his attempt though, so there will be others." The Master said this as if it were a common enough thing- nothing at all above the ordinary.

Cadrissa was shocked as the tower groaned under the howling winds.

"Have no fear. My tower will hold against him," he moved up the stairs leaning on his staff like a very old man. "It has been so before. Come, I have need of you once more."

Together, the mages ascended the long steps up to the top of the tower. It was there they found the study of The Master. It was filled with books, charts, and vials from when the Elyelmic Empire was first formed. In the center of it all though rested a great tome on top of a stand crafted with silver, and made to look like a hunched skeleton supportting the weight of the book above him with his own effort.

Cadrissa stood transfixed by such an accumulation of knowledge before her. She felt as if she had gone to the realms beyond. Indeed, the whole room was something she would have loved to explore if she had the time and wasn't a prisoner in The Master's tower. The tomes alone could grant her insight into things she hadn't even begun to fathom;

things she hadn't known existed. What more could have been gained from the scrolls or the relics that dotted the shelf and room as well?

The Master ran to the skeleton-supported tome, placing his staff to rest at his side. He embraced the old tome on its stand with an enthusiastic, if not physically-awkward hug.

"Now bring the tome I had you get from the magic shop."

"Tome?" Cadrissa questioned.

"Remember," The Master moved his bony hand before her face. Instantly Cadrissa recalled all the events in the shop in Elandor, and her getting the tome. Then she understood how The Master had possessed her to do so.

"You possessed me, and took this tome?" Cadrissa dug out the book from one of her hidden pockets, and peered at the cover in confusion as it grew in size before her.

"Yes, let me have it," he put the book on top of the stand, and laughed with the most cruel laughter Tralodren had ever heard.

"Do you hear me Ganatar, Gurthghol, and the rest of you so-called gods? I have more power now than ever before. After I have learned the secrets of this book, which I have been denied these long centuries, I shall be greater than even you!"

The tower then shuddered as if it were being uprooted, followed by a series of loud thunder and deadly lightning which lit up the tower both inside and out. The Master paid it no mind in his ravings, but Cadrissa shrieked with fright as she tried to keep herself upright.

What had she been put in the middle of?

"The Master has returned to Tralodren!"

THE DIVINE GAMBIT TRILOGY continues in…

Path of Power
Coming Late 2006

They thought it was over.

They were wrong.

As the former mercenaries have scattered, the force which first drew them together has started to pull them back. None know why, even fewer noticed this pull, but each is being brought back to the other for something grander than their own imaginations and fears can envision.

With Cadrissa held captive by the Master, she is privy to a large piece of the puzzle as the full extent of this dark mage's plan is laid bare before her trembling eyes. She too though is just another piece in a game in which she and even her captor are being used as pawns. What is this game and who is playing it? Why them? Why now?

Mysteries within mysteries; wheels within wheels; the gambit continues to grow. No one can resist it, merely hope to survive it as the true revelation of what they are and have been about, come to light amid this growing turmoil.

Hatred flares, love blooms, fear corrupts, potential is unleashed, and honor is frustrated in this exciting continuation of The Divine Gambit Trilogy. Following the events from Seer's Quest, this second volume expands the ever growing saga of Dugan, Rowan, Clara, Cadrissa, Gilban, Vinder and Hoodwink as they look for answers while dealing with their own inner struggles and weakness. Struggles and weaknesses which could very well destroy them in the process.

Welcome to The World of Tralodren™, a place rich in history, faith, and tales of adventure of which this story is but one of many.

A Minnesota native since his birth, Chad Corrie has long had a love affair with his creative side. Dabbling in art, film, music and acting, it wasn't until he found writing that he began to excel at something with which he'd found a healthy outlet and addiction.

Since that time he has written a wide array of material from such varied genres as horror, sci-fi and contemporary fiction amid comic scripting, poetry, screen plays, stage plays and more. It wasn't until recently that he discovered fantasy and began to work more in this interesting and very broad genre.

Read the whole Divine Gambit Trilogy!

The Divine Gambit Trilogy
Seer's Quest
Path of Power (2006)
Gambits End (2007)

Visit Chad on the web at **www.chadcorrie.com** for all the latest updates and insights into **The World of Tralodren**™ and his other projects and events.

Romans 16:27

Chad Corrie

𝔄𝔭𝔭𝔢𝔫𝔡𝔦𝔠𝔢𝔰

Maps

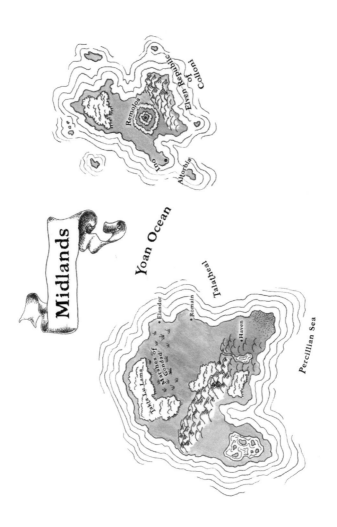

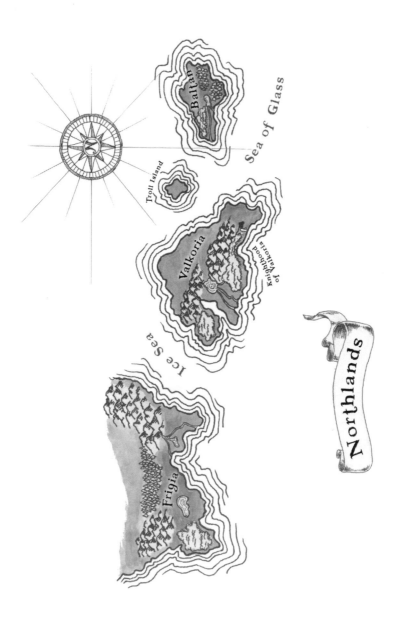

Appendix A: Basic Pronunciation Guide

Nations/Lands

Altorbia	Al-TOR-be-ah
Baltan	BALL-tan
Belda-thal	BELL-DAH-thall
Colloni	Co-LOAN-ee
Elandor	EE-LAND-oar
Frigia	FRIDGE-ee-ah
Gondad	GONE-dad
Gondadian	GONE-DAD-ee-un
Ino	I-KNOW
Rexatious	REX-AH- toy- US
Romain	ROW-main
Takta Lu Lama	TALK-tah loo LAH-ma
Talatheal	TALA-theal
Tralodren	TRAH-low-DRIN
Tralodroen	TRAH-low-DROW-in
Valkoria	Val-CORE-re-AH
Yoan Ocean	Yown

Races

Ajuba	Ah-JEW-bah
Celetor	SELL-ah-TOR
Celetoric	SELL-ah-TOR-ick
Elonum	EE-LONE-um
Elyellium	EL-YELL-e-um
Elyelmic	EL-YELL-mick
Napowese	NAH-POW-ease
Nordican	NOR-DUH-kin
Pacoloes	Pak-COAL-lees
Patrious	PAY-TREE-US
Telborian	Tell-BOAR-e-UN
Telborous	TELL-BOAR-ohs

Tralodroen™ Pantheon

Aerotription	Arrow-TRIP-tee-ON
Asora	AH-soar-RAH
Asorlins	Ah-SORE-lynns
Asorlok	AS-oar-LOCK
Causilla	CAW-SILL-ah
Dradin	DRAY-din
Drued	DRUID
Endarien	EN-DAR-en
Gurthghol	GIRTH-gaul
Ganatar	GAN-AH-TAR
Khuthon	KOO-THONE
Olthon	OLE-THONE
Panian	PAN-ee-un
Panthor	PAN-THOR
Perlosa	Per-LOWES-ah
Remani	Rah-MAN-ee
Rheminas	REM-MIN-noss
Saredhel	SAIR-RAH-dell
Shiril	SHAH-RIL

Main Characters

Cadrissa	CAH-DRISS-sah
Clara Airdes	CLAIR-rah AIR-DEES
Dugan	Do-GAN
Gilban	GILL-ben
Rowan Cortak	ROW-in CORE-tack
Vinder	VIN-DER

Supporting Characters

Balon	BAY-lawn
Cirmelian	Cur-MEAL-lee-un
Dranor	DRAN-OAR
Hoodwink	HOOD-WINK
Kylor	KI-lore
Nabu	NAH-boo
Relforaz	REL-FORE-as

Appendix B:
A HISTORICAL OVERVIEW OF TRALODREN™

Tralodren is a world with a long, rich history. Provided here is a brief overview broken down along with a short synopsis of what happened during each section of time.

THE FOUR HISTORICAL DIVIDES

Tralodroen scholars (primarily Patrician Dradinites) have made four basic divisions when it comes to documenting the history of Tralodren. The first two divisions are unrecorded and recorded time.

Unrecorded time is the span of years that came before the first known written documentation was put down by the ancient ancestors of the mortal races who now inhabit Tralodren. Because of this understanding, it is widely held that recorded time is the beginning of not only written history, but mortalkind as well.

Before recorded time, there is nothing but oral legends and myths, uncertainty, the creation and reign of the gods and the Dranors. Seen mostly as somewhat reliable, unrecorded time is approached with a grain of salt whenever it is studied by scholars who feel a bit uneasy without their written documentation to vouch safe their own historical ideas.

Recorded time is than divided into two more sections. The Divine Vindication, which all see as a watershed moment in history, marks all recorded time into two distinct historical periods: all that came before, B.V. (Before Vindication), and all that came after, P.V. (Post Vindication).

With this explanation let's examine the history of Tralodren...

UNRECORDED TIME
This is the time before 5,000 B.V. None know how long this collection of years was; how many centuries, decades, or millennia each of the following ages covered. It is the realm of myth and legend, story and speculation. Be that as it may, it has been recognized to contain five separate ages:

THE BEGINNING
This was the beginning of everything. Myths speak of two powerful and unknowable forces causing all things to be; everything that was, is, and ever will be was created from just these two entities.

THANGARIAN AGE
Myths also speak of a time when the Titans came to power. They ruled a great empire spanning many worlds, centered on their home world, called Thangaria. As the empire grew it came to be ruled by the first gods: Vkar and Xora who would later give birth to the Pantheon.

PANTHEONIC AGE
Following the fall of the Thangarian Empire, and the death of their parents, their children took power and ruled instead, forming the Pantheon. It was during this age the gods created Tralodren and many of the races came to live on the world. Each god also increased their realms, power, and influence; and of the stories from this time, there seems to be no end.

TITANIC AGE

The first powerful empire on Tralodren, these Titans, now expelled from Thangaria, were the rulers of the world before any other race came to dominate the planet. At first childlike in nature, they soon grew jealous of the gods and wished to be like them, then greater than them. Mighty in nature and ability, they nearly ravaged the world in their battles with the linnorm, who where their equals, in trying to have their dreams become reality.

DRANORIC AGE

With the defeat of the Titans, the gods left the Dranors in charge of Tralodren. Sadly, they too, though they started out with the best of intentions, and as pure and innocent as babes, wound up as despots in the end. According to the Patrious, the gods cursed them to a slow death and caused them to bring forth the mortal races of elf, human, dwarf, gnome and halfling. With the Dranor's final demise there was a great shaking of the world that split up the once massive continent which dominated much of Tralodren - burying almost all of it beneath the waves, and pushing pieces beyond the Boiling Sea.

RECORDED TIME

Recorded time starts at 5000 B.V. and continues until the Present Age. While every continent and people has its own rich history, this overview concentrates on the basic universal events effecting a large portion - if not all - of Tralodren. That being said, recorded time is considered to have eleven basic ages (demonstrated via capital letters with a further breakdown of the age following):

SHADOW YEARS
(5000 B.V. - 1155 B.V.)

This was a time of societal darkness as those who had survived the great shaking of the world had to rebuild, and repopulate the new Tralodren presented them. In time they did this, but they weren't able to reclaim or create any civilizations for quite some time. It was in this age that the Origin Cities arose, and soon swelled into empires.

The Time of Beginnings (5000 B.V. - 3120 B.V.)

These years are fragmented in terms of recorded documentation, growing more detailed as time progresses. Encompassing a time at the very dawn of history for the mortal races, following the collapse of the previous age and The Great Shaking, it sees the five Origin Cities come to power and the development of all the other creatures, nations, and races that called Tralodren home at that time.

The Imperial Wars (3120 B.V. - 3000 B.V.)

As the races grew, they began to rub up against each other more and more. In time, fueled by ambition, greed and other darker traits all fanned by the Dark Gods, a period of warfare erupted covering the whole world. Each nation either tried to defend itself from being taken over or was trying to take over its neighbors.

During this time the Dradinites claim the Race Gods appeared, being raised to godhood as heroes from the wars. Others don't hold this view claiming the Race Gods were the ones who created the races in the first place. The matter has not been resolved, as others hold to yet other beliefs on the matter. What is known though is that the wars destroyed all the Origin Cities save Remolos, which was rebuilt and has been inhabited to the modern day.

The Great Unrest (3000 B.V. - 2400 B.V.)

Taking advantage of the rubble and bedlam the Imperial Wars caused, a great wave of murderous migrations exploded from the lands beyond the Boiling Sea. From here came Jarthals, Ryu, and their offspring along, with more monstrous races who took over lands and ransacked ruins; slaughtering at will.

The wave of death and violence spread up from the south, all the way to the far west and to the extreme north. The whole tract of their carnage-laden migration serving as the seed bed which would in modern days become the tribes and clans and pockets of goblins, hobgoblins, ogres, giants, and lizardmen that now sprinkle the lands.

The Whispering Years (2400 B.V. - 2250 B.V.)

Here the recorded knowledge available grows scarce and any insight into this era is dim and fleeting, like straining to hear whispers in the wind. All that is known for certain is it was a time very close to the Years of Perdition. and depressed in poverty and ruin. Further, the people were very faithful at this time, indeed looking to do penance to the gods for a release of the hardships many suffered during these years.

The Years of Restoration (2250 B.V. - 1600 B.V.)

This time period was just a shorter version of what had happened in the Time of Beginnings. Rebuilding and repopulating the lands and world that had been ravaged by the Imperial Wars, and then the Great Unrest. This was when new kingdoms arose, independent cities emerged and nations began to define themselves anew by race, culture and other social means.

There were still a few minor skirmishes here and there but the general trend was of an upward nature. In time much of the scars had healed and smoothed over, and a new era was dawning over the horizon.

The Great Ascent (1600 B.V. - 1155 B.V.)

On the heels of the Years of Restoration, the increase didn't stop once things were restored. Indeed many new discoveries were found, and the knowledge of all was increased from the lowest of peasants to the greatest of kings. Architecture, art, and the sciences soared in progress as well as a great many matters of social justice were also addressed so as to bring about, as what many called the time in which they lived "Tralodren's Golden Era."

FIRST AGE OF THE WIZARD KINGS (1155 B.V. - 905 B.V.)

For the most part what marks this age is the discovery and rise of mages. People began to understand the nature of magic, and many found that they had the ability to wield it. While just fledglings in skill, well below even what present-day apprentices can master, they grew in understanding, and recorded what they learned.

It was during this time that the Tarsu, the first school and organization of mages, was founded. In time they would give birth to the rise of the Wizard Kings, but during this age they were scholars and scavengers of lost knowledge and mystical insight.

The War of Spoils (1155 B.V. - 1097 B.V.)

As the Tarsu began to teach students, non-mages began to rediscover the Dranors and sought out their ruins with fervor. Lost treasure, hidden secrets, and forgotten mysteries from long ago, all caused a massive campaign funded by merchant, faith, and king alike to try and gain as many of these relics and riches as possible.

While not a true war, in the sense that no one fought battles against one another for these so called "spoils", the drive to get them was equal in pitch to the energetic din of combat. Eventually, this craze died down as many of the known sites were picked over, and very few - if any - new locations were found to keep the flame of looting burning.

SECOND AGE OF THE WIZARD KINGS (905 B.V. - 655 B.V.)

When true mages started to appear it marked the beginning of this age. More skilled than their previous teachers, they had begun to approach the talents of most mages in the present age. The Tarsu had also become more political, gaining much influence from the royal, rich, and highly-esteemed citizens who had joined their ranks.

The Second War of Spoils (820 B.V. - 743 B.V.)

As with the first case of this "war", new discoveries of ruins and secreted wealth lead to searching out many relics, riches, and tempting insights into greater arcane power. However, this time it became a more wide-scale event as many kingdoms, headed or influenced by Tarsu members, pushed the issue to increase their knowledge. As with the previous collection of spoils, this craze soon burned out when the trickle dried up and was picked over.

THIRD AGE OF THE WIZARD KINGS (655 B.V. - 405 B.V.)

It was during this age mages first ascended into Wizard Kings. Many took up ruling their own territories as kings and queens, and started to amass followers and subjects as a true ruler would. Seeing the rising power of these figures, many turned to them for aid instead of the gods and their priests. This caused a decline in the faithful and worship of the Pantheon in favor of the Wizard Kings - who some followers took to rise closer toward a divine rank with each new generation of devotees.

The Years of Perdition (640 B.V. - 590 B.V.)

This was a chaotic time with the rising of wizards, and the fracturing of faith and society. Poverty and other calamities came upon the land, forcing many to crime and other vices - further adding fuel to the fire. To combat these troublesome matters, the Gartaric Knights were created (an order of knights dedicated to Ganatar, god of order, justice and light).

For forty years they waged a massive campaign, gaining support all over Tralodren in a war against crime and injustice. These wars led to a massive recruitment to their ranks, and decreased unrest on a large scale, helping cement the knighthood into one of the oldest, and most respected institutions in the world.

The Great Apostasy (590 B.V. - 465 B.V.)

While the Gartaric Knights were respected, not many held to the old ways of things as did their ancestors before them. As more and more people turned to the Wizard Kings than the gods, the temples and priesthood faltered, shrank and faded. Many smaller shrines and places of worshiped were emptied, and the clergy who attended them left to serve the Wizard Kings instead.

With the increase of this new godless faith in the masses, many faithful saw a great threat looming over the horizon, and dreaded the day when it would fall upon them - taking out the last bastions of fealty to the Tralodroen Pantheon.